DARK HORIZONS

DAN SMITH

A PHOENIX PAPERBACK

First published in Great Britain in 2011
by Orion
This paperback edition published in 2012
by Phoenix,
an imprint of Orion Books Ltd,
Orion House, 5 Upper St Martin's Lane,
London WC2H 9EA

An Hachette UK company

1 3 5 7 9 10 8 6 4 2

A CIP catalogue record for this book
is available from the British Library.

ISBN 978-1-7802-2009-3

Typeset at The Spartan Press Ltd,
Lymington, Hants

Printed and bound by CPI Group (UK) Ltd,
Croydon, CRO 4YY

The Orion Publishing Group's policy is to use papers
that are natural, renewable and recyclable products and
made from wood grown in sustainable forests. The logging
and manufacturing processes are expected to conform to
the environmental regulations of the country of origin.

www.orionbooks.co.uk

For Anisha and Ashwin

Acknowledgements

The publication of a novel is a collaborative affair so I'd like to take a moment to extend my thanks to all the people who've had a part in bringing *Dark Horizons* to print: to my agent, Carolyn Whitaker, to my editor, Genevieve Pegg, to Jon Wood, and to all the people at Orion who've worked so hard to bring this novel to life.

Thanks, as ever, to my wife, for giving me a first opinion and for putting up with all the day-dreaming.

I'd also like to acknowledge all those who have travelled and found themselves in deep water – particularly those touched by the terrible events in Bali, October 2002.

1

I had never before witnessed the exact moment at which life passes from the body; the instant it becomes nothing. With only twenty-five years behind me, I had collected just a few experiences of death, which I kept hidden in a place I rarely visited. A neatly dressed body lying in the velvety folds of fabric in the confines of a carefully chosen box. The wax-like effect of once living skin now tended by the mortician's expert hands. I had stared down at the sunken features of a mother I had loved and cared for; empty now, reduced to a motionless collection of skin and wasted bone. Mourners dressed in black. Sombre faces, hands shaken, drinks taken. These were my experiences of death. I had participated in the act of farewell, but I had never seen *that* moment. The exact moment at which life evaporates.

But I saw it that day. Sprawled on my stomach, with my head turned to one side, pressed to the hot tarmac, I watched life disappear. I saw it vanish as if it had never existed, leaving nothing but the ruined shell it once inhabited.

For a while before I opened my eyes, I was content to be where I was. The sun warm on my back, the air quiet around me. My head was filled with a pleasant, bleary feeling, as if I were just waking from a long, deep sleep. But the silence was punctuated by the first stunned groan, and as consciousness clawed its way back into my mind, I became more aware of the sounds around me.

A child crying. A man moaning, or perhaps it was a woman,

it was hard to tell. Both, maybe. More than one person. More than two. Then the world popped into focus and I heard many people. Many voices. Shouting, crying, screaming. The sound of twisted metal settling into place.

I opened my eyes, alarmed that I could see nothing more than a blur of light around the periphery of what I should be looking at. My whole body was numb. A wave of nausea swept over me and I retched. Disorientated and muddled, I was shamed as my stomach heaved and I vomited so publicly.

Blinking hard, I tried to move but was unable to do more than shuffle a few inches before another wave of nausea came over me. I closed my eyes tight and fought the feeling, pushing it back down.

When I opened them again, the world came to me in a bright flash of light and colour. The first thing I saw was the bubbles of tarmac, which had bloated and popped under the intense heat of the sun. A smell of oil and petrol crept into my nostrils and clawed into my lungs, making me retch again, forcing me to fight it. I wriggled my fingers, moved my hands, brought my arms up towards my face. I planted my palms on the road, trying to push myself up, but the effort was too great, so I let my head fall back onto the warm tarmac and shifted my eyes to take in the scene around me.

I'd been lucky, that much was clear. I had survived, but others had not been so fortunate. An old woman was facing me, her mouth opening and closing, her voice producing little more than a weak, breathy moaning. Blood ran from her nose and formed tributaries as it slid into the wrinkles around her lips and chin. Her eyes were wide, her hand outstretched towards me as if she knew she was dying but refused to relinquish her life without the touch of another human being. To me, she was an unfamiliar face in an unfamiliar land. Her skin was different from mine, her eyes were not shaped like my own, and our culture was not shared. Yet there are some things that we all have in common. No one truly wants to die alone.

I watched her for a moment, keeping my eyes on hers,

summoning my strength, then I manoeuvred my right arm up and reached across to take her hand. But she was too far away. There was a space of an inch or so between the tips of our fingers, and yet we continued to stretch towards each other, desperate for that last moment of human contact.

I began to pull myself towards her, dragging my weight along the tarmac so that I could take her hand. I struggled to close the gap between us, seeing that she was unable to move. The weight of the bus pinning her to the road was far too great.

Around us, the sounds of suffering grew. The ringing in my ears and the fuzziness in my head was dissipating, and my eyes didn't hurt so much any more. I tried not to listen to the creaking metal, the screaming, the crying, the moaning. I tried to ignore the smell of oil and petrol and blood that saturated the thick, hot air. I tried not to notice the other people around me. The dead, the dying and the dismembered. I tried only to concentrate on the old woman, her mouth opening and closing like a fish left to die in the sun, her final ounce of strength channelled into the act of stretching her fingers towards mine. I pulled myself closer and grasped her hand, squeezing it so that I felt the bones rubbing together beneath her thin, leathery skin. Old life and new life.

She squeezed my hand in return, closed her eyes in relief, then opened them again and looked at me.

And *that* was the moment. A life-changing moment. The moment when her deep brown eyes emptied in front of me as if her body were a vessel and her life were a liquid that had been poured from her. Her eyes died. One moment they were alive and a person lived behind them. A woman with memories, a place in the world, a purpose. And the next she was just lifeless skin and bone and flesh. In an instant she had changed from something of incredible value to something of no importance at all.

I was still holding the old woman's hand when I forced myself to look around once more.

The bus in which I'd been travelling was lying on its side, its rusted orange and green markings looking up at the cloudless azure sky. Its nose was crumpled, the windscreen shattered into crushed ice spread across the soft tarmac. Skewed at an angle in the dirt at the side of the road was another large vehicle, this one a truck. The cab had come away from the flatbed.

Seeing the rotting monstrosities like this reminded me of the moment they had collided. I'd been sitting at the front of the bus, in the 'death seat' as I have since heard it called. After waiting almost four hours in the terminal in Medan, and after two failed attempts to board other buses, I had followed the crowd onto this ill-fated vehicle, only to find myself pushed down into the backless seat beside the driver, my face only inches from the windscreen.

I'd heard that bus travel in Indonesia was a game of Russian roulette, but I hadn't expected to find myself in such a position on my first day in the country – in an overcrowded bus, surrounded by a foreign language, baskets of chickens, screaming babies, sitting beside a driver for whom life was a race. For an hour I'd tuned out the whining, high-pitched eastern singing that blasted from the internal speakers. I'd persuaded myself not to care that some travellers were actually *out*side the bus, clinging to the sills around the windows and the roof-rack. I'd ignored the open door beside me and I'd tried not to think about what would happen if the bus were to come to a sudden and terrifying stop. But I was certain that of all the passengers in the bus, I would be the first to die.

As it happened, though, I was wrong. Our collision was not head on, as I'd expected it to be. Travelling with my eyes half open, I'd assumed that when the impact came, as it surely would, it would be at the moment when our driver made one of his reckless overtaking attempts – at high speed round a blind corner, giving only a toot of his horn to indicate he was on his way. I was wrong. Our contact came, in fact, at a fork in the road, and the oncoming Mitsubishi truck hit us at the front

4

side, knocking me from my seat, propelling me through the open door before the bus twisted, slid, turned and toppled.

The people who had been clinging to the near side of the bus were crushed immediately, leaving a ragged red stain across the potholed grey tarmac as the vehicle slid to its final resting place.

I could see the tide left by the runaway bus. It was a gruesome wake of crushed bodies, dismembered limbs, blood drying in the sun.

I lingered over the sight for longer than I wanted to, unable to take my eyes from it. I wanted nothing more than to rub it from my mind, to reach inside my head and disinfect such a view, but I was compelled to look. I'd never seen such a thing before. I imagined that it was how it might look if a bomb had exploded. Bodies separated from limbs. A head. An arm. A leg protruding from beneath the overturned bus. A man whose lower body was so crushed that he had split, burst like a wet balloon, and his viscera had spilled onto the road. The flies had already begun to feast on the shiny mass of grey and red that had emptied from him.

I turned away and looked back at the old woman, then I forced my arms to move, pushed myself up onto my elbows, brought my legs around and dragged myself into a sitting position.

My head swam as I scanned around me. Chickens running in the road. People strewn all about. Thirty, thirty-five bodies that I could see. Many of them dead. One or two people were dragging survivors away from the wreck. Others were wandering in a dazed stupor as they searched for relatives.

At the side of the road, a few onlookers, unable or unwilling to help.

People's belongings, too, were scattered around the wreckage. A suitcase burst open, clothes distributed across the tarmac. A shoe. A basket full of chickens, intact. A soft-drinks crate containing only glass and the last fizz of what had been contained within. My backpack, bright blue, spotted with blood. It held everything I'd brought with me except my passport and the money, which I kept hidden beneath my shirt in a thin canvas belt.

I stared at my backpack, trying to focus on it. It had made it all the way here from England. From a small camping shop on a steep street in Newcastle. I'd bought it on a wet Thursday afternoon, the sun already set, the streetlights on and blurred behind the rain. A cold, wet, ordinary afternoon marked by the purchase of a bright blue rucksack that was to be my travelling companion for the months to come.

Only now it was lying on a bloodied road under an intense sun in an alien world.

A motorbike passed me, its engine chugging as it made its way around the wreckage. The rider weaved in and out of the people, the body parts, scanning, witnessing, then picking up speed and heading back onto the open road. Somebody had somewhere to go and a crash wasn't going to stop them from getting there. They'd seen it before and they would see it again.

I tried to get to my feet, but once more the nausea surged over me and I waited for it to subside before I began shuffling towards my backpack. My one symbol of home. The only thing I had that made me who I was. I kept my eyes on it, focusing on nothing other than the bright blue canvas.

On my hands and knees, I made my way past the old woman, not looking down at her as I struggled forwards, keeping my eyes only on the bag, until I was distracted by a young boy who came into my peripheral vision, making me turn my head to follow the movement. The boy, maybe twelve years old, had come from the side of the road where a small gathering of people had grouped to stare, none of them making any effort to come to my assistance. He stepped over a piece of debris that lay between me and my goal, then headed for my backpack. He stopped beside it, glancing across at me before bending at the waist and picking it up. He felt its weight, and then used both hands to swing it round and drape it over his back. He hunched under its load as he began to move away. I tried to call out to him. He was taking my bag. Perhaps he was moving it to a safer location; perhaps he was helping to clear the road. Or perhaps he was just stealing my belongings. Whatever he was doing, I called out, but my tongue was lazy and my mouth was dry. My confused mind rebelled against me, refusing to send the right messages to any part of my body. I was unable to stand and now I was unable to speak. The only sound I heard myself utter was a fumbled one, as if my tongue had grown too large for my mouth.

The boy stopped and stared at me, the way I mouthed my words, the way I held out one hand in protest. He watched me for a moment, then came towards me. He had seen sense. He realised I was trying to tell him the rucksack was mine.

I lowered my arm, fell back onto my knees and waited for the boy to come closer. When he reached me, he placed the backpack on the ground and squatted beside me. He waved a hand in front of my face and I tried to smile, nodding like an idiot. The boy looked around, glancing up at the people who'd gathered to survey the mayhem, then at the mayhem itself. When his eyes came back to mine, he reached down and took my hand. He lifted my arm, slipped my watch from my wrist and put it round his own. He smiled at me before standing again and slinging my backpack over his shoulder.

I stared, helpless, as the boy disappeared among the spectators.

I slumped, my shoulders sagging under the weight of my head, and I felt a mesh of darkness creeping across my mind. There was pain behind my eyes, which reached up and spread its fingers around the top of my brain, squeezing in rhythmic pulses, tightening its grip. I felt woozy again, the sounds of the crash fading in and out. I struggled to a sitting position, leaned back against whatever was there to support me. My vision began to swim and I closed my eyes, wanting to stay right there, curl up and go to sleep. I wanted to enjoy the warmth of the sun, to find a comfortable spot to lie in.

I felt a tugging at my feet and opened my eyes enough to allow a little light to needle in. Everything seemed brighter than it ought to be, the glare from the sun forcing its way into my eyes, shaded only by the figure crouched at my feet, tugging my shoes from me.

Then a voice, shouting in a language I didn't understand. Nasal, foreign, not sounding like words at all, but more like a staccato attack of consonants and vowels being fired from a rifle. The tugging at my feet stopped, my shoes slipped away, and the shadowy figure disappeared from view, replaced by another image, this one looming close to me, running a hand over my head.

An angel. An earth-bound angel, or a heaven-bound one, I wasn't sure, but an angel nonetheless. She took my head on her lap and she lifted a bottle to my lips. I drank the warm, sour water, grateful for the liquid on my parched and raw throat. I complied with her every touch when she moved me onto my side, brought my legs up and turned my head. I let her manipulate me and move me, and then my mind slipped away into the abyss as she ran her hand across my forehead and spoke in her soothing tone. Then, darkness.

2

A warm breeze on my face. A large ceiling fan above me, churning the air over my head, wafting the smell of disease and affliction, swirling it around me. The blades spinning without sound, the stalk swivelling in its fixing.

I watched the predetermined motion of the fan, allowing my eyes to adjust to the afternoon light, collecting my thoughts into a coherent pattern. I'd been in a crash. I remembered that. I remembered the old woman, and the angel, too. Although, she couldn't have been an angel because I wasn't dead. At least, I didn't think so.

I moved my toes against restrictive sheets which were pulled tight across me and tucked into either side of the iron bed. I pushed my feet up, loosening the stiff cotton, giving myself room to move. I looked around at the other beds in the ward. Ten in total. Five on my side and five on the other. All occupied.

To my left, a man with a bandage across one eye, the centre of the gauze rusted brown with old blood. To my right, a man with one of his legs kept from under the sheets, the limb wrapped in bandages, again with the same coloured stain seeping through the cream material. All of the other beds were occupied by men in similar states of disrepair. Bandages and stains seemed to be the requirement for accommodation in this particular ward, and I found myself lifting a hand to check for injuries. Sure enough, the top of my head was bandaged.

I pushed up, manoeuvring into something close to a sitting

position and studied my surroundings. A plain ward, with white walls and a green painted concrete floor. No tiles, nothing fancy, everything functional. The smell of full bedpans evaporating in the tepid air. Ten iron beds with tight white sheets. Two windows on the opposite side of the room, both filled with green mosquito netting, the shutters thrown open to the day. I could see a glimpse of foliage outside, the top of a tree which might have been a palm. The mosquito netting gave everything outside a strange fuzzy hue.

None of the men in the other beds was talking. They either slept or sat and stared. The man beside me, the one with the bandaged face, caught my eye as I looked around the room, and he smiled, nodding his head once. '*Salamat siang.*'

I processed the words, remembering them from the phrase book I'd bought before leaving England just a day or two ago. I waited for them to digest, turned the sounds into written words inside my mind, searched for the translation as I remembered it from the pages of the book. Once that was done, I returned the words, pronouncing them as best as I knew how.

'*Salamat siang,*' I replied. Good afternoon. A polite formality, but contact was made.

The man smiled at me again, 'Ah, *salamat siang,*' he said again, giving me a thumbs up before launching into another sentence, which, to me, was nothing more than a jumbled collection of sounds.

The brown stain in the centre of his bandage was looking more and more like a strange and sinister eye, so I tried to concentrate on his good one.

I held up my hands. '*Saya . . . tidak . . . bisa . . . bicara . . . bahasa . . . Indonesia,*' I said with my best accent, telling him I couldn't speak his language.

He stopped talking and nodded knowingly. '*Baik, baik.*'

After that we just looked at each other, smiling and nodding, sharing the common experience of being strapped beneath tight sheets with bandages wrapped around a part of our body.

Then he had a thought. He leaned across and offered me his hand. 'Muklas,' he said. 'I Muklas.'

I took his hand, surprised at his limp grip. 'Alex,' I told him. '*Saya* Alex.'

Once again we fell into an awkward state of smiling and nodding before his face lit up again as if he'd come to a sudden and significant conclusion. He took a hand of small bananas from his bedside table and ripped one from the bunch. He passed it to me saying, '*Pisang. Pisang tuju.* Ba-na-na.'

I took it from him. '*Terima kasi*' – thank you – words I'd committed to heart – and opened it immediately, my stomach grabbing for the food. It occurred to me at that precise moment, though, that I didn't know where I was, nor how long I had been there.

It was a strange realisation that dropped into me like a weight, especially when I remembered the fate of my rucksack. I stopped, with the banana touching my lips, and I put my free hand to my waist where my money-belt had been.

Gone.

I dropped the fruit on the sheets and turned to check the table beside my bed. I leaned down to open the small door, feeling the blood racing to my head where it pumped and pounded, beating in my ears. The cupboard behind the door was empty. The weight that had dropped into my stomach began to mutate. It was no longer just a weight, it was now a living thing, which was expanding and rising inside me, threatening to cause panic in every cell of my body.

The man beside me was speaking again but his voice sounded different as my breathing quickened. I had lost everything that gave me any identity. I had lost myself. *Every*thing.

I wrestled with the constricting sheets and swung my legs from the bed. My ankles skinny and pale, dangling from the mattress as I lowered my feet onto the floor. The glossy paint covering the concrete was cold under my soles as I pushed myself up to stand. I crossed the ward as quickly as I was able to, my head numb and the sickness returning to my stomach. I didn't know where I was going or what I would do, but I needed to do something. My clothes had been taken from me, somebody must have undressed me, put the gown over me, and that meant someone must know where my belongings were. My money and my passport. Without them I was nobody.

I leaned on the swinging doors, pushed my way into the corridor and stopped. I put out a hand, leaning against the wall for support, and looked around. One side of the long hallway was lined with beds and trolleys, many of them old and broken, all of them full. Men and women, some with limbs missing, blood draining from their bodies as ill-equipped doctors and nurses struggled to help them. The other wall of the corridor provided a place to lean on for yet more patients. They were sitting in the stifling heat, no fans above their heads to break the air.

I stayed where I was, taking it all in, the sounds and the smells and the sights overloading my mind. I put my free hand over my eyes, my head swimming, wondering where I was and what I was going to do. When I took it away again, a middle-aged man in a long white coat was standing before me. He put his hand on my shoulder and spoke, but his words meant nothing. I shook my head. 'I don't understand.'

He tried to look sympathetic, nodding, still talking, but the look in his eyes was unfamiliar. His expressions were not like those I was used to. I tried to move away from him, but he smiled, taking my arm.

'No.' I snatched away. 'No. I need to . . . I need to . . .' I needed my life back. I needed to know where I was, but I didn't know how to ask him and he didn't know how to tell me.

Once again he reached out and took my arm, a reassuring look that I recognised.

'No.' I pulled away again, but with less conviction this time. He was trying to help. So I held up my hand and nodded, letting him take me and lead me back into the ward. He helped me to my bed and waited until I was beneath my sheets before he held out both hands, palms towards me.

'You want me to stay?' I asked him. 'Wait here, is that it? You want me to wait here?'

He backed away, still keeping his hands up, making small movements with them, reinforcing the idea that he wanted me to wait.

So I waited.

For how long, I don't know. From time to time I glanced at my wrist, forgetting that my watch had been taken from me on the road. So I waited a while longer, and a while longer still, staring at the door, wondering when the doctor was going to return, hoping he would bring my identity with him.

I ignored Muklas, the man in the bed beside mine. I avoided any contact with him, keeping all my attention on the swinging door.

When the doctor returned, he was not alone. This time he was accompanied by the angel I had seen on the road. But of course, she wasn't an angel. She was quite real, and she brought with her a breath of fresh air, a relief and a beauty that made her the next best thing to an angel.

3

Everything around me was alien. I knew little of the language and the customs. These were things I had intended to experience first-hand, to soak up and infuse into my consciousness. I came here hoping that I would grow and find myself in the way I'd heard other travellers speak of. I'd intended to broaden my horizons, unsuspecting of how dark those horizons were going to be. If I had known that my journey was to begin and end in death, perhaps I would never have stepped foot from my empty home.

I imagined I'd return from my travels a different person. More rounded and experienced. A *bigger* person. I envisioned an improved me; someone who would somehow stand out from others because I carried a knowing and accomplished air, but so far I had reached no further than an hour or so beyond my first foreign airport. My intentions had been derailed by a manic driver and an incredible road system where the only law was the unwritten *nasib saja*. Only fate. A law that allowed overtaking on blind corners because if it was your time to go, it was your time to go and there was nothing anybody could do about it. When your time was up, Allah would take you.

So, instead of the worldly-wise individual I was hoping to become, I'd been obstructed at my first attempt. I was left as myself. An inexperienced, self-conscious individual who'd had just enough confidence to buy a ticket and tell the handful of people he knew that he intended to travel. I'd even managed to surprise myself by boarding the plane in England and making it all the way across the world.

That's why she was a godsend. She wasn't a familiar face, but at the same time she *was* a familiar face. She had the kind of face I was accustomed to seeing. She looked more like me. I knew, even before she opened her mouth, that she would speak the same language as I did.

She had an open and relaxed manner about her, not a trace of affectation or self-consciousness. An air that suggested overwhelming confidence in herself. She came in without much more than a glance around the room, unperturbed by her surroundings.

'How ya feeling?' she asked, putting down her bag and sitting on the bed, turning towards me, her body close to my waist.

'You know what happened to my stuff?' I asked.

'Sure.' She lifted her bag onto her lap and took out my most precious belonging. 'Managed to save it for you,' she said. 'I was there when they took your kit off, got you all cleaned up.' Her eyes slipped from mine, an unwitting glance along my body. 'The clothes, they're gone, but this . . .' She handed me the belt that I'd kept hidden under my shirt, and I immediately opened the pockets, relieved to see everything still inside. Cash, cards, passport.

'I used some of the cash,' she said, provoking no reaction from me. I was just happy to see the essentials were still present. I was me again.

'It was the only way to get you a bed,' she went on. 'Money does a lot of talking here, you'll learn that quick enough. You can have anything you want, long as you got the cash to pay for it.'

'Thanks,' I said, zipping the pocket, and putting the belt on top of the sheet, gripping one end of it in a tight fist.

'Quite a fuckin' bump we had there, wasn't it?' If she'd been disturbed by the experience, she didn't show it. She just smiled, reached up to deal with a stray hair that had crept round to

15

hang over her forehead and across her right eye. It was fair but not platinum; a very light golden-brown, sun-kissed, waved and touching her shoulders. Like her clear brown skin, it had seen sunshine and felt fresh air. Beside hers, my own skin was pale, as if I'd been hiding from the world, holed up in a sunless place.

I nodded. 'Yeah. Quite a bump.' A bump that had separated people into individual parts. A bump that had left a stain of blood and viscera in its wake. She must have seen the expression on my face, or perhaps she felt the darkness of my thoughts, because she put a hand on mine.

'Don't think about it,' she said. 'You'll get used to it. Happens all the time round here.'

I looked down at her hand. Her brown skin on my pale skin. Like the old woman at the crash, only this girl's fingers were slender and strong, the knuckles not protruding like my own. Her short nails decorated with green varnish, a silver ring on her thumb. Blonde downy hairs on her forearms, bleached by the sun and standing out against her tan. She squeezed my hand in a familiar way. As if we knew each other.

'You were on the bus, too?' I asked, already feeling renewed. She had returned my identity and given me contact with the world.

'One of the lucky ones, I guess. Not much more than a few scrapes.' She pulled up the skirt of her dress to show me her right thigh, the skin broken. A raw patch no bigger than my hand.

'That's it?' I asked.

'That's it.' She smoothed out her dress. 'Skinned leg, a few bruises. Bump on the head. Nothing like yours, though.'

I lifted my eyes to hers, feeling her smile radiate from her full lips to the corners of her mouth, to the very edges of her green eyes, and I thought of Rachel, the girl who'd outgrown me. She'd had eyes almost as green, but her features were not as fine and her manner had not been as welcoming. I had loved Rachel, or at least I thought I had. We were to stay together for ever. Her going to university while I stayed back to care for my mother would not break us apart. We were meant for each other. But while she moved on, I stayed the same. I was left behind to play catch-up in my own life.

'Where are we?' I asked the angel who had come to my rescue.

'*Rumah sakit*,' she said. 'Hospital. Not a bad one either, to tell you the truth. I've seen a lot worse.' I caught the accent now, not too strong, but it was there. Australian.

I was about to thank her for helping me, but my thoughts were interrupted by the doctor who began speaking. She listened to him, nodding, and when he finished, she turned back to me.

'Doc here says you've had a concussion. Says you might feel sick for a while, a bit dizzy. Maybe even have a few blank moments, like you don't remember what happened. Bit of a cut on your head, too, but other than that you're OK. Looks like you're gonna live.'

I touched a hand to the bandage on my head.

'Don't worry about it,' she said as if she'd read my mind. 'You look great.'

The doctor spoke again, then turned and left the ward.

'He says you'll probably need a couple of days, and after that you'll be fine.'

'A couple of days? I have to stay here for a couple of days?'

She nodded. 'That's what he said.'

'Bollocks.'

'What? You don't want to get better?'

'It's not what I had in mind, that's all.'

She made herself more comfortable, taking her hand away from mine. I could still feel the warmth of her on my skin; it was moist from the sweaty closeness of our touch. I had enjoyed the contact and I wanted it back.

'I guess not,' she said. 'But what are you gonna do, eh?' She rubbed her fine nose with the back of her hand, then flicked a few stray hairs from her face.

'I suppose I could just leave.' Back home, in England, the

thought wouldn't have crossed my mind. Here, though, I felt less bound by the orders of the doctors. Everything felt less real.

'You could,' she said. 'But what if you collapsed out there? Somewhere nobody saw you? Concussion can do that, I reckon, and you might end up lying there all night.'

I shrugged. 'You're probably right.'

'I *am* right. I'm always right, Alex.'

Her use of my name made me look up with a start. 'How d'you know my name?'

'I looked at your passport. You had long hair, eh?'

'A while ago.'

'You're only twenty-five,' she said. 'That makes you a couple of years younger than me. Nothing was *that* long ago for us. Why d'you cut it?'

I ran a hand across my head, feeling the bristle of close-cropped hair. 'Thought it would be better that way.'

'Out with the old?'

'Maybe.' Rachel had liked it long. She wanted me to grow it that way.

'Suits you better short. Skinny guy like you, it makes you look . . . I dunno . . . tougher maybe.'

'Tougher?'

'Yeah. Older, too. Goes well with this,' she said, touching a finger to an old scar on my chin. 'Oh, and I like skinny guys; it wasn't an insult.' She pursed her lips as if she were hiding a smile, then reached out her right hand. 'Domino,' she said.

I took her hand and shook it like we were business people meeting over lunch. 'Domino? Like the song, you mean?'

'Song?'

'Van Morrison.'

'OK, yeah,' she said. 'Like that then, I guess. Like the game. Or the Bond girl.'

I watched her eyes, wondering if she was winding me up. 'For real? That's your name?'

She smiled. 'For real. My parents were kind of hippies, I guess.' She kicked off a flip-flop and lifted her right foot onto

18

the bed, her toes flexed. These nails were green, too. 'See.' She pointed at a small tattoo on the outside of her ankle. A single domino. Double six.

'I like it,' I said. 'It suits you.'

'Thanks. I think.'

'So,' she said after a moment. 'Have you been here long?'

'You mean Indonesia?'

'Well, I know how long you've been in the hospital, so yeah, I mean Indonesia.'

'About a day.'

'A day? You crashed on your first day? Shit, you're a veteran already. I know people who've been here years and never crashed.'

'You say that like it's a bad thing.'

'Where you headed?' She took her foot away.

It struck me that she asked where I was going, not where I'd come from, but then I remembered she'd seen my passport. She'd know exactly where I'd come from.

'Lake Toba,' I said.

'Danau Toba? Any reason? Most people, they go to Brastagi first. It's closer.'

'I saw some pictures, photos on the internet, and it looked . . . I don't know. Beautiful. As soon as I saw it, I knew I wanted to go.'

'It *is* beautiful,' she said. 'I think you'll like it there.'

'You've been?'

She nodded and we lapsed into a comfortable silence. I considered asking her more about my destination, but instead I enjoyed the moment, watching her look out of the window. Domino sitting right there on my bed, a musky scent of sandal-wood, sun cream and sweet body odour masking the stale air that pervaded the room.

I watched her profile, seeing the line of her narrow nose, the curve of her defined jaw, the rise of her cheekbones. A strong face. Striking and quite beautiful. The sweep of her neck dropping to her chest where the dress remained untied, showing the tiniest glimpse of the top of her small breasts.

She turned to look at me again, biting her lower lip and nodding before speaking. 'Well,' she said, 'I better get going. Maybe I'll see you around sometime.'

I hid my disappointment. Not only was she beautiful, but she was also my saviour and my translator. 'Yeah,' I said. 'I hope so.'

Domino stood, straightened her dress and threw her bag over her shoulder. 'Well, you look after yourself.'

I nodded. 'OK.'

She flicked her hair back from her face. Her wavy, sun-bleached hair. 'See you around, Alex.'

And with that, she turned and walked away. I watched her hips swing, the flesh of her buttocks firm beneath the dress, and a surge of desire ran through me.

'Domino,' I called after her.

She stopped and looked over her shoulder. 'Hm?'

'Thanks. For what you did back there. The bus, I mean.'

'Don't mention it.'

'If I can do something for you . . .' I said, not really knowing what I was saying or why I was saying it. I didn't know anything about her more than her name and her tattoo. I had no idea whether I'd even see her again.

'Sure,' she said, kissing her hand and lifting it in a half-wave. She smiled once more, then pushed through the swing door and walked out of my life.

4

For the rest of the evening I sat in silence. Dumb not through my own choice, but because there was no one I could speak to. The man in the bed next to mine, Muklas, called my name from time to time, and we smiled, gave each other the thumbs up and nodded in spasmodic bursts of attempted discourse, but that was the most either of us could manage. After some time, I decided it was best to not look in his direction, because my mouth ached from the forced smile and my head swam from the concussion. I felt stupid, in the most literal sense of the word, and embarrassed at my inability to do much more than wave my hands. I wished I'd spent more time with my Indonesian phrase book. But then, *most* of my thinking time was occupied with wishes. I wished I hadn't lost my rucksack. I wished I hadn't climbed onto the bus. I wished it hadn't crashed. But most of all, I wished Domino was still here.

It was absurd that I should think about her so much. I'd only known her for the briefest moment, yet she'd come to my aid twice, and that made her more than just another traveller.

I don't know what time it was when they turned out the lights. I repeatedly looked to my wrist, each time remembering that my watch was gone, whisked away by a boy who'd seen an opportunity and taken it. It made me angry to think about it, and every time I did, my hand went to the belt that Domino had brought back to me. My money and my passport. Without them, I was screwed.

The ward was quiet. The occasional moaning, snuffling, snoring from the other men, but nothing more than that. I could hear traffic outside, somewhere not far from the hospital, and I wondered why I hadn't noticed it during the day.

Part of me wanted to sleep, to rest my mind and sink into blackness, but something wouldn't allow it. I wasn't supposed to be here. I was supposed to be in control of what was happening to me, and it bothered me that I wasn't.

I watched the fan rotate above me. I concentrated on the warm draught of air it pushed at me, and I studied the shaft swivelling in its bearing. I listened to its blades as they cut through the air and I tried to relax my mind. Footsteps out in the corridor, the gentle swish of loose clothing, the squeak of rubber-soled shoes on glossy floors.

I thought how different this room was from the one my mother had been in. There were no electronic gadgets here, no intimacy, and yet the feeling was much the same. The feeling of being surrounded by the sick and the dying. It was something I'd never grown used to. I'd never felt comfortable with the polished floors and the turned-down beds and the blankets and the nurses and the machines. It all felt wrong.

I drifted in half-sleep for a while, my mind playing events back to me, jumbling them together, making a nonsense of what had happened. I tried to push them out, to think only of what I would do when I left the hospital. But still the memories and the unease crept in and, as a thin veil of sleep finally fell over me, so my thoughts were filled with the memories of my most recent hours. I saw the bus, felled like a giant beast, the blood disgorged from its bloated carcass, bright where it was still fresh, and shining under the sun. The stench of death was all around me, petrol fumes spinning in my head, the cries of the wounded and the dying filtering through me. And I saw the face of the old woman, her eyes watching me, fading, draining of life, unseeing and dry and empty. Now I was drifting too, my own life leaving me as the ache in my head pulsed to the irregular beat of the screaming and the crying. Then a quieter voice, my angel, whispering. Gentle at first, shaking me awake, then harder, more insistent, and I opened my eyes to the darkness of the hospital and there she was, her face close to mine.

'Alex,' she said. 'Shit, I thought you were never going to wake up.'

I stared at her. I wanted to say something, but nothing came to mind. I was still emerging from the horror of the crash. My head still pounding, but not from the screaming as it had been in my dream. This was the throbbing of the wound.

'You OK?' she asked. 'You all right?'

'Hm? Yeah. Yeah, I think so. What—'

'Something you should know,' she said.

I looked around, but the ward was dark and quiet.

'There's police coming to talk to you.'

'What?' I closed my eyes, fought through the pain in my head, feeling it subside.

'Something to do with the crash. They already talked to me but they didn't give much away. I think they found drugs or something.'

'Drugs?'

'In the wreck. Look, the doctor's taking them round to talk to everyone.'

I was still not recovered from my sleep. 'Drugs? I don't . . . What's that got to do with me?'

'We're white, Alex. They see young whiteys like us, they think we're only here for one reason. If there's drugs, it's our fault.'

'What?'

Domino held up a hand to quieten me. 'Just listen to me, Alex. You know the police here are not like your English police, right? I mean, they're *nothing* like your English police.'

'What're you saying?' I asked, the horror of the crash being replaced with a different feeling. Something less concrete. More unsettling. 'Why are you telling me this? I haven't done anything.'

'That doesn't make any difference.' Domino looked around. There was a light outside in the corridor, an orange glow leaking through the small, round, frosted windows on the swing doors. 'You seem like a nice guy,' she said, turning back to me. Her voice was a beautiful whisper, her hair close to my face, her scent in my nostrils. 'But – and I don't want you to take this the wrong way – but you seem a bit green.'

'Green?'

'Yeah. Like you don't know what you're doing.'

'I guess you're right.' The unease I felt before was masked now, masked by my proximity to Domino. She was intoxicating.

'I think they're looking for somebody, and that means they're not going to want you to leave.'

'Don't leave the country, you mean?' I tried to smile, but working the muscles tightened them around the back of my head, bringing pain. 'Well, I don't think I'm going anywhere right now.'

'They'll try to take your passport and your money.'

Now the unease returned. Only this time it was stronger, pushing any excitement about Domino to one side. 'But I'll get it back, right?'

She sighed and pursed her lips, tilting her head. 'Maybe. I mean, that's what they'll tell you, but I've heard about people who . . .' She shook her head. 'Look, Alex, it's just better if they don't get it. And if they see all that money you've got, they'll be wondering what you're planning on buying with it.'

I'd seen films and I'd read books. I knew that I had to keep hold of my passport. No matter what. It was all I had to prove who I was. If they took it away from me, I would be no one again. 'I'll tell them I don't have one,' I said. 'I'll tell them I lost it . . . Will they search me? You think they'll search me?'

Domino shook her head. 'Probably not, but it would be better if you had somewhere to hide it. Someone to—'

'You could take it for me.'

'No, I don't think so.'

'If I don't have it, I can't give it to them, right? You can bring it back to me tomorrow.' I don't know why I felt I could trust her, but it seemed like the best thing to do. Maybe she had already proved herself to me. She had come to my help at the crash. She had come as my translator earlier that day, returned my identity, and now she had come to warn me. And if she took my belongings, it would mean she'd have to come back. She couldn't just abandon me.

I had no idea that keeping her in my life was a mistake.

'I'll be gone by tomorrow,' she said. 'I can't.'

'Then wait until they've gone.' I put my hand on hers. 'Please.'

Domino paused, looked away, then nodded. 'OK,' she said, running her thumb over the back of my hand. 'I'll look after it for you.'

I slipped my hands beneath the sheet and removed the money-belt.

For the second and last time that day, I watched Domino leave through the swing doors, and I hardly had time to consider whether or not I'd made a mistake, when a shadow crossed the rounded windows, blocking the weak light that passed through them.

The indistinct shapes shifted, stopped, swayed like spectres waiting just out of sight, then the doors opened a touch. They cracked along the centre, a hairline of illumination that filtered into the ward and slipped across the floor, touching the foot of my bed. I watched as the doors inched open further, the sound of muffled voices as the visitors finished their conversation, the doors moving ever inwards until their discussion was over and they finally swung to their full extent. The men who walked in came without regard for whoever was inside. Their boots were loud on the concrete floor, their keys jangled, and the paraphernalia hanging from their belts clattered and creaked.

Some of the men in the ward remained still. Others stirred,

looked up with mild interest, then turned over in their beds, realising this visit was not for them.

The doctor who accompanied the men made no attempt to stop them. There was no consideration for the sick. Authority had stepped into the ward, and nothing was going to halt its procedure. There were no pleas to return tomorrow when the patients had rested.

The two policemen came to a halt beside my bed and looked down at me. Intimidating in their military-style uniforms, both of them with pistols on their hips. They wore peaked caps, pulled low to obscure much of their faces. If they were trying to scare me, it was working.

The one who was chewing gum was the first to speak. '*Dari mana kamu?*'

I looked at him.

'*Dari mana?*' he said again.

I shook my head at him. 'I . . . I don't speak. *Saya tidak bisa bicara*—'

'English?' he interrupted.

'English. Yes. I'm English. You speak—'

'*Siapa namamu?* Name.'

'Alex. Alex Palmer.'

'Passport.' He held out his hand.

Again I shook my head with a sigh, but inside my heart was racing. I'd been in a crash, I'd seen blood and death, and now I was lying to the police. 'I don't have it,' I said. 'I lost it in the crash. It was stolen. A boy stole my things.'

The policeman stopped chewing and looked at his partner, who shrugged and looked directly at me, saying, 'Passport.'

I searched my memory for a phrase. '*Saya tidak punya*. I don't have—'

'No passport?'

I shook my head. 'Stolen.'

'*Dicuri?*' He seemed to understand.

'Yes,' I said. 'Stolen. On the road.'

The policeman who was chewing spoke to his partner, his

26

language fast, the words spilling from his mouth, and he pointed at the cabinet beside my bed. The partner nodded and squatted down to open the door and check inside, then looked up saying, '*Tidak ada.*'

The other one stared at me, his jaws taking a rest from chewing as he considered me, then he spoke to the doctor, who replied, causing both policemen to look at me again. He began chewing once more, motioning at me with his chin. His partner stood, pulled back the sheet.

'What—' But before I could protest, he put his hand on my waist and ran it over me.

Finding nothing, he shook his head and then a rapid conversation broke out among the three of them. By now some of the other patients were beginning to take a little more interest. One or two had propped themselves up on an elbow to watch the show. In the bed beside me, Muklas was looking on with something like an expression of sympathy on his face.

'You wait,' the policeman said, putting one hand on the butt of his gun. I don't think it was intended as a threatening gesture, more like he was finding a place to rest his hand, but it felt threatening nonetheless.

I nodded.

'You don't go from here.'

'OK.'

'*Besok.* Tomorrow. We. Come – back – tomorrow.'

'OK.'

'You stay.'

'OK.'

They stood for a few more seconds, then they pushed past the doctor and marched from the ward, the doctor hurrying to keep up with them.

When they were gone, I stared at the doors, watching the decreasing arc of their swing. There was a kind of laziness to the way they flopped back and forth. When they came to a final halt, I cast my eyes around the room, watching the men avoiding my eyes, turning and settling beneath their sheets. Only Muklas would look at me. He gave me a nod and showed me a thumbs up.

'OK,' he said. 'You OK.'

I forced a smile around my fear and returned his thumbs up, then I slipped down in the bed and studied the ceiling, wondering if the policemen were going to come back right away. I was afraid of what they might do to me. The doctor had obviously told them about my money-belt, and now they thought I was hiding something from them. Perhaps they had gone to look for a translator. Domino, even. Or maybe they'd gone to find her for a different reason, and when they came back, they would drag us both away. I should have been honest. They were the police after all, and I'd only known Domino a few hours. Maybe when they came back tomorrow, I would tell the truth. Domino would bring back my passport and I would do the right thing.

But Domino didn't return.

I waited for a long time. I turned onto my side and watched the doors, waiting for her. But as the evening progressed and the room filled with the sound of snoring, I began to wonder if I had been wrong to trust her. I imagined her spending my money, selling my passport, but told myself that if she'd wanted to do that, she wouldn't have returned it the first time. It had to be something else. There had to be a good reason why she hadn't come back, and I felt helpless, lying there, not knowing. The only way I would ever know was if I found her.

So I shook my head and sat up in bed, looking round the ward in the semi-darkness, illuminated only by the glow from the windows in the swing doors. I slipped off the loose bandage, touched the crusty scar on the back of my head and inspected my fingertips. Clear. I threw back the sheet and swung my legs over the side of the bed. I waited, sitting upright, testing my stability. My head didn't spin. I didn't feel faint, no head rush. Satisfied I wouldn't collapse, I moved forward, placing my feet on the painted floor, enjoying the coolness of it on my soft soles. I stood and straightened my unflattering gown, then I began walking towards the light, keeping my eyes ahead of me, fixed on the two circles of dim orange.

I pushed against one of the swing doors and moved into the corridor, allowing it to close behind me, an eerie, quiet sound, the arc of its swing decreasing until it came to a stop as I looked around.

It was calm now, nothing like it had been earlier in the day. There were still trolleys lined along the far wall, perhaps fifteen or sixteen in all, but almost half of them were empty. I wondered if the patients who'd been lying on them had beds now or if they were in boxes somewhere down below, keeping cool.

An occupant of the gurney nearest me rolled her head to one side, straining her eyes to the corner of their sockets to see who had come from the ward. She stared at me, a vacant, tired stare, then rested her head back, a quiet moan escaping her open lips.

I waited, looking both ways along the corridor, deciding which way to go. Now that I was up, I wanted to stretch my legs, feel as if I were something other than bedridden, to be free of the walls, the smell and the pitiful noises of the sick. I wanted to feel alive, not muted, suffocated, languishing in the turgid atmosphere of the ward. I needed to breathe something other than the stale stench of sickness and death, to be outside where the air was fresh. I wanted to find Domino, take my passport and run from this place. Do what I had come here to do. To live and experience a different life, to escape from the emptiness and regret I had left at home.

Behind me a sound, making me turn and see a doctor coming towards me. The same doctor who had been with the policemen. I expected him to try to stop me, to take hold of me like I was a patient in a mental institution, to guide me back to my bed, but I spoke to him before he could react.

'Domino,' I said to him. 'Where's Domino?'

He held out his hands to show he didn't understand.

'Does no one in this fucking place speak English? Domino. The girl. *Girl*,' I said, becoming frustrated. I shouldn't be here. This wasn't where I was supposed to be.

'Girl?' He stopped. '*Perampuan?*'

'Yeah, yeah, that's it. *Perampuan*. Where is she? Where?'

The doctor glanced at the floor and shook his head.

'What? Where is she?'

He met my eye and put a hand on my arm. '*Perampuan mati*. Girl dead.'

'What?'

He nodded.

'No.' I stepped back, pushing his hand away. 'No way. She was here. She was right here, not more than an hour ago. You're lying.'

The doctor approached, extending a hand, but I knocked it away and turned, moving quickly along the corridor, looking for a way out. It was a bad dream. Death piled on death. I had to get away from here. I had to be outside where life was real. I needed to see normality, even though it wouldn't be my own. Right now any kind of normality would be enough. And as I hurried away, I glanced back, but the doctor did not follow. He simply stood and watched.

There was nothing to indicate which might be the way out, so I just picked a direction, my bare feet slapping on the cold concrete. I looked down at each trolley as I passed, seeing blank faces. One or two glanced up at me, their eyes drowsy, but no one spoke. Once I was past them, I came to an intersection where the corridor was crossed by another. I stopped and scanned both ways. There was no sign of anyone and I began to move forwards again when the door at the far end to my right opened and two men entered. They weren't doctors. Doctors would be wearing white, but these men were not. As they passed they left in their wake the smell of cooking and the scent of outside, and I guessed they were visiting the hospital, so I headed in the direction from which they had come.

I picked up my pace, a prisoner making a break for freedom,

and found myself checking behind me, looking to every door I passed, expecting a doctor, a nurse, an orderly to hurry through and confront me. But no one appeared.

Still in my bare feet and my flimsy gown, I approached the doors and pushed one open just enough to look through. On the other side was a reception area. Nothing big, just a square entrance room with seats on either side, forming a path, which led to a large double door held open to the night. Facing the two rows of seats, just to my right, was a counter where two nurses were stationed. They were busy with the patients who'd formed an untidy line at the counter.

All of the seats were occupied, and there were a number of people milling around. Some of them, I was relieved to notice, were dressed like me, and I guessed I wouldn't attract too much attention if I stepped in.

I was wrong. I did attract attention, but not because of my attire. It was because of the colour of my skin. As soon as people noticed me, they kept their eyes on me, and I tried hard to ignore the stares. I made my way among them, heading for the open doors, and I passed out into the night.

I stood at the top of a short flight of wide, shallow, concrete steps, which sloped down to a tarmac circle surrounded by thick-bladed grass. Behind me, on the wall of the hospital, bright lights illuminated the lawn and the palms that grew on it. Insects flitted in the cone of light, bumping into the bulbs. The air was warm but agreeable, and the smell was exotic and exciting.

Beyond the modest driveway and garden of the hospital, a pair of large, wire mesh gates, and then the road. A busy road, full of life and movement. All manner of vehicles passing, engines coughing fumes into the night. And beside the road, a line of stalls. From the top of the steps I could see a cart loaded with fruits and, beside it, a woman grilling chickens on a rotisserie, the scent of the spices and the cooking meat coming over to me on the breeze. For a moment all thoughts of passports and policemen and Domino were banished. This was what I had come for, and I felt myself drawn down the steps. I wanted to go out there, to be surrounded by the life. I wanted to be away from the hospital right now.

'I wouldn't go out there,' she said. 'Not dressed like that, anyway.'

'What?' I was so wrapped up in everything that had happened, I hadn't noticed her sitting on the edge of the step to my right. Domino. She was looking up at me now, making no attempt to stand, her elbows on her knees, a cigarette in one hand, held near her pale lips so the smoke was drifting across her face. She squinted one eye as she looked up at me, then took a drag and looked out at the street. 'It's like going out in your pyjamas,' she said, blowing smoke into the air. 'You look better without the bandage, mind you.'

'You're . . . you're alive.'

Domino looked taken aback. 'Um. Yeah. Reckon I am.'

'They said . . . the doctor said . . .'

'Well, come on,' she smiled. 'What did the doc say?'

I shook my head, pressed the heels of my palms into my eyes. 'Fuck,' I said, smiling down at her. 'What a night I'm having. They said you were dead.'

'Dead?' She didn't seem surprised. 'Well, clearly I'm not.'

'Clearly.'

'Wonder why they said that.'

I shrugged. 'Maybe I misunderstood.'

'Maybe. Oh,' she pulled my belt from her bag, 'this is yours.'

I took it from her, wanting to check it but not wanting to offend her. I felt a pang of shame when I remembered I'd considered she might have stolen it.

'Check it if you like,' she said. 'I don't mind.'

'It's OK. I trust you.'

'You do?' She took a drag and blew it away from me. She held the cigarette between the ring finger and the middle finger of her right hand. I'd never seen anyone hold it like that before.

'Smoke?'

'No, thanks.'

'Suit yourself.'

I sat down beside her, catching the strong smell. 'What the hell *is* that?'

'This?' She held up the cigarette. '*Kretek*. Clove cigarettes. Taste like shit, but it's all they had.' She nodded out towards the road, indicating that she'd bought them somewhere out there in the strange, new world. 'The coppers came and talked to you, then?'

'Yeah, and they were pretty scary. They searched me. The doctor must've told them I had a belt.'

'Good job you gave it to me, then.'

'Maybe I should've let them have it.'

'You did that, you'd probably never see it again. Probably not the passport, *definitely* not the money.'

'I don't want to get into trouble.'

'If you were in trouble, I reckon you'd know about it by now. And if they'd seen that money, you wouldn't be sitting here. You'd be sitting in a cell trying to explain what you were going to buy with it. First thing they'd think of is drugs. Trust me, I know. You did the right thing, Alex.'

'So what did they say to *you*?'

'Not much. Asked me a few questions.'

'You said something about drugs.'

'They showed me a bag of dope, told me they found it at the crash. Asked if I knew anything about it and I said no.'

'And they just let you go?'

Domino shrugged.

I studied her face. 'Thanks. For helping me.'

'Don't mention it. I'll keep you right.' She leaned round and touched a finger to the back of my head. 'Doesn't look too bad,' she said. 'They've not made a bad job of the stitches. Should dissolve nicely. Good job you had your hair cut, though. Don't want those buggers leaving you with patches.'

I looked out at the heavy traffic. A bus rolled past, faster than it should, the roof laden with baskets and battered suitcases. It was smaller than the bus that had crashed, this one painted blue with a yellow bonnet and elaborate lettering etched on the side. I watched for a while, distracted only when I felt something brush against the exposed skin of my leg. A cat, scabbed and dirty, rubbed its nose against me, then passed the length of its body along my shin before turning and doing it again. Its white fur was grey with filth, its face scarred from its life of survival. I put out a hand and stroked it, feeling the vertebrae and ribs beneath skin that was painfully thin. It brought memories of the old woman in the road, of the way her bones had rubbed together when I held her hand, and I snatched my fingers back, pushing the cat away with my foot.

'You got the time?' I asked her.

She held up both hands to show me her wrists. All she wore on them was bangles. 'What you *doing* out here, anyway?' she said, putting her hands down. 'I thought you were supposed to be resting.'

The cat loped down the steps, spotting something in the grass, and crouched low to the ground.

'I was looking for you. I've had enough resting,' I said, seeing the cat jump, the muscles twisting under gossamer skin. 'I had to get out. Thought I was going crazy in there. What about you?' I looked away from the cat and studied her. She didn't have the same strength about her I'd seen earlier that day. She had an air of vulnerability now, and it was an attractive quality. It was a side of Domino I wouldn't often see; a side that was kept hidden, crushed beneath the dark weight of the true influences in her life.

Domino shrugged. 'I was with someone on the bus,' she said. 'She wasn't as lucky as you and me.'

I wasn't sure exactly what she meant but I could guess. 'I'm sorry,' I said. It seemed to be the right thing.

'Not your fault. Not anyone's. Shit, I didn't even know who she was, not really. Some kid I sat next to on the plane coming over from Sydney. Could've been anyone. Maybe that's who the doc was talking about when he said someone was dead.'

I didn't say anything. I went back to watching the cat, which

34

now had an insect in its mouth. A praying mantis, its unnatural arms locked onto the cat's whiskers, the cat shaking its head and pawing at it.

'She died about half an hour ago,' Domino said. 'They wanted me to stick around 'cause I can speak the lingo, but . . .' Her words trailed off and she took another drag on the cigarette. 'Weird, isn't it? She got so banged up she was bleeding inside. I was sitting next to her and all I get is a skinned thigh and a few bruises. Maybe it was just her time.'

Out on the road, life continued to speed past, the stall owners continued to trade. The cat had managed to release itself from the mantis's grasp and was hunched in the grass, chewing and snapping at its stick-like body.

'So what about you?' she said after a few moments. 'What's your story?'

'No story.'

'You gotta have a story. Guy like you . . . on your own.'

'Who says I'm on my own?'

'Well, aren't you? I mean, you never asked about anyone, you didn't ask to make any calls, nothing. It's like you've got no one else to think about but yourself.'

I rested my chin in my palm.

'You must be brave, I guess; it takes guts being alone like that. Not many people come out here on their own. Normally you see mates, couples, people seeing a bit of the world before they go to uni or whatever, but not on their own. And normally they're a bit younger.' She looked at me. 'Younger, but not so green.'

'Lucky I found you, then.'

'Lucky *I* found *you*. You should've brought someone with you.'

'Couldn't find anyone,' I said.

She ran her eyes over me and smiled. 'Something tells me you didn't look too hard.' The smile broadened her mouth, stretched her full lower lip, changed her whole face.

I put my forearms on my knees and watched another bus pass on the road beyond the gates.

'So what *is* it with you?' she asked. 'You don't look like the backpacking-before-uni type. Well, you don't look like the uni type, anyway.'

'Don't I? Why not?'

She shrugged. 'You just don't.'

'I wanted to go. Filled out my applications, posted them in, but things didn't turn out how I'd hoped.'

'Plans change,' she said.

'Yeah.'

'It happens. The path is clear, then . . .' she shrugged, 'then something blocks it and we take a new direction. It's fucked up, but it's life.'

'Maybe I'll go to university one day,' I said, more to myself than anything. 'When I get back.' She didn't seem to hear, though.

'So what is it, then?' she asked. 'You're looking for something? An adventure? That's why you're on your own, right? You're hoping to find yourself?'

I turned to look at her now. 'Sounds cheesy when you say it out loud.'

Domino nodded. 'That's 'cause it is cheesy.' She finished her cigarette, smoking it as far as it would go, right down to the filter, before dropping it at her feet and grinding it into the rough concrete.

She cast her eyes over me again, looking at every part of my face but not making me uncomfortable. Something about the way she did it made me feel wanted rather than studied. When she was finished she smiled a wistful smile and looked out at the road, allowing a light sigh to escape her lips.

'My mother died,' I told her, not really knowing why. 'I looked after her a long time.'

'Sounds shitty.'

'It was. I took care of her at home, but eventually she needed more than I could give.'

36

'That's tough.' She flicked her head back. 'I guess you've had enough of hospitals, then?'

'You could say that. Seeing her hooked up to machines all the time, being pumped with this drug or that drug. Christ, you should've seen the tablets she had to take every day. I didn't really have to be there all the time, she hardly even opened her eyes, but . . . somehow it seemed like the thing to do, you know.'

'Look after your own, right?'

'Maybe, I don't know.'

'Funny what makes us do things. No brothers or sisters?'

'Uh-uh. No one.' I pinched the bridge of my nose and sniffed hard.

'*No* one?'

'I barely even have any friends,' I told her.

'No one waiting for you back home?'

'Nope.'

'That's tough.'

'You know, I did things I never thought I'd have to do for my own mother. Clean her up, wipe spit off her chin, wipe her . . . well, you can guess.'

I wondered why I was telling her this. Maybe it was because I'd never had anyone to talk to about it before. Not someone who was going to be a fleeting part of my life. Someone who'd walk into and then straight out of my life. I was here on a journey. I'd pass through this place and leave no trace of myself behind. It didn't matter what I said.

'It went on for so long it's like there was no end to it,' I told her. 'She hated every minute of feeling like that; I hated every minute of *seeing* her like that . . .'

'You put me in a situation like that,' she said, 'I reckon I'd have to do something.'

'What do you mean?'

'Give her meds, switch something off, increase the dose. Anything. It's not right to be like that; to let someone suffer. I mean, I wouldn't want it, would you?'

'I don't know, I . . .' I let the words fall away. I'd said as much as I wanted to; the conversation had taken a difficult turn. I didn't want to think about it any more; the guilt of what I had or hadn't done.

'So then you ran away.' It was as if Domino had sensed my discomfort and now she steered me in a different direction.

'Not ran away,' I said. 'No.'

'But you had to get away. Do something? It's what I'd want.'

'After she died, I felt like I didn't know who I was any more.' I stopped, wondering if I was saying too much, but Domino looked at me as if she were expecting me to go on, so I said it anyway. 'I spent so long looking after her, I had no life. Nothing. I was going to go to university. I had a girlfriend. All gone.'

'There's always a girl,' she said, lighting another cigarette. 'What was her name?'

'What difference does it make?'

'Good answer.'

'If things had been different, maybe I would've come out here with friends, who knows? Maybe I never would've come at all.'

'Maybe.'

I shrugged. 'What happened happened. So I had enough money to come out here. She paid for it. My mother. So I have to make it worth it. Make it mean something.'

'Because you don't know where you fit in. You don't know where you *belong*. You're looking for yourself.'

I felt a smile cross my lips. 'Only place I found myself is in a hospital ward that smells of piss.'

'Yeah,' she said. 'I noticed that when I came in. Wasn't yours, was it?'

'No,' I laughed, but thinking about the ward reminded me that I'd lost everything I owned except for the belt that was strapped to my waist beneath my gown. And sitting out here, I knew I wanted to get away from this place, leave this part of my trip behind me. I looked at Domino. 'You know, I heard somewhere that you're never free to do what you want until you've lost everything you've got.'

'I like that.'

My attention was drawn to a car pulling up by the entrance to the hospital, white and blue, the word *Polisi* across the bonnet. It looked cleaner than the other vehicles that passed. Newer. For a moment, there was no movement, then both doors opened at once.

'And . . . ?' Domino asked.

'And what?'

'And is it working? Is it true? You've lost everything, right? Are you free to do whatever you want?'

'The jury's still out on that one.'

Domino put the cigarette to her mouth, that strange way of holding it, her middle finger touching the tip of her nose. She raised her eyebrows as she took a drag. 'I was like you once, Alex,' she said around the scented smoke.

'Yeah?' I glanced at her, seeing that she, too, was looking at the police car.

'Mm. Lost, I mean. In a different way, though. Foster care with my brother before we were split up. After that I was trouble all the way.'

'What kind of trouble?' I asked her.

'Kids' stuff mostly.' She continued to watch as two policemen stepped out of the car and headed towards us. They were not the same ones who'd come into the ward, but her words became slow, more considered. Distracted. 'But then I came here. Found a home and a purpose.'

Dressed in short-sleeved khaki shirts, black trousers and boots, pistols in leather holsters, the policemen reached the steps and started up, both of them with their eyes on us.

'Don't look at them,' Domino said.

'What?'

'Don't make eye contact.'

'Why?'

'They don't like it.'

'OK.'

'You know, there's places for people like us,' she said, lowering her voice as they passed, their boots heavy on the broken concrete, one of them his feet almost touching my thigh.

'How do you mean? What places?' I turned my head just as one of them looked back and down at me, so I glanced away, watching from the corner of my eye as they went through the hospital doors and disappeared from sight. 'What kind of places?' I asked again.

'Good places.' She jumped to her feet as if a sudden change of mood had overcome her. 'You hungry?' She took me by surprise.

'What? Yeah, starving.'

'Let's get something to eat, then.'

'Maybe we should go back inside.'

'What for?'

'I dunno. The police—'

'You give them your name?'

'My name? Um. Yeah. Yeah, I did.'

'But they don't know where you're going, who you are, anything about you?'

'I suppose not.'

'So what's your problem?'

'I—'

'Let's get out of here, Alex. Before they decide it's got something to do with us. Let's just go. You and me.' Now she was back to the confident woman I'd met before. The melancholy and the worry had evaporated as if she had something else to concentrate on. 'You'd like that?'

'Yeah, I suppose—'

'You *suppose*?'

'I mean yes. I do want to get out of here. More than anything, but . . .' I looked back at the hospital doors.

'Somewhere you need to be?' she asked. 'Something you left behind?'

I shook my head. 'I haven't got anything.'

'You've got your money.'

'Yeah, I got that.'

'So, you want to get out of here or not?'

'I—'

'You can stay here if you like. Fester in that bed, surrounded by all those people, wait a few more days and then follow your guidebook if the coppers let you. Or maybe they'll just drag you down to a cell.' She looked at me. 'Or you can come with me, Mr Anonymous. Test that theory about losing everything so you can be free to do what you want. I'll take you places you won't find in your guidebook, show you things you didn't even know existed.'

'Like what?'

Domino shrugged, her body language telling me she wasn't going to give anything away. If I wanted to know her secrets, I would have to follow her. And that was the decision I had to make. All my life I'd been starved of choice. I looked after my mother, that's what I did. During that time most of my decisions were made for me by other people. Doctors, nurses, solicitors. I'd only ever had to make one real decision, and I still felt the weight of it now, still wondered if it had been the right one. But I told myself even *that* hadn't been a real choice. There was never a real alternative for me. But now my choices were limitless.

I looked up at her. 'You said I should stay here. Get better.'

'Did I? When?'

'Before. When you came to see me.'

'Are you feeling better now?'

'I think so.'

'What are you worried about, then? Anyway,' she winked, '*I'm* with you now. You'll be fine.' She held out her hand.

I could stay right here; go back and lie in my bed to wait for the police. I could miss an opportunity. Or I could take her hand and let her show me things that were not in the guidebook. 'Like this, though?' I glanced down at my gown. 'Running away from the police – like *this*?'

Domino laughed. It was a warm sound. Not too loud. Not raucous and unpleasant. Not the kind of laugh that would attract attention. It was an intimate and comfortable sound, and it made her mouth turn up more at one side than the other. It was a laugh that reached her eyes, made me want to keep looking at her.

'No,' she said. 'Not like that. We'll have to get you something to wear.' She threw her cigarette out onto the grass where it continued to glow. 'Come on.' She slung her bag over her shoulder.

I looked up at her, still wearing the same dress she'd had on when she came to see me. Her calves were inches from my face and I could smell the last remnants of cream on her, mingled with the scent of her body. There were fine, light hairs on her calves and around the front of her legs. The domino on her ankle.

I pushed to my feet, standing only a couple of inches taller than her now, and looked into her, feeling a connection. Her green eyes fixed on mine, serious now, flitting gently from side to side as if constantly focusing on different points of my face.

'Come on,' she said again, and this time I let her take my hand.

'Where are we going?'

'Round here,' she said. 'Something I saw earlier on.' And she took me across the front of the hospital building, into the night beyond the arc of the lights.

I had made my choice.

5

Domino and I moved without sound as we made our way round the white-painted building, passing shuttered windows, and rooms that slept in darkness. The thick-bladed grass was coarse on my bare feet, but it wasn't uncomfortable, and the ground itself was warm and spongy. From the trees and the bushes the cicadas chirped their music into the night. Ahead, a shaft of light poured from an open window, projecting a stream of orange, which met an impenetrable hedge. The dense foliage broke the light into a thousand shadows that stained the grass.

Domino stopped moving and turned to me, raising a finger to her lips. She ducked onto her haunches and beckoned me closer. I squatted beside her and she brought her face close to mine, brushing her hair back and putting her mouth to my ear.

I could feel her lips against me, and I could hear the sound of her moist tongue in her mouth as she spoke. Some of her hair loosened and fell against my cheek. 'Quiet now,' she whispered. 'There might be someone inside. I'll take a look.' Her words were warm against my ear, the sibilants a delicious mix of hard and soft. Her breath tickled my neck, sending shivers down my back.

Domino let go of my hand and put her bag on the grass. She crept to the window, keeping low. When she was below the sill, she raised her head, peering into the room. She paused, stood and turned to me. The light illuminated her face and she smiled, beckoning, so I crept closer and stood to look inside the room.

Directly opposite the window was a closed door. Above and to the right, in the high corner of the room, a small television perched on a shelf. It was not switched on. Below it, a bare wooden table was home to several stacks of glasses, a large kettle and three or four tins. The other side of the room was lined with shelves, most of which were filled with piles of white and dark-blue clothing. From where I was standing, they looked to be trousers and tunics, the type of thing worn by hospital staff.

'You should find something to fit,' Domino said.

'What? No, I can't take that.'

'Sure you can. All you have to do is climb in and grab something.'

'No way.'

'What you worried about? No one's going to come in.'

'How do you know? And there's bloody police everywhere.'

Domino shrugged. 'If you won't, then I will.' And with that, she pulled herself onto the windowsill and jumped down into the room. She went straight to the shelves of clothes and took a pair of navy-blue trousers from the top of the pile, holding them up for me to see. I stepped back, spying both ways along the side of the hospital, not quite believing what she was doing. I looked back at her, wide-eyed and questioning, but she stayed where she was, waiting for an answer, so I shook my head. Too small.

After two or three tries, she held up a pair of trousers that might fit me, so I nodded and she threw them at me and moved on to the shirts.

Once she had found a suitable shirt, she came back to the window and passed it to me before pulling herself back onto the windowsill. 'Give a lady a hand?' she whispered, so I put my hands under her arms and was helping her through the window when the door opened behind her and a man walked in. He was dressed in clothes not unlike the ones Domino had just stolen for me, except his were white. There was a streak of blood across the front of his tunic.

He stopped in his tracks, the door held open, and everything hung in time for a split second. The man frozen in the doorway, Domino halfway through the window, me with hands under her arms, pulling her through. Then the moment of suspension broke. He opened his mouth and shouted a string of words that had no meaning to me. Anger in his eyes, he ran towards Domino, grabbing her legs and yelling at the top of his voice.

Domino gripped the windowsill hard, pulling against him, and I put all my effort into helping. The man wasn't big, but he managed quite a fight, tugging and shouting until eventually Domino made it through the window. She slid through the opening, fell onto the grass in a heap, then leaped to her feet, grabbing my arm and saying, 'Run!'

I was still shocked and I hesitated, wanting to apologise, to return the clothes we'd taken, but Domino pulled at my arm.

I held up a hand to the man, offered him a pleading look and then followed Domino's lead, grabbing the clothes as we made our escape. We ran back to where she'd left her bag, Domino bending to scoop it up before turning and heading directly for the hedge.

'Jump over,' she shouted.

I didn't have time to think about what I was doing. I saw Domino jump over the hedge, but not make it. She landed on top of it, swimming through the leaves and branches, making her way across. I did the same, reaching a little further than she had done but still struggling to get over, feeling the branches raking at my exposed skin as I went.

We tumbled onto the ground on the other side, picked ourselves up and ran as fast as we could until we came to a small copse of trees, where we stopped to catch our breath. Domino collapsed to the ground, her back to a gnarled trunk, and I squatted beside her, my breath coming in palsied gasps.

'You're not supposed to exert yourself too much,' she said between breaths, beginning to laugh through her pained expression. 'Bloody hurt my leg, too.'

I looked at her, wondering if she was crazy or fun, enjoying the feeling of adrenaline in my body as I sat down beside her. She put her head on my shoulder, laughing into my neck, and when the laughter died, she lifted her face and kissed my cheek. 'Thanks,' she said. 'I think I needed that. Something to pick me up.'

I nodded, surprised by the kiss. 'Me too.' I was sore where the hedge had scratched me, the tops of my legs, my arms, but I felt alive again, not like a patient any more.

'Back there,' she said. 'When I was in that room, and you were standing outside, getting all antsy?'

'Yeah?'

'That gown you're wearing looked almost transparent from my angle.' She raised her eyebrows and looked me up and down. 'Nice.'

I smiled and glanced back at the hedge. 'Will he come after us?'

She shook her head. 'I doubt it.'

'Really?' I said, feeling relieved. It had been fun, but I didn't want it to last too long.

'Probably send a guard instead. Or maybe some of those cops.'

'For real?'

'Yeah,' she nodded. 'Probably. We should go.'

I looked back at the hedge again, fancying that I could see figures moving behind it.

'You better get changed.'

I looked down at the clothes in my hands. 'Yeah.'

I pulled on the trousers, slipping them up my legs and underneath the gown while Domino watched. They were tight, but I could fasten them, no problem. Then I lifted the gown over my head, Domino's eyes on me the whole time, not embarrassed to look me over as I dressed.

'We'll get you something else later on,' she said. 'And some flip-flops from one of those stalls.'

'Shouldn't we go further away? I mean, it'll be obvious it was us, won't it? If a guard comes looking. Me walking around in hospital clothes. And there's the police . . .'

'Stop worrying about the police,' she said, standing up. 'But yeah, I guess you're right.'

As she spoke, I felt a sharp stinging sensation in my toe and I let out a yelp, slapping at my foot as if I'd been stung by a wasp. 'What the hell was that?' There was something small and hard between my fingers.

As I lifted it closer to my face, so that I could see what had bitten me, I felt another sharp bite. Then Domino was slapping at her legs, too, saying, 'Bloody red ants. Come on.'

And once again we were running, as if all I would ever do with Domino was run. We were running and slapping our legs at the same time, coming out onto the road, and laughing as we slowed our pace, caught our breath and began walking away from the hospital, making our way among the stalls.

'You know what?' I said to her as we approached a *warung* with all manner of knick-knacks, including flip-flops, hanging from hooks around its frame. 'I don't know where we are. I don't even know what time it is.'

Domino shrugged. 'It's not late, I reckon. Just after nine, maybe.'

'Feels later,' I said.

'It gets dark early.'

We stopped in front of the *warung* and Domino turned to me. 'We're about half an hour away from Lake Toba. And that's where you're going, right?'

I nodded and looked around, seeing things in a new light now I had some inkling of where I was. I thought it strange that everything should look so different just because I had a vague idea of my location on a map. And yet it made the place more real. I smiled and breathed deeply. 'Yeah,' I said. 'Lake Toba. That's right.'

Domino nodded and turned to the woman at the stall. She was wearing a sarong and a cotton top, a second sarong strung around her shoulder, a heavy bundle inside.

Domino said something to the woman and pointed at a pair of flip-flops, looking at me and asking if they'd be big enough.

The woman reached up to take them down, turning so I caught a glimpse of a small baby wrapped within the sling of the sarong over her shoulder. She passed the flip-flops, new and smelling of rubber and plastic, and I slipped them on, nodding, telling Domino they were fine.

I paid, putting a few notes in my pocket so I didn't need to reach for the money-belt every time, and then we moved on, stopping at another *warung*. We bought a couple of spring rolls and something wrapped in green leaves before Domino grabbed my arm and indicated a policeman further down the road, close to the hospital entrance, where the car was still parked.

'Let's go over here,' she said, leading me away. 'Where it's dark.'

So we hurried off the roadside, heading to where the grass was thin and a banyan tree grew with prop roots so thick and so many that they were indistinguishable from the main trunk. The tree was like a forest of its own, and we slipped into its cover.

'You think they're looking for us?' I asked.

'I don't reckon. He's just standing there smoking a cigarette, doesn't look like he's in a hurry to do anything. Anyway, they won't come over here; most of them think these trees are haunted.'

'You're sure?'

'Relax,' she said as she sat down on the compacted dirt. 'We'll sit where we can watch him. If he looks like he's coming this way, we'll leave.'

I checked the ground for ants, then settled beside Domino, close enough that our hips were touching but neither of us moved away. The banyan roots fell around us, some thick and woody, giant fingers reaching for the ground, penetrating the soil, others clumped together, winding round one another, coiling like serpents.

I watched the policeman through the trunks of our strange

forest and bit into the spring roll, burning my tongue on the vegetable filling.

'So you want to go together?' Domino said.

'Hm?'

'Lake Toba. It's where I'm headed, too.'

'Really?'

'Coincidence, eh?'

I took another bite.

'There's a place,' she said. 'I'm meeting some friends there. You can probably stay awhile.'

I stopped eating and looked at her, thinking for a moment.

'No pressure,' she said. 'I mean, do what you like, but it would be fun, I can promise you that.'

'Yeah, that would be good.' Already I felt a sense of excitement. Domino wanted to be with me.

'Maybe we'll get to know each other better. I'll show you those things I told you about.'

'I'd like that.' I didn't want to sound desperate, but I wanted to be with her. She was exciting and beautiful. And she was strong. Being with her made *me* feel stronger. I had thought I could do this alone, but the crash had killed my confidence. Domino could bring it back for me. Maybe she'd even travel with me awhile.

'So,' I said. 'Are you a traveller, or . . . ?'

Domino laughed.

'What?'

'Traveller,' she said. 'Sounds like a gypsy or something.'

I felt a little embarrassed and turned away. 'No, I meant . . .'

'Don't worry, I know what you meant. Yeah, I guess I am, sort of. You? You a "traveller" now?'

I shrugged. 'For a while, I suppose. Couple of months here, then I'm going to Bali.'

'Bali's nice.' Domino nodded and passed me one of the banana-leaf bundles.

I turned it over in my hands, seeing how the maker had put it together.

'*Nasi bunkus*,' she said. 'Take the leaf off before you eat it.'

I removed the leaf, handling the package of hot sticky rice inside, biting into it and finding a delicious spicy mince.

'I'm not really travelling,' she said. 'Not like you. I kind of live over here. We have a place on the lake, we hang out. Every now and then I go back to Oz, but I always come back. I like it here.'

I continued eating and looked out at the road where the stall lights glowed in the night. The policeman had finished smoking his cigarette and was talking to his partner. I could feel Domino's hip against mine, feel the warmth coming off her. I glanced at her legs, pulled up towards her, the dress riding up her calves, the tattoo on her ankle. 'So how do we get there?' I asked. 'This place of yours, I mean. Bus?'

'Can do.'

'Is it going to be like the one I was on before?' I asked. 'People hanging off it?'

She wiped her mouth with the back of her hand and smiled. 'They're all like that. You don't fancy going through it again, eh?'

'Nope.'

'You want to walk? Might take a while. Or there's always a taxi,' she said, pointing at a couple of cars pulled over by the roadside. 'Bit more expensive, probably just as dangerous, but it's not a bus and it's not walking.' She dropped her arm, her skin brushing against mine as she reached for her bag, digging for cigarettes. 'And it's another experience.' She lifted out a red packet and took one of the cigarettes.

I could smell them before she even lit it. She offered me the pack but I said no.

'You don't smoke?'

'Not really.'

'Not really? Either you do or you don't.'

'I did,' I told her. 'But I stopped.' I didn't tell her it was lung cancer that killed my mother. Drained her life like an insect sucking away her blood.

'You should try one.' She put the cigarette between her full lips and lit it with a plastic lighter. She took a drag and then lifted it to my mouth. 'Try it,' she said. 'You can't come to Indonesia and not try one of these.'

I hesitated, then allowed her to put her cigarette in my mouth. The way she held it, right down in the nook between her middle finger and her ring finger, her palm was across one of my cheeks, her fingers stretched across the other. In that intimate pose I dragged on it, swallowing the smoke down into my lungs and tasting the sweetness of it.

I blew it out and nodded. 'Yep,' I said. 'It's pretty much as disgusting as I thought it would be.' I grimaced and shook my head, but I'd enjoyed the sensation of the smoke in my body again. Most of all, though, I'd enjoyed her touch, having *her* cigarette in my mouth.

'You see that?' she said, pointing towards the hospital. The policemen had moved away from their car and were walking among the stalls, looking around them as if searching for something. I had forgotten about them, been too busy talking, feeling the arousal of being close to Domino.

'They're looking for us,' I said.

'You might be right.'

'Shit. Maybe I should—'

'Too late for that.' She stood up and offered me her hand. 'Come on.' She pulled me to my feet. 'Let's go.'

6

We climbed into the back of the first taxi we came to. A yellow Toyota. I'd thought that, like the bus, it would have tassels and hangings dripping from the ceiling and around the windows, but it looked much like any taxi at home. Mock-leather seats that had seen a few backsides, floor mats that needed changing, and everything squeaked.

The driver turned down the music and asked where we wanted to go. Domino told him and he thought about it before nodding. They spoke for a moment longer, seemed to be haggling over a price, then he flicked his music back up and pulled away from the side of the road without much more than a quick glance in his mirror.

Domino looked out of the back window, putting her hand on me as she twisted for a better view.

'You think they saw us?' I asked.

'No,' she said. 'You can relax now, Alex. It's all behind you.' She smiled at me. 'Or maybe it's all in front of you.'

Once we were away from the hospital we headed out of the nameless town, the taxi braking and accelerating, dodging the traffic until we left the lights behind us and moved into the real darkness. I could see the shadowy shapes of trees and buildings out there, but not much else. We were on a narrow road, only the occasional glare of oncoming lights, and there was a sensation of climbing. The air coming in through the open window was cooler and I felt my ears pop.

'How long?' I said to Domino. We'd been travelling at least twenty minutes.

'Not long. We're not going straight to Toba, though. Gonna make a quick stop-off.'

I strained to see her eyes, but one side of her face was in shadow, while the other was cast with a yellow glow from passing headlights. I could tell that she was smiling, but I couldn't read her expression too well. 'What kind of stop-off?'

'I'm taking you for a surprise. See something of the local culture.'

'Something like what?' Now that we were calm, enclosed in the taxi, I felt the first stirrings of doubt since we'd run from the hospital. Unease dribbled into me, a loose sensation that tingled around my stomach. I didn't know Domino. I'd followed her on a whim, run from the police. I had no real reason to trust her.

'Don't worry.' She reached across and put her hand on mine, as if she had heard my thoughts and seen my need for reassurance. 'I'm pretty sure you're going to like it.' She leaned over and kissed my cheek, taking me by surprise again, making me pull back to look at her, get her in focus. She smiled at me, her eyes holding mine, then she kissed me again, this time on my lips, before breaking away, saying, 'We'll be there soon. A few more minutes,' and almost the second she stopped talking, the taxi slowed and the driver leaned closer to the windscreen as if searching for something.

He spoke aloud, his voice disturbing whatever it was that had passed between Domino and me, then she looked away and replied, nodding her head.

Taxi-man slowed even further and pulled off the road, turning onto a dirt track that led through trees rising tall on either side of us, killing the sky. The Toyota was squeaking even more now, away from the relative smooth of the broken tarmac. The road here was not covered, just a cleared track, loose and potholed.

'Where the hell are we going?' I asked, feeling the nervousness folding its arms around me again.

Domino squeezed my hand. 'This is going to be fun. You want to experience the place, don't you?'

'Sure.' But I didn't want to disappear without trace.

'Well then . . . sit back and enjoy the ride.'

I wasn't sure if I was seeing the real Domino now or if she was showing off to me, demonstrating that she knew the place, that she could show me things I wouldn't otherwise see. Either way, I strained my eyes at the window, hoping to see some memorable landmarks, just in case I had to return this way on foot. Alone. But we were on the track for no more than a few minutes before we finally saw lights coming at us through the trees.

'Here we are,' Domino whispered. She sounded excited.

I couldn't see much, it was too dark, but I could see that there were large buildings in a clearing, around which the trees had been thinned. Just a smattering of dark shapes among the pines, slivers of lamplight. No discernible roads or paths other than the one we'd arrived on.

The taxi stopped and the driver turned round and spoke to Domino. She shook her head, put her hand on the back of the seat, talking in Indonesian. The driver cut her off, raising his voice, then they were talking over each other, both voices at the same time, growing louder until Domino raised her hands and leaned back beside me.

'He wants too much. Not what I agreed back there.' She sighed. 'Taxi drivers. They'll always try to con you. You speak the language, you stand a better chance with them. You know the place, you stand an even better chance, but they still try to con you. They think because you're white, you got money. Like it's their duty to charge you more.'

I hesitated, then stretched my leg and dug a hand into my pocket. I didn't see I had much choice other than to pay. I pulled out a handful of notes and offered them to Domino but she pushed my hand down against the seat.

'Keep it,' she said. 'Only one way to deal with this. We're going to have some fun.'

'What?'

'You never did anything you shouldn't have?'

'Like steal clothes, you mean? Run away from the police?'

'Yeah, like that. Or maybe something like this.' She opened the taxi door and began to climb out. 'Run,' she said.

It took me a moment to shake off the feeling of déjà vu and register what she was doing. I looked from her, running away, to the taxi driver, sitting in his seat, head turned, mouth open. His reaction was similar to mine. Like me, he couldn't believe what was going on, so we stared at each other for a fraction of a second, then he was moving, reaching for the handle.

I took my chance, doing the same, throwing open the door hard enough for it to bounce back on its hinge. I pushed it again as it hit my outstretched hands, caught my foot as I stepped out, tumbled onto the ground, picked myself up and ran round the car, hoping to see where Domino had disappeared into the trees.

As I rounded the car, though, the driver caught hold of my shirt, grabbing and pulling me closer to him. I tugged back, pushing him away, knocking him against his car, and I wheeled my arms to stop myself from falling and collapsing at his feet.

Regaining my poise, I broke into a sprint, following Domino into the trees.

In the relative safety of the darkness, I stopped and crouched low, looking back at the driver, who was now standing beside his car, peering into the shadow, deciding what to do.

I kept low, tucked in at the base of a tree a few metres inside the main line of foliage, and continued to watch him as he paced back and forth. He waited for what seemed like a long time before he slapped a hand against his thigh and shouted something at the trees. Then he climbed back into his taxi and turned over the engine, throwing one last look from his window before driving away.

I stayed where I was, listening to the sound of my own heart thumping in my throat, the blood pumping through me, echoing in my ears.

It was cooler here than it had been near the hospital. The air was fresh, almost sweet with the taste of the pines around me. This was not the dense jungle, or the regimented rows of rubber trees I'd passed on my bus trip from Medan, damp in the sticky heat. These trees were more thinly spaced, their smell more familiar to me. There were smaller plants, too, tufts of growth that sprouted in patches around my feet. The ground beneath me was carpeted with pine needles and I reached down to touch them, pick them up, rub them between my fingertips and lift them to my nose.

'Alex,' Domino's voice came at me out of the darkness. I looked around, but saw nothing of her. No shape, no shadow, just the slats of lamplight from the buildings among the trees, the slivers from the moon playing in the undergrowth.

'Alex! Where are you?'

'Here,' I called back. 'I'm here.'

I waited for Domino to find the sound of my voice, follow it to where I was, and within a moment or two, I heard soft footfalls behind me. I turned to see her silhouette coming between the trees. She called my name again and I replied the same way, leading her to me.

When she reached me, she held out a hand to touch me, to know where I was, then she sat down, breathing hard.

'What the hell was that all about?' I asked. 'You have a habit of running away from people?'

'He tried to rip us off,' she said.

'I can't believe you did that. You have no idea what's out here, what we were running into. You had no idea what he might do, either. He might've come after us.' I wasn't sure if I was angry with her for making me steal clothes, run from the police, from taxi fares or for not warning me. I wasn't sure if I was angry with her at all. It had been fun. The rush, the excitement, it all made me feel alive. And sitting here, in the night, under the pines, with the cool breeze playing through the treetops above me, everything felt good. Better than I'd felt in a long time.

'He wasn't coming after us,' she said. 'And I know where we are. There's nothing out here but trees.' She paused. 'Unless you run about three hundred metres that way.' She took my hand and pointed it behind us, away to the left.

'Why? What's there?' I asked.

'A kind of cliff,' she said.

'*A kind of cliff?*' I imagined myself running too far, disappearing into the abyss. 'What kind of cliff?'

'You'll see,' she said. 'It's what we're here for.'

I took a deep breath, opened my mouth to speak, but felt Domino come closer to me, her face in front of mine, almost shining in the light cast from the moon.

'Don't ask,' she said. 'It's a surprise.' And she touched her mouth to mine. Soft and wet. Taking my lower lip between hers, the tip of her tongue pushing into my mouth, drawing back before I could respond. 'Something we have to do first,' she said.

'Like what?' I said, feeling teased. She was building me up, dropping me down. 'I'm supposed to be in hospital, remember. This might all be too much for me.'

'Oh, I think you'll survive.'

I moved my face towards hers but she put her fingertips on my mouth, saying, 'Uh-uh. Not now. We don't want this to be too much for you.' She was both exciting and infuriating. Being with her brought something to life inside me.

'OK,' I said. 'So what is it we have to do?'

'Someone we have to see,' she said, standing and making her way through the trees.

7

I stayed where I was, watching Domino's silhouette moving away from me, stepping among the pine needles before she stopped and turned in my direction. 'Well, then?' she asked. 'You coming?'

I sighed and shook my head. It was hard to believe that just a couple of days earlier I had been in England, everything grey, rainy and cold.

I followed Domino onto the path where the taxi had dropped us and we walked together, towards the buildings I'd seen when we arrived.

Here, where the trees were thinner, the moon was able to cut through the canopy enough to give me an idea of what the place looked like. There was a collection of no more than five houses. Three of them side by side, two further away, behind the others, a small area of open ground between them. There was a cleared space in front of the main buildings, which looked as if it might be used as a communal area, perhaps a place for children to play.

The buildings were traditional Batak houses made from wood with high roofs, saddle-backed, pointed at each end and bowed in the middle, reminiscent of the horns of a water buffalo. Two of them were thatched with palm fibre, but the others were roofed with rusted corrugated iron, bent and hammered into shape, the moon catching and shining on the few patches that hadn't been aged by the rain. The houses were not so much on stilts as they were on a kind of rough wooden frame, with fixed ladders leading up to the front entrance to each building. One or two of them had large stones laid out in a square, pressed into the dirt around the base of the ladder as a rudimentary front-door step. At the far end of the row I could make out a washing line, dark shapes hanging limp, swaying in the weak breeze. And here, close to where we were standing, there were a few open tins, like large paint cans, pulled together into a kind of mosaic, their contents catching the moonlight, glittering like jewels. There were other signs of life here, too. A motorcycle outside one of the houses, leaning against the building's wooden frame, a pair of bicycles, a solitary chicken scratching the ground at the edge of the clearing. And as we approached, I could hear the strum of a guitar, a man's voice singing.

I looked around, moving my head in the direction of the music, trying to ignore the whisper of the breeze against my ear, taking in as much as I could. Everything so different from what I knew. A small gathering of unusual houses in the middle of the forest. A new song. A place without roads. Narrow paths leading in and out of the trees.

There were lights on in only two of the houses, the glow peeping not from windows but from cracks in the walls, flickering as if they were lit with lamps.

'What is this place?'

'*Kampong*,' she said. 'Village.'

'How d'you know about it?'

'It's not some mysterious secret,' she said. 'It's just a *kampong*. A place where people live.'

'Like this?'

'Why not?'

'I just . . . I dunno.' A touch of embarrassment crept around the edges of my mood. With it being so isolated, it seemed that the people here were hiding from what lay beyond the trees.

'Mostly they're workers,' she told me. 'They tap the trees.'

'Tap them?'

'That smell,' she said. 'They cut the trees and collect the

59

resin. They make turpentine out of it. That's what these cans are for. They're full of resin.'

I looked down at the cans as we passed them, taking in the smell. It was good, sweet, not at all like the pungent and oily liquid I was familiar with at home.

'The people here, they're pretty poor,' she said. 'Always happy to get some extra cash.'

We stopped outside the first of the five houses, this one sporting the more traditional thatched roof, and I looked up to see the large, swollen-eyed *singa* that adorned it like the figurehead of an ancient ship. An angular, mask-like carving, at least four feet high, part animal and part human. A painted devil staring down at us.

'You should wait here,' Domino said, stepping within the stone square planted around the base of the ladder. 'I won't be long.'

Apprehensive, but feeling that Domino was familiar with where we were, I took a step back and watched her climb the short ladder. At the top, she rapped her knuckles on the rudimentary wooden door. Immediately the music stopped and the singing was replaced by the sound of silence. I heard nothing but the wind in the treetops and the beating of my own heart. Then voices; the language fast and garbled to my untrained ears.

When the door opened, a weak glow leaked out, folding itself around the edges, oozing over Domino's feet, sliding its fingers through her hair. A face followed it, dark and undefined in this light. A boy, his voice low as he spoke to Domino, hesitating only when he caught sight of me. He stared, his eyes just dark holes, his body language a mixture of mistrust and bravado. I glanced up at the carving above his head.

Domino spoke to him again, her voice louder, making him turn to look at her, consider her, while repeatedly looking back at me. Eventually he nodded, leaned back into the house to say something, then waved Domino down the steps. She backed down the ladder, her dress tightening around her, smoothing her silhouette, and the boy followed, pulling his sarong up to his thighs, closing the door behind him.

Domino stepped onto the ground, waiting for the boy, and when he reached the bottom, he headed round the house, beckoning us to follow. Domino nodded at me and we took the path in single file, skirting the building as the music resumed inside.

We headed across to the two houses that stood alone behind the others and, as we drew near, the boy turned and said something to Domino. But I could see now that he was not a boy. His height had fooled me. He was a man, maybe in his thirties, it was hard to tell.

Domino responded to him and then spoke to me. 'We're going inside,' she said. 'Both of us.'

'You sure this is safe?'

'I'm sure. You ready?'

'OK.' I looked up at the building, seeing the ladder but not a front door. 'How do we get in?'

'Magic,' she said.

The man climbed the ladder and went through a trapdoor into the house. Domino followed him, and I stayed close behind her, wondering what she was getting us into.

The space inside was black. In here, the light from the moon was unable to penetrate and the darkness was complete. I could hear the man moving somewhere in there, but I could see no sign of him.

'Wait here a moment,' Domino said, putting a hand on my back and keeping it there as if to reassure me that I was not alone in this place.

Outside the air had been fresh, scented with pine, but in here, it was still and thick and dusty. It smelled of wood and smoke, an exotic mixture of spices and unfamiliar smells.

Domino and I stood in silence, sampling the atmosphere, listening to the man delving deeper into the house, moving about, searching. After a minute or two, a match flared and in its glow I could see the man, twenty feet away, crouched low to the floor, hunched over a lamp. As the match burned down, he breathed in, a sharp intake, and the room was once again plunged into darkness. The rattling of matches in a box, scraping, the flare of phosphorus and, once again, there was a small arc of light in the black. This time, the flame spat and grew before the man waved it out and stood up holding a lamp with a weak glow that expanded and became brighter.

Domino took her hand from me and we both approached as the man beckoned.

The house was like a cave. A large open space without windows, partitions or rooms. There were several low tables at the far end, half obscured in the gloom, and to my left was a pit filled with ashes and charred pieces of wood. Along from the dead fire, a lopsided and basic chest of drawers that someone had made from thin planks of wood. In the centre of the room, a carved wooden pole reached up from floor to ceiling. Even in this light I could see that it was intricately decorated with faded red and white paint, carvings of lizards and spirals. Several sets of buffalo horns had been bound to it with rope, the points jutting out at irregular angles.

The man led us to an area at the back of the building, towards the low tables, and sat down on a tattered woven mat behind one of them. As he sat, he hitched up his sarong and indicated that we should sit on the mat opposite.

He placed the lamp on the table and reached across, holding out his hand to me, saying, 'Alim.'

I could see him more clearly now and, although I had mistaken his short, slight frame for that of a child, there was no mistaking his face. Thick black hair, skin that was dark and lined, his mouth scarred in the centre where a cleft lip had been corrected. His front teeth were crooked and stained, almost black in this light, except for two on the right side of his mouth, which caught the lamplight and looked to be made of gold.

I took his hand and nodded, telling him my name. 'Alex.'

He didn't smile, but he tested the name, trying to say it, not getting it quite right. I thought about correcting him, but didn't bother. Particularly when I saw what was on the table in front of me.

A bottle of clear liquid, next to a stack of small glasses. A small set of brass scales. A machete with a long, dark blade and a rudimentary wooden handle bound with copper wire. The scabbard that lay beside it was ornately carved, also bound with wire at the top and bottom. The other object on the table, however, was the one that made me most nervous. Something that amplified my fear and exaggerated the sensations in my stomach. A pistol, the metal marked and scratched, the wooden grips scored and nicked. A mysterious and prosaic amalgamation of wood and metal, angular and rounded, created for only one purpose. And what made me most nervous was the way it had been left there, as if it were unimportant. Something kept to hand in case it needed to be used. A knife, a bottle, some glasses, a gun. Everyday items to this man.

As soon as he was sitting, legs crossed beneath him, Alim reached for the pistol, quickening my heart as he took the magazine and pushed it into the weapon with the heel of his palm. He pulled back the slide, and thumbed down the hammer before placing the pistol on the floor beside him.

Alim then took three dirty glasses from the stack and placed one in front of each of us. He picked up the unlabelled bottle, removed the cork and poured us each a generous measure.

'*Tuak*,' he said with a grin that wasn't a smile.

I looked at Domino for an explanation, wondering what I was going to have to drink.

'It's fine,' she said. '*Tuak*. Liquor brewed from coconut palm. Tastes like shit, makes your breath stink, but it's OK. Just drink it and smile.'

I followed Alim's lead, lifting the glass in the air in a silent toast and throwing the contents into my mouth. Domino was right, it *did* taste like shit, and it burned like hell on its way down, but I didn't cough and my eyes didn't water. I showed no weakness, whether it mattered or not.

Domino did the same, downing it like water.

I wiped my mouth and steeled myself as Alim poured us another. This time, though, we didn't drink it straight down. We left it in front of us, lukewarm and unpleasant, stagnating in the dirty glasses.

Alim spoke, the sounds alien and confusing.

'English,' said Domino. 'Speak English.'

Alim rolled his eyes. 'So you want to buy something? For yourself?' The words were awkward and hesitant, his accent thick. 'Why not take it from what you collected yesterday?'

'Haven't been back yet,' said Domino. 'I just came in from Medan.'

'You couldn't wait?'

Domino shrugged.

Alim returned the gesture. 'Who is this?' He tipped his head at me, but kept his eyes on Domino. 'This one I don't know.'

'A friend.'

'Someone new? He's cool?'

'Sure. Where's Hendrik?'

'Gone.'

Domino narrowed her eyes. 'Gone?'

'*Gone.*'

'I've only been away a couple of weeks. What—' Her lips began to form more words, but she glanced at me and stopped herself.

'A lot can happen,' Alim said. 'Even in just one day. It was only a matter of time.'

Domino shook her head and sighed. 'So Danuri's in charge now? And Kurt knows?'

'Of course he knows.'

'What did he say?'

'What *can* he say? We're here now. It's better this way for everyone, business as usual. More or less.'

Domino erupted into Indonesian, the words coming easily to her lips, her face serious. Alim crossed his arms and smiled, before cutting her off, saying, 'Speak English.'

Domino looked at me, choosing her words. She opened her mouth to speak, a light intake of breath, then she closed it again and turned to Alim. 'What you got?' she asked.

Alim pulled a wooden box from under the table. Long and flat, the size and shape of three shoe boxes side by side. He lifted it onto the table with two hands and centred it between us, removing the lid and saying, 'I got whatever you want.'

I leaned forwards for a better look as Alim lifted the lamp to light the contents of the box and I wondered if there was a connection between Domino and the drugs the police had found at the crash. Maybe *she* was the reason I'd had to hide my passport and run from the police.

There were small bags containing lumps of resin and powders, both white and brown. Clear plastic boxes of pills, tiny squares of what looked like blotting paper, and larger bags filled with herbs in different shades of green and brown. There were a number of empty syringes, too, maybe ten or eleven in all, their needles capped, their plungers down. Accompanying them, an assortment of medicinal bottles, the kind with the rubber caps, just right for tipping upside down and sliding in a needle.

I'd never seen such things other than in a hospital, sterile and offered up on kidney dishes of pulped brown paper. Tablets were for prescriptions, and syringes were for use by white-clad nurses and doctors who smiled empty smiles betrayed by eyes that tried for sympathy but never quite managed it. My experience of drugs was limited to healing and pain relief. Prolonging and preserving. They were the things that had kept my mother alive and unhappy for longer than she wanted. For longer than I should have allowed. They had been dispensed with good intention, but had extended her wretched existence. But this was a different world now; a world where tablets and tinctures were intended to bring pleasure, not heartache. I didn't want to expose my naivety. I didn't want to show my fear. Not of Alim, not of his gun and not of his drugs. I was here to experience new things, to see a side of life I had never seen, and I tried to relax myself, give nothing away, and hope that I would walk away from this place in one piece.

I sensed Domino watching me and I turned to see her gauging my reaction to Alim's box of goodies. A smile trickled over her lips, touching the corners of her mouth, then disappeared as she went back to her dealer. 'Nothing too heavy,' she said. 'Something to smoke, that's all.'

Alim took a syringe from the box, removed the cap, held it up for us to see. 'You sure?' he said, putting down the lamp and reaching for one of the small bottles. 'You could shoot right now.' He slipped the needle into the rubber top and raised his eyebrows, waiting for an answer.

Domino shook her head. 'I don't do that shit.'

'Just pass it on, eh?'

'Smoke is all we want.'

Alim hesitated, holding the syringe at eye level, one hand securing it with the bottle, the other hand ready to pull the plunger, suck the clear liquid into the shaft. He remained that way for a moment, watching Domino, then nodded slowly and withdrew the needle. 'I have something from Aceh,' he said, putting the syringe back in the box. 'Strong. I think you like.' He took a bag of what looked like dried herbs from the box and held it out. 'You wanna try?'

Domino nodded. 'Sure.'

'Cigarette.' He put out his hand like a beggar asking for money.

Domino took a packet from her bag and passed it to him. Alim removed one cigarette and began to roll it between his forefinger and thumb, loosening the tobacco, tipping it out onto the table. When he was done, he held the empty cigarette upright, filled it with the herb, tapping it firmly on the table, packing the dried plant right down into the paper. He finished by rolling the filter until it loosened enough for him to pinch it with his fingernails and pull it from the cigarette. He flicked it to one side and replaced it with a small piece of rolled card, which he tore from the cigarette box.

66

The whole process took no longer than a couple of minutes, and when he was done, he put the cigarette in his mouth and lit it with a match. He pursed his lips around the end and sucked hard, holding the smoke in his lungs as he passed it to Domino. She received it without hesitation, not even a pause to wipe it, took a long drag and held it out for me to take.

I knew what it was, but I'd never tried it before. Part of me wanted to say no, to smile and tell Domino I didn't want it. I'd been so controlled for so long that I didn't know what I'd do if I lost even the tiniest amount of that self-constraint. But that part of my life was gone now. I didn't have the same responsibilities any more. I only had one person to take care of. I could try anything I wanted, *do* anything I wanted. It was why I had come away.

I took the cigarette from Domino, touching her fingers as I did so. The smoke stung my eyes, and my mouth was filled with the scented taste of the dope when I inhaled it, but I didn't cough. I nodded, as if I knew what I was doing, as if I'd smoked a thousand joints and knew the difference between good shit and bad shit, then I passed it back to Alim with a smile.

'*Baik?*' he asked. 'Good?'

'It's OK,' Domino said, her eyes on me.

'You want?'

'How much?' Domino asked.

'How much you want?' He wasn't giving anything away.

Domino reached into her bag and took out a two-ounce tobacco tin. She used her fingernails to prise off the top, then removed a number of photographs contained within. She slipped the photos back into her bag and pushed the tin across to Alim. 'Fill that,' she said.

Alim laughed, throwing his head back, showing us his gold teeth.

'I'm serious,' Domino said. 'How much?'

Alim stopped laughing as if someone had turned off the volume. He levelled his head and stared at Domino. 'That's all? One tin of ganja?'

'It's all we need,' she said. 'We want more, we can take it out of what Kurt has.'

Alim shook his head. 'Danuri said to watch you people. This some kind of joke?'

'Just fill the tin, Alim. It's all I want right now.' She was strong, determined. If she was afraid of Alim, she gave no sign of it.

Alim handed her the joint and stood up, taking the pistol from beside him. He looked down at us for a second before turning and moving out of the arc of the lamp. He melted into the shadow and we heard him moving around somewhere out of sight. I felt exposed and anxious, sitting there in the light, listening to the man with the gun rummaging in the back of the oversized building. I half expected to hear a gunshot, feel the lead pierce my skin.

Domino nudged me and passed the joint, so I took it from her and smoked some more, starting to like the taste of the herb, feeling a buzz from it now.

Alim came back from the shadow, the silhouette of a boy holding a gun in one hand, the steel hanging limp at his side, and he dropped a clear plastic bag onto the table. It was roughly the size of a carrier bag.

He sat down again, placed the pistol on the table, close to his hand, and opened the bag. He filled Domino's tin, then tipped the contents onto the scales. He told her the price, then refilled the tin, replaced the lid and pushed it across the table to her.

Domino smiled at him. 'I'll pay you along with the rest.'

Alim shook his head. 'This is a different deal.'

'C'mon, you know you'll get your money.'

'You pay now.'

'What's the matter with you, Alim? Power gone to your head? You think that 'cause Danuri's your—'

Alim touched his fingers to the pistol.

'OK,' Domino backed off. 'OK.'

'You got money, right?' Alim asked, gripping the butt, lifting the weapon from the table.

'Not enough,' she said. 'I'll leave it for now, come back later.'

'Maybe you give me something else?' Alim smiled, leaning forward and looking at Domino's chest. He reached across with the pistol and used the tip of the barrel to flick the loose ties at the front of her dress.

Domino knocked it away. 'Get that off me.'

Alim's face changed in an instant, the pistol coming back to press against Domino's soft cheek. 'Hendrik's not here any more,' he said. 'Remember that.'

Domino closed her eyes as Alim released the pressure, used the pistol to push back a strand of her hair.

'I'll get it,' I said, taking the last of my notes from my pocket. My hand was shaking. 'I'll pay.'

Alim pursed his lips and glared at me. The barrel of the pistol traced a path down Domino's cheek, across her neck, along her breastbone until it reached the top of her dress. He sniffed hard, withdrew the pistol and sat back again, placing it by the bottle of *tuak*. 'Good,' he said. 'Good.'

I could hardly take my eyes from the gun as Domino counted the money from the fold and put it on the table. And when she was done, Alim's hand whipped out and pinned hers to the wood, turning it over and taking another note from the wad. 'Something for me.'

The rest she gave back to me, and Alim's eyes followed it back into my pocket. Once again I looked at the pistol, thinking how easy it would be for him to take everything we had and send us out the door with nothing more than the clothes we were wearing. Or perhaps he would take our lives, too. No one knew we were here. No one would come running to our aid if they heard shots in the forest. No one would miss me.

But Alim relaxed, moving his hand away from the gun and reaching for his glass. He left the money where it was, a few lonely notes on the table, and raised his drink. Domino and I ignored ours and got to our feet, my legs stiff from having been folded beneath me. I shook away the discomfort and waited for Alim to light our way. He came alongside us, and stopped beside Domino.

'Come to me anytime,' he said, moving his face close to hers. 'I give you what you want.' And as he spoke, his eyes went to her chest again, looking down the top of her dress. His raised his hand to her hair, taking a strand of it between finger and thumb, lifting it to his nose. 'Your hair smells like gold.' He held it a moment longer, then flicked it away with a laugh.

Domino forced a smile and waited for him to move on ahead, light our path to the trapdoor where he stood to one side as we descended the ladder. Once we were out, he followed us, jumping the last few rungs onto the dirt beneath. He nodded once as we left.

As we walked, I couldn't help glancing back to see Alim making his way towards the other house. 'Christ, I thought he was going to kill us,' I said, feeling my heart beating so hard in my chest it threatened to outrun itself. Now that Alim was gone, and we were away with our lives, my body slipped into a kind of shock. I had never felt so afraid and so alive. My whole body was raging, my limbs shaking, and yet, fight or flight, I don't think either would have been possible. If Alim had pulled the trigger, put a bullet into Domino, I think I would have frozen like an animal. I would have frozen in fear and waited for him to do the same to me.

'He wouldn't,' she said. 'He needs us too much.'

I hardly even registered what she said. 'What now?' I asked as we reached the line of the trees. My legs felt as if they belonged to someone else, as if I was learning to walk for the first time. 'Where we going now?'

Domino took her bag from her shoulder and put her hand inside, searching, then stopping. Her movements became more erratic as she searched further.

'What's wrong?'

'Dropped something,' she said. 'My iPod.'

'You dropped it in there?'

'Mm-hm.' She stopped and looked back at the longhouse.

'I didn't hear anything drop.'

'Must've been when I was looking for my tin. Shit, I'll have to go back for it.'

'Go back in? You're joking, right?'

'Wait for me here,' she said, starting towards the longhouse.

I went after her, putting a hand out to stop her. 'He went the other way. The other house. Don't you think you should tell him first?'

'Alim? You gotta be joking.'

I shook my head, not understanding.

'You saw what he's like. What you think he's gonna say if I tell him I dropped my iPod in there? You think he's gonna let me go look for it, or d'you think he's gonna say tough shit, what's yours is mine? You have any idea how much he'd get for it?' She began walking and I followed alongside.

'And if he catches you in there?' In my mind I saw the gun pressed to Domino's chest.

'He won't.' In the other longhouse, the music started up again, one or two guitars playing, men singing. 'Wait here for me.' She stopped at the base of the ladder and looked at me. 'I'll be two seconds.'

'I'll come with you.'

'I'll be fine,' she said. 'You'll slow me down.'

'I don't trust that guy. What if he comes back? He's weird. Dangerous.'

'He's weird all right, but I reckon he's harmless.'

'Harmless? After what he just did?'

'He didn't do *any*thing,' she said. 'He wouldn't dare. And keep your bloody voice down.'

I thought about the pistol and the *parang* machete. 'Didn't look harmless to me,' I whispered. 'You're not going in there on your own. What if—'

'He's in the other house, for fuck's sake, he won't come back.' She put one hand on her hip as if she were thinking about something. 'You ever smoked before?'

I looked at the joint in my hand.

'It's making you paranoid,' she said. 'You need to relax.'

'No, I'm—'

'Wait for me over there.' She pointed to the line of trees. 'Finish the joint, chill out, be quiet, I'll be back in one second. Maybe two.'

I started to protest again, but she cut me off, saying, 'I'll be fine,' and climbed the ladder, pushing on the underside of the trapdoor, looking down and smiling when it opened.

The music from the house next to us stopped and we looked at each other for a moment before Domino spoke again. 'Go,' she said. 'Quickly. Wait over there.'

'All right,' I agreed, but let her hear the reluctance in my voice. 'I'll wait.' I backed away from the ladder, watching Domino climb the last few rungs, her legs disappearing into the darkness.

Then the trapdoor shut behind her and I was alone in the night.

8

I stopped and watched the door, straining to hear any noises from the other house. Nothing but the wind and the insects. I considered following her, then sighed and walked to the edge of the trees. I placed my feet carefully, rolling from the heel to the ball of my foot, keeping my tread light so that I'd hear anything out of place. But still there were no sounds. Nothing.

When I came to where the trees grew thicker, I sat down and leaned against the trunk of a tall pine, the dead needles a cushion under me, the old bark rough against my back, and I raised the cigarette to my lips and dragged on it, exhaling a rush of scented smoke. I held it up in front of my eyes and studied the place where Domino's lips had been, adjusted my focus to look at the Batak house, the ladder and the trap-door, then refocused on the place where Domino's mouth had been.

I was beginning to feel a vague sense of panic now and I told myself that Domino was right; it was the dope. I shouldn't smoke any more; it was making me anxious. I took another drag and cleared the pine needles in a small circle beside me. I brushed them away until my fingertips touched dirt, then I scratched a small hole and crushed the glowing end of the cigarette into it. I watched the last wisps of smoke dissipating, then looked over at the house again.

Domino had been gone longer than I expected. She said she'd dropped her iPod, so all she had to do was go in and get it. Pick it up, put it in her bag and come back out again. I shook my head, rubbed my face and told myself she was probably looking for it. It was dark in there; maybe she couldn't find it straight away.

I stared at my wrist, cursing the boy who had stolen my belongings, left me to bleed and die in the road. The absence of my watch gave everything a surreal edge. I had no way of tracking what was happening to me. And as the memory of the crash came back, the trapdoor in the occupied longhouse opened, spilling light in a crooked rectangle across the cleared ground. I shuffled back, around the thick trunk of the tree, thankful for my dark clothing, and watched Alim descend the ladder, followed by a second, slightly taller man. They stopped in the shard of light and looked back at the longhouse, as if expecting someone else, but no one came. The weak glow from the building cast across their faces and I could make out Alim's features, but it was his partner who caught my attention. He had a lazy, arrogant manner about him, the way he stood with a slight hunch, his legs bowed, and he carried a rifle over his shoulder. He was heavier built than Alim, and the way they spoke, although I couldn't understand the nasal tones, I could tell that he was talking down to Alim. He lifted his hand and pointed at the smaller man, then he looked around again, as if he had sensed my presence in the forest. I squatted further, seeing the way he squinted out at the dark, and I imagined I saw something hard and unpleasant in those searching eyes as he stepped forward, unslinging his rifle and tucking it into his shoulder, pointing it into the night. He turned on the spot, slowly, as if his eyes could pierce the night, then he relaxed, lowered the rifle and turned back to Alim to continue his castigation. When Alim answered him, the second man struck out and slapped Alim's face. His movement was fast and vicious and I heard the sharp smack of skin on skin, and watched as the two men became silent and stood facing each other until Alim looked away, adopting a submissive pose. And then the altercation was over, and the taller man slung the rifle over his shoulder and came straight towards the line of trees and stopped. Alim stayed where he was, head bowed, then he too came into the shadow and after a few moments I heard the sound of them urinating onto the ground.

Now I looked away from the shapes of the two men, over to the other longhouse where Domino was, and I was shocked to see that she was now on the ladder. She wasn't much more than a dark shape, but it was definitely her descending the rungs, and she had no idea the two men were there, camouflaged against the trees.

I tried to wave my hands, catch her attention, but I knew it was useless. I turned my head, looking from Domino to the men and back again, hoping, *praying*, that Domino would spot them first. And when one of them spoke, his voice carrying in the stillness of the night, I saw Domino's shadow stop dead on the ladder. She hung in time for a heartbeat, then her torso and legs disappeared back up into the longhouse.

I returned my attention to the two men. They'd finished their business and were heading back in the direction they'd come until Alim stopped, spoke, then broke away and made for the longhouse that Domino had just re-entered. When he reached the ladder, he paused to scratch his foot, then stepped up and climbed into the building.

The next few minutes happened to someone else. I was a spectator, looking down on myself, frozen, not knowing what to do. An impossible situation in an impossible place.

A lump rose to my throat and all I could taste was the bitter flavour of the weed. I told myself she was OK. Domino was fine. She would be out in a minute. I looked at my wrist again and swore. I couldn't tell how long she'd been gone. There was no way of knowing.

I counted seconds in my head, trying to keep track of how many minutes I was waiting, but it was difficult to concentrate. There was a numbness across my forehead, the feeling that my skin was pulling tight around my skull. My thoughts spiralled with

75

concern for Domino and what Alim might be doing to her. I couldn't let him hurt her. I couldn't just stand here. I had to do something to help.

I pushed myself up, putting one hand against the tree, bringing it away with a sticky resin on my fingers. I rubbed it on my stolen blue trousers as I headed towards the house. Domino had been gone too long. I couldn't wait any more. Fearing the worst, my breathing became shallower and I set my mind to what I had to do. My body was preparing itself for what might lie ahead in the darkness of the longhouse. Images flickered through my head. Violent images of what Alim might have done to her, what was now lying behind the trapdoor. I pushed them away and approached the building, making as little sound as possible.

I braced myself when I reached the ladder, took a deep breath, placed my foot on the lowest rung and began to climb. It wasn't high, perhaps eight rungs, and I was at the top, my hand reaching for the underside of the trapdoor, when it yawned open before me.

It took me by surprise, I'd heard nothing from within, and I flinched, my immediate reaction to move away, to escape whatever it was I was going to see. I stepped down, missed my footing and slipped. I reached out as I fell, grabbing for the edge of the ladder, but my weight was too much and I was falling too quickly. My feet caught on one of the lower rungs, buckling my legs, toppling me backwards and dropping me to the ground. I landed on my back, the air escaping my body in a quick release, and my chest hitched, desperate to take in more breath.

At the top of the ladder, Domino looked down at me. 'Shit. What the fuck are you doing?' Her voice was quiet, almost inaudible.

I shuffled away from the ladder, trying to stand. 'I thought . . .'

'Shh. Quiet. You trying to kill yourself?' She came down face forward, her heels on the rungs, pulling the trapdoor behind her. 'Jesus Christ, Alex, you scared the shit out of me.' She reached the bottom and came to my side. I could see, in the moonlight, that there was a film of sweat across her forehead. 'Come on,' she said, helping me up. 'We have to get out of here. All your bloody noise.'

We hurried back to the line of the trees, to the safety of the darkness.

'I was worried,' I said. 'You were gone so long, and that guy in there—'

'I was only in there a couple of minutes, Alex.'

'I thought . . . Shit . . . did he see you?'

'What do you think? Course he didn't bloody see me.' We moved further into the shadows, quickening our pace. 'You think I'd be in one piece if he bloody saw me?'

'Then how the hell did you get out?' I imagined a different scenario now – one in which Alim was not the aggressor. 'How did you get out without him seeing you?'

'I hid,' she said. 'It's dark in there. Loads of places to hide. When he went to the far end, I slipped out. Mind you, with the amount of bloody noise you made, it's a wonder he didn't follow me.'

I let out a long sigh, feeling like I was releasing ten years' worth of tension. 'So did you get it?'

'Get what?'

'Your iPod.'

'Oh yeah,' she said. 'Yeah, I got it.'

We were away from the houses now and I stopped, turning to her. 'Don't *ever* do that again.'

'Sure,' she said. 'I mean, why would I?' She touched a hand to my cheek, then put her arm through mine. 'You were scared for me?'

'Yeah. And for me.'

'Come on,' she said. 'Over here.'

I wanted to say something else, but I didn't know what.

She led me past the place where she'd told me to wait and she stopped, shoving me against a tree and moving close, pressing herself against me, pushing her tongue between my lips. I opened my mouth wider to receive it.

'You feel that, Alex?' she said, breaking away.

'Hm?'

'The adrenaline in your veins.' She kissed me again, hard, uncontrolled.

'Adrenaline?' I said, catching my breath. My hands were still trembling, my heart still pounding, but maybe it was for another reason now. I could taste her saliva on my lips.

'Doesn't it make you horny?'

'Horny? I don't know if *that* did, but—'

She put her hands on my face, ran them over my head, across my shoulders, down my chest. 'It does *me*. Makes me feel fantastic.'

Her actions were unexpected. I thought she'd want to get away, but we were far enough from the houses now, no sign of Alim coming out, so I responded by kissing her again, wrapping my arms around her. I slipped one hand behind her head, tangled in her sun-bleached hair; the other ran across her slim back, pulling her into me, crushing her pelvis against mine.

We stayed that way, moving together, tasting each other, before she leaned back, smiling. 'That's good,' she said, breathing hard, her mouth wide. 'Really good.' She put her hands either side of my head and kissed me again, pulling away, saying, 'God, I want to fuck you.'

The words startled me. Dirty. Passionate. Lustful. No one had ever said it to me before. Not like that. She stared right into me, no embarrassment, no shame, no looking away. She knew what she wanted.

'Then why don't you?' I said, pulling her dress higher around her waist, sliding my hands underneath and feeling the flesh where her buttocks met the back of her thighs.

'Uh-uh.' She moved my hands. 'Not here.' She looked

back at the longhouse. 'Not yet. Something I want to show you.'

'Show me?' I pulled her towards me, feeling teased.

'Not yet.' She broke my embrace. 'Not yet.'

9

I followed her through the woods, not knowing where we were going or what I might walk into. There was light, but not much, and I kept my eyes fixed on her shape just ahead. We circled away from the village, keeping among the trees until they began to thin out. When we finally emerged from them, Domino stopped. I came alongside her and stared out at the night, understanding this was what she wanted me to see.

About twenty metres from where I was standing, the ground fell away down the hillside. A gentle slope at first, then sharper, trailing perhaps four hundred metres to the ground below. Beyond that, an area of flat ground, dotted with tiny lights, and then nothing but water.

'That's it,' she said. 'Danau Toba.'

I stared out at the water, the moon reflected on its calm surface. A slice of silver, resting on the lake beneath a clear sky of pinprick stars. A lake that stretched to infinity, never reaching its furthest shore.

'That's what you wanted to see. It's what the tourists come for, but they never see it from here. Not like this.'

I sat on the dirt, among the tufts of grass and taut saplings that sprang from the earth, and I wrapped my arms around my knees. I could still feel the buzz from the ganja, but I no longer felt anxious. Kissing Domino had pushed it aside. The walk had expelled it from my system. Seeing the lake stretched out below me replaced it with a different feeling altogether.

'Like looking into heaven, isn't it?' Domino said. She sat down beside me, squeezing herself close.

'Hm?'

'The lake,' she said, taking something from her bag. 'Do you know where it came from?'

'Sure.' I continued to gaze at it, remembering what I'd read. Something prosaic that could, in no way, capture the beauty of what I was seeing. 'A volcano did that. Bigger than Krakatoa. Bigger even than Vesuvius. A *super* volcano. There's still a fault under there,' I said. 'Pushed out another volcano in the middle of the lake. Did you know that the island of Samosir is nearly as big as Singapore?'

'Sounds like you read the guidebook,' she said, taking a cigarette and rolling it so the tobacco came loose and fell onto the ground. 'Anyway, that's not what I meant.' She scooped marijuana into the emptied cigarette, tapping it on the lid of the tin to settle it, just as Alim had done.

'What *did* you mean, then?'

Domino finished making the joint and lit it, lying back on the dirt. Her dress pulled tight across her flat stomach, her hip bones protruding on either side.

'There's a legend,' she said. 'About a fisherman who caught a golden fish. He took it home to eat, but decided it was too beautiful.' Domino passed the joint to me.

I took it, considered whether or not to smoke it with her, but decided to go ahead. I wouldn't get anxious here. Not with such a beautiful view, not with Domino lying beside me. 'A golden fish,' I reminded her.

'Yeah. Golden fish. So anyway, he decided not to eat the fish because it was too beautiful. Instead, he put it in a pond to keep as a pet. But the fish turned into a princess, the most stunning woman he'd ever seen, and he immediately fell in love with her.'

I glanced down at Domino and then lay back beside her, staring up at the stars. She shuffled to make herself more comfortable, put one leg over mine, wrapped her arm around my own.

'So he asked her to marry him and she said yes, but on one condition.'

'There's always a condition,' I smiled.

'Always,' said Domino. 'Women always like to have a condition.'

'They do?' I looked at her.

'Sure,' she shrugged. 'Why not?'

'So what's yours?'

'Do you want to hear the story or not?'

'Go ahead.' I took a drag of the joint, beginning to feel even more relaxed now.

'Well, the condition was that he couldn't tell anyone she was a fish. I mean, he wasn't allowed to ever talk about it, probably not even *think* about it.'

'OK.'

'So they got married and had a kid – a boy. The boy turned out to be a bit naughty, though, and one day when he was taking his dad some lunch out to the field, he got hungry on the way so he stopped to eat it.'

'Sounds like trouble,' I said.

'Exactly. He yells at the kid, calls him a stupid son of a fish or something, and his wife, the princess, she finds out straight away. She just *knows*. And she also knows that something bad is going to happen now that her secret is out. And that bad thing is the mother of all storms. The gods are angry. So she tells her kid to run up into the hills just as the storm comes. There's thunder and lightning and a volcano and all kinds of nasty shit, and as the princess runs away, every time she takes a step, a spring wells up where her footprint was, and they gush with water and they join and the whole place floods, making Danau Toba.'

'What happened to her after that?'

'She turned back into a fish.'

'And the man?'

'He turned into an island, right in the middle of the lake. Samosir.'

'And the kid?' I said. 'What happened to him?'

Domino shrugged. 'Fuck knows.'

I propped myself up on one elbow and smiled down at her, liking the arch in her narrow eyebrows, the way it made her look like she was always seeing the world with surprise. Her hair was splayed out around her head like a melted halo, lying on the dirt, traces of it stretched out among the tufts of grass like threads of gold and silver. 'You know, seeing all that stuff in Alim's place, I was thinking about the drugs they found on the bus—'

'I can guess what you're thinking, Alex. They weren't mine.'

'Really?'

'Really. I just came over from Oz; you think I'd be carrying dope?'

I nodded once and she reached up to touch my face.

'You were pretty cool back there,' she said. 'The way you came with me from the hospital, running from the cops. And in Alim's place, I could see you were uncomfortable, but you went with it. I like that. I reckon you've got balls, Alex.'

'And you really weren't scared?' I asked, thinking she was far stronger than me. Either things didn't bother her, or she buried them deep.

'When I went back? Nah, not until he came in,' she said.

'I thought . . . I dunno. I mean, I don't see how you managed to get out without him seeing you.'

'I told you, I hid by the trapdoor. He came in, went to the far end, and I slipped out. What did you think? You think I did something to him?' She looked at me, amusement in her eyes, and she retracted a little as if to study me. 'You did, didn't you? You thought I did something to him?'

'No, I . . .' I shook my head. 'Well, maybe it crossed my mind.'

Domino moved quickly, lifting her head and pressing her mouth to mine. She kissed me and let her head fall back to the ground. 'You're funny,' she said. 'You really think I could do something like that?'

I looked down at her and shook my head. 'No. Of course not. It was just a thought. I was scared for you. There was another guy there, with some kind of rifle. He looked like he wanted to use it.'

'I saw them. You get much of a look at him?'

'A bit. He had a kind of wispy moustache and beard. Bandy legs. He looked pretty mean, actually.' I couldn't help smiling to myself now that I was away from it. 'You know, he looked kinda like he was a bad guy from a film.'

Domino nodded.

'You know who it was?'

'Sounds like Danuri,' she said. 'And yeah, I suppose he is pretty mean, but he wouldn't have done anything. Not to us. Too much to lose.'

'How d'you mean?'

'Without us, they'd be fucked. Hendrik understood that. It's what made him such a good guy.' She sighed. 'Wonder what they did to him, poor bastard.'

'You want to tell me what you're talking about?' I asked, passing her the joint.

She took it and banished all curiosity from my mind by moving to kiss me. 'Forget it,' she said against my lips. 'Thinking out loud, that's all.' Then she withdrew to drag on the joint. She filled her mouth and pressed it against mine, blowing the smoke into me. It felt as if she were reaching right down inside me. I held the smoke in my lungs, keeping my mouth against hers until I could hold it no longer, and raised my head to blow it out into the night.

'It's time,' she said, pulling me back to her, bringing our mouths together again.

As we kissed, I moved my hands over her body, fumbling the dress up over her thighs, over her waist, reaching underneath and running my hand over her cool breasts. Alim's gun was forgotten now. The crash, the hospital, the running away – all that was gone. All that remained was the beauty of the night and the air, and the intoxication of closeness. I didn't stop to think of the speed with which it was happening because, since coming here, everything had happened in a tidal rush. Everything was cascading around me and below me, lifting me and carrying me along. I just closed my eyes and went with it. Enjoyed it, as Domino crushed her mouth against mine, showing me she wanted me to go on, pushing my head down onto her chest, wanting to feel my warmth on her skin. I broke away, kneeling before her, using both hands to lift her dress as she reached to unfasten the stolen trousers. I slipped her underwear from her, taking care not to touch her injured thigh, the material twisting as it came past her tattoo and over her feet. I sat back and looked at her, naked in the moonlight, her skin tightening into goose bumps, her breasts flat against her chest. The scrape on her thigh, the bruises that spotted her body, were nothing more than discoloured patches of skin in this light.

'Now,' she said to me. 'Now.'

I put my hands under her knees, ran my fingers down her calves, and only then did I sense my own hesitation, knowing that something was still to be said. 'Maybe we . . .' I shook my head, feeling awkward, not wanting to spoil the fluency of the moment. 'I mean, what about . . . you know. Protection?'

'You don't need protecting from me,' she said, taking my hands, guiding them where she wanted them to go.

'No, I mean . . .'

'I know what you mean, Alex.' Her hands still over mine, still moving. 'But it's time to let go. Lose control and enjoy the moment.' Then she was sitting up, pushing me back, pulling off my trousers and straddling me, moving me inside her and leaning over, her hair in my face, her lips on mine, and I had never known it could be so wonderful, never imagined this had been waiting for me.

10

We lay together, side by side, feeling the cool air on our skin until it became too cold and we gathered the clothes that we'd strewn around us in our rush to be together. I pulled on the stolen trousers and sat down to put on my shirt as Domino slipped the dress over her head, stretching her arms and letting it fall over her.

'I need some new clothes,' I said, looking down at myself.

Domino rubbed my thigh in an absent-minded way. 'We'll have something for you. Maybe in a day or two we can go into town, buy some things.'

'A day or two?'

'There's something else you might want to see.'

'Out here? For a day or two?'

She shrugged, leaned back and pulled me down beside her. 'You don't have to come,' she said, turning, running her hand under my shirt and stroking my chest. 'You can do whatever you want. Isn't that why you're travelling?'

I sighed and closed my eyes to the stars, basking in her touch, still feeling the hazy sensation in my head left by the dope.

'You can be whoever you want. Go anywhere, do anything,' she whispered. 'No one can make you do anything you don't want to.'

I felt myself smile.

'You could get up right now and leave,' she said. 'Or you could stay with me a while longer.'

I turned to look at her. 'I think I might stay awhile. Do you want me to?'

Domino took her hand away. 'It's not up to me, Alex, it's your choice.'

'What if I said no?'

'Then it would be what you wanted.'

There was no sunrise of any note, the sky just grew light. As the day brightened, though, and the air filled with the scent of damp earth, I saw the full beauty of the lake below me. From where we sat, overlooking a small, natural bay, the water was a sheet of glass reaching out from one mountainous shore to the other. Far below us, where the ground levelled out, the land was a mix of colours, a patchwork of light and dark green. One or two points of white, toy villages dotted along the shore, an obvious spot for fishermen to make their homes.

To my right, beyond the village we'd visited last night, beyond the line of the highest and furthest pines, the mountains of the Batak Highlands rose into the clouds. Sheer, dark walls, two thousand feet high, erupted from the lake and burst into the sky, their craggy surfaces streaked with the foam of young waterfalls.

To my left, at the foot of an abrupt drop, the land was softer, rising and falling in gentle undulation, the dull green of rice paddies visible on the hillsides. Further away, perhaps two miles from where we were sitting, the trees began again, a wilderness of pines and thicker, leafier trees, laurel and tanoak and beech, clinging to the hillsides, securing the land, keeping it from falling into the lake. Even in the misty light of a cloudy morning, the view was enough to take my breath away. Heaven on earth.

'That's where we're going,' Domino said into the grey dawn. 'Where you're looking right now. Those trees. That's where we're going. But we have to go down before we can go up.'

I turned to her.

'If you want to, that is.'

'What's there?' I asked.

'Wait and see.' She stood up. 'You want to come, or you gonna stay here?' She looked down at me. 'It's up to you.'

'There's something I need to know first.'

'What's that?'

I stood up beside her. 'Can we get something to eat anywhere round here?' I opened my arms to the wilderness. 'Other than pine cones and soil, I mean.'

'You got munchies?'

'Call it whatever you want,' I said. 'But if I don't eat soon, I'll not be going anywhere.'

Domino kissed me and headed for the slope in front of us. 'Come on, then, Mr Traveller, let's go find some food.'

It took us twenty minutes or so to make our way down the gentle stretch of the slope. The ground was bare here, the soil exposed and damp, hampering our progress. We were wearing only flip-flops and they gave no grip on the slippery dirt. Nearing the end of the more placid gradient, though, it became obvious that my initial observation had been incorrect. The ground did not continue to slope at a steeper incline towards the flat, but fell away at a sharp angle.

'We'll never get down there,' I said, coming to a standstill.

'Sure we will. There's no other way.'

'In flip-flops?'

'It'll make it harder, but yeah, why not?'

'Why not?' I put my hands on my hips and looked down. 'Because we'll go arse over tit,' I said. 'Break our necks and die if we're lucky; break them and live if we're not.'

Domino sat down and rolled a joint while I walked a hundred metres or so in either direction along the top, looking for a way down. I scanned the hillside, hoping to spot a quick way out, but there was nothing. We were in the middle of nowhere. Apart from the few buildings below us, I could see no sign of life whatsoever. No other route down.

'Come and sit here,' Domino called to me. 'Don't be so fuckin' antsy. We'll smoke awhile, then make our way down.'

'Where?' I said. 'Where are you planning on doing that?'

'There's a path,' she said, lighting the joint and patting the ground beside her. 'It's hard to see, but it's there.'

'A path? You're sure?'

'Well, I should be. I've been up and down it a hundred times.'

'A hundred times?'

'Well, maybe not a hundred.'

'But more than once, right?'

'Sure. I mean, it's a little tricky, you wouldn't want to lose your footing but yeah, it's there.'

'Wouldn't want to lose your footing?' I asked, eyeing the joint in her hand. 'So is *that* a good idea?'

'Course it is. It's a great idea. The best. Help chill you out on the way down.' She smiled and beckoned me over again. 'Loosen you up. And when we get down there, we'll get something to eat. Curb those munchies.'

I shrugged and went to her. 'You know, I think you might be mad.'

'Isn't that what you like about me?'

She was probably right. It *was* what I liked about her. As if the rules that applied to everyone else didn't apply to Domino. She did whatever she wanted to do, and I found that enticing. Part of me wanted to be like her, to throw off my cloak of conservatism and guilt and allow myself to be free like she was. And in that moment, standing in the hills surrounding Toba, I thought maybe I was coming close to what I was looking for. Back home I'd been a caring son who'd cut the thread of his own life to care for a decaying mother. I'd been left with a gaping hole when she was gone, filled only with the nagging doubt about the decision I had made for her. Now I could see that I was running away from that as much as I was looking for a new direction. And here I was picking up my life thread again. Here, I could be different. If I wanted to be brave, I could be. If I wanted to be carefree and reckless, I could do that, too. I could rise above myself or fall below. At least, that's what I thought. But the truth is always different from what you imagine in a moment of intense feeling. What I didn't understand then was that I couldn't just change myself. I couldn't just be someone else.

Domino had said it would chill us out, but I still wasn't sure the ganja was a good idea. I tried to give myself over to it, think the way she did, feel the things she did, be what I wanted to be, but I didn't have her confidence and I couldn't help feeling anxious as we began the descent.

For a time, we walked the crest of the drop, close to the edge where the ground was unstable and looked as if it might break away at any moment. In some places the vegetation was thick, sparse at first, but thickening as we progressed along the edge until it was at my waist, lush and green, firming the soil.

Eventually Domino stopped and pointed to a small gap – a narrow, worn patch in the dirt that cut through the undergrowth and snaked down the hillside, twisting from side to side like a poisonous and treacherous reptile. 'I'll go first,' she said. 'Probably safer that way.'

I showed my hand and bowed like a gallant knight, waiting for her to lead the way.

At first the path was manageable. It was wide enough and dry enough for us to pass without too much trouble, tacking our way down the steep face. But as we progressed, the dirt became firmer, worn down to the rock by countless years of weather. Here the smooth stone was damp where it had retained moisture from the first morning air, and I felt less secure. The treadless rubber of my flip-flops offered no grip at all, and we were both forced to slow our pace.

'Thought you said it was easy,' I mumbled.

'Where's your sense of adventure?'

'I think I left it up there,' I said, looking up and behind me, immediately regretting it because it made my head spin.

'Well, it's not far now,' she said. 'Maybe you'll find it again when we get to the bottom.'

'Find what?'

'Your sense of adventure.'

'Oh. Yeah. Maybe.'

I watched her moving along the path, admiring how she managed it with apparent ease, despite her attire. She'd pulled the dress up to her thighs, tied it in a thick knot, and I wondered if perhaps it was forcing her to take small steps, if that was how she made it look so easy. I tried to tighten my own steps, keep my feet steady on the slippery rock, but it was a mistake to change my method and as soon as I did, my foot slipped and I collapsed to one knee, reaching out for the undergrowth above me, between two sections of the snaking path. 'Shit.'

Domino stopped and looked back. 'You all right?'

I took a deep breath, steadied myself, crouching on the path. I nodded and looked down at the settlement below, not far from the lake. We were about two hundred metres up now, and the water looked different from here, more choppy. There was a breeze channelling down the hillside, buffeting the flat land below us and launching itself across the lake, raising the water into small waves, which curled and crashed at their peaks.

There were a couple of boats, not much more than dark pencil lines on the surface of white-tipped waves. Early-morning fishermen in their dugouts, feeding their families, making a living.

'Not too far now,' Domino reassured me, but I could see for myself that there was still a fair distance to go. If I were to head straight down, as the crow flies, or as the body would tumble, I guessed I'd reach the bottom in good time, but the way we were moving, snaking from side to side, it would take us a while to reach level ground. It would be far easier to approach the settlement by boat, from a safer place across the lake, and I wondered if Domino had brought me this way for the adventure. If that were the case, then I needed to show her I was up to the challenge.

'Come on, then,' I said, getting to my feet. 'Let's do this. I'm starving.'

'That's the spirit,' she said, taking the next bend in the path, turning and looking up at me. 'Getting pretty peckish myself.'

She was about eight feet below me, facing the opposite direction, and as I looked down at her, the cloud over the mountains in the distance split in two for a brief moment and a tiny arc of the sun glanced over the dark crags. It spilled light across the lake, catching the surface of the waves, glittering like gold dust and lighting the world before me. All I could see was brilliant water and an orgy of greens and blacks, stretching ahead of me. It was as close to paradise as I had ever seen, and I felt as if a hand had reached over the Batak Highlands and touched my heart.

I drank it in, soaked up every last drop of it and looked down at Domino's face, seeing her remarkable green eyes and her glorious figure. Everything was forgotten. Nothing mattered but what I could see in front of me right now.

Then I slipped.

I shifted my weight without thinking. I was too wrapped up in what I was seeing to be aware of what I was doing. I adjusted my balance on the smooth rock, my right foot slipped, and I came off the path, my other foot going out from under me. I was able to grasp my fist around a tuft of grass, tall and thick, but the soil it used for purchase was thin and infirm. The plant came out of the ground with little resistance and, with a handful of vegetation, I began my rapid descent to the valley floor.

I hurtled past Domino, hearing her call my name, then I bumped, slid and tumbled more than forty feet, coming to a halt when I crashed into a well-placed outcrop at the side of the path – a black mass of rock, formed as a short, low wall, which stopped me dead in my tracks when I struck it at speed. I was lucky not to hit it with my head, but that was where my luck ran out. My contact with the solid wall came with a sickening crunch, which sent pain like nothing before it coursing through my right shoulder, spinning down my spine and reverberating back to the base of my skull. The pain was overwhelming. An intensity of physical sensation that I hadn't experienced before. It was as if I'd been hit by a charging bull; an outrageous and sudden feeling that was accompanied by a grotesque sound. A combination of dry cracking and wet popping, and then all I could do was release the agony from my body in the only way available to me. I opened my mouth and howled.

11

I tried to sit up, but my right arm was useless. It lay limp beneath me. I rolled to one side, using my left arm to lift my right into what I thought would be a more comfortable position but, once again, pain rocketed through me, burning outwards from my shoulder as if someone had exploded napalm in my armpit.

Instead, I shuffled back against the rock that had stopped my fall, caused the discomfort that now smothered me. I shook my head and looked up, seeing Domino coming down the track. She was close, just five metres away, following the twists of the path. I wanted to call out to her, tell her not to hurry, tell her to be careful on the rocks, but I'd spent my last energy howling to the sky like a wild animal. All I could do now was watch her approach.

When she reached me, she dropped her bag onto the hard ground and crouched at my feet. 'Shit. Shit, shit, shit,' she was saying. 'Fuck, fuck, fuck.'

I nodded my head in agreement.

'That looked bad. Do you feel like anything's broken?' She looked over my shoulder as she spoke, assessing our options. Down the mountain or up the mountain. Either way we went, there was little civilisation. We were a good hour's hike from the *kampong* we'd been to last night, and that was at least a few miles from the main road, which, in turn, was a long way from anything, as far as I remembered from our trip last night. In the other direction there was the settlement I'd seen from above, but it didn't look like much, and I doubted it would have hospital facilities. A doctor maybe.

'There'll be boats,' I reassured myself, not realising I'd spoken aloud until Domino asked me to repeat what I'd said. I just shook my head and closed my eyes against the pain.

'Alex? Alex? Did you hit your head?'

My face contorting.

'Is it your head, Alex? Did you hurt your head again?'

Unable to speak. The pain coming in tidal waves.

'Open your eyes. You need to sit up.' She grabbed my shoulders and hefted me up, eliciting another howl. 'Don't pass out on me,' she said, running a hand over my head.

I tried to nod.

'You think you can move?' Her voice insisting. 'We'll have to get moving. Can't stay up here.'

'Just for a moment,' I managed, my breath coming back to me. 'Give me a moment.' I adjusted my position, tried to make myself more comfortable.

'It hurt?'

'Yeah. Yeah, it fucking hurts.'

'Where? Your head?'

'No.'

'You think you broke something?'

'Feels like I broke *every*thing,' I said, the stabbing sensation subsiding now that I'd moved.

'For real?'

'I dunno. Feels like my shoulder.'

She seemed to relax, pursing her lips, breathing hard through her nose. 'You're not exactly the luckiest guy I've ever met, Alex. Gave me a fucking scare there. Thought you were a goner for sure.'

I forced a smile. The pain was lifting a little now. 'Me too.'

'Thought you were going all the way down.' Domino looked over my head once more. 'You seen? This rock hadn't stopped you . . .' She made a whistling sound.

I shuffled to a kneeling position, turning round to put my left hand on top of the rock and pull myself up to look over.

On the other side was an escarpment, the most vertical part of the climb. An almost sheer face of black rock, virtually no vegetation growing there. A narrow path was cut into the rock, two feet across, cracked and damaged.

I swallowed. 'Who made it?'

'What?'

'The path,' I said. 'Who made it?' I mean, why would anyone want . . . ?'

'Don't know. It's always been here. Me and Kurt found it a couple of years ago, but I guess the people down there know about it, too.'

'Kurt?'

'Yeah. Never seen anyone else on the path, though.'

'Who's Kurt?' I'd heard her use the name at Alim's place and, even through the pain, I felt piqued to think that she'd shared this journey with someone else.

'You'll meet him soon enough,' she said. 'In fact, he's the one who's going to make your shoulder better.'

I looked at her, wondering what she was talking about. 'I need a doctor, not some old boyfriend called Kurt. This pain is—'

'Kurt *is* a doctor,' she said. 'Well, kind of.'

I wanted to say more, but a wave of nausea washed over me like a thick, oily blanket and my clear vision became clouded. I closed my eyes and waited for the pain to subside.

'Still hurt?'

'Yes.'

'I'll skin up. It'll take the edge off.'

I started to shake my head, feeling a pang of anger towards her. It was her answer to everything. Smoke dope. But she was only doing what she could. A doctor would give me something to kill the pain and nausea, so maybe she was right. Maybe it was exactly what I needed. It might take the edge off and give me enough strength to make it down the mountain. There was a path, after all; it wasn't like I was going to fall. 'Yeah,' I said. 'OK. That might work.'

She sat beside me and reached for her bag, taking it by one handle and pulling it towards her. 'I'll sort us out,' she said as the loose handle caught on a lip of rock, tipping the bag onto its side, spilling some of the contents.

The tin of dope was first, the packet of *kretek*, a lighter, a flat yellow box of Chiclets chewing gum, a clear bag of white tablets, knotted at the top, a book. The cover was a montage of photos – cars and clear blue skies – but I couldn't read the title. The glimpse I had was too brief because as soon as the bag tipped and the contents spilled, Domino moved to block my view as she gathered everything together. Before she could totally obscure it, though, I caught a hint of something that made me want to look closer, see what she was concealing. But I had to be wrong. I shook my head. It was probably the shock of the fall, the pain from the bump.

I thought I saw the grip of a pistol. The marked, dark steel of the gun I'd seen in Alim's hands.

Domino tucked the bag beside her and made a start on the joint.

'What's that in your bag?' I said.

'Stuff for the plane, mostly. Never carry much more than something to read, some music.'

'I thought I saw . . .' Even without saying the words aloud it sounded ridiculous.

Domino stopped what she was doing and looked at me.

'Pills,' I said. 'And . . . and Alim's gun.'

Domino continued to stare at me. She studied my eyes, tried to read my mind, then sighed and put the joint down. 'I didn't really drop my iPod,' she said. 'I wanted to see what else he had in his little box.'

'The pills I just saw?' I shifted and winced as a sharp bolt flashed through my shoulder.

'You OK?'

'No. Hurts like fuck.' I waited for the pain to subside. 'What about those pills, then? What's that all about?'

She looked away from me, clenching her beautiful, serious jaw. I watched the muscles twitching there before they relaxed and she turned back to me. 'I was pissed off at the way he treated me, leering like that. I thought maybe we could get something for free.'

'And the—'

'Gun?' she said, putting her hand in the bag, taking out the pistol, holding it up.

'Yeah. The gun.'

'Don't look at me like that. I didn't do anything to him.'

'I know. You told me.'

She turned it over in her hand. 'I grabbed it when I heard him coming back in. I thought if he caught me . . .' She shrugged. 'I wouldn't even know what to do with it.'

'He left it on the table? Didn't take it with him?' I said, thinking maybe it was what he went back for. Maybe it was what *she* went back for.

'I guess.'

'And he didn't notice it was missing?'

'Don't know. I guess not.'

'But he will. Eventually.'

'Probably,' Domino nodded, her expression suggesting it was a consequence she hadn't considered. She was a hit-and-run girl, I'd seen that already. An animal of instinct.

'And what happens then?' I asked her.

'Maybe he'll think he lost it.'

'No way.'

'Or that someone else took it?' she offered.

'He'll know it was you.' Her impulsive nature was attractive, but it had its downside.

'How could he *know*?'

'Would he have to?' I asked, looking back up the hill. 'Maybe he'd just have to *suspect*.'

'It'll be fine.'

'Does he know where to find you?'

She ignored me and returned to the task of making the joint.

'You shouldn't have kept it,' I said. 'You should've put it back.'

'Too late for that now,' she replied, putting the joint in her mouth and lighting it.

'Yeah,' I said. 'Too late.'

12

Coming down the steep crag, every movement intensified the pain in my shoulder. It was a feeling that consumed all. Like a flesh-eating disease, it affected every part of my body. As if someone had slipped a narrow, hot knife into the front of my shoulder, pushing it back into the socket, and was grating it against the dry, sensitive bone inside. Twisting muscle and sinew. Every time I moved, bumped on the track, it was as if the stiletto was raking deeper, pushing harder.

The gun now lost to the Technicolor of my pain, I tried to concentrate on the ganja buzz in my head, keep my eyes on the path at my feet. Domino stayed close, keeping just behind me. She wanted to go in front, watch for potential hazards that I might miss in my inattentive state, but I told her not to. The way I was right now, I might slip again, and if she was too close to me, I'd take her with me.

We managed the remainder of the descent without incident, reaching the flatter ground within half an hour.

'Not far now,' said Domino. 'We'll go straight through the village. Find Kurt. He'll fix you up.' She was sweating. Blonde hair pushed back, a few darkened strands clinging to the dampness along her sharp jaw line, her temples, around the top of her forehead.

I nodded. 'Lead the way.' From where we were, I couldn't see any sign of life, nor could I see the lake. In front of us there was a maze of paddy fields reaching out towards a low line of traveller's palms, which spread dark-green feathered leaves, fanning like peacock's tails to hide the village. The collection of regular-shaped fields stretched from one side of the valley to the other, maybe seven or eight fields across and five deep. They were kept separate by shallow walls of dirt arranged into irregular squares like a surrealist's chessboard. Each was filled with water, something I'd been unable to detect from above because they were overgrown with bright green rice plants. In one of the furthest fields I could see a group of people, knee deep, their bodies bent low.

We kept to the raised walls between the paddies, following the worn paths through the grass that tried to grow there. We moved more quickly now, and it wasn't long before we neared the line of palms, their upright branches spreading wide like Chinese fans. The group of workers looked up as one, stopping to watch us pass.

Three women, their skin weathered and dark, each wearing an arrangement of material – a kind of flat turban – on their head. Their check-print sarongs were pulled high and tied between their thighs like oversized nappies. They nodded in greeting, one of them raising a hand, saying, '*Horas*'.

I raised my good hand in return, looking down at them in the water, and forced a smile as best as I could. They watched us pass, and when we'd cleared the field I turned to see that they were still looking in our direction.

At the far edge, beside a pump spewing water into the fields, a water buffalo lay on the dry land, enjoying the morning air. The beast's ribbed and nicked horns reminded me of those that had been roped to the central post in Alim's longhouse. But while those had felt macabre and cautionary, these were benign and almost without purpose.

Just as the women had done, so the *kerbau* watched us pass, its brown eyes unblinking behind long eyelashes, its tail swishing flies from its hindquarters. It turned its head, its jaws moving slowly in rumination.

Through the palms and bamboo and banana plants and I could see the lake again, and up ahead, at the end of a short path lined with elaborate shrines, the small village stood on the bank, a collection of houses without pattern. There were several Batak longhouses like the ones I'd seen last night, but there were other buildings here, too. Mostly they were made from wood – rickety affairs with rusted corrugated roofs and slats missing from their walls. One or two were made from brick but these, too, were in poor repair. And there were people here. Enough people for this to be a village. Not like the place we'd visited last night, where there had been a handful of houses and we had seen only two men. As soon as we came out of the trees here I could see many people going about their daily business.

'Through the village and out the other side,' said Domino, running a hand across her brow. 'We still have a little way to go. You gonna be OK?'

'How far?'

'There's a track out of the *kampong*. Maybe ten minutes, then we're on our way. We'll be there in forty minutes.'

'Forty minutes?'

'You can do it.'

'There's no one *here*?' I asked. 'No one who can help?'

Domino shook her head. 'Nope.'

I squeezed my eyes shut, trying to force away the pain. 'Right, then.'

Domino hesitated and watched me. We'd been travelling for a good hour since the fall and she'd heard every wince, yelp and sharp intake of breath. Domino knew I was hurting. Perhaps she could almost feel it herself.

'Maybe there's someone,' she said. 'I mean, he's not . . .' She broke off and looked down. 'Maybe we'll go to him. He might help.'

I glanced at the first in a row of shrines to my left. A brick-built block, decorated with two white crosses, on top of which was a miniature Batak house – a perfectly scaled version, intricately painted, adorned with carvings and topped with a thatched roof. A shrine could not change who a person was, no matter how much attention the builder paid to the detail, but it made for an exuberant reminder that someone had stepped foot on this land; that they had touched other people's lives and meant something to someone. I wouldn't mind such a legacy myself. It was a far more colourful and celebratory acknowledgement of someone's life than the plaque my mother had on the crematorium memorial wall. Not even a carved headstone and a small piece of land to rest in. Just a scattering of ash into the surf of the North Sea and a brass plaque on a wall. It didn't change who she was, but it was grey and inadequate by comparison.

'If there's someone who can make this pain go away, I'd like to meet him,' I said, taking my eyes off the shrine. 'Right now I reckon I'd let someone cut my arm off.'

Domino smiled at me. 'Let's hope it doesn't come to that.'

Despite the pain, I smiled too.

'OK,' she said. 'I reckon there's someone who can help.'

Coming into the village and walking among the ill-repaired buildings, people looked up from their work to follow us with curious eyes. A group of women, sitting in a huddle, talking in conspiracy, leaning to spit red gobs of betel nut through tombstone teeth. A woman using a long, thick, wooden pole to pound rice in a stone bowl, the rhythmic thumping of wood on stone halting when we approached. A black dog, its fur coated with dry dust, slinking between two buildings, pausing to watch us pass. Children stopped playing, some of them running over to touch us, the taller ones reaching up to feel Domino's golden hair.

'Most of these people,' she said, 'they don't get out of the village much. They have boats, and there are towns on the lake, places for them to go, bring in supplies, but mostly they stay here. Grow rice and catch fish. They don't see that many whiteys.'

I looked around, the nausea coming in waves again. The buzz from the dope was wearing thin, the pain seeking out the worn patches and pushing through.

Offset from the road, a smallholding, not much more than

wire mesh wrapped round two-metre fence posts. There were a couple of pigs in there rooting around, looking for scraps. There were chickens, too, some inside and some outside the fence. Scrawny and dirty, their white feathers marked with grime. A young girl, not even ten years old from the look of her, was squatting by the fence holding a chicken tight under her arm. With her free hand, she set down a glass bowl and a knife, adjusted the chicken so its neck was over the bowl. Picking the knife from the dirt, she drew it across the chicken's throat in a sawing motion, the bird jerking in her firm fingers, the glass bowl filling with deep red. She looked up as we went by and she nodded once, saying, '*Horas*', before turning her attention back to the chicken, which she released, allowing it to tumble for a while, frantic in death. I watched with fascination, even through the haze of my pain.

'I guess that's something *you* haven't seen much of,' Domino said.

'Usually I just get them from the supermarket,' I told her.

We passed a small collection of shops, more like stalls, selling knick-knacks and general household items. Pots and pans, piles of cloth wrapped in plastic, sacks of ground spices and leaves I didn't recognise. The aroma from these was exotic and exciting, but tainted by the smell of the open drains, which ran along either side of the street.

A brick building, this one painted pale green, stood out from the others. The walls were decorated with film posters for movies that might have been made in India. Long-haired beauties entangled in the arms of young, handsome men, almost effeminate with their high cheekbones and full lips. I couldn't understand the words, the names of the films, and some I couldn't even read because they were written in letters I didn't recognise. The building had a wide shutter door at the front, the metal rolled high so that customers could walk straight in. I could see trays of fruit, sacks of rice, brightly coloured sweets and pretzel-shaped snacks. Bright pink and shocking green, the sort of thing no westerner would pick from a shelf. Above the door, in scripted letters, the word *kedai* was painted. Simply stated, this was a shop. The man inside, sitting in a rattan chair sipping black coffee from a glass, looked up as we passed, mumbling, '*Horas*', his head turning to follow us until we were out of sight.

We walked for a couple of minutes along the main street of the *kampong*, heading straight for the lake. At the water's edge, things were quieter and I could hear the slap of the waves against the stone shore. An old man squatting on his haunches, untangling a fishing net, didn't even look up as we passed.

Domino led me along the shore towards a line of houses, just a few feet away from a short stone jetty with iron moorings. Here the villagers kept an eclectic collection of vessels, ranging from rowing boats to basic dugout canoes laden with nets, floats and what looked like lobster pots. There was even a bright red pedalo and, beside it, two single-engine motorboats. One of them had a pair of water skis and a couple of dirty yellow life jackets in the back.

Domino muttered something under her breath as we passed the boats – 'Shit. *He's* here,' it sounded like – and took me straight past all of these things.

We went to the first house in the row, a whitewashed brick building, surrounded by tall, fan-shaped palms. It was topped with a distinctive saddle roof, made from rusted corrugated iron, but it didn't have a trapdoor and it didn't have a ladder. It was smaller than the traditional Batak home and it was more modern, with a front door and windows lined with mosquito nets. It was in keeping with the general style of what I'd seen of Toba, but it had a more up-to-date twist.

Domino went straight to the front door, shooing away a mangy cat, and lifted her fist to knock, hesitating before rapping her knuckles on the edge of the screen. It was a hard, shallow tone, weak in the cloudy morning. The sound of the lake behind us was louder, the water lapping at the shore, buffeting the boats enough for them to bump together. A rhythmic, lazy thumping as the vessels nudged each other on the surface of the water.

Domino knocked again, harder this time, but still the sound was dead.

We waited a moment longer.

'No one in,' she said. 'We should go. We leave now, we'll get back home within the hour. Kurt will sort you out.'

That name again.

'One more time,' I said through my teeth. 'Please.' I cradled my right arm with my left, trying to ease the pain.

Domino raised her fist but stopped when she saw a shadow moving behind the green screen. 'It's him,' she said, and before she could say any more, the figure was there, a large silhouette reaching out for the catch, pulling back the door, looking out at us. What surprised me most of all, apart from his size, was that he was European. His tanned skin was almost native in colour, but his features were not of this place. Fair hair, rounded eyes that might have been grey or blue. I guessed he was at least twenty years older than me, but might have been more. It was difficult to judge because he had a weathered look, as if he spent a lot of time outdoors. A face that had felt the wind, hands that had seen hard work.

'You?' he said, looking down at Domino. 'What the hell do you want? You people—'

'Hidayat,' Domino said. 'We need Hidayat.'

The man stopped, raising his eyebrows and looking Domino up and down before saying, 'What for?'

'We need his help.'

'That's a good one. Why the hell d'you think he'd want to help you?'

'He slipped.' She motioned her head towards me. 'On the path down the hill.'

'Tough.' The man looked at me now, running his eyes up and down me in the same way he'd done with Domino. 'You're new,' he said. 'I've not seen you before.'

I nodded. 'Please. I really need some help.'

The man raised his eyebrows again. '*Please?* That's a new one from you people. First time I ever heard one of you say *please*.' He stayed where he was, one hand on the door, his arm stretched to hold it open. 'Came down the path, eh?'

I nodded.

'Braver than you look.'

'Let's go.' Domino touched my arm. 'He's not gonna help. I shouldn't have even brought you here.'

'I can't,' I said, thinking I couldn't go any further.

'Kurt will fix you,' she tried to reassure me. 'It's not too far now.'

'Kurt?' the man scoffed.

'Please.' I looked up at him. The dope was wearing off and the pain was intensifying. I tried to lean against the door-frame, but I was too far away and I stumbled.

The man stepped forward and grabbed me. He held me firm, shaking his head. 'I'll probably regret this, but you need more than Kurt. You need a proper doctor.' He ran his free hand over his head and nodded. 'OK, then, you better come in. I'll wake Hidayat.'

13

Domino followed us into the house, coming straight into the sitting room. Although the building looked like a modern version of the traditional Batak house from the outside, on the inside it was more like the kind of home I was used to. There were no wooden pillars adorned with buffalo horns here. No mats to sit on, no fire pit in the ground. It wasn't luxurious either, but it had furniture. A glass-topped rattan table served as the focal point for a two-seater sofa and two armchairs also made from rattan. The orange covers were worn through in places, but they looked comfortable.

On the walls, large glass cases, six or seven at least, each one of them filled with the preserved colours of more than a hundred butterflies. The wings spread wide, the narrow bodies pinned to boards like Gulliver staked out by Lilliputians. They were beautiful and distasteful at the same time. Removed from the world outside so they could bring a cruel and tainted beauty into this place.

'You better sit down,' the man said, guiding me to one of the threadbare armchairs. 'Wait here.'

It was a relief to be off my feet, but Domino remained standing. She watched the man leave the room, her pale lip almost curling, her fine nose wrinkling. It was a look I'd never seen and it reminded me that I hardly knew her.

'What is it? What's the matter?' But before she could reply, the European returned, followed by a smaller man, thin and wiry, this one Indonesian. He was less weathered than his friend. His skin was clearer, his features finer, his manner more delicate. He was wearing a plain white T-shirt and was tightening a checked sarong around his waist as he came. His hair was tousled and his eyes were hooded as if he'd just woken from a deep sleep. As he walked, there was a hint of him dragging one foot.

'There.' The European pointed at me. 'Some kind of fall. Coming down the path, bloody idiot.'

The Indonesian nodded and ran both hands over his face to wake himself. 'What's the matter?' he asked in English. His accent was good.

'It's his arm,' said Domino. 'I think—'

'Not you,' said the European. 'Him.'

He and the other man looked at me, waiting for me to speak.

'My arm,' I said, looking at Domino. 'I fell.'

'Hm,' said the European. 'Coming down the path. Fit for nothing more than mountain goats and snakes. Which are you?'

The smaller man shook his head and smiled at me. 'Don't mind Richard,' he said. 'He acts like a bear sometimes, but he's a very nice man. I'm Hidayat, by the way.'

'Alex,' I said.

'An Englishman? Just like Richard.'

I nodded.

'No need to shake, I suppose,' he said, indicating that I should stand, and he put his hands on me, taking my right arm, moving my left out of the way. He felt around the top of my bicep, probing higher, his fingers pressing around my shoulder. 'It's not your arm,' he said. 'It's your shoulder.'

'Broken?'

Hidayat smiled. 'No, no, not broken. Dislocated.'

'Can you fix it?' asked Domino, making Richard snap his head in her direction, daring her to speak again. She held up her hands and threw them down again.

'Anterior dislocation,' said Hidayat. 'I can fix it, but it won't be nice.'

'Are you a doctor?' I asked. It seemed an unlikely place to find a doctor.

'I trained at one of your London hospitals, believe it or not, but I prefer a slower pace now. And the air here is so good.' He took my left arm and guided it back to where it had been before, cradling my right. 'Why don't you lie down?'

'Here?'

'There's somewhere you'd prefer?'

I looked at Domino, who nodded once, very slightly, almost impossible to notice.

'You want the pain to go away?' asked Hidayat.

'Yes.'

'Then lie down and I'll fix it for you.'

I took a deep breath and eased myself onto the floor, lying on my back and looking up at Hidayat.

'You want something to help you relax? Nicotine, caffeine, something stronger?'

'No, thanks,' I said, glancing at the butterflies on the wall.

'You sure? It can help. I have some hash if you want it. It's good stuff.'

'I've had enough already.' The pain was crisp now, clear and biting, not fuzzy and dulled as it had been before. It was unpleasant, almost unbearable, but I wanted to feel the moment when he put it right. I wanted to feel the pain disappear, to sense the relief of removing a splinter, magnified countless times.

He squatted down on one knee and took hold of my right arm, bending it at the elbow and rolling it across my body, then away. 'You like butterflies?'

'Not really. Maybe when they're alive, but . . .' The pain was intense and I squeezed my eyes shut, trying to think of something other than having a stiletto forced into my shoulder socket.

'A macabre pastime you'd think. Catching beauty and pinning it to a board. Naming it and keeping it.' He repeated the movement, rolling backwards and forwards.

'Not for me to say.' My words were laboured.

'Each to their own?' He began to push a little harder. 'How very English.' He glanced back at Richard. 'You'd be surprised how relaxing it can be. Catching, pressing, cataloguing. Not that I do so much of it these days.'

'I—' On the fifth or sixth iteration, there was an audible wet crunch as my shoulder slotted back into place and I felt an immediate release from the pain.

I took a deep breath and let out a long sigh. I opened my eyes and looked at Hidayat, not knowing how to thank him for doing such a thing.

'Don't mention it,' he smiled.

'No, really. *Thank you.*'

Hidayat stood up as if it were an effort for him, using the couch for support, then he offered me a hand. 'You need a sling for that. For a couple of days, that's all.' He turned to Richard and spoke to him in Indonesian. Richard hesitated, rolled his eyes, but when Hidayat didn't reply, Richard left the room, returning with a folded cloth, the pattern red and indigo.

'This is a traditional cloth. *Ulos ni tondi*,' Hidayat said. 'Cloth of the soul.' He opened it out and re-folded it in a different way, making a sling for my arm. 'We can wear it on our shoulders or around our hips. Sometimes on our head. We Bataks wear it for rituals and ceremonies, and we give it as a gift – an act of giving warmth and honour. And love.' He looked at Richard as he reached around my neck to fit it in place, slipping behind me to tie it. 'And it's a way of blessing you with good health, so today we can use it to make you better, OK?'

I nodded.

'Just promise me that you'll return it one day.'

'Thank you. I will.'

'There,' he said when he was done. 'You should be OK. Anywhere else, I'd tell you a hospital visit would be a good idea, but here . . . well, you'll probably be all right.' He glanced at Domino, who remained standing, looking uncomfortable.

Hidayat cleared his throat. 'Are you hungry? You should eat something. Let me get you some food.'

I opened my mouth, but Domino spoke first, saying, 'No. Come on, Alex. We have to go.'

'Wait.' Hidayat held up a hand. 'I'll get you something. To take with you.' And before either of us could answer, he swished from the room, his ankles pounding the edges of his tightly tied sarong. Again, I noticed the way he dragged his left foot. It seemed more pronounced now.

The three of us stood in silence. Beyond this room, there were sounds of movements, clattering and clinking, but in here, there was nothing. Richard watched Domino, a scowl fixed on his face. Occasionally he glanced at me, but only for the briefest moment before he looked back at Domino.

When Hidayat returned, he handed me a small bundle wrapped in paper. 'You need something after pain like that. Something sweet. Make sure you eat it, Alex.' He looked me in the eye when he used my name.

I took the package and thanked him, wanting to show more gratitude. Hidayat struck me as a good man, and my instinct was to avoid insulting him, but my loyalty was to Domino.

'How about the cut?' Hidayat asked. 'What happened there?' He put his hand to my head, turning it gently to look closer.

Domino came forward, knocking his hand away from me. 'Enough,' she said. 'Time to go, Alex.'

Hidayat jumped in surprise and Richard moved towards Domino, raising his hands.

'No.' Hidayat stepped in front of his friend. 'No, it's OK.'

'Who the hell does she think she is?' said Richard. 'Coming here for help, then—'

'Leave it,' said Hidayat.

'No, I won't leave it.' Richard moved around him, coming for Domino, pulling himself to his full height and staring down at her. 'Get out,' he hissed at her. 'Get the fuck out of our house.'

Domino stared up at him, and I noticed that her bag was still over her shoulder, but one hand was now hidden inside and I remembered what I'd seen up on the path after I'd fallen.

'We should go,' I said, stepping between them.

'Yes, you should,' said Richard. 'You should go now. Fuck off back to Kurt and tell him not to come down here again.'

'Thank you,' I said to Hidayat; then I looked at Domino. 'Come on.' I took her arm, the one that was now half buried in her bag, and I pulled it out, grasping her hand and turning her round to face the door.

I wanted to stay longer, to thank Hidayat once more for what he'd done. Richard was aggressive and unpleasant, but Hidayat had been gentle and caring. It was unfair of me to leave like this, but the animosity between Domino and Richard was crackling in the air around us.

I ushered her towards the door, pulling back the screen and encouraging Domino outside. I stopped and turned to look at the two men, Richard standing defiant, Hidayat embarrassed, a half-smile on his face, one hand lifted in a wave. 'Rest your arm . . .' said Hidayat.

'Thanks. And I'm sorry about—'

'Just go,' said Richard. 'And don't come back with her. Or any of the others.'

I nodded, wanting to leave now.

'Kurt will take care of him,' Domino said from behind me.

'Kurt's bloody dangerous.' Richard stared over my shoulder at her.

'Come on.' She was leading me now, pulling at the back of my shirt. 'Let's get out of here.'

I began to turn, following her as she stepped down from the house and walked out past the boats, but Hidayat put a hand on his friend's chest and came to me, his movement laboured. He touched my arm, stopping me and speaking in a quiet voice.

'Be careful. Those people. I don't know how you know them, but, well, maybe you don't want to get mixed up with them. You seem so . . . so nice.'

'What people?'

'Her.' He glanced over my shoulder. 'Kurt too. And the American. He's the worst of them.'

I opened my mouth to speak, to ask what he was talking about, but Richard was coming over and Hidayat shook his head. 'Don't take any notice of Richard. If you need to come here, then come. If we can help you, we will.'

'Come on,' Domino shouted.

'Even the smallest thing, you can come. But them?' He shook his head again. 'Don't bring them here. Not any of them. You seem like a nice guy, Alex. Whatever happens, don't let them get under your skin.'

14

Skirting along the edge of the lake, past the boats and away from the houses, I stopped and looked out at the water. Domino urged me on, telling me it wasn't so far now. Into the line of trees ahead and up the hill. Half an hour maybe, no more than that.

'Let's sit for a moment,' I said. 'It feels like we've been walking for ever.'

'It's what travellers do. They travel.'

'Yeah, but they also stop and look around from time to time, otherwise what's the point?'

'New places? New people?'

'Like them back there, you mean? Hidayat and Richard.' I adjusted my sling and sat down in the long-bladed grass, watched a tiny grasshopper make room for me as I opened out the package Hidayat had given me.

'Them? You don't want to know them.'

'Why not? They seemed OK. And look: cake.' There were four squares of yellow sponge. It looked simple, homemade, and when I took a bite, it was soft and delicious. 'Maybe Richard was a bit scary but Hidayat seems like a nice guy. And this cake is pretty good.' I gestured at the three pieces remaining in the package, but Domino shook her head.

'Do you reckon he was all right?' I said. 'Hidayat, I mean. It looked to me like he was limping.'

'I didn't notice. And he didn't scare *me*.'

'Hm?'

'Richard. You said he was scary. Not to me.'

I wasn't sure *any*thing could scare Domino, but I remembered how she had slipped her hand into her bag. 'Because of what's in there?' I kept my eyes on the lake as I ate. It was beautiful from every angle. On the hill where we'd been this morning it had taken my breath away. Here, up close, the sound of the water lapping at the shore, it *was* my breath. I could smell the lake, drink its odour right down inside me and feel it touch every part of me. I'd not seen anything like it. The size was almost impossible to comprehend. It stretched for miles.

I ignored Domino as she reached into her bag and removed something heavy. 'You mean this?'

I glanced down, seeing the pistol in her hand. 'Yeah. That.'

'It was stupid of me to take it, wasn't it?'

'Maybe you should just throw it in the lake.'

She shrugged. This wasn't the carefree girl from last night; this girl was introspective and quiet, like she had been on the hospital steps, and I wasn't sure which version I preferred. When she was like this, she was vulnerable and it made me feel as if I had something to offer her. When she was like this, she needed me. The other side of her, though, was edgy and sexy. Like that, she was intoxicating and blinded me to her faults. Faults that ran far deeper than I knew.

I touched a plant at my feet and watched its leaves curl and close to protect itself.

'*Kucing tidur*,' said Domino.

'Hm?'

'Sleeping cat. It's what they call that plant.' She kicked off a flip-flop and touched it with her toes. 'People aren't always what they seem, Alex.'

'Like Kurt?'

She ignored me, stretched out her legs and turned the pistol over in her hand.

'They said he's dangerous, Domino. Who is he?' I finished

the first piece of cake and took another. 'Sure you don't want some? It's very good.'

'He's not dangerous,' she said, shaking her head and tightening her fingers around the grip. 'Not at all.'

'Then why did they say it? And who's this American guy he mentioned?'

'They don't get on.' She ran her fingers over the steel, touching the various catches and moving parts. 'They don't like the way we live; we don't like the way *they* live.'

'Because they're gay?'

Domino looked at me as if I were mad. 'No, because they're troublemakers. Especially that guy Richard.' She shifted her eyes back to the pistol, using her thumb to push a catch at the bottom of the handle. The magazine slipped from the grip of the pistol, dropping onto the ground between Domino's knees.

'Be careful with that,' I said, narrowing my eyes. 'I wish you'd just get rid of it.'

'He might come back for it,' she replied, studying the magazine like a curious child, then sliding it back in.

'You said they're troublemakers. Why? What kind of trouble do they make?'

'The kind that nearly ruined us.' She took the magazine out again, slid it back in.

'Ruined you how?'

'So many questions,' Domino sighed, forgot about the pistol for a moment. 'Some guy went missing. About a year ago. Last anyone saw of him, he'd been staying with us.'

'Where?' I watched her as she thought about it, the tiniest movement creasing her brow, transferring along the bridge of her nose where a few freckles nestled, almost invisible. 'Staying where?'

'You'll see. Anyway, Richard made sure we got our fair share of hassle, that's all.' She rushed the explanation.

'Why would he do that?' I pressed her.

'Because he's a wanker. He fell out with Kurt over something else, something to do with money, so he went out of his way to make people think we'd done something.'

'Something like what? Why did he think it had anything to do with you?'

'Fuck knows.'

'So what *did* happen to him?'

'Who?'

'The guy who went missing.'

'He didn't go missing,' Domino said. 'He decided to leave, that's all. Left without telling anyone where he was going. Our life isn't for everyone, I suppose.'

'What life is that?'

'Like I said, you'll see.'

'I'm intrigued.' I looked back out at the water. I couldn't even guess what I was getting into, but I was prepared to go further because Domino excited me and I wanted to spend more time with her. Besides, I was curious. I wanted to know what was so special up there in the trees and I couldn't help wondering what sort of a person Kurt was to have made such an impression on people. Perhaps someone like that might be able to inspire something in *me*. 'So what kind of hassle did you get?' I asked.

'The police kind. Questions, intimidation. Wouldn't happen now, of course, not with . . .' She shook her head. 'Anyway, there was even stuff in the papers, and the guy who left, his parents came up to see where their son had been.'

'Pretty bad for them, eh? The parents, I mean.'

'Yeah. Pretty bad.'

'So now you want to shoot him?' I asked, tilting my head at the weapon in her hand.

'Richard?' She raised the pistol. 'For giving us some hassle?'

'Mm-hm.'

'Nah. Of course not.'

'Well, that's something, at least.'

'But that doesn't mean I have to like him.'

'Why don't you put that away? You're not going to get rid of it; you might as well just put it away.'

Domino slipped the pistol back into her bag.

'And have this,' I said, taking another piece of Hidayat's cake and offering the last of it to Domino.

She looked at it for a moment. 'You know, I'm glad you came with me,' she said. 'I mean, I'm not glad about you falling and everything, but I'm glad you're here. With me.'

'Me too.'

'Maybe you're the right one.'

'The right one?' I tested the words. 'Yeah, maybe I am.'

She took the cake and we ate in silence, then dusted the crumbs from our fingers.

'Are we going now?' I asked.

'In a minute.'

I looked over her head at the line of trees, seeing how they arced upwards, the hill rising sharply. 'Another steep climb,' I said.

Domino smiled and nodded. 'The last one. You won't regret it.'

I started to get up. 'Come on, then.'

'No,' she said. 'Not yet.' She took my hand and pulled me down towards her. She put the tip of her finger on my chin, tracing the scar that ran an inch along my jawbone. 'How d'you get that?'

'I fell over when I was a kid.'

'Did it hurt?'

'I don't remember.'

She brushed her finger along my lower lip. 'One more time.'

'Hm?'

She kissed me, her lips sweet from the cake, and then leaned away to look right into my eyes. 'I want you again.'

'Now?' I glanced down at my arm, still in the sling.

'It hurt?'

'A little.'

'Then maybe you need something to take your mind off it.'

She smiled and slipped her dress straps over her shoulders and allowed the material to fall down and expose her breasts. 'Unless there's something you'd rather do?'

'But . . . here? And with my arm like this?'

'We'll manage just fine. Come on, Alex, don't leave me like this. Don't embarrass me.' She took my hand and put it to her chest. 'I really want you.'

I looked around, reassuring myself that we were far enough from the village, that we were well hidden by the vegetation growing around this part of the lake. I smiled at Domino, nodded and sat back, bringing her towards me with one hand.

15

The final trek wasn't as bad as I had expected. It was steep in parts, but not as steep as the hillside we'd come down that morning, so it wasn't too difficult to traverse with one arm in a sling. The ground was more or less clear to begin with, the trees growing a good few feet from each other, mostly pines, forty, fifty metres tall, with deeply fissured red-brown bark. As we pressed further, they grew closer together and the ground cover was thicker. Dark-green shrubs dotted with purple flowers and pink blooms the shape of broken hearts with their life essence leaking away.

'Bleeding hearts,' Domino said as she brushed past one of the plants, trailing her fingertips along a row of flowers that hung from an arching stem. 'That's what they call these.' Some were intact, a trail of pink falling like a single drop of blood, while others had split open from the bottom, white tips protruding like tears.

'I've seen them before.'

'But did you know there's a little heart inside each one?' She plucked a flower and tore away its outer layers, holding out her hand with the tiny heart in her palm. 'For you,' she said with a laugh.

I took it and she turned, pressing on to where other plants joined the cacophony, these ones more leafy, not as tall, bringing the canopy lower, blotting out the sky in some places. To begin with, Domino appeared to be walking among the trees at random, but as we moved on, I realised she was looking for signs, following a route she'd taken before.

The sound of our footsteps crunching over the dry, fallen pine needles and twigs. The swish of our clothes brushing through the undergrowth. Birdsong and the constant chatter of insects.

'You know where we're going?' My voice was small, an insignificant disturbance.

'Yeah,' she said. 'I know.'

'How?' I couldn't see any path – nothing worn on the forest floor, no obvious breaks in the undergrowth.

'The trees are marked. You have to know where to look.'

'So tell me.'

'Not yet,' she said. 'You're not ready.'

'Not ready?'

'You haven't even seen where we're going yet. How d'you know you'd want to come back?'

'I was thinking more about how I might *leave*.'

Domino stopped and turned to me. 'Maybe you won't want to. Come on.' She turned and continued walking again, moving among the trees, looking up from time to time, checking for signs that only she could read.

Within half an hour or so of trekking, we came upon a series of more obvious paths, narrow worn areas snaking through the thickest undergrowth, but the one we followed wasn't long. It writhed through the vegetation for no more than fifty metres, penetrating the wall of trees ahead of us, breaking out into a clearing, which burst upon me without warning. One moment we were among the trees, blinded by the explosion of green, broken only by the purple and blue petals of the *melastoma* and the bright pink bleeding hearts of the *spectabilis*, then I was in a large clearing, Domino stepping to one side, watching for my reaction.

Totally encapsulated within the trees, the clearing would be almost invisible from anywhere but the sky, and yet it was hard to believe it could be here, as large as it was. Seeing it brought home to me how big the lake really was, and how much of its surrounding area must be uninhabited.

There were two traditional Batak houses here, side by side and in remarkable condition. Their great saddle roofs were not corrugated like many of the houses I had seen; these were thatched in the old way, with sugar-palm fibre. Nor was their paint so faded. The furthest looked as if it were being renovated, but the colours etched into the dark wood of the nearest to me were vivid, and the many carvings around its sides had been highlighted with green and red and white. Even the massive wooden *singa* masks that hung over the fronts of the houses were intact, the paint bright, the markings clear. It was amazing that they were in such good condition, not plundered for sale to tourists as trinkets to take home to distant lands.

In front of the houses, in the centre of the clearing, there was a circle of flat-topped stones, big enough to sit on and set around a circular stone table no bigger in diameter than a cart wheel. At the far end, there was a rice granary – a smaller version of the traditional house, built on a stilted frame, with the same shaped roof, intricately decorated but open at all sides. Beside it, there was evidence of another path, another way into the clearing, or perhaps a way out, leading in what I thought was the direction of the lake.

The clearing was not empty. In fact it was alive with movement and it struck me that I hadn't heard any sounds when I was inside the forest. The wall of trees and thick vegetation encircling the community not only made it difficult to see, but also blocked the sounds that came from it. Anybody exploring the forest could easily miss it if they walked just a few metres to either side.

On the edge of the clearing furthest from where we were standing, close to the granary, there was a lean-to made from wood and roofed with palm fronds. Beneath it, three people were standing at a table, preparing food. There was a fire to one side, set in a pit lined with stones. It was a rudimentary kitchen from what I could tell, but the people were busying themselves without complaint.

Near to them, sitting at a wooden table, another group was playing mahjong. On the table there was a large brass water-pipe, the players intermittently taking hits, the sound of music drifting over from a portable CD player.

There was a young woman sweeping leaves from the ground, brushing them back into the undergrowth, a man standing on a ladder, touching up the paint on the side of one of the houses. Two people coming through the path at the right-hand side of the clearing, a young man and a woman, probably similar in age to me, their hair wet. The man glanced up as he stepped into the clearing, looking over at us and stopping dead in his tracks. The girl beside him continued walking, not realising that her partner was no longer beside her. Then the man spoke. Or rather he shouted. 'Domino!' And everybody else in the clearing looked up. At first their faces turned to him in unison, but as soon as they saw where he was looking, the way he raised his arm and pointed, they followed the line of his finger until all eyes were on us.

'Domino,' he said again, and he came towards us, his pace quickening, throwing his arms around Domino when he reached her, squeezing her hard like she was going to pop. He held her for at least a minute before stepping back and holding her at arm's length, looking her up and down, his face beaming. His hair, braided into cornrows, was still wet, water glistening on the black skin of his naked torso.

'Shit, we missed you, girl.' He spoke with an American accent. 'Thought you were never coming back.' He gave her another lingering look before turning to me. 'And who have you brought?'

Domino smiled. 'I brought Alex. Alex, meet Michael. Michael, Alex.'

Remembering Hidayat's warning, I held my hand out to the American, ready to shake, but Michael opened his arms as if to ask what I was doing. He grinned and threw his arms around me, ignoring the sling, and squeezed me just as hard as he had squeezed Domino. He smelled of clear water and fresh air.

'Welcome to the family,' he said.

16

'What is this place?' I asked, thinking I had slipped into another world, hidden here among the trees. I wondered if I had stepped through a looking-glass and found myself in a gentle hippy paradise, or stumbled upon a Manson-like cult that was awaiting its next recruit. There in the clearing, looking around at the people watching me, I had no inkling of what richness I could draw from my time here, and what wickedness would take place in it.

'This is home,' said Domino.

She took me round the clearing, telling me the name of each person, but I couldn't remember them all. My short time in this country was a blur of movement in my mind, from the confusion of the bus terminal to the nightmare of the crash and the unreality of the hospital, but there was something calming about this place. I didn't know what it was, nor did I know the people who lived here, but they spoke my language and they greeted me with conviction. Seeing their relaxed faces and their smiling eyes, and with Domino by my side, I nodded and shook hands and greeted each person, but every face washed over me, most names forgotten as soon as I turned away to hear the next.

Michael, the one who had hugged me, was now hanging by my side like he was my new best friend. He was probably older than me by a couple of years, but not much more. The woman he'd been with seemed younger, though; her face had that look as if she hadn't quite decided who she was going to be. She introduced herself as Helena, her English clear but her accent obvious. Scandinavian. Maybe Swedish, although she didn't have the platinum blonde I associated with the Swedes. Her hair was dark brown.

Helena didn't throw her arms around me like Michael had done; she offered me a hand, which I took, and a smile, which I returned.

After Helena, I met Matt, with his short, blond dreadlocks, his skinny frame and his surfer-dude drawl. He looked like he spent most of his time stoned and there was a relaxed, loose quality to the way he carried himself. As if he were made out of something softer than the rest of us. Putty instead of muscle and bone. I met his best friend, Jason, whose cheeks were pitted with old acne scars and whose chin sported a few days' growth of dark beard. His hair was long and lank, and he had the same relaxed intonation as his friend Matt. I met Freia, who was tall and masculine; Alban, who was stocky and clean-shaven with a head of blond spiky hair; Morgan, who had too many facial piercings to count; I met Kate, Evie, Sandy, Chris, Eco, Apsara, and I tried to remember all their names and faces. I shook hands with each of them, working my way round the clearing, meeting everyone who came from the trees, or stepped down from the longhouses, emerging to see what the disturbance was.

And, finally, I met Kurt.

He wasn't as I'd imagined. I'd seen *Apocalypse Now*, I knew what people called Kurt should look like. Although, maybe not having the 'z' on the end of his name made all the difference. He was more Kurt Cobain than Colonel Kurtz. I'd expected someone older, bald and fat, not a young man with long fair hair hanging loose around his face. He had bold features, a strong face to match his athletic body. He was wearing just a sarong tied around his waist, his slim torso bared, a golden tan on his white skin. Around his neck, a red and white patterned bandanna tied in a loose knot.

He stepped down from the longhouse on the left and went straight to Domino, hugging her, holding her long enough to spike something in me that made me want to dislike him. They looked too good together.

'Good to have you back, D,' he said. 'Everything OK?' His voice was calm and even. Like Domino, he had a slight hint of an Australian accent. It made sense; Australia wasn't far away. Many people came across to travel around Indonesia.

She nodded. 'Everything's fine.'

He broke off the embrace, extended his arm, grasping my hand in his, squeezing it and smiling before looking at Domino. 'And this is Alex?' he said.

'This is Alex,' she replied.

'Kurt,' he said, releasing my hand and putting his arm round my shoulder. 'So what happened to *you*?'

'Alex took a dive,' said Domino.

'Coming down the hill,' I told him. 'Down past Alim's place.'

'Alim's place? You've been up there?' He glanced at Domino. 'You see anyone?'

'We bought a little something. I see Alim's in charge now.'

Kurt looked back at me, watching me with interest, then he shrugged. 'Yeah. Took over a few days ago. He's a bit more difficult, and Danuri likes to show us who's in charge, but . . . well, did you get everything you needed?'

Domino nodded.

'Does it hurt?' he asked, looking at me.

'Not so much now. Hidayat did a good job. Hurt like fuck before that—'

'You met Hidayat as well?' His eyes narrowed, his mouth tightened, his whole face darkening. 'What the hell you take him there for, D?'

'He was in pain,' she said. 'I had to do something.'

'And he helped? Hidayat helped?'

Domino nodded.

'Was *he* there? *Richard?*' There was venom in his voice when he said the name. As if it was a word that dirtied his mouth.

'He was, but he was OK.'

'So you've really given him the tour, D. Alex must be a special guy.'

'Yeah.' Domino looked at me. 'Yeah, he is.'

'So what you do to it? Broken?' He shook away his former expression. The smile came back.

'Dislocated,' I said. 'Knocked it right out, so he just popped it back in.'

'Popped it back in, eh?'

'Yeah.' I told him how Hidayat had rolled my arm until everything went back into place.

'Anterior dislocation,' Kurt said. 'Easy enough to put right. Even for a *datu* like him. But it doesn't hurt now?'

'Not really.'

'You shouldn't need this any more, then.' He turned me round and untied the *ulos*.

'You some kind of doctor?'

'Yeah,' he replied. 'Some kind.'

I let him remove the sling and I stretched my arms in front of me. Everything seemed normal. No pain, no feeling of weakness, just a dull ache. 'What's a *datu*?'

'Witch doctor.'

'He said he trained in England. What he did was good.'

'Hm. Could happen again,' Kurt said, bundling the *ulos* in his hands. 'Probably more chance of it now, I suppose, but you should be fine.'

'I should take that.' I reached out to take the cloth. 'I promised I'd—'

'You don't need it any more.' He walked over to the charcoal pit by the kitchen and tossed the *ulos* into it. 'Come on,' he said, walking back in our direction. 'Let's go inside.'

We followed Kurt into the longhouse, leaving the trapdoor open behind us. Despite the lack of windows, the inside of the house was light during the day. The construction was such that the gaps in the wood allowed enough daylight to pass into the building for us to be able to see what we were doing. And, because it wasn't exposed directly, it was cool inside.

The interior was unlike the longhouse I'd been in last night. This house was a home. The pit by the entrance was filled with a small charcoal fire, beside it a collection of cooking utensils and pots. Close to that, there was a low table with mats on either side, big enough for at least eight people to sit around. There were thin mattresses along the floor, bordering the trough that ran the length of the house, splitting it into two. Most of the mattresses had sausage-shaped pillows on them, folded sheets. Halfway down, a hammock was strung from one side of the house to the central pole. There was room to sleep around twenty people and I guessed the other house would be the same, meaning there was enough room to sleep far more people than I'd seen outside. I wondered if there were others, away from the settlement, or if Kurt was hoping to attract more travellers.

'Sit down.' He pointed to the mats on either side of the table.

I lowered myself onto crossed legs and leaned my forearms on the table. A slight discomfort in my shoulder, but not much more. Domino sat beside me, not touching, though, not as close as usual, and when I put my arm on her thigh, she tensed and moved away. I watched her, looking for a sign that something was wrong or that I'd done something I shouldn't have, but she kept her eyes on Kurt.

'So was it painful?' he asked, still standing.

'Yeah. It was.'

'And did Hidayat tell you to get to a hospital? That you should get it checked out?'

'Yeah. There somewhere round here?'

'Round here?' Kurt ladled water from a barrel into a pot. He hung the pot over the fire and came back to the table, sitting opposite us. 'Nearest place would be where Michael was that time.' He looked at Domino.

'We've already been there,' she said.

'Really? After you went to Hidayat? When did you do all this?'

Domino shook her head. 'Before. Alex's had some shitty luck since getting here. We both have.'

Kurt looked concerned. 'What kind of shitty luck?'

'Bus crash kind of shitty luck,' said Domino, her words bringing everything back to me in a powerful surge. All the things that had happened since leaving the hospital had been so fast and unexpected I hadn't had time to think about where it had all started — lying face down in the middle of the road, surrounded by the dead and the dying.

'A few scrapes, a bit shaken up . . .' I could hear Domino saying. 'Concussion . . . lucky to be alive . . . hospital . . .'

I put both hands on my face and rubbed hard.

'. . . all right . . . ?'

I breathed deep, my head spinning.

'. . . all right . . . ?'

I felt a hand on my shoulder and I looked up. 'Hm?'

'You OK, dude?' Kurt was standing, coming round the table. Domino had one hand on me, a concerned expression. I looked at her fingers, the green varnish on her nails.

'Are you all right?' she asked. 'You look like shit. Kind of went all spaced out on us.'

I nodded. 'Yeah. I'm fine. Tired, but fine.' I remembered that I hadn't slept much since leaving the hospital.

'No shit you're tired,' said Kurt. 'You've had concussion, then you dislocated your shoulder. I reckon just about anybody would be tired after all that.'

'You should sleep,' said Domino.

'Yeah. Have some tea, then sleep,' Kurt agreed, going over to the fire where the water was boiling. He made strong, sweet tea, no milk, and poured it into a glass. He put it on the table in front of me. 'It won't make your shoulder feel better, but you need to drink.' He looked at me like he suddenly remembered something. 'Hey, when was the last time you ate anything?'

*

So I drank my tea while Kurt brought food for Domino and me. We ate *mie goreng* from a tin plate, the noodles hot and spicy, a couple of small bananas to finish off, another glass of sweet tea. And when we were done, Kurt showed me to a wafer-thin mattress that didn't belong to anyone, told me that the sausage-shaped pillow was a Dutch lady.

'Squeeze her nice and tight between your legs,' he said. 'You get sweaty, she'll soak it right up for you.'

I thanked him and waited for him to leave before I lay down on the mattress, asking Domino if she was going to join me. She was a part of this adventure now, I'd been with her every moment for almost twenty-four hours and I didn't want her out of my sight.

'I'm gonna go catch up with some of the guys,' she said.

'You mean Kurt?'

'Among others.' She watched me. 'Something bothering you? About Kurt?'

I shook my head, pretending not to have noticed his healthy good looks, his easy nature, his confidence.

'You're jealous,' she said with a hint of a smile.

'No.'

'You don't need to be. He's—'

'It doesn't matter. I don't care.' At least, I didn't *want* to care. I didn't want to talk about Kurt. I could feel the sleep rolling over me now that my stomach was full and I was lying down. I just wanted to lie here, with Domino in my arms. 'Aren't you tired? You don't wanna . . . ?'

'Not just yet,' she said. 'I'll come back later.' She made to stand up, but I grabbed her hand and pulled it towards me. I kissed it and held it to my chest.

'I'm worried I'm going to see her face,' I said. 'When I close my eyes.'

'Whose face?'

'The woman on the road. I don't want to see it.'

'Shh.' She ran a hand over my head. 'It's OK. Close your eyes.'

'It hasn't affected you,' I said. 'The crash. That girl. It doesn't bother you. We didn't really talk about it.'

'I'll talk it through with Kurt.'

Again. Kurt. 'No, stay a while. Stay with *me*.' My eyes were closing.

She nodded. 'OK. Sure.'

'Just while I fall asleep.'

17

I don't know how long I slept, motionless, like I hadn't been in a bed for days. I was exhausted and my body shut down, repairing itself, allowing my mind to settle and process everything that had happened. Images came to me – the bus, the hospital, the old woman reaching out to me, my mother asking for my help – but they came as dreams, not nightmares. They flitted past as images flickering across a screen, haphazard and disjointed. They manifested as the experiences of another person, and I watched them from afar, seeing them in a new light, as if for the first time. And I saw the bright colours of butterflies – butterflies that had been plucked from the air and impaled.

There was nothing to disturb my sleep except for those broken sketches of the past days, but I remember waking, my eyes drowsy, the lids heavy, not wanting to open. It was a moment when everything seemed far away. I wasn't asleep and I wasn't awake; I was somewhere between worlds. There were voices, not loud, but agitated. Not shouting, not talking, not whispering, but a combination of all three.

'What the hell did you think you were doing . . . You know what'll happen . . .' Snippets of conversation.

'I didn't think . . .'

'No, you never do.'

Just words, not meaning anything, no context to them.

'. . . coming up here . . .'

'. . . Danuri's not like Hendrik, poor bugger . . .'

'What did they do to him?'

I lifted my head, despite the weight of it. Like trying to pull a cannonball from a ship's deck.

'Fuck knows. They probably—'

'Shh, keep your voice down.'

I saw two figures through my half-open eyes. Figures that were blurred by my eyelashes; figures that hushed and became quiet when they saw me moving.

'He's waking . . .'

'He's just turning. Dreaming.'

Then Domino was beside me, running her hand over my hair, easing my head back onto the pillow, whispering sounds in my ears, then sleep again.

When I woke it was dark inside the longhouse, but for a lamp at the far end, and I had the distinct feeling that I was alone. I sat up and looked into the shadow reaching out on either side of me, wondering at first where I was. It took a moment for all my senses to come back to me, and I stayed there, rubbing my eyes, finding my bearings, remembering the layout of the enormous room. Outside, there were voices. A guitar strumming, perhaps even someone singing, it was hard to tell.

I stood and walked the length of the longhouse, looking down at the other mattresses as I went, but seeing no signs that anybody else was sleeping here. I came to the trapdoor, which was now shut, and pulled it open, stepping down the ladder into the night. It was much cooler outside than in.

The sounds popped from muffled voices to clear conversations as I climbed down to the clearing below. The lean-to kitchen was lit with two lamps, one on either side, each of which was mounted on a pipe, which in turn was planted in the top of a blue bottle of butane. Close by, but not too close to the butane, a charcoal pit glowed in the half-light. A couple of people were working there, and another was sitting on the open wall of the nearby rice granary, swinging her legs against the carved, painted wood.

On the other side of the circle of stone chairs, close to where Domino and I had first come into the clearing, a small fire crackled, oozing orange across the dirt and merging with the people around it to cast strange and misshapen shadows, which flickered and danced at the edge of the trees. One of those sitting by the fire was playing a guitar, strumming it lightly as if not to disturb the peace of this small pocket of wilderness.

At the wooden table the mah-jong tiles were out again, playing cards too, the animated faces of the players illuminated by the glow from the lean-to kitchen on one side and the orange fire on the other. In all, there were probably a dozen people in the clearing that night.

Helena, the dark-haired Swede whose name I'd managed to remember, was in the kitchen, putting rice onto plates, scraping it from a large metal pan, which she'd taken from its place over the charcoal pit. Beside her, Michael was stirring another large metal pot, lifting a spoon to his lips to taste whatever was inside. As before, he was shirtless, the muscles clear even from where I was standing, some forty feet away.

I glanced around the clearing, taking in everything I could see. A small group of like-minded and friendly individuals coming together to make something for themselves. No aggressors, no arguing, no disagreements. There was no harm here, just a group of people living their life in the manner they chose to live it. Already I had forgotten Hidayat's warning.

I smiled and soaked it in, thinking I could stay here a while. I sat down on the last rung of the ladder and stayed in the shadows, watching how they went about their lives, and thought this was a good way to spend some time. There weren't any worries here, no greater responsibility than looking after yourself.

I watched for a while longer, wondering where to go first, who to talk to. I couldn't see Domino or Kurt anywhere among the people. The only other names and faces I remembered were Helena and Michael, so I made up my mind to head over to the kitchen. Besides, I was starting to feel hungry again.

I moved into the light, catching one or two eyes. I was the new guy and I expected to draw some attention, so I just kept on and hoped I'd get the same welcome from Michael and Helena that I'd had when I arrived. But before I could reach the lean-to, Kurt and Domino emerged from the trees at the far end of the clearing, stepping into the circle of diffused light, just a few seconds later than I did. They were arm in arm, their faces set as if they were deep in serious discussion, then Domino threw back her head and laughed like I'd never seen her laugh before. She had never laughed like that with me.

When they saw me watching them, Kurt and Domino shared a glance before heading over towards me. 'How ya feeling?' Kurt asked as soon as they were close. Most of the others had returned their interest to whatever it was they'd been doing before, but I still felt a few eyes watching me.

'Much better, thanks,' I said, not liking that he and Domino had been alone together. I was confused by their relationship.

'Your shoulder?'

'Good.'

'You want a drink?'

'Sure.'

We didn't go to a table, we just sat down in the clearing, close to the charcoal pit, feeling the heat coming off it, warming the side of my face. Domino sat beside me, not Kurt, offering me a bottle. I took it and looked at the clear glass, no label at all.

'Water,' she said.

I took a swig and swallowed the lukewarm liquid. It slipped down my throat, clearing away the gritty feeling, soothing it, and I took another drink before returning it to Domino.

'So what d'you think of our home?' Kurt asked, putting his arms behind him, leaning back, his hair falling over his shoulders. His confidence reminded me of Domino. His easy nature, his healthy appearance made me even more aware of myself. I felt pale and constrained in comparison. My own hair cropped short, my skin ashen, my eyes dull.

'It's cool,' I said. 'I like it.'

'Domino tells me you're on your own. No family.'

I looked at Kurt, seeing just one eye because the other was in shadow.

'You want to stay? Let this be your family?'

I bit the inside of my lip and thought about what he was saying.

'It's not everyone gets an offer,' he smiled. 'Don't think about it too long.'

The way he said it made me feel uncomfortable, but I was about to tell him that yes, I would like to stay a while, when he spoke again. 'Domino tells me you're a traveller, is that right?'

I rearranged my thoughts and nodded. 'Might be a while before I use the bus again, though.'

'You must've been very frightened. You want to talk about it?'

'Not really. Nothing to talk about.'

'I guess it was lucky Domino was there.'

'Yeah.' I turned to see her watching me, something personal passing between us.

'But it was quite an experience, right?' he went on. 'Life-changing, even.'

'You could say that.'

'So is that why you're travelling?' Kurt sat up, came closer to the fire and crossed his legs. 'Because you're looking for new experiences?'

'I . . .'

'What made you decide to travel?' he asked without giving me a chance to reply. 'Because you want to see something of the world, or because you want to *feel* something? Is it because you want to pack it away inside your head, tick the box, say you've been there, or are you looking for something else? Something *more*.'

Beside me Domino lit a joint, taking a drag before passing it to me. Her reassuring touch lingered on my hand as she gave it over. I accepted it and watched Kurt sitting opposite me, half his face obscured by shadow, the other half a bizarre mix of white and orange, light thrown from the fire and the lamps.

'A bit of both,' I exhaled. But there was something else, too. A grey doubt that I carried with me. The lingering memory of things I wanted to leave behind.

'What I mean, Alex, is are you a tourist? 'Cause it's the same thing, you know. Traveller, backpacker, tourist, they're all the same thing.' He leaned forwards, his face in full view. 'That what you are, Alex? A tourist? A *backpacker*?' He made it sound like an insult.

'I don't even own a backpack.' I sensed that more eyes were on me now. 'Not any more.'

'Good.' Kurt turned his head and looked about. 'Because there's no backpackers here, Alex. We're something else altogether. We're *look*ing for something else. Something to experience, not something to see, and that kind of makes us like brothers and sisters. We share a common ideal. We're looking for the examined life, because the unexamined one isn't worth living. Do you know what that means?'

I didn't reply. I wondered where he was going with this, and figured he was a little stoned, getting deep, telling me about this place where people came to chill out and be themselves.

'It means we want to do something different. It means we want to look inside. It means we want to enhance ourselves with a life we can't get anywhere else.' His voice was calm and soft. 'We're not tourists. You want to be one of them, you should go to Tuk Tuk, see the tombs. Go to Parapat market, stay in the hotel that's shaped like a fish. Watch a cultural show. But if you want something else, something to enhance your life, then stay a while. Hang out. See what we can give you. See what you can teach your*self*. You want all that, Alex, then you're welcome here.'

'Sounds good to me,' I said, taking another hit from the joint, thinking if he was going to get stoned and spout a load of shit at me, then I'd have to join him. Maybe he'd make more sense.

'I mean, where else can you live like this? Our own little paradise. Undisturbed and untainted.' The guitar continued behind me, someone singing in a low voice.

'People don't know about this place?' I asked.

'Of course they know, but they leave us alone. Most of them think we're the same as all the fucking hippies who come out to live in longhouses on Samosir and smoke dope . . .'

'But we're not?' I said, with a half-laugh, hoping to lighten his mood a bit.

'Of course we're not. We're different.'

I was almost afraid to ask. 'Different how?'

'You been listening to anything I just said?' Kurt looked right at me, grinning, white teeth. 'Maybe it's something you should find out for yourself.' I detected no joy in that grin, only a kind of gentle malice hiding behind it. It was as the spider might look when it opened the parlour door and invited the fly to step in. 'So you say you want to stay?' Kurt raised his voice, looking around the clearing.

I'd almost forgotten that Domino was beside me, but now she put her hand on my thigh and squeezed.

'Yes,' I heard myself say, and then I sensed people moving around us, getting up from the table, leaving the fireside, coming over to where we were sitting. The guitar had stopped; the other voices had stopped. There was only Kurt's voice. 'Say it louder,' he said.

I looked around me, embarrassed and confused, but trying to go with it, taking another hit from the joint. 'Sure,' I said, feeling self-conscious. 'Yes.'

'Make him do it,' someone said behind me. I turned round to see everybody closing in on us, coming closer. Some were smiling, some were not. Some looked excited as if anticipating a special event. My embarrassment lurched, shifted, became something else. Not fear, but something like it.

'Yeah. Make him do it,' said another.

Then Michael was beside me, smiling. 'He wants to stay,' he said. 'Make him do it. Just like everyone else.'

'Do what?' I asked, not liking the smiles.

'Jump,' said Kurt. 'You gotta jump.'

Then a second voice joined in, saying, 'Jump,' then a third and a fourth, the voices growing in number until they were all chanting one word at me. 'Jump. Jump. Jump.'

Their voices were almost mesmerising, the constant whisper-chanting of that single word combined with the buzz from the dope, the surge of anxiety, and I looked around me in bewilderment, wondering what was going on, what the hell I'd got myself into.

Finally, Kurt stood and held up his hands. As soon as he did so, the chanting stopped.

Kurt removed the bandanna from round his neck and handed it to Domino. She moved behind me, slipped the cloth over my head and pulled it against my eyes, tying it tight at the back of my head. I could smell Kurt on it.

I raised my hands, a natural reaction, and touched the cloth, but my hands were grasped, pulled behind my back and tied. 'Wait,' I protested. 'What the fuck is this? What the fuck is going on?'

'Don't worry,' Domino whispered in my ear. 'Everything's going to be fine.'

'No. Let me go. Untie my hands.' Panic touching me, creeping around the bandanna, seeping into my pores.

'You said you want to stay here.' Kurt's voice was measured. 'You've made your choice. Now you have to make the jump.'

'No. No jumps. I'm not fucking jumping anywhere.'

'Push, then,' said a voice, sniggering.

I was taken, hands at every part of my body, and I was pulled and pushed, at times lifted from my feet as I was led from my place by the fire and taken away with my eyes blindfolded and my hands tied. I felt the panic rising inside me, a wild animal desperate to get out, a fear and loathing, a great feeling of nausea. All these emotions mixing and frothing, making my head spin as they took me to God knows where.

'Don't worry,' I heard Domino whisper again, then another voice, a man's, telling me everyone had to do it.

'No,' the fear clawing to my throat, welling in there, preparing to burst from me like a rampaging animal, wanting to tear my bonds and rip flesh from those around me. 'Get off. Fuck. Let me go.'

Then I was out of the clearing. I could tell because the ground was no longer hard beneath my feet. It was soft here, the same as the ground among the trees. I could hear the whoops and cat-calls of the others, the chirrup of the cicadas amplified a thousand times in my frightened state. I felt thin branches bend and give against me, the brush of pine needles and leaves against my skin.

I struggled against the rope, feeling an awkward tension in my shoulder as I tried to move this way or that, but each time I was blocked, each time I was held firm. I don't know how much later I heard the rush of water, but the sound grew louder as we moved on, the heavy spill of liquid on rock, until I was halted, hands on every part of me, holding me back.

'We're here,' said Kurt's voice. 'It's time.'

Hands moved from me, taking some of the panic with them, replacing it with a dread curiosity. I could feel the wind on my face. The sound of water falling close by. I could smell the pine but now there was a strong scent behind it, mingling with it to make something unique. I could smell the lake.

Then, a warmth on my ear and Domino's voice speaking to me. 'If *I* can do this, *you* can do this,' she whispered, and I felt her hands slip under my shirt and unfasten my money-belt. 'I'll keep this safe for you,' she said. 'And don't be afraid. You're strong, Alex. Show them how strong you are.' And then she was gone.

I took a deep breath and waited for what was coming next. If Domino could do it, I could do it.

I felt the ties on my hands loosen and the rope slip away. I stood for a moment before raising my hands to my eyes, expecting them to be restrained again, but this time no one touched me as I reached for the blindfold and removed it.

To my left, a sharp rise in the land from which a steady stream of water cascaded from a crack in the rocks. It fell into a shallow pool surrounded by wet black stone, blanketed with ferns and moss. The pool frothed and welled, overflowing, spilling its innards, dropping water further into the mass below.

I was above the lake. Forty feet of sheer black rock fell away just inches from my toes. The surface of the water beneath me was pitted with waves caught and whipped by the breeze so it looked like the sea.

'You want to stay, you have to jump,' Kurt's voice said from behind me.

I turned to see the others in a semi-circle, close behind me – Kurt standing one step in front – and I watched them, looked at each and every face. All attention was on me, gas lamps raised to head height and held out towards me so that I was the focus of our gathering. I looked at Domino, saw my belt bundled in her hands, and lingered over her features, looking into her eyes, seeing something that I thought was concern, before I finally came to Kurt. His head was cocked to one side, his unkempt, sun-bleached hair, not unlike Domino's, hanging across his naked shoulders.

'You gonna jump?' he asked.

I took a deep breath. 'What does it prove?'

'That you want to stay.' He straightened his neck and smiled. 'That you want this life.'

'And if I don't?'

The smile fell from his lips. 'Good luck finding your way out of here.'

I glanced behind me at the drop, then looked at Kurt again. 'You mean you don't have somewhere higher?' I took a step back from him, turned and threw myself out into the night.

I didn't close my eyes on the way down.

18

The world rushed around me. The darkness enveloped me. The air buffeted under my shirt, slipped up the cuffs of my trousers, tore my flip-flops from my feet. There was just enough moonlight on the surface for me to see the water hurrying up to meet me and I had a brief moment to wonder what would happen if I landed badly; to worry that my shoulder would once again break free from its socket and leave me floundering in pain, drowning in a giant lake thousands of miles from home. No one to take my hand as life slipped away. A final snatch of breath. A terrible descent into the weedy blackness. Fighting, clawing my way to the surface. One arm struggling against the motion of the water. Then, without oxygen to feed my body, I would sink, drifting among the tendrils, convulsing and jerking as life ebbed from me.

A fraction of a second was all it took for those things to flash through my head. An instant data transfer, information darting from one place to another at extraordinary speed. Electrical impulses chattering in my brain, brought to a sudden halt when I hit the water, my body straight, my shoulder braced.

I went deep, my clothes drenching immediately, my weight increasing, but I was a strong swimmer and my instincts overrode anything I had been thinking or feeling. As soon as my descent into the water was slowed, I struck out, kicking upwards, thankful I could use both arms to pull me through the lake towards the surface. I was hastened by the stroke of the weeds on my feet, an eerie sensation that probed a primitive spot inside me. I hurried away from them, escaping their touch, afraid they might entangle me and pull me down, or that they weren't weeds at all, but something dark and animate waiting for me in the cloying depths.

I reached the surface, my shoulder still intact, glad to be away from the clinging plants, and burst out, opening my mouth and taking a deep breath of clean air. I rubbed my eyes while treading water and turned round, scanning the shoreline for somewhere to come out of the lake, but there wasn't an obvious spot. Behind me, Danau Toba stretched out towards Samosir. I would tire if I had to swim that far, and the thought of striking out into the darkness, heading for the distant shore, filled my stomach with a heavy sensation and made the water feel colder.

In front of me, the black cliff reached up to the place from which I had jumped. Nothing but rock from water to sky, no visible way out. I thought if I moved a little further into the lake, I could get a better view, find a place to land, but as I began to swim away, I heard someone shouting, the voice coming closer, then a splash just a couple of metres away from me. A heavy sound, followed by another and then another.

I stayed where I was, watching the choppy surface until something broke just ahead of me. Then something to the left. Another, this one closer.

'Hey, you think we were gonna let you have all the fun?' Michael's voice, the unmistakeable American accent calling to me from the darkness, followed by the other two coming to the surface and shouting, one of them whooping like a cowboy.

'Some of us liked it so much we just can't get enough of it.' As Michael came closer, I could see his head above the surface of the water. 'And anyway,' he was beside me now, his smile still there, like it was impossible to wipe it away, 'how you gonna get out without us to tell you where?' He was breathing steadily, pursing his lips, blowing the water away from his mouth.

'He figured he'd have to swim all the way to Samosir,' said another voice, its owner coming close. 'Like Jason did.'

'It was a nice night, Matt. I like to swim.'

Matt laughed, a short sound, trying to conserve his breath and his energy. 'Set off before any of us got down here. Thought he'd drowned, all of us shitting ourselves he'd wash up somewhere. Turned up next afternoon. Big grin on his face.' In the limited moonlight, Matt's head was a peculiar shape, the short dreads sticking out at angles like Medusa's serpents.

'Come on,' Michael spoke to me. 'Stay close. There's an easy way out.'

We kept together, close enough that we didn't lose sight of each other. There was light from the moon, but not enough for us to see more than a few feet, and there was a slight wind cutting across the top of the water, raising the lake into waves big enough to obscure our view. Matt and Jason swam ahead, Michael keeping closer to me, all three of them knowing where to go despite the lack of visibility. But as we swam, we heard another shout, almost a scream, and the sound of rushing wind followed by another loud splash.

We stopped swimming.

'Someone else jumping tonight?' said Michael.

'Don't think so,' Matt replied. 'No one else said . . . You hear anything?'

We moved as slowly as possible, treading water but trying not to make any sounds, straining our ears.

'I don't hear anything,' I said. 'Why?'

'We should hear something,' said Jason. 'Someone coming up. Breathing. You hear any of that?'

'Maybe if you shut the fuck up,' said Michael. 'Maybe then we'd—'

'Shh,' I interrupted. 'There.' I was whispering, keeping my voice quiet so it wouldn't hide the sounds. A weak splashing in the water not far from us. Not the sound of swimming, not a regular sound, but an erratic sound like something repeatedly hitting the water. Then a cough. Unmistakeable.

'Shit,' I said. 'Someone's in trouble.' I turned and struck out towards the source of the noise, Michael following, telling me not to go too far.

I swam back towards what I thought to be the place where I had first entered the water, the noises of struggling closer yet weakening. I kept my head up, my neck strained as high as possible to see over the top of the waves.

There. Up ahead. Something on the surface, a froth of white, then nothing but black as the bubbles dissipated. It could have been anything, but I headed for it, swimming faster now.

A hand broke the surface and I knew for sure now that someone was struggling in the water, perhaps drowning as I'd feared I would. I felt horror surge in my body, a glimpsed memory of the tendrils brushing my feet, and I pushed harder to reach the spot where I'd seen the hand. I took a breath and dived under, not wanting to sink deep into the thick black below, but knowing that I had no choice.

I felt around me, spreading my arms, swimming deeper, afraid to become turned round in the water, lose my sense of direction, forget which way was up.

My hand brushed against something solid – not a weed, but something more substantial; something that reacted to my touch, turning and grabbing, fingers gripping my forearm like a vice, dragging me with it, deeper into the lake.

The oxygen I'd taken before I dived was thinning. My lungs were tightening and I knew that my fear might now become a reality. To die at the bottom of the lake. Like the old woman on the road who'd reached out for me, a stranger, I was to die with someone I did not know.

But I was not going to drown here, I was not going to breathe the water and sink to the weeds and the detritus that littered the floor of the lake. I was going to survive. I would live.

I twisted in the grip of those tight fingers, wrenching my arm free and snatching at the swish of cloth that brushed my skin as I sank. I grabbed at the clothing, pulling, finding something solid so that I was controlling the drowning person instead of them dragging me deeper. I could feel their panic, almost more tangible than my own as I struggled to remain in control of them, trying to keep away from flailing limbs, and I kicked my legs, used my free arm, and pushed towards what I hoped was the sky.

As I came closer, I saw the disturbance on the surface, the waves buffeting the water. My lungs were burning, desperate for oxygen, my head clouding, and I pushed hard, dragging the weight of another person with me, believing that time was running out; that once my body and brain were starved, I would weaken, drop, sink, die.

I burst into the air with a great gasp, relieved to find the others right there, coming to my aid, reaching for the body I was dragging with me.

Matt took hold of me, pulling me up, placing a hand under my chin as I gasped for more air, and I let him hold me in the water for a moment as the burning sensation that had drenched me began to subside. I was thankful not to have to use my limbs, happy to let them hang limp in the water.

Behind us, Michael and Jason took care of the person who had jumped.

Within just a few minutes we were on land. A flat, rocky outcrop at the base of the bluff, no more than six feet wide. My body was warm but shaking; high from the thrill of being so close to death. For an instant, I understood why people would risk their lives in the pursuit of that exhilarating rush.

And I had saved a life.

On my first day in this country I had watched life pass, I had seen nothing but death and distress, and today I had prevented it. It was as unreal as the things that had come before it, and I had to remind myself that all of this was happening to *me*. I had swum down and I had saved someone from drowning. If it hadn't been for me, she might still be down there, her flooded body moving with the ebb and flow of the current.

'Jesus Christ, Helena, you gave us a fright,' Matt was saying. 'What the fuck were you thinking?'

We were sitting in a line, the outcrop not big enough for anything else. Helena was in the middle beside me. The dark-haired girl who had emerged from the forest that day with Michael. She was now huddled with her knees drawn up, her chin resting on them, her hair plastered tight against her head. 'I wanted to do it again,' she said in a weak voice. 'I wanted—'

'You're supposed to tell someone,' Michael said. 'You know that. We agree before we do it. Remember how we all felt after Jason was gone so long? You remember how we all thought he drowned?'

Helena nodded. 'I know. Sorry. I just thought—'

'No. You didn't think,' Michael sounding like someone's father. 'You didn't think at all.' It gave me a strange sense of comfort to hear him speak that way. It mattered to him that Helena was all right. These people took care of each other.

Helena turned and looked at me. 'I'm sorry. I nearly pulled you with me.'

'He's fine,' said Michael. 'Don't worry about him. He's a tough guy, aren't you, Alex?'

'Yeah.' I forced a smile. My throat was still tight with the panic and relief.

Jason leaned forward to look past Helena, see me. 'Shit, Alex, I like your style. *You got somewhere higher?* Isn't that what you said up there before you jumped?'

'Something like that.'

'You see him throw himself off?' said Matt. 'Like a fuckin' madman. Even *I* nearly shit myself when they made me do it the first time. But you, Alex? I think you're even crazier than me.'

'So how do we get back up?' I asked. 'How do we get out of here?'

Michael told me there was a path up the cliff face, right from where we were sitting on that outcrop. Something like tiny steps cut into the rock, he said, that looked as if they'd been there for years. They made for a quick way up but in the dark it was impossible and far too dangerous. That meant we'd have to swim further along the shore, where there was an easier way out, and a gentler climb up the hill from a different angle.

'You ever been that way?' I asked. 'Up the cliff?'

'Once,' he told me. 'But I wouldn't do it again. *You* might, now you're a hero, but one wrong foot and you're off the edge.'

Once we were rested, we slipped back into the water and began our return to the settlement. We swam along the line of the cliff, Michael leading, Jason and Matt bringing up the rear. I kept alongside Helena, feeling a kind of responsibility for her now.

'I'll be fine.' She slowed to speak to me.

'Sure,' I said. She had to be strong to do what she'd done and still be in one piece. She'd come out of it quickly, no crying or feeling sorry for herself, but it had shocked me to see someone in such distress.

Michael called back to us, saying, 'Swim out a bit. We're getting too close.' The waves wanted to push us into the rock, buffet us on the crags.

We didn't have to swim for long, just a few minutes before the black rock at our side began to drop from the sky, its level falling, and eventually there was a clear spot for us to come ashore.

We pulled ourselves out and I sat on the rocks, my hands still trembling. I caught my breath and looked back at the way we'd come. I could see that we'd rounded a gentle corner, explaining why I hadn't been able to see this spot from where we were before. During the day it would have been clear, but at night the shoreline was a long, dark smudge.

'So you got all the way to Samosir?' I said to Jason as we started walking, the rush of excitement finally beginning to subside. 'The long way round, I guess.' My hospital clothes were uncomfortable; cold and heavy, sticking to my skin.

Jason laughed. 'Not quite. It's a good story, though. I mean, I might look stupid, but I'm not. Not really.'

'Not *too* stupid,' said Matt.

'I'd have to be bloody mental to think I had to swim all the way over there. There's a village right here, just along the shore. Everyone knows it. We all had to come through it to get up there.' He pointed to the tops of the trees that covered the hillside. 'Nah, I just swam along the shore until I found it.'

'But you were gone for a day?'

'Almost. Thought I'd give 'em all a scare for making me jump. Especially Matt – he's the one brought me here – so I hung around in the *kampong*, got a bite to eat, went back the next day.'

'So what did you do?' I turned to Matt. 'You look for him?'

'Look for him?' Matt shook his head. 'How?'

'Course you looked for me, Matt. I heard you were out in the woods all night.'

'We didn't do anything,' said Michael. 'We just waited for you to come back.'

'You hear that?' said Jason. 'They're nothing on you, Alex, they just waited for me to come back. But you? I bet you wouldn't have just waited for me to turn up. Man, you just saved someone's life.'

'Yeah.' Matt slapped me on the back. 'I gotta admit, that *is* cool. And look at you, it's like you do it every day. Me, I'd be high on it.'

I listened to their banter as we made our way back up the hill, the ground harsh on the bare soles of my soft feet. I'd lost my flip-flops when I jumped – they'd be drifting on the surface of the lake, probably wash up and make someone a lucky find. I was about to ask one of the others if they'd have some for me to borrow, when Helena took my arm, pulling me back.

'Thank you,' she said. 'For . . .'

'It's OK,' I told her, not knowing what to say. 'Anyone would have done the same thing.'

'You could have drowned, too,' she said. 'I grabbed you.'

'It's natural. A natural reaction.'

She tugged harder on my arm, bringing me to a stop while

the others carried on ahead. She put her arms around me. 'Thank you,' she said again, pressing her cold face to mine.

I didn't know what to do other than pat her shoulder. Here she was, an attractive woman, putting her arms around me, thanking me for saving her life, and I didn't know what to do other than pat her shoulder.

'If there's anything I can do for you,' she said.

'No,' I replied. 'Nothing.'

She pulled her head back to look at me. 'Anything at all.'

'Alex? Helena? What the fuck're you two doing back there?' Michael's voice was loud and had an edge to it. It wasn't the congenial tone I was used to hearing from him.

'We should catch up,' I said, then called out into the darkness, 'Coming.'

'Yes,' she nodded. 'We should.'

I broke away from Helena and together we quickened our pace, joining the others.

'You two sharing a moment?' Michael asked when we reached them. He glared at me, then Helena, but neither of us replied as we fell in line with them, pushing on through the trees.

'You need a drink?' said Michael, putting an arm around Helena, eyeing me again. 'I'm damn sure I do.'

'I reckon I could go for that,' I said. 'No tricks?'

'Tricks?' asked Matt.

'Should I be worried?' I looked at Helena. 'I mean, the last time I went somewhere with you guys it was to make me jump off a cliff.'

Helena shrugged away Michael's embrace and smiled. 'No more jumping,' she said. 'No more water.'

'No more water?' Jason replied. 'You can say that again. No more water passing these lips tonight.' He slowed his pace and encouraged me to do the same, dropping us back so that he and I were walking with Matt, a few paces behind Helena and Michael.

'Pretty awesome what you did back there,' Matt said,

lowering his voice. 'Saving Helena and everything, but you need to . . .' He screwed up his face, searching for the right word. 'Stay cool. Yeah, you need to stay cool.'

'I don't understand.'

'Sure you do.'

'Michael and Helena are kind of a thing,' Jason said.

'So why do I feel like he's pissed off with me? I saved her, didn't I?'

'Yeah, you did, but . . . I dunno, maybe it's 'cause you handled the goods. Michael gets jealous,' Matt told me. 'And he can be pretty touchy when he's pissed off.'

'OK, but all I did was—'

'Save her life,' said Matt. 'I know.'

'I reckon Michael's wishing it was him, though,' said Jason.

As we came closer, I could hear noises from the settlement. Music, laughter, just the occasional sound carried on the air, and a few people looked up when we came into the clearing, one or two of the people playing cards at the table putting down their hands and clapping. When the others heard the noise, they all looked across, a few cheers, raised glasses and bottles. Smiles all round. Everyone had made the jump at some time or another so they all knew what I'd just experienced – for the most part. I even caught myself wondering if I'd ever do it again and realised that I was already planning on staying a while. I felt as if I'd been accepted.

Domino was by the kitchen, talking to people I didn't recognise, and I noticed her straight away. There was something about her that stood out. The way she carried herself with such confidence. I'd never before met anyone who affected me the way she did. Just looking at her, seeing her talk, watching her flick her hair from her face, it made me forget about everything. I just wanted to go to her, take her inside so that we could be alone. I wanted her to myself.

She glanced across when she heard the others clapping, and she paused, smiled. She spoke to the people she was with, touched her hand to someone's shoulder and started to come over, but Jason and Matt came either side of me, taking my arms and raising them high.

'Alex the fucking hero,' said Jason. 'He didn't just jump, you lot, he fucking saved Helena's life.'

People exchanged glances, hesitant, disbelieving, then came to crowd around, hands on Helena, concerned voices. I hadn't felt like a hero when we were traipsing back up the hillside, but now I did, and I looked around at their happy faces, smiled acknowledgement of their congratulations. But when I caught sight of Michael, standing to one side, there was no sign of pleasure in his expression.

When the excitement died down and the story had been told a dozen times, and people returned to their drinks and their games, Matt and Jason started walking me over to join the others, but I stayed back, telling them I wanted to talk to Domino. They winked and nodded, nudging like schoolboys, then left me alone.

'You made it, then?' she said, coming close, but stopping short, as if she were keeping her distance, maybe not wanting other people to see us share affection. 'And you're quite the hero.'

I looked round, wondering if Kurt was nearby. She only acted this way when he was close, but I couldn't see him. Michael and Helena were standing away from the others, Michael talking down to her, trying to take her hand. I watched her snatch it away, shaking her head, then she glanced over at me, catching my eye before joining the others in the kitchen. Michael watched her, then turned, looking over at me.

'Michael doesn't look so pleased about it,' I said.

'Probably thinks *he* should've saved her,' she echoed what Jason had said. 'Worried she'll take a fancy to you. Maybe I should be worried, too: she's pretty.'

'I hadn't noticed. Anyway, you could've warned me.'

'About what?'

'About the jump.'

She pursed her lips, suppressing a smile. 'I could've. But that would be against the rules.'

'Rules?'

'Rules.'

'What rules?'

'Doesn't matter where you are,' she said. 'There's always rules.'

'Even here?'

'Even here.'

On the other side of the clearing, Michael nodded to me, then went to the table where some of the others were playing cards. He took a long hard drag on the pipe that was smoking in the middle of the table, and he spread his arms, saying, 'Damn, I feel good.' He dropped to the floor in a bizarre display, and began doing push-ups beside the table, counting them off. The others joined in the counting, and when he reached fifty, he stood up, barely out of breath, poured himself a glass of whatever was in the bottle on the table, and drained it in one shot.

'I'm wet,' I said to Domino. 'And I'm gonna need some new flip-flops.'

'OK, then, let's see what we can do.'

Inside the longhouse, Domino lit a lamp and led me to the back of the building, to the mat I'd slept on earlier that day. She put the lamp on the floor and went to a small cupboard against the wall, opening it and taking out a folded sarong. She threw the sarong onto the mat, following it with a folded white T-shirt.

'Should fit,' she said. 'It'll do until those dry.' She took out some other clothes and put them on top of the cupboard. 'There's some shorts here, too. A couple of T-shirts. Plain, but they'll do.'

'Whose are they?'

'They were . . . nobody's. They're spares.'

'And *my* things?'

Domino reached into the cupboard and held up my money-belt. I stretched out to take it from her, but she kept hold of it. 'It's safer in here. No one's going to take it.'

'My life's in there. I can't afford to lose it.'

'You remember what you told me when we first met?'

'About what?'

'You said something about having to lose everything before you can really do what you want. Well, why not lose everything for a while? See how it feels. You can come back and get it any-time you want.'

I didn't release my grip on it.

'You trust me?' she asked.

I hardly knew her.

'Alex?' She narrowed her eyes. 'You do *trust* me, right?'

'Sure,' I said, letting her take the money-belt. It was a risk, letting it out of my sight, but it only had to be for now. Later, I would come back and get it, put it back round my waist where it was safest.

'It'll be here whenever you need it.'

I watched her stuff it into the cupboard and close the door.

'Tell you what,' she said, turning the key and taking it out of the lock. 'You can keep this. Make you feel better.'

'No, it's OK,' I half protested, but she unwound one of the thin leather thongs from her wrist and slipped it through the key, tying both ends together and coming close to me.

'Wear it,' she said, putting it over my head. 'That way you won't be worrying about it.'

I lifted my hand to the key and looked down at it. 'Thanks. I appreciate it.'

'Sure you do. Now come on, let's get you changed.'

'I'm going to need some new stuff of my own,' I told her. 'Clothes. A watch. Maybe we can go down to Parapat to-morrow; there's a market there, right?'

Domino came closer to me, helping me take off the wet shirt, pulling at the sodden material as it clung to my skin. 'You should stay a while first. It's better that way.'

'Better?'

'Let people get to know you. Let them see you want to be here.'

'I *do* want to be here.'

'Then stay. You go running off the first day, they'll think you *don't*.'

'It's not running off, it's buying new clothes.'

Domino dropped the wet shirt to the floor and reached down to unfasten the button on my trousers. 'Trust me,' she said. 'There'll be plenty of time to go to Parapat.' She struggled with the button, her fingers not strong enough to push it back through the tight hole.

'I heard you,' I said.

'Hm?'

'When I was asleep. I heard you and Kurt talking. Arguing.'

'You were dreaming.'

'No. I was awake. You were arguing, I'm sure.'

Domino stopped, resting her hands. 'Yeah.'

'He was pissed off about something.'

'I don't want to talk about it.'

'Was it about me? You in trouble for bringing me here?' Again, I wondered if there was something between them, something more than just friendship. A reason why she kept her distance from me when he was around.

'No.' She shook her head and went back to what she'd been doing. Waggling her fingers then going to work on the button again. 'Not that. He's glad you're here. Glad for me.'

'Yeah?'

'Yeah. I told him about what happened with Alim, that's all.'

'Going back in, you mean? Taking the—'

'Yeah.'

'So what did he say?'

'That it was a stupid thing to do.'

'He's right. It was. There's something else, though? Something *between* you two?'

'No.'

'You sure?'

'Would it matter?'

'I . . . don't know.'

'So you want to talk all night?' she asked. 'Or you want to do something more fun?'

'OK,' I said, reaching down, helping her with the button.

Domino knelt so she could unfasten the zip, loosen the trousers and drag them down my thighs to my ankles. She waited for me to step out of them.

'You know how to wear a sarong?' she asked, discarding the stolen trousers.

I shook my head, not wanting to speak, feeling her warm breath on my cold skin.

'I guess I'll have to teach you, then.' She leaned forwards a little further. 'In a moment.'

Domino looked up, her eyes on mine, and slipped her warm lips around me.

19

Later, when Domino and I rejoined the others, I was dressed in a white T-shirt and a check-print sarong. I had a pair of borrowed flip-flops on my feet, and a glow in my face that I'd never had before. Stepping out of the longhouse, I found myself thinking that I'd already had enough experiences to last me a lifetime. I believed I was already changing. And when I looked at Domino walking ahead of me, I wondered if it was possible to fall in love with someone after such a short time.

I stopped and watched her, the way she slipped among the people, joined a group with ease, became a part of their conversation without any effort. She was mesmerising. She was beautiful. She had confidence beyond her years. I could hardly believe that I was here, that she'd met me, that she wanted me, but somewhere at the back of my mind, a voice was telling me that I was a gatecrasher in another person's story. A whisper, warning me that it was all too good to be true. People like Domino don't give themselves to people like me. People like Domino don't give themselves to *any*body. They're wild animals, mischievous sprites, flitting from one experience to the next, never committing themselves to anything. Domino would come into my life and disappear from it just as quickly and I should make the most of it. Enjoy her while she was still mine.

'You're wondering where to go.' A voice beside me, startling me.

'Hm?' I turned and looked at Kurt. I hadn't heard him approach and guessed he must have come from one of the longhouses behind me. I felt a sudden injection of embarrassment and anger when it occurred to me that he could have been inside the longhouse Domino and I had been in. He might have been watching us; watching us in our intimate moment. I tried to push the feeling aside, to make myself believe that if he *had* been in there, it didn't matter. The person I'd been a week ago would have cared, but the person I was now had no reason to worry about what others thought. I tried, but the feeling was still there.

'You're wondering who to talk to. Wondering where you fit in. If anywhere at all. Should you follow Domino, or should you go talk with someone else you know?'

'I don't really know anyone else,' I said, looking at my wrist, repeating that involuntary action.

'What about Michael? You know him, right? Matt, Jason. You shared something.'

I looked over at them, sitting round the table playing cards. Matt and Jason, the surfer dudes who'd leaped from the cliff for a thrill. Matt with his dreads and his wispy goatee. Jason with his lank black hair, his stubble beard and his acne scars – a darker, heavier and less good-looking version of Kurt. And there was Michael with his muscles, his head back, laughing at the clear sky above us. I followed his gaze and stared at the stars.

'Or how about Helena?' Kurt said. 'I heard what happened.'

I looked at him now, tearing my eyes away from the countless stars dotted over our heads.

'You saved her life.'

I shrugged, hid the feeling of pride. 'I did what anyone would do.'

'Not anyone. And now maybe she thinks she owes you.'

'Owes me? No. No, she doesn't owe me anything.'

'*She* probably thinks she does, though. But you need to leave her alone. Don't confuse her. She and Michael . . . they have some issues they need to resolve.'

'Like what?'

'It doesn't matter. Just know that it could upset the balance. Michael has a short temper. I've seen him angry and it's not a pretty sight, so I wouldn't want the two of you to fall out.'

I wasn't sure what to say.

'So, remember, she doesn't owe you anything. If anyone owes you, it's me.'

'How's that?' I asked.

'Because Helena's my sister.'

'Your sister?'

Kurt nodded and put his arm around my shoulder. 'Sure,' he said. 'In the same way that you're my brother.'

I didn't like the feel of his arm around me and I made myself relax, not wanting to offend him. He was offering me his thanks for what I'd done; I needed to be gracious enough to accept it despite there being something about him I didn't like. I couldn't put my finger on it, though. He was good-looking, charismatic, accepting. There was nothing specific that he'd said or done to make me dislike him. There was just a general air about him that made me uneasy. And the relationship he had with Domino.

We were quiet for a while, him with his arm round my shoulder, me looking out at the people. Matt and Jason had left the others and were standing in the shadow at the edge of the clearing to my left, smoking and laughing, but my eyes were drawn to Domino, watching her without seeing her because my mind was here: my inner eye was watching Kurt, sensing his touch like the coils of a snake wrapped loosely round my neck, preparing to tighten. And halfway through our silence, intruders came into our community.

One moment we were alone, and then they were there. Two men coming into the clearing, stepping in and looking around, checking their surroundings, taking in each person they saw, sizing them up.

I recognised both men immediately. The first was Alim. The man who had taken Domino and me into the darkness of his longhouse. The man who had put his hands on her. His eyes darted across the clearing, picking out faces, seeing bodies. He had the air of a gladiator entering the arena to be faced with multiple opponents. He was expecting trouble and he had prepared himself for it. In his hands, the *parang* I'd seen in his longhouse. The copper wire wrapped round the wooden sheath catching the light from the lamps and torches.

The second man was the one who had been with Alim outside the longhouse that night, and he carried himself in an arrogant and calculated manner, just as he had done when I first saw him. Perhaps that was his nature, or perhaps it was because the object he held in his hands gave him a greater feeling of power. It was something far more brutal than the pistol I'd seen on the table, surrounded by Alim's drug paraphernalia. This was something I associated with revolutionaries and guerrillas, men piled into the back of Toyota trucks. It had been obscured the first time I saw it, the night it had been pointing into the forest around me, but now it was an instantly recognisable rifle. An AK47, the stock battered and nicked, the blued steel magazine curved beneath it. A wicked half-smile that carried brass and lead designed to pierce a man's flesh and fragment his bones. And the man who held it was even more severe in this light than he had been that night. The way he slowly turned his head, scanning the clearing with dark eyes; the way he sniffed, turned and spat.

Kurt looked at the ground, exasperated yet knowing. He'd expected Alim to come.

He released his hold on me, smiled and approached the two men, speaking in Indonesian. Michael fell in behind him, watching.

Alim's partner swung the rifle up, pointing it at Kurt, making him come to an abrupt stop and raise both hands to waist height. They stayed like that, the rest of us holding our collective breath, then the man relaxed, slung the rifle over his shoulder and came forward to meet Kurt. They shook hands and stood for a while in conversation.

The others in the clearing were silent, all eyes on the intruders, watching with interest as the two men spoke in hushed tones. It wasn't long before Alim came forward, trying to dominate the conversation, and when his voice began to rise, Kurt held out his hands, shaking his head, speaking words I wouldn't understand even if I could hear them. Then Kurt dropped his hands and turned, looking round the clearing, seeing Domino and beckoning her closer.

As Domino went over, I felt an urge to stop her. I'd seen the way Alim had looked at her. I knew what he wanted to do to her, and my suspicions were heightened by his reaction to her, the way he raised his voice further when she came closer. He pointed at her, gesticulating up and down.

Kurt shook his head and Domino halted, Alim advancing to close the distance between them. When Kurt moved to stop him, Alim forced him aside, reaching out and slapping Domino's face. Her head whipped back, but she was quick to recover, to look Alim in the eye.

My reaction was to step forward, but I was held back. 'Nothing you can do,' Jason said in my ear. 'Just stay calm.' I'd been too busy watching Kurt to notice him coming close behind me.

'Yeah, be calm, dude,' Matt added. 'The guy's a fucking wanker, but Kurt will sort it out. Kurt always sorts it out.' And they were right. Already Kurt had recovered and was talking to Alim, holding out his hand to keep him at arm's length, then speaking to Domino, who nodded and came back in my direction.

'And if *he* doesn't, Michael will,' said Jason. 'He's even harder than he looks. Fuckin' black belt in chop-socky or something. I heard he once killed a man with his bare hands, if you can believe that.'

'More likely split 'im open with his machete,' countered Matt.

Domino passed me without a glance and climbed inside the longhouse. When she came out again, she was carrying the pistol. The hard, deadly metal was big and out of place in her small hands.

She went back to Alim and held it out to him, handle first. He took it, allowing the barrel to point at her for a moment before he dropped it to hang by his hip. He looked at Kurt and spoke. I imagined this was the point where he was telling them not to do it again, that they were lucky to be alive.

Business concluded, Alim and his friend turned to leave, looking back just as Matt made a gesture with his right hand, raising the middle finger at their backs. Without hesitation, Alim raised the pistol and pointed it at Matt. He fired one shot, the bullet zipping past at head height, hitting something behind in the forest. An intentional miss or not, I didn't know, but the moment was surreal. Someone had shot at me – well, perhaps not at me, but at the person close beside me – and yet it was undramatic. Just a loud report, the sound of something disturbing the air, then a cracking among the trees. As if a small animal had stepped on a twig. That was it.

I ducked, as if it might protect me, but before he could fire again, Michael was there, pressing his hand on top of the pistol, pushing the barrel so that it pointed only at the ground. His other hand rising, putting a blade against Alim's throat.

Alim's friend reached round to unshoulder his rifle, but Michael shook his head and pressed a little harder with the *parang*. Alim spoke, the words tripping from his mouth faster than usual, and the man stayed where he was. Alim then tucked the pistol away and held up his empty hands.

Michael released him and the two intruders melted back into the trees. Gone.

'Jesus Christ,' I said, watching the spot where they'd disappeared into the forest. 'Jesus Christ.'

'He fucking shot at me,' said Matt, still standing exactly where he had been. 'He fucking shot at me. You see that?' This wasn't fear, though, it was disbelief. Excitement. 'Man, that was *cool*.' He put one hand to his head, rubbed it across the stumpy blond dreadlocks. 'So cool.'

'I saw it, man. I saw it,' said Jason. 'Shit.'

'Whoa, I need a drink after that,' Matt told him.

'Maybe something stronger,' Jason replied. 'I need something special after a thing like that.'

I stayed where I was while the two of them went away, wide-eyed and shaking their heads, enjoying the excitement of it all as the others crowded round them, asking how it felt to come so close to death. I, on the other hand, had taken no enjoyment from the episode. My hands were trembling as they had done when I pulled Helena from the lake. My heart was thumping, my whole body was starting to shake. My mouth was dry, too. I forced my legs to work, going over to where Kurt and Domino were standing, still watching the trees where the two men had gone.

'I told you it was a stupid thing to do,' Kurt was saying. 'Danuri's hard enough to deal with, but this is gonna make things *really* fucking bad, D. How long you think it's gonna be before we patch this one up? What the hell were you thinking?'

Domino looked up at me as I approached. 'I don't know,' she said. 'I guess I just do things sometimes, you know. He came back in and I saw it sitting there and—' She stopped. 'I'm sorry, Kurt. I was scared.'

Michael slipped his *parang* back into its wooden sheath and watched the line of the trees.

'Will they come back?' I asked.

Kurt whipped round as if he were about to challenge my presence. His face was tight, angry, a flash of menace, but he made it relax and took a deep breath. 'No, I don't think so.'

'How can you be sure?'

'They need us and we need them,' he said. 'We have a kind of agreement.' He shifted his eyes to glare at Domino. 'A kind of symbiosis.'

'Symbiosis?'

'We can't survive without them, and they can't survive without us.'

'And—'

'And I don't want to talk about it right now.' He held up a hand, making it clear this was all he was going to say.

For a moment we stood in silence, the three of us by the line of trees, the others further away, still grouped around Matt and Jason. Then I spoke to Domino, asking her if she was all right.

'I'm fine,' she said, leaning forwards to embrace me. 'Thanks for asking. Yeah. I'm fine.' She kissed me on the mouth, glared at Kurt, then strode away, leaving us alone.

'D does things,' he said after a pause. 'Without thinking about them.'

'She's not the only one.' I looked across at Matt. It was his finger that had caused the shooting, not Domino's.

'She's . . . impulsive.'

'That's what I like about her.' I was still shaking.

'It can be endearing,' he said.

I nodded.

'But it can cause trouble, too.'

'So I see.'

Kurt studied my face. He glanced at the woods, then looked at me again. 'You really like her?'

I thought for a moment. 'I do.'

'And you want to stick around? Even after . . . you know. What just happened?'

Again, I thought hard. I wanted to be sure about what I was going to say. An inch or two in the other direction and the bullet might not have been just a rustle in the forest. It might have pierced Matt's skull, torn through his brain and taken his life. Further still and it might have been *my* skull, *my* life.

I glanced away to see Domino by the fire, talking to some of the others, the group now fragmented. I watched her move and remembered our moments together, alone, then I turned back to Kurt.

'Yeah,' I said. 'I do.'

20

After the intensity and excitement that had led to and included my arrival in the community, the following days were uncomplicated and free. I did, more or less, as I pleased, and it wasn't difficult to understand why people wanted to stay here. There was something numbing about the way we lived; everything was encapsulated in a bubble of ether. Nothing reminded me of my life before I came here. I had no past. No duty, no betrayal, no loss. There was nothing else; everything was forgotten.

Each night I slept entangled with Domino at the back of the longhouse, and each morning we bathed together beneath the waterfall on the bluff overlooking the lake. It was cold, but it was part of this life, and it didn't take long to become accustomed to it. We ate mainly fish and rice, but those who cooked knew a hundred different ways to prepare the *mujahir* fish that was our staple.

By day, there was always something to do; it was just a matter of slowing to the pace. I learned to play mah jong; we had a badminton net, which we put up across the clearing; we swam in the lake, fished for our food. Domino and I spent a lot of time alone, walking in the forest, watching the lake.

It was a kind of paradise I hadn't expected to find. A place with no rules bar those of our own making. And yet I didn't feel as if I were seeing the whole picture. There was a sense that I was not yet part of the community. Everybody treated me like a friend, but I was not yet one of them and I didn't know why.

On a few occasions I thought Helena wanted to talk to me – she threw expectant glances my way – but each time I approached her, or she approached me, Michael found a way to come between us.

It was Kurt who eyed me with the greatest suspicion, though, despite his efforts to conceal it. This was most apparent when I was with Domino. As if he were interested in every move we made together. I tried to keep away from him whenever possible, which was why we spent much of our time away from the clearing, only joining the others when Kurt was busy in the second longhouse. The longhouse that, I discovered, was always kept locked.

The way Kurt watched us reinforced my belief that he and Domino had been together at some time, that he didn't like me replacing him. The thought of them together stung with jealousy, and I had been, once or twice, on the verge of broaching the subject with Domino, but decided not to. I was enjoying my time with her and didn't want an uncomfortable conversation to damage that.

On the fourth day, though, Domino wasn't there when I woke.

I dressed and went out into the clearing but the place was quiet and there was no sign of her. There were a few people sitting at the table, eating breakfast. Matt and Jason together as always, Alban and Evie sitting close.

I went over to the lean-to kitchen where Helena and Freia were preparing food. Helena in a vest top and a short skirt, nothing on her feet. Freia's masculine frame draped in baggy shorts and an ill-fitting T-shirt.

'Where is everyone?' I asked.

Helena looked up and smiled. 'Hi, Alex.' She straightened, used both hands to brush her hair behind her ears.

'A few went out,' Freia said without looking at me. She was on her haunches by the fire, stirring a pot of something that smelled good.

'Out?'

'Hm. For supplies. Parapat probably. Or Samosir.' She wiped her forearm across her nose.

'And Domino went, too?' I asked, feeling a little angry. Domino knew I wanted to go to Parapat. I'd been living in borrowed clothes for three days. I wore borrowed flip-flops on my feet and drew a borrowed razor across my face. My whole life was borrowed. I wanted to buy a watch, too. It was hard to keep track of time up here – no real sense of it other than day and night.

'I saw her go,' said Helena. 'She was with Kurt.'

'Don't worry about it.' Freia looked up at me, seeing my expression. 'They'll be back this evening. Maybe tomorrow morning.'

'*Tomorrow?*'

'Sure,' Freia shrugged. 'Sometimes it takes longer.' She rested the spoon on a plate beside the pot and wiped her large hands on a cloth as she stood up. I hadn't really noticed until now that she was taller than me. Wider, too, her large breasts heavy beneath the loose material of her T-shirt.

'What does?' I asked. 'What takes longer?'

Freia shrugged again. 'Whatever it is they need to do.' She put the cloth on the table. 'I'm sure you'll find something to do while she's gone, though. Someone else to talk to.' She flicked a quick glance at Helena. 'But I'm going for a *mandi*, so it's not going to be me. You want to talk to me, you'll have to come to the waterfall.'

Freia stalked away, her large feet wrapped in leather sandals. I watched her go, saw her stop and turn to us. 'You know,' she said, 'Helena talks about you a lot. How you saved her. That kind of thing can . . . how you say . . . put the cat in with the birds.'

'Pigeons,' I heard myself say.

'Exactly,' Freia replied. 'Pigeons. And Michael's quite a cat.' She raised a hand and left us.

When I looked back at Helena, I could see she was blushing.

A tint of red around her cheekbones that contrasted with her pale skin and dark hair. It looked good on her.

'So,' I said. 'They left this morning?'

'Early.' Helena didn't look at me. Instead, she twisted round to see the table where the others were sitting. 'Alban,' she raised her voice, 'it's your turn to clean this place up, you lazy sod.'

Alban smiled and leaned back. 'Nah, it's Evie's turn,' he said with a light accent. 'I already did it a couple of days ago.'

'Fuckin' liar.' Evie slapped Alban's shoulder, making him laugh, saying, 'All right, all right, I'll do it in a minute.'

'And you really don't know when Domino'll be back?' I asked Helena.

She shook her head.

'So why wouldn't she tell me she was going? I could've gone with her.' It should have been me instead of Kurt.

'Maybe you're not ready yet,' she said, taking an interest in something behind me.

'Not ready? What do you mean, not ready?'

But Helena didn't have the chance to reply because Michael's voice was in my ear. 'Not ready for anything, pasty boy.'

Surprised, I turned to look at him. 'Michael. I was just saying I wanted to go somewhere. You know, Parapat maybe.'

'Why d'you want to go there when you've got all this?' He spread his arms wide. 'There's nowhere better.' In one fist he gripped a long-handled axe, the blade almost black apart from the edge, which had a freshly ground gleam. In the other hand, he carried a two-man saw.

'There's some things I wanted to get,' I told him.

'Don't you have everything you need? Clothes, food, company?'

Yeah, but—'

'Can you do anything other than jump off cliffs?' he asked, putting his arm around my shoulder, letting the saw hang down my chest. 'And, by the way, I hope you're not chatting up my girl,' he said, lifting the teeth towards my throat.

'Eh? No, I was—'

'Just kidding with you, Alex. You English have no sense of humour, you know that?' He put the axe into my hand and stood back. 'So, *are* you good at anything other than jumping off cliffs?'

'I don't know. I suppose I can do one or two things.'

'You can swing an axe, though, right?'

'Sure. I think so.'

'Oh, you think so? Well, then now's the time to find out. Let's go get some exercise.'

Michael strode away towards the line of trees in the direction of the waterfall, expecting me to follow.

Behind us I heard Alban asking if we needed some help, but Helena's voice told him to get on with cleaning the kitchen, then she came after us, her footfalls light, Michael asking, 'You coming too? Great.'

We waited while she slipped on a pair of light plimsolls, then we traced the path towards the bluff for a good two hundred yards before veering off the track into the denser trees. Michael wandered for a while, stopping from time to time, studying trunks, testing their width, leaning back to check their height, until eventually he tapped one with his knuckles and said, 'Perfect. Time for you to do your stuff, Alex.'

'You want me to cut it down?'

'About here.' He drew a *parang* from the wooden sheath that hung from his shoulder by a loop of twine and swung it into the soft wood about three feet from the ground. The blade connected with a dull but satisfying thud, biting a good inch into the tree.

'OK.' I moved forward to tug it out. I handed it to Michael and readied the axe. 'Stand clear.'

Helena and Michael watched for a while as I made a deep enough cut for the three of us to put our strength behind it and push the tree down. I felt a vague ache in my shoulder as I worked, but I ignored it and enjoyed the labour. There was sweat running down my back by the time I was finished and the physical exercise was like a purging tonic. All thoughts of leaving the community were vaporised.

The tree came down with a crash that satisfied all the fantasies of my boyhood games. Insects, pine needles and narrow cones rained down on us.

'So what's it for?' I stood back to inspect the fallen tree.

'Renovating the kitchen.'

'Make it bigger?' I flicked a bug from my arm, dusted the back of my neck.

'Bigger and better. Onwards and upwards.'

'OK, well, give me a minute and I'll do the branches.'

'Let me,' said Helena, tying back her hair into a stumpy ponytail. Some strands were too short and she pushed them behind her ears before coming close to me. She took the axe from my hands, allowing her fingers to touch mine, before she turned and went to the felled tree.

Helena's build was slight, her arms sinewy, her legs slender. She didn't look suited for physical work like this, but I was surprised by her strength and stamina. She went straight to the tree, raising the axe and working her way along its length, removing the branches. Some she took with one clean heft, others with repeated blows.

When she stopped to stretch her back, her vest top was soaked with sweat and her face was flushed. She leaned on the axe handle, immersed in what she was doing, and it was hard to believe she was the same person who'd struggled in the water on my first night.

'Beautiful,' said Michael beside me.

'Yeah,' I replied without thinking. But as soon as I realised I'd said it, I turned to look at Michael, who was staring at me. 'But she's not Domino.'

Michael raised his eyebrows.

'No, I didn't mean . . . Oh shit, you know what I meant.'

Michael grinned and punched my upper arm harder than necessary. 'Course I know what you meant.'

Helena glanced over at us. 'You two having a nice time?'

'Sure am,' said Michael. 'You?'

'Yep.'

'You need any help yet?' he asked.

'No,' she replied. 'Not yet.' And with that, she raised the axe and began cutting again.

As the blade continued to swing, so Michael began to grow restless, finding a low sturdy branch and jumping up to hang from it. He pulled himself up, raising his chin to the bark. 'Gotta keep fit,' he said, lowering himself and repeating the movement. 'Stay in shape. You should try it. Get some muscles on you. Domino would love it.'

I wished he wasn't there and I tried to think of a reply, but Helena broke the moment by shouting and jumping back from the tree, saying, 'Snake.'

Michael dropped from the branch he was using and took up his machete, hurrying over to where Helena was standing. A bright green snake, no thicker than two of my fingers together, and about eighteen inches long, was uncoiling itself from one of the half-stripped limbs. It was impossible to tell what its tiny black eyes were looking at, but it was clear that it was in a hurry to escape from us as its impossible body relaxed, released and headed for the safety of the undergrowth.

Michael stepped after it, raising his *parang*.

'No,' I said, making him turn his head to look at me. 'Don't kill it.'

When he turned back, the snake was gone. He stared at the spot where it had been, letting his arm drop before he looked at me again. 'Why not?'

'Why would you want to kill it?' I asked.

'Because it was there.' Michael looked confused. 'What?' He glanced at Helena for support. '*You'd* kill it, right?'

'Actually, no, I don't think I would.'

'You wouldn't kill it?' Talking to me again. 'It's a snake, Alex. What if it bit you? What if it bit Helena? Or Domino?'

'Why would it do that?' I said.

He watched us, studying us like we'd spoken a language he didn't understand, then he walked over to Helena and grabbed the axe. 'You people.' He went to the felled tree and vented his frustration on the remaining branches.

Once the tree was stripped, we used the saw to cut it into two logs and we carried them back to the clearing, laying them beside the kitchen.

'Another one of those should be enough,' Michael said as we put down the second log. 'We'll go back out after lunch.'

Lunch was *nai tumur,* another variation of fish and rice. This time the *mujahir* fish was boiled with a spicy saffron sauce and it tasted good, especially after the physical work.

There were several of us at the table, all of us eating our food with spoons, scooping it off tin plates.

'So, Alex, you had the shits yet, man?' said Matt, looking up from his food.

'Do we have to talk about this now?' Alban put down his spoon in disgust.

'Just wondered,' said Matt, slurring his words a little.

'Must have a strong stomach,' said Jason. 'Mr "haven't you got anything higher".'

'Well, if you get 'em, just you remember to starve those mothers out,' said Matt. 'That's what Kurt told me. Rice, water, tea. Nothing else. And *definitely* no fruit.'

'Can we please finish eating?' Alban said from across the table.

'He needs to know,' Jason backed up his friend, trying to look sincere, but it was hard to take him seriously. He was stoned, his pupils dilated, his hair held back with a tortoiseshell Alice band.

'So what *do* you guys do if you get ill?' I asked. 'You go find a doctor?'

'We don't get ill,' said Michael.

'We got our own doctor,' added Jason.

'You mean Kurt?' I asked. 'What kind of doctor is he?'

'The *almost* kind of doctor,' Matt said. 'Dropped out of med school.'

'Dropped out? He do something wrong?'

'Yeah.' Matt waved his hands at me. 'He liked to cut people up. Like Doctor Frankenstein or something.'

I noticed Michael stop eating and look up to stare at Matt.

'Nah, did he fuck,' said Jason. 'He finished. He's a fuckin' doctor.'

'No way, dude,' Matt replied. 'He's not old enough.'

'I'm telling you, the man finished med school. Came out here, found this place and decided to stay. He's, like, a hippy doctor, man.'

'Whatever,' said Michael, pushing his plate away. 'Come on, Alex, we got more work to do.'

I shovelled in the last of my food and drained my cup before sliding out from the table.

'You coming?' I asked Helena.

She thought about it, looking up at Michael, then shook her head. 'Not this time,' she said. 'I got other things to do.'

Back out on the path, I asked about Kurt, saying, 'So what's the deal, then? Is he a doctor or not?'

Michael pretended not to hear, so I asked him again, making him stop. 'He's doctor enough for me.'

I put my hands up and told him I didn't mean to cause offence. He seemed to relent a little at my submissive gesture and he allowed his chest to deflate, letting out a long sigh. 'He dropped out. Least that's what he told me. And if that's not what happened, then I guess he had his reasons for telling it to me that way.'

'And he came here?'

'After he met me.' Michael started walking again, keeping his pace slow. 'In Bali. We travelled a few weeks, but he didn't find what he was looking for. Didn't like the buzz, the people.

He liked the quiet adventure, so we came looking for something else. Found this place.'

'The two of you?'

'Just us,' Michael said, veering off the path, looking for the spot where we'd left the tools. 'We stayed, set the place up, made a few contacts.'

'Like Alim?'

'Alim?' Michael looked back at me. 'How d'you . . . Oh yeah, I forgot you saw him the other night. And Domino took you to his place, right?'

'Hm.' I remembered the exhilarating night in the woods, running from whoever would give chase. The morning after, with Domino, on the hill overlooking the lake.

'Only it wasn't Alim back then,' he said. 'Hendrik was the one in charge. Alim just worked for him. Then Alim introduced him to Danuri.'

We came to the place where we'd cut down the tree and Michael handed me the axe, telling me I could do the next one if I wanted.

I took the axe. 'Danuri. He's the one who came here with Alim, right? The other night? He seems like a tough guy.'

'Yeah, sure, he's a tough guy when he's flashing the hardware around. Take the gun away, though, and he's nothing but a . . .' Michael shook his head. 'Hendrik I could get along with, but this guy Danuri? He likes to be the one in charge.'

'In charge of what? He make you pay more, or—'

'Or never you mind right now,' he replied. 'Let's find a tree.'

We headed deeper into the forest until we found one similar in size to the last one, and I set about cutting it down.

'So who was the first to come?' I asked, taking a rest. 'I mean, after you and Kurt.'

'Domino. Kurt brought Domino in.'

I nodded, thinking it confirmed what I already suspected. Domino and Kurt had once been together. 'He cares about her,' I said.

'You better believe it, white boy.' He raised his eyebrows at me. 'Hurt her and you'll be hurting bad yourself.'

I half smiled, unsure if he was joking, then took up the axe again. 'Anyone ever leave?' I asked.

'Why would anyone want to do that?'

'Domino mentioned someone. Some guy who left without telling anyone. Disappeared.'

His face fell. 'She told you about Sully?'

'Sully?' I asked. 'His name was Sully?'

Michael shrugged and stared. 'Yeah. Maybe.'

I waited for him to say something else, but he didn't. Instead, he found a sturdy branch and started with the pull-ups again. I watched him for a second, then lifted the axe over my shoulder. I took a last look at Michael, then swung at the tree.

The blade bit hard.

21

By the time Michael and I brought the next two logs from the forest, it was growing dark and some of the others had returned, bringing with them sacks of rice and sweet potatoes.

Morgan and Chris, whom I'd met on my first day but hardly spoken to since, were in the clearing, starting a fire. Their sacks were stacked by the entrance to the permanently locked longhouse. There were others there, too, setting the table, preparing food, playing cards, football, but there was no sign of either Domino or Kurt.

'Shit,' Michael said as we dropped the last log. 'Something else for me to do.' He straightened up, looking across at the sacks, then at Morgan. 'You refilled the containers?'

'Sure did,' Morgan said as she rotated one of the three rings that pierced her lower lip. I wondered what the local people in the village made of her, with all that metal in her face. She said something to Chris, then stood and came over. 'Everything's topped up. You want a hand storing the rest of it?'

Michael nodded. 'Let's get it done.'

The pair of them headed over to the longhouse, Michael slipping a key from his pocket and climbing the ladder to open up before coming back down to carry the sacks into the forbidden darkness.

'So that's like a store?' I said, going over to where Jason and Matt were kicking a football between them.

'Something like that,' Matt said, flicking the ball up,

bouncing it on his knee, then passing it over to Jason, who headed it to me.

I fumbled the ball, ran over to the edge of the clearing to retrieve it. 'So why's it locked?' I asked, coming back with the ball at my feet. 'You guys can't be trusted, is that it? You eat all the food?'

'It's where we keep the bodies,' said Matt.

'Right. Seriously, what's in there?'

Jason tapped his nose with a grubby finger. 'All in good time, dude. All in good time. You been to the stone yet?'

'The stone?'

'The execution stone.' Matt swayed his body and waved his hands to suggest he was telling me something spooky. 'The *blood* stone. The place of blood and lost souls. The place where all crimes are purged.'

'What the fuck are you talking about?'

'Wait and see,' Jason smiled. 'Wait and see.'

'Oh, come on, guys, you're winding me up, right?'

'Nu-uh.' Matt shook his head. 'There really is an execution stone. I tell you, man, it's crazy, but you'll love it. Kurt'll take you there when you're ready.'

'Ready for what? Why does everybody keep saying I'm not ready? Ready for what, exactly?'

'All in good time, dude. Everything comes to he who waits.'

I tried to press them further but they refused to elaborate, so we ended up kicking the ball around until it was too dark to see, then Matt and Jason went to smoke a joint. I went with them, all three of us lying on our backs at the edge of the clearing, looking up at the canopy because that's how they liked to do it. The early stars were visible in the greying sky.

'So you going to tell me about this rock?' I asked.

Matt laughed. 'Got you worrying about that, eh? Just chill out, it's all cool.'

I took the joint he offered me and dragged on it. 'So what about this guy Sully, then?'

Matt and Jason remained quiet. I sensed them exchange glances.

'You knew him, right? Domino said he left, and that there was all kinds of trouble.'

'Why you asking about him?' Matt said.

'Just making conversation, I guess. I was curious. Domino said he just disappeared.'

'Upped and left in the night,' Jason offered.

'In the night?'

'Fuck, I don't know, could've been anytime,' said Jason. 'One day he was here, the next he was gone.'

'Probably chilling out on some beach somewhere,' Matt said.

'What was he like?' I asked.

'What difference does it make? Anyway, we didn't know him so well. He was Michael's friend.'

'Michael's?' I said. 'Seemed to me like he hardly knew him.'

Jason sat up. 'You talked to Michael about Sully? Shit, Kurt and Michael don't like to talk about it. I'd keep it to yourself if I were you.'

Now Matt got to his feet and reached down to pull Jason up beside him. 'Let's go see what the others are doing,' he said. 'We'll see you later, Alex.'

I watched them go, wondering at their sudden departure, certain I'd said the wrong thing. I sat up and tried to remember Michael's words from earlier that day when I'd asked about Sully. He hadn't mentioned that they were friends – but he hadn't said they *weren't* friends, either. Maybe Michael was pissed off that Sully had left without him; that's why he didn't want to talk about it. I looked across at him sitting by the fire with Helena. She was slightly turned away from him, her body language telling me she didn't want to be with him, but he either didn't notice or didn't care. Perhaps he was blind to it because his feelings for her were so strong, and it occurred to me that the same might be true for me and Domino. In her more vulnerable moments, I felt that Domino needed me, but maybe she just needed *someone*. And in her stronger moments, I doubted that she really needed anyone at all.

Now that I was thinking about Domino again I brooded for a while, wondering where she was and what she might be doing with Kurt. With nothing much to do besides sit there and reflect on our relationship, it began to smart again that she hadn't told me she was going. The only reason I could think of was that she'd wanted to be alone. With Kurt.

I closed my eyes and hung my head, wondering if I had been as blind as Michael. So much had happened since I'd arrived in this country and I'd barely had time alone to think. This was the only moment I'd been able to snatch and, for the first time, I thought this might not be the right thing for me. I had always intended to travel alone; perhaps I shouldn't have come here at all. I'd put too much trust in Domino. Relied on her too much.

'Hey,' a voice broke into my despondency. 'You want to come join us?'

I opened my eyes and looked at a pair of feet clad in leather sandals. The toes were large and squared, the nails uneven. Freia.

'Come on, Alex,' she said. 'No reason for you to sit here when you've got friends around you.'

I willed a smile to my lips and raised my head. 'Just taking a moment.'

'No need for that. Best thing to do when you don't know people is throw yourself in there and get to know them better.'

'I hardly even know people's names,' I said. 'I mean, I know some, but . . .'

'The names will come. You know, it took me weeks to remember everyone's names. I'm crap at names.'

'How many people are there?' I asked. 'Is this everyone?'

Freia turned and scanned the clearing. 'Well, Kurt and Domino are missing, but you know that, right? Apart from them, everyone's here. There's no other names to know.'

'Sixteen people,' I said. 'Including me, that is.'

Freia shrugged and her breasts shook. 'As many as that, eh? I think there were maybe eight when I came.'

'Yeah? How long you been here?'

'Long time. I love it here. Came just before Matt and Jason. Met Kurt on Samosir one time, we got talking; one thing led to another.'

'You and he . . . ?'

'No,' she laughed. 'Domino's more my type.'

'Oh.'

'But I'm not her type, Alex. I don't think she goes that way. And, of course, now she has you.'

'You think so?'

'Oh, I'm sure about it. I see how she looks at you.'

'Really?'

'Yes, really. You shouldn't be so insecure. But no more hunting for compliments.'

'Fishing.'

'What?'

'No more *fishing* for compliments.'

'Whatever. You gonna come get something to eat – join the rest of us – or sit and feel sorry for yourself 'cause Domino's not here?'

'Do you know where she went?' I asked.

Freia shook her head. 'Who knows where they go? I wouldn't worry about it, though, she'll come back. She always comes back.'

'And you really have no idea *when*?'

'Sometimes they're gone a day, sometimes longer. I don't know what they do, but it takes time. Come on,' she said. 'Come sit with us.' But I told her I wanted to be on my own a while, so she left, saying, 'Suit yourself.'

'Hey,' I called her back. 'Domino mentioned some guy called Sully. Did you know him?'

'*Michael's* Sully? Sure, I knew him. Why you asking about him?'

'Curious, I suppose. Domino said he's the only person who left and didn't come back. I wondered what made him leave.'

'No idea.' She held up her hands. 'Anyway, it's probably better not to talk about it. Michael gets . . . Well, keep it to yourself, Alex.'

I watched her go, helping herself to food, sitting beside Helena and Michael, leaning across to speak into his ear. Michael looked over at me as he listened.

I slid down the tree again, and the way Michael looked at me made me feel cold. I had said the wrong thing, I could see that, and I had said it to the wrong person. I had thought I was comfortable here, that it was a good place to be, but without Domino it felt wrong, as if I wasn't supposed to be here. As if I was only a part of this group because of her, and now she had left me. Without any word, she had gone and I was alone, and the longer I dwelled on it, the more angry I felt until eventually I made up my mind what I was going to do.

I headed back to the longhouse and went inside, taking up a torch from beside the entrance. I picked my way to the far end where my bed was and took the key from round my neck. I opened the cupboard and removed my money-belt.

I was putting it round my waist when I heard someone come in and a beam of torchlight shone towards me.

'Alex?' It was Helena's voice. 'You coming to eat?'

I didn't reply. I felt as if I'd been caught committing a crime.

Helena came closer, her footsteps light, the torch pointed low. 'What you doing?'

In the thin light I could just make out her fine features, the focus of her eyes. She was looking at the money-belt, seeing me halfway towards fastening it round my waist.

'You're leaving?'

Again, I didn't answer. I felt foolish. Petulant. Like a spoilt child who hadn't got his way. Domino had gone, left without a word, so I was planning my retaliation.

'I'm not a prisoner,' I said eventually.

'Of course not.'

'So it should be all right if I go, then.'

'Now? At night? You'll get lost in the forest.'

I stopped fastening the belt and let it hang in my hand.

'You want to leave, Alex, do it tomorrow. In daylight. I won't tell anyone. Maybe I'll even come with you.'

'I was planning on coming back,' I said. 'I just need a few things, some time to think. This place—'

'Maybe you *shouldn't* come back.'

'What?'

'I'm not so sure Kurt would let you anyway. He likes people to be here a while first.'

'Why?'

'Get to know them better? Let them prove their loyalty, maybe. Who knows?'

'Loyalty?'

As we spoke, I heard noises at the entrance to the longhouse and I knew immediately that it would be Michael. Whenever I was alone with Helena, he appeared like a ghost.

Sure enough, within a few seconds I heard his voice calling, 'Helena? You in here?'

'Yeah,' she replied. 'I'm here.'

'Who you talking to?'

There was a pause and I spoke out. 'Me,' I said. 'Alex.'

'What you two up to?'

I heard him come right into the longhouse, take up a torch that he shone down the length of the building.

'Helena came in to make sure I'm all right. I wasn't feeling well.'

'Hm,' he said. 'So you coming to eat, then, or what?'

'We're coming,' Helena said, her hand reaching out to touch mine for the briefest moment, sharing the lie. And with that touch came a realisation. I felt something for Helena not because I had stopped her from drowning, or because of some misconstrued responsibility for her. It was not because by saving her I had somehow made a difference. I felt something for her because she was a good person. And, like me, she was probably in the wrong place.

'Not me,' I said. 'Think I'm gonna get my head down. Get some sleep.' I smiled at Helena. 'I'll see you guys in the morning.'

When they were gone, I stayed where I was, with the belt hanging from my right hand. It was all that made me who I was. Without it I was nobody. Without it I had no connection to anything outside this small community. I looked down at it, a dull shape in the dark, my mind torn between putting it on and leaving this place – leaving Domino and Helena, disappearing into the forest – or returning it to its place of safekeeping and giving this place one more chance. But now my anger was calmed, I knew I would stay. I couldn't go into the forest alone at night. Helena was right, I'd probably get lost. And I didn't want to lose Domino just yet. Maybe we had other places to go.

Eventually, I sighed and stuffed the money-belt back into the cupboard and put the key round my neck. I changed my shorts for a more comfortable sarong, then lay down on my mat and pulled the sheet over me. I stared at the darkness above me, listening to the sound of the others outside, wondering if I had made the right decision.

I dozed for a while with those thoughts in my head, and after some time, I heard someone come into the longhouse, fumbling footsteps coming my way. Then someone whispered my name in the darkness, 'Alex,' and I knew it was Domino.

I heard the sounds of her undressing, saw a dark silhouette standing over me, then she was lying beside me, running her hands over me, pulling off my T-shirt, putting her fingers on my skin. 'I'm sorry I was so long,' she said. 'I didn't want to go.'

'You should've told me.'

'I didn't want to leave you.'

'So why *did* you?'

'Shh,' she whispered.

'Where did you go?'

'Errands,' she said. 'Supplies. Does it matter? I'm here now. I couldn't wait to see you again.' She pulled me on top of her and wrapped her limbs around me.

'Where's everyone else?' I asked.

'Still outside,' she said.

'You're sure?'

'Of course.' She pulled me into her and held me there. 'We're alone.'

Later, in the darkness of the longhouse, Domino breathing deeply beside me, I listened to the night, hearing no familiar sounds.

Close by, Helena would be sleeping alone. I remembered how she had looked that day in the forest, her sinews working as she swung the axe, and I recalled how we had touched that night. The briefest touch. I shook the thought away and eased myself from Domino's arms. I wanted to feel fresh air, see the stars.

I crept the length of the longhouse, glancing down at Helena as I passed her, and climbed down into the clearing.

The fire was dying in its grave. The sky above me was clear. All was quiet and still.

I walked to the middle of the clearing and turned my face to the sky. Everything about the day was forgotten; blown away by Domino's breath. Her touch had cured my jealous thoughts and I remembered, now, why I wanted to stay here.

'Nice night,' a voice startled me.

'Make you jump?' Kurt was behind me. 'I heard you come out. Thought I'd come with you.' He raised his arm, brandishing a large plastic yellow torch. 'Something I'd like to show you,' he said, approaching me and hanging one arm over my shoulder. Without giving me the chance to refuse, he began walking, his arm still around me, only slipping away when he was sure I was coming with him.

We moved around the edge of the clearing towards the lean-to kitchen, stopping a few feet before we reached it. He glanced at me, a mischievous expression in his eyes, then he inclined his head at the trees edging the clearing. I looked at them, but saw nothing of any significance.

'Like it's not even there,' he said.

I shook my head, not understanding.

'You see nothing,' he said. 'You've been here a few days now but have no idea it's here.'

'You're going to have to put me out of my misery.'

'Let's hope it doesn't come to that.' His face became grim. The change in his eyes took me by surprise, a dark moment passing like a flash storm. There for just a second before the twinkle returned. 'Hold this.' He passed me the torch and pulled up his sarong, tucking it up as I'd seen the workers do in the paddy fields. When he was done, he took the torch from me, saying, 'You might want to do the same.'

He gave me a moment before speaking again. 'This way,' he said as he clicked on the torch and stepped between two of the gnarled trunks, pushing the fir branches to one side. 'Not our last secret, but one of them.'

He waited for me to put out a hand before he released the needled branches, and pressed on ahead, tramping through the ground cover, filtering among the pillars of pine. I focused on the back of his white T-shirt, careful not to lose him and, after a few minutes, we came to a narrow, overgrown path that snaked among the dense trees.

Kurt pointed the torch beam at the hidden track ahead. 'We don't come down this way much,' he said.

'You're not going to make me jump off something again, are you?'

'No.'

We followed the path a few hundred yards, moving further away from the clearing behind us, the only two people in the entire forest.

'Just down here,' he said, and then we were in another clearing. This one was smaller from what I could tell, but it was difficult to see much because the torch beam was narrow and did little more than light a small patch on the ground.

'Wait a moment,' Kurt said, and he slipped into the darkness.

I watched the beam of the torch moving to and fro on the forest floor before it came to a stop. The beam lowered, becoming more concentrated and then the circle of light was half-deadened when Kurt placed it on the ground, diffusing it in a wide arc.

In the faint light I could see him squatting on his haunches and I heard scraping. A small glimmer of a match, then another, larger flame. The flame grew, and the clearing began to flicker in the glow of fire taking hold on the end of a wooden torch that was wound with black rope.

'There.' Kurt stood, holding the burning torch away from him. 'That puts some light on everything.'

I stayed where I was, scanning the small clearing. There were pine needles littering the ground here. Nobody had come to sweep them, to leave the smooth circle of hardened dirt that was a constant of the main clearing. The trees around the edge were denser than in the other clearing, too, as if they were closing in, hiding it from the outside world like a guilty secret. The forest was wrapping itself around this place, sending out roots to burrow beneath it before pushing upwards and breaking the floor. Lifting in humps like aquatic monsters showing their backs above water.

The flames from the torch jumped in the breeze that filtered through the trees like the devil's breath, casting shadows behind the protruding roots, giving them movement, as if they were living creatures, writhing across the clearing to escape our intrusion.

Without speaking, Kurt made his way around the area, lighting other torches, these ones almost as tall as me, thrust into the dirt like fence posts. When they were alight, they created further shadows, the whole place alive with movement. I could hear the flames twisting and flickering.

In the centre of the clearing, a boulder was half-buried in the dirt. Large, rounded, smooth. Like a giant blind eyeball, sunk into the forest floor, it stared up at the clear sky, seeing nothing. Its surface was blotched and mottled. White in places, dark in others, where moss and fungus had left their mark.

Kurt thrust his torch into the ground, collected his flashlight and switched it off. He stalked over to the stone and ran his hand across the top. 'They say that once you've laid eyes on Lake Toba, you can't ever bear to be away from it.'

'I like that.'

'It's just for tourists, though. Something to write on the brochures to get the foreigners to come and spend their money. Take only photos, leave only footprints, that kind of shit.'

'But they'll never forget it,' I said, thinking about the first time I'd laid eyes on it. 'You don't forget something like that.'

'True, but it doesn't mean you can't live without it. And there are other things here that'll stay in your heart. Things you *really* won't want to live without. Things that'll keep drawing you back. The lake is just one of them.'

'What other things?'

'One of them I can see in your eyes every time you look at Domino.'

He paused as if waiting for a reaction. I gave none.

'And this community,' he said. 'We're part of this place now. All of us who live here. The lake is as much ours now as anyone's. Did you know the Batak people believe this is the centre of the world? That all life originated here?'

I shook my head, wondering if this was what he'd brought me out here for: to open his arms and tell me we're all children of Toba. I hadn't yet seen anything in Kurt to inspire me in the way he'd inspired others, but maybe this place wasn't about him at all. Like he'd just said, it was about the *place*. Maybe that's what he was trying to tell me.

'The stone chairs,' said Kurt. 'The ones back there?'

'In the clearing?'

'Hm. We put them there. Michael and me. We couldn't find the real ones, the *original* ones, but there would've been some so we made our own. Took us days to get the rocks where we wanted them. We found a place out behind the longhouses where they were littered all over the hillside, so we picked out the right ones, pushed and rolled them into the clearing. They're not carved, but they're good enough.'

He leaned against the boulder and crossed his arms. 'You know why I was so sure there should've been stone chairs?'

'No.'

'Because this was here. This rock.' He unfolded his arms and put his hands on it again. 'You see, back there, where we live, that's where the village elders would've sat. I dunno, maybe hundreds of years ago. Discussions about daily life, meetings, judgements, that kind of thing.'

I walked further into the clearing, moved around the boulder, ran my hand over its smooth surface.

'But here,' he said, slapping the rock. 'This is where people died. Right here on this stone.'

I removed my hand, snatching it away as if the rock had instantly become hot.

'I just can't believe how no one ever comes here,' I said. 'I mean, if you're right, then this place must be of interest. Historically.'

'If I'm right?' said Kurt. 'Why wouldn't I be right?'

'I didn't mean—'

'There are other places like this. On Samosir you can see something like this in Ambarita.'

'I read about it.'

'In a guidebook.'

'Yeah. In a guidebook.'

'I guess people don't know about this one,' he went on.

'Someone must know.'

'*We* know. And we keep it to ourselves.'

'No one ever comes up here?'

'Occasionally they come. They've heard about us or they stumble on us, and we welcome them. But it doesn't happen often and they never come this far. Why would they? Why would anyone find *this* unless they were looking for it?'

'And the people who come,' I said. 'They don't tell others?'

'We ask them not to.'

I raised my eyebrows. 'You must ask them very nicely. For them to actually not tell anyone, I mean.'

'It doesn't make any difference, Alex. Who would they tell, and what would it matter? People leave us to it.'

'Except for Richard,' I said. 'Didn't he send the police up here one time?'

'We don't have to worry about that kind of interference any more,' Kurt replied. 'We have someone to take care of that now.'

'How d'you mean?'

'We have a good place here, Alex; we like to keep it that way. It's calm, relaxing. A kind of haven. It's a way of life and we like to keep it. Domino told me you have no family; no ties to the outside world. No one to give a shit. Except for us, of course; we're your family now.'

I didn't like the way he said it, but he was right.

'It's best that way. It means we can be here without any interruption. Without any influences.'

'What about Sully?'

'Sully? Who told you about him?'

'He had ties, right? That's why you had trouble with Richard. That's why he sent the police up here.'

'Sully's gone,' Kurt said. 'We don't talk about it any more. And the thing with the police . . . well, I guess that's why outside influences need to be kept low. We don't want that to happen again.' Kurt smiled, the orange glow from the torches smothering his face, giving life to shadows that distorted his features. 'Michael heard you talking to Helena. Asking about going down the hill.'

'And you're worried that if I go down, I'll do something to jeopardise this place?'

'Maybe.'

'I won't,' I assured him.

'Domino must see something in you otherwise she wouldn't have brought you here. We've accepted you, shown you something of our home. I'm hoping I can trust you to be part of our way of life.'

'Sure,' I said, thinking maybe Kurt was a little too strange for me to want to spend a lot of time with him. 'But I'm not sure how happy Michael is about it. He doesn't like me.'

'He just takes a while to get used to new people, that's all.'

'Seemed friendly enough when I first arrived.'

'What matters is that Domino wants you here.' He leaned across the stone. 'You like her.'

'I do,' I told him. 'And so do you.'

'Of course.'

'You and Domino—'

'But she likes you,' he interrupted with a smile that looked more like a grin, 'and that's what's important right now. She likes *you*. Maybe more than you realise.'

I wondered once again where he'd been when Domino and I had been alone in the longhouse on my first night. Had we, perhaps, not been alone at all?

'I wanted to show you around,' he said. 'That's the real reason I brought you here. You need to see everything before you decide whether or not you want to stay.'

'I thought I already decided,' I said, not believing this was everything. There was more to this place. More to Kurt. 'I did that when I jumped off the cliff.'

Kurt made a noise that sounded like it might have been a laugh but I couldn't be sure. It might have been a dismissive sound, as if to say that jumping off the cliff had been nothing, just child's play, and that the real test was to come. 'Yes,' he said. 'The cliff. You did well. You looked brave when you did it.'

'Anyone ever refuse?'

'Of course.'

'And what do you do?'

'We push them off. After that, it's up to them.'

I waited for him to laugh, smile, anything, but I realised he was serious. 'You just push them off? And they don't get hurt?' My mind went back to the night I had jumped. The sound of another person hitting the surface, struggling. Distress in the water. I imagined something like that happening to Sully. I wondered if he had sunk into the depths of Lake Toba and this community had kept it hidden. I could believe such a thing of Michael and, maybe, Kurt. But Domino? Helena? I wasn't sure they would be a willing part of such a conspiracy.

'It was Domino who pushed Helena off,' he said.

It explained why she was so determined to jump that night. She hadn't done it before. Not herself.

'Some of the guys went down to make sure she didn't drown. After that it was up to her if she came back up. She decided to come.'

'Why?'

Kurt shrugged. 'She wanted to be here. There was some-one . . . waiting for her.'

'Michael?'

'Not exactly.'

'Who, then?'

Once again Kurt shrugged as if to say, 'What does it matter? Things are what they are.' He sat down and leaned his back against the smooth stone, beckoning me over to sit beside him. I hesitated. I considered whether or not I wanted to sit, almost as if I were deciding whether or not I wanted to stay with him in this place; stay with *any* of them in their strange little community, living together in their longhouses, pretending the outside world didn't exist other than to provide them with supplies and something to look down on from their tower. But then I saw Domino's face in my mind and my resolve softened. If she was here, then I was prepared to stay a little longer.

I went over to Kurt, lowering myself beside him, leaning against the rock.

He was silent for a while before he spoke. 'The Bataks who lived here,' he said, 'they were cannibals.'

I didn't look at him.

'I don't mean like bones through their noses, explorers in a pot kind of cannibals. They didn't just eat *any*body.'

When he paused, I caught a hint of sound from somewhere in the forest: a primal, animal noise that shrilled and was then gone.

'Criminals mostly,' he said. 'They'd bring them right here, to this rock. That's what it was for. They'd put him over the rock and torture him to scare away the evil spirits. Chop off his head, cut him into pieces, eat his heart and his liver, drink his blood. Village elders first, then the rest of the villagers got their share. Ate him till there was nothing left but bones that they'd throw into the lake.'

'Sounds disgusting.'

'Yeah, disgusting all right. Sometimes they tied a man to a stake, worked themselves into a frenzy, then ate him alive, cutting pieces off him. Took a long time to die, I reckon, but they only did it to convicted criminals – and people who consented. The ill and the old.'

'Well, that makes it all right then.'

Kurt made that noise again, the one that might have been a laugh and might not. 'They had some strange customs but they weren't savages. You know, most of them are Christian now?'

'Yeah, I know.'

'Sure you do; you've read the guidebooks. You prepared yourself before you came. You knew you were coming to Toba to see the lake. You'd go to Samosir to see the longhouses, maybe go to Tuk Tuk to smoke some dope like a hippy, score some Frank Sumatra and kick back. After that you'd go to Brastagi, see the volcanoes, say you'd been up Gunung Sibayak, maybe even Sinabung if you're really brave. Aceh, Bukit Lawang, all the tourist spots. Then Bali, to Kuta, to dance and drink and live like a westerner abroad.'

It was, pretty much, my intended itinerary.

'You came here as a tourist, Alex, and we're giving you the opportunity to live here as something else. Not as a native, though. Something . . . *else*. Like nothing else. You live here, Alex, you're like nothing else in the world.'

I wondered if Kurt really believed we were *that* unique. There might be people living in places like this all over the world, all of them thinking they were the only ones. Perhaps another community, right here on the banks of Lake Toba.

'Like I said before, Alex, the day you jumped: do you want to be a tourist, or do you want to be something different? Do you want to see this country, or do you want to see into your*self*? Find out who you are?'

For all his bullshit, Kurt understood. He'd seen what I was looking for. My life had stopped when my mother's illness deteriorated, and I had stagnated. I hadn't felt like a person, more like an extension of someone else. I had watched her die while I weighed my choices, wondering what I could do for her, and then I'd had to carry the consequences of the decision I made. But now I was free, I wanted to find myself again. Be who I wanted to be. If I even knew who that was.

'Stay with us a while. See what we have here. Find a new peace. That thing you're looking for?' He leaned across and tapped my head. 'It's right here. All you have to do is find it. Happiness isn't about getting what you want, Alex, it's about appreciating what you have.'

'How would we ever get any better, then?' I said. 'If we never try to get something we don't already have – or be something we aren't already.'

'Don't overcomplicate things, Alex. Just sit back and let the experience wash over you.'

I looked at him now, nodding. 'I think I'd like to stay a while,' I said. But it wasn't because of him and his speeches. Him, I could live without.

'So do that. Settle in. Be one of us before you go looking for a way out.'

'A way out?'

'Michael said you were talking about leaving, remember?'

'I was planning on coming back.'

'Stay a while longer,' he said. 'For Domino. No more talk of leaving.'

'OK.'

'Good.' Kurt tipped his head back against the rock and looked up at the sky. 'She'll be pleased.'

I thought about her, pictured her as I had first seen her, an angel coming to my rescue as I lay on the warm road, surrounded by blood and death. Then I saw her as she had been when we were together on the hillside, watching the lake and making love for the first time. I remembered the way she had looked with her hair spread on the uneven ground, tangled among the grass, her eyes squeezed shut one moment then locked on mine the next.

Kurt reached into his top pocket, his fingers working to grip something, but I ignored him, thinking only of Domino now.

'Just one last thing,' said Kurt. 'And then you'll be part of our group.'

'Hm?'

'Just one more thing.'

I looked down at what he was holding. A small box, wooden from the look of it, but it was difficult to tell in this light. He opened it and took something from inside. Tiny, almost invisible in the fingers he held out to me.

'What is it?'

'You eat it,' he said, taking my hand and placing a small tablet in my palm. 'And you enjoy it.'

I stared at the small white object, innocuous and yet sinister, staring back at me. Something unknown. Another part of the adventure.

'Eat it?' I asked, feeling my throat become dry, my tongue click in my parched mouth. I could feel the hard rock of the execution stone against my back. 'You're not trying to drug me up,' I said, trying to lighten the moment. 'Put *me* over the stone?'

'Don't joke about that,' Kurt said. 'There are souls all around us, watching everything we do. I've seen them. We all have. You will too.'

'Souls?'

'Swallow it,' said Kurt. 'And stay here a while. Think about . . . well, think about whatever you want to think about. Whatever is most important to you.'

'And then?'

'And then Domino will come.'

I looked at the tablet again. 'What is it?' I asked.

'It's an eye opener,' he said.

22

When Kurt left, I looked at the tablet resting in the palm of my hand. I picked it up between finger and thumb and turned it around. No markings. Just a white tablet. I didn't know Kurt and I didn't know what he'd given me to swallow. I felt like I did when I had looked over the edge of the cliff and considered jumping. The risks were almost the same, or at least that was the way I saw it at that moment, sitting in the dark, resting against a rock that had been used as an execution block in some distant past.

I mulled over the possibilities in my mind. I could go back to the others, tell them I'd taken the tablet, but I didn't know what effects I was supposed to feel. There might even be someone out there, right now, watching me. Kurt, maybe. They'd know I hadn't taken it and they'd send me back down the hillside, make me leave Domino behind. I wasn't ready for that yet. I wanted to be with her despite my reservations about Kurt.

If I had thought about it more deeply, though, I might have realised that I had broken free of the prison that had been my mother's illness just to stumble into another incarceration. The only way I was going to be free was if I left it behind me, turned away from Domino and Kurt and everything that had happened to me. Right then, I couldn't see that, and I stared at the tablet, wishing it could tell me whether it was something sinister that would make my kidneys bleed, or if it was something else: something that would show me a new experience. But I couldn't back out now, and for ever wonder what would have happened, so I made a choice. I put the tablet between my teeth and closed my lips around it. I shut my eyes and swallowed. Then I opened my eyes and looked at the sky.

The stars were clear and the dark heavens were full of them, the tiny pricks of silver touching almost every part. And they were brighter than I had ever seen them. Not like the faint stars at home. Here the sky was a sequinned curtain, every inch decorated and glowing.

I felt nothing from the tablet. No obvious signs of pain or discomfort. Normal. Perhaps it wouldn't show me anything other than my ability to let go. I had let go for just one second and taken a risk.

For a while I stayed as I was, staring up at the sapphire sky above me. I watched the stars, tried to identify the constellations using my rudimentary knowledge of such things, but mostly I just saw patterns with no meaning.

Still I felt nothing from the tablet and I began to wonder if it was a joke; another initiation into Kurt's group.

After some time sitting with my shoulder blades against the smooth surface of the execution rock I shifted my weight, pushed myself away from the stone that had seen blood. I stood and looked at it, pondering how many people had been stretched across it, their organs removed for eating, their blood spilled for drinking; how many souls had touched it and then moved up into the cleared circle in the canopy above me.

I contemplated the rock, not sensing that I was spending longer over these things than I usually would. At first I didn't notice the increased awareness, but as soon as I did, I wondered how I could have missed it, and my thoughts opened like a flower. My tunnelled mind, which had once been a pin hole, was now a gaping chasm. A small receiver which had become an entire listening station – an *array* of satellite dishes hungry for input. I became alert to everything around me, as if I were a part of the forest. I was the rock and I could sense the tiniest traces of each soul that had passed across me. I could feel the anger and the pain and the sadness of every body that had been stretched across it. I was the earth beneath my feet, the collector of the blood that had been spilled. I was each individual tree, the silent spectators at every execution, every banquet of human flesh. I was the curtain of stars above me, each one having looked down without judgement on events that had unfolded in this place.

I was part of it all, but my mind was not too tangled with its surroundings to understand that I was feeling the effects of what Kurt had given me and it inspired in me a great respect and love for him for having given me this opportunity. But as quickly as I had begun to feel love and respect, so my mind switched, like a train reaching a series of points, changing rails in rapid succession.

I turned from clear, pure feelings to tainted jealousy and disgust. He had been watching us. Domino and me. He had been watching us when we were in the longhouse. I knew it because I was part of the trees again, and I knew what they were thinking, what they had seen. So now I was there, like a bird on a branch, watching Domino and myself coming out of the longhouse, Kurt sneaking out behind us. Only he wasn't Kurt any more. He was something else. Something darker. His body was stooped, his shoulders enlarged, his legs short and crooked. He moved like nothing I'd ever seen before, a stuttering move-ment, his body rolling from side to side as he twitched and spasmed from the longhouse. He stopped and sniffed the air, jerking in my direction, cocking his feral head towards me and looking up into the trees. He knew I was there, watching the watcher. He stayed like that for an eternity, staring up at me, his eyes dead wood, his carved face devoid of expression, like the dreadful facade of the *singa* masks that hung over the doorways, then he moved away, flinching and twitching into the forest, lost in the darkness.

Then I was no longer in the trees, but back in the clearing, touching my hand to my head, staring at the rock in front of me, now soaked in a dark syrup, which I knew was blood. And when the word passed into my head, the liquid on the rock sprang into focus, glowing the brightest red, the thick rivulets sliding down the rock, pooling in the dirt and forming clotted clumps around its base. I stepped back as if the blood might come to life and reach out for me, but it remained where it was, glowing, unnatural in the night.

I turned to look at the trees, approaching the nearest and seeing the tiniest detail on its bark, the orange glow from the torches casting a rainbow of glittering colours across the ancient wood. And as I contemplated stepping among them, the trees merged into a solid wall around me, their trunks becoming one as they enveloped me, blazing in their new colours, their surfaces singing to me, their odour powerful and intoxicating. I knew I would be able to pass among them like a ghost, though, and I dissolved, melted into a cloud of invisible vapour, ready to become one with them, to be a part of something bigger.

But as my being began to melt into nothingness, so an angel appeared before me, dispersing the trees and coming into the clearing like a divine messenger parting the clouds and dropping to earth as a feather. The angel glowed with a billion colours shimmering around her body, a halo illuminating her entire being. She held her arms out to me, my widening eyes almost incapable of swallowing such a wondrous sight.

She came to me with open arms and a smile so knowing that I felt as if the angel had looked into my heart and seen all that was inside.

'An angel,' I heard myself say, the words having substance as they escaped my lips. Like a glowing vapour, scented with earth and pine needles and sweet water, each aroma surpassing the next, like a rolling cloud of ever-changing odour.

'Not an angel,' she said. Her words, too, were tangible in the night, the colours mingling with those of mine, the two breaths snaking around each other, both visible for some time before they became one, glimmering together, rising over us, reaching for the curtain of dazzling stars.

The angel stood before me, watching, smiling, before coming right to me and putting her arms around me, melting into me, her limbs sinking into mine, becoming part of me. I put my mouth on hers, drawing us together even further and I felt her breath pass through me, warm and sweet.

'Christ, I want you,' I heard my voice say.

Then, with a sensation of two things being torn apart, an almost painful feeling, she stepped back and stared into my eyes. 'Really?'

'I want every part of you,' I said, as if someone else were speaking the words for me. 'Everything.' I pulled her to me again. 'I want to be inside you. Come into the woods. Let's feel what it's like to do it under the trees.'

'This isn't you talking. This is . . . something else.'

'No. Take me into the trees.'

'You're sure?'

'More than anything.'

So the angel took my hand and turned to lead me back into the forest, but my legs were rooted into the ground. I could feel their extensions, burrowing under the dirt, clinging to the earth. They weren't my own. They were numb, hardened like wood.

'Come on,' she said, no longer an angel now. Now she was Domino, her golden hair bathed in the glow of the stars.

'I can't. I can't move.' And I felt a panic stir in me; a panic that grew like a fungus, rapidly spreading, gripping me, smothering me, tightening its fist around my heart.

'You *can* move,' she said. 'It's just the trip. Try thinking through it. *Break* through it.'

I closed my eyes and concentrated on moving my legs, breaking them free from the ground, and after a few moments one of my legs was my own, then the other, and I pulled them away, moving them in front of me, one at a time.

'Good,' she said. 'That's good.'

I let her take me among the trees.

'Let's go further in,' she said. 'Let's go where no one can see us.'

When she stopped walking, I brought her down to the ground beside me where I could smell her, sense her odour emanating from every pore on her skin. I leaned towards her and kissed her, my lips tingling with the heat from her body, my fingertips electrified as they caressed her face and ran through her hair. She put one hand on my face in return and it sent a wave of colour and sensation through me that made me want to explode with joy, burst into tiny fragments and scatter myself across the forest. This was what life should be. It should be about joy and love and this incredible intensity of feeling. It shouldn't be about boredom and existence, living just so that we may die.

'We should do it,' I said, pushing her back onto the ground. 'Right here. Now.'

'Are you sure?'

'It'll be amazing. Like nothing ever before it.'

'It's really what you want?'

'Yes. It's what I want.'

And as we joined together, in the forest, my skin alive with a battery of feelings, my mind awash with colour and scent, I looked down at my angel. But the face that looked up at me, contorted with pleasure, did not belong to Domino.

It belonged to Helena.

23

When I woke, it was light and Domino was leaning over me, looking down. 'Shit,' she said. 'I've been looking for you for ages.'

She held out a hand and I reached up to take it.

'You need to get up,' she said as she helped me to my feet.

My head felt peculiar. Detached. The pressure of a headache but the euphoric memory of last night's experience. The confusion of what I saw coloured by unusual pleasure.

'The others are looking for you.'

'You weren't here before?' I asked, rubbing my eyes and glancing around. The trees were just trees, the sky was just sky, and I was just Alex.

'No,' she said.

It was still dark, but not as dark as it had been when Kurt and I were resting by the boulder. It felt as if our conversation had happened quite some time ago – days, although I suspected it was more like hours – and the atmosphere was very different. There was a duskiness to the light, as if the day was breaking somewhere over the lake, and the first traces of reality were seeping among the trees like mist.

'I don't understand,' I said. 'You sure you weren't here before?' It had felt so real.

'You mean someone was here with you?' She looked concerned, and for the first time since opening my eyes I really saw her expression. She was pale and tired, her eyes ringed red, the whites shot with tiny rivers of blood.

'What's the matter?' I asked.

'Something happened last night.' Domino kept hold of my hand and pulled, taking me back towards the clearing. The torches were out now, no flame from them at all, not even a hint of smoke. I slowed and stared at the rock, remembering how I had seen it last night. The detail on the surface, the blood, the wisps of soul. I had to tear my eyes from it as Domino dragged me in the direction of the path leading back to the main clearing.

'What's the hurry?' I said. 'What's happened?'

'An accident.'

I stopped and pulled against her, making her halt. 'What kind of accident?'

Domino tried to tug at me one more time, but I was stronger and she gave up, her shoulders slumping. Defeated, she leaned against the nearest tree and slid down it. She put her hands on either side of her face and gripped her hair, pulling it back. 'It's all going to shit.'

'What's going on, Domino? What kind of accident?'

She looked up at me with glazed eyes. Dark lines on the soft skin below.

'Tell me.'

'It's Matt.'

'Matt? What about him?'

'He's dead, Alex. Matt's dead.'

I stared at her, collecting my thoughts. I'd felt a great sense of belonging last night, a sense of intoxication that had stayed with me even when I woke, but now it was gone. As if someone had stepped into my opium den and whipped back the curtain to let the harsh light in. I processed Domino's words. I let them spin around my hazy thoughts, clearing away the last remnants of last night's exhilaration, wondering. 'Is this another one of Kurt's games?'

'Games? No, Alex. No . . . he . . . he was just there, lying on his back.'

'For real? This is for real?' The sensation of falling. The

approach of fear. Not the kind of fear that grips you and squeezes, but the kind that slips up your spine, sinks its roots into your stomach and feeds on you.

'Kurt told me to come get you. He wants everyone there. Wants everyone to see.'

'To see what?'

'I found him,' she said. 'I came out to look for you. I was supposed to come and get you. I should have come earlier, but . . . but I found him.'

I sat beside her, not knowing what to say, putting my arm around her shoulder. She was shivering, and being beside her like that, I realised the air was cold, the sun hadn't yet begun to warm the trees. I held her closer, tighter. I pushed away any fading memories of last night, of the incredible feeling of being inside her, being part of her. 'What did you find?' Comforting her gave me a feeling of strength that wrapped itself around the fear. I admired Domino's confidence but when she was like this I felt more connected to her. Like this she was mine, not Kurt's, not the community's.

'I walked into him,' she said. 'Just walked into him. I think I stepped on his hand. Something under my foot. Hard, like a twig or a branch or something.' She stopped and stared as if seeing it all again. 'It was still dark.' She gripped the fingers of her right hand in her left, bending them backwards then releasing them in a quick movement. 'I thought it was just a twig.' She repeated the action over and over as she spoke, taking the fingers in her fist and crushing them together. Her joints cracked. 'But it wasn't a twig.' Her eyes unseeing. 'It was his fingers snapping. When I stood on them. I can hear them now. I can hear them snapping under my feet.'

I squeezed her tighter, letting her shivering rattle through me. I wished I had something to give her. A drink. A cigarette, maybe. Something for her to do with her hands instead of wringing them together like that. 'It wasn't your fault,' I said, feeling their emptiness as soon as the words fell from my mouth. Of course it wasn't her fault.

Domino stopped shivering and looked at me. She opened her mouth as if to say something but stopped. She closed her eyes, tightened them like she was trying to squeeze out what she had seen. 'We have to go back,' she said. 'Kurt's waiting for us. He wants us all to be there.'

'He can wait.'

'No.' She pushed my arm away and got to her feet. 'We have to go. He's waiting. They're all waiting.'

I stayed where I was, watching her stand. Now it was her turn to look down at me and I saw that she'd changed, as if she'd slipped on a mask. She was no longer the fragile and distraught girl who'd been shivering beside me just seconds ago. I'd seen this before. She flicked a switch and she was Domino again. Strong and in control. I wondered how she did it. How she managed to shift her emotions from one state to another so quickly. Like a chameleon changing its colours to suit its environment.

'Come on,' she said. 'They're waiting.' And she turned, began walking along the path.

I watched her, half expecting her to stop and turn again, but she didn't. She kept on walking until she was out of sight, so I hurried after her, catching her as she reached the end of the path, and we came into the clearing together, Domino leading by a footstep.

The others were gathered in front of the longhouses, standing in a group around the body that lay on the ground.

He was lying face up. Matt. His eyes closed, his stumpy dreadlocks dusted with soil and pine needles. His arms crossed on his naked chest and his legs stretched out beneath his sarong.

As we approached, I was unable to look away from him. I had played football with him, jumped with him, smoked with him, but now he was nothing. Lifeless. Like my mother lying in her coffin; like the old woman on the road whose life had vanished before me. The sight neither disgusted nor shocked me, but it disturbed me. Everything about what I saw was wrong.

This wasn't where he'd died and it wasn't the position in which he had been found, and it was wrong, to my modern mind, that someone had moved him. My knowledge of death was that it was left to the authorities; that it was *they* who should move the body. Not us. Particularly because Matt was young, healthy, and his now cold and waxen face was bruised.

Nevertheless, Matt had been arranged and now his friends were watching him. Most of them were there – everyone except for Michael and Jason. Kurt, as usual, was in the centre of it. All eyes were on the body, as if some grim acceptance had gripped each of them, but they looked our way when we joined them.

Kurt was the last to look over at us, as if he were unable to take his eyes from what lay before him.

Domino stopped, facing the others, and I came alongside her, reaching down to take her hand, but she pulled it away from me. She waited for Kurt to reach out to her, then she went to join him, to take her place in the semi-circle. The others looked away, their eyes back on Matt. All except for Helena. She continued to watch me, her face less hardened than the others.

I stayed where I was, wondering if Kurt's invitation extended to me. I felt a strong sense of not understanding a ritual that the others seemed to know. A sense that the scene before me was wrong. Unnatural. As if some other force had taken them over, made them different from me. I was an outsider again, while they behaved as one, all knowing how to react. Perhaps that was why Domino's mood had changed so suddenly. For a moment I had seen her as she really was – vulnerable and fragile – but *this* Domino, the one I was seeing right now, was the person who belonged here, with Kurt and the others, standing in their semi-circle, staring down at the body of a fallen brother.

In that moment I despised Kurt, the self-appointed leader for these people, but then he extended his hand to me, and I had a sudden and overwhelming feeling of belonging that made me believe these were my people, too. I was one of them, just as Matt was. I had been accepted and I could take my place with Domino. I would do as they did. Perhaps this *was* where I truly belonged.

24

I hadn't known Matt well, and I didn't feel the loss the others felt, but he'd treated me as a friend, and I understood their grief. A part of the community had been torn off and cast away.

We stood in silence for some time before Michael brought Matt's best friend to join us. Jason must have been forewarned because his face was white beneath his scant beard. It was the face of someone preparing for something terrible.

He didn't look at any of us as he came to kneel beside his friend, staying like that for a moment before easing back and sitting on the ground. He bent his head forwards, and we stood in silence.

When he looked up at us, his face was a curious mixture of sadness and fear. 'I told him not to take it,' he said, as if the words were rehearsed, speaking them like an automaton. 'I fucking told him.' He shook his head. 'He wouldn't listen, though. You all knew what he was like. Always looking for the next thing. The next way to get high.'

He stopped and we waited for him. We waited because Matt was *his* friend.

Jason wiped the palm of his dirty right hand across each eye and went on. 'He was all fired up. Doing the jump the other day. The thing with Alim. Someone new coming. He wanted to celebrate, do something he'd never done before. I fucking told him not to, though. I told him not to take it.' As he spoke, he looked only at Kurt, and when he was finished, he lowered his head and stared at the ground, his hair falling forwards to cover his face.

The others standing with me were watching Jason with intent, digesting his words, believing them. But I was concerned that no one was asking any questions, and when Jason lifted his friend's head into his lap, a livid mark was visible around Matt's exposed throat before Jason leaned forward to cradle the corpse, hiding it from view. I looked around at the others, but saw no reaction. It was as if they didn't see what I did. Or as if they didn't want to.

It was Kurt who broke the silence. He took a step away from the semi-circle and bowed his head for a few moments before beckoning Jason, hugging him and patting his back. With that done, he turned to us, sweeping his eyes across each one of us. His gaze fell on me last, as if he were gauging my reaction, then he took a deep breath and cleared his throat. 'As hard as this is, we all have a decision to make.'

I glanced across and saw that Helena was watching me again.

'There's no decision to make,' Jason said, standing up. 'He wouldn't want to be anywhere but here. We're all he had.'

Kurt nodded and scanned the group once more. 'Does everybody agree?'

A few people nodded, some mumbled, Michael spoke aloud, his voice clear. 'Yes. We all agree.'

Kurt let his eyes meet mine again, holding them there. 'We *all* agree?' he said again. 'We sure?'

'Yes,' I heard myself say, and I shifted my gaze to see Helena still watching me. I had no idea what I had just agreed to, but the way Kurt looked at me, I didn't think I had any other choice.

'Then we should start right away,' said Kurt. 'Michael, bring the *cangkuls*.'

The semi-circle began to break apart now, some leaving alone, others in pairs, but they all headed in the same direction into the trees. I looked about me, wondering what to do next. Everyone else seemed to know what they were doing, as if they had specific roles to play in such a situation. But I remained where I was, because Domino stayed still beside me.

'You're one of us now,' Kurt said, coming closer. 'Go with Michael. We have a burial to attend to.'

I looked at Domino. 'A burial? I don't—'

'Go on,' said Kurt. 'What are you waiting for?'

I hesitated, once again glancing at Domino. 'You're going to bury him?'

'*We're* going to bury him,' Kurt said.

'But we can't.'

'What else would you have us do?'

'I don't know, maybe—'

'Please,' Domino said. 'You're with us now.'

I faltered, torn, looking for an alternative. There were two paths for me to take. I could stand alone and be apart, or I could fall in line and be one with the others. With Domino.

'Your choice,' Kurt said, as if he knew what was in my mind.

'Please,' said Domino. And still I was under her spell, so, with terrible doubts, I chose what I thought to be the easier path. I turned to follow Michael, catching up with him as he reached the back of the longhouse.

He snapped his head round when he heard me approach, his whole body stiffening. 'He send you to help?' His manner was suspicious.

'Yeah, but I'm not sure what's going on here. I mean, shouldn't we get a doctor, or the police or something?'

Michael came close to me. 'Matt's dead. He doesn't need a doctor, and he sure as hell doesn't need the police. What you think *they'd* do?'

'I don't know. Help?'

'They'd turn this place over and move us all out, *that's* what they'd do. Put us all in prison.'

'Prison? I thought Kurt said he had someone . . .'

'They know the kind of shit we get up to,' he butted in, too fast, not waiting to hear what I had to say. 'Drugs, that kind of thing, but they leave us to it. They leave us alone to get on with it because we don't disturb anyone and we don't get in anyone's way. And because Kurt has a guy in the police and because every now and then the right people get a nice little gift that keeps them happy. But we bring a body down, one that's died from OD, what the hell you think's gonna happen?'

I shook my head.

'They'll have to come up here, that's what. They'll come up here and they'll steal our way of life that we got. They find all these drugs and they see the way we live, they have to do something about it. They can't turn a blind eye when we stick it in their faces.'

'But we have to tell someone. I mean, what about his family? Doesn't he have any family?'

'Does he? Shit, I don't know. But if he had people out there he cared about, then he never mentioned them to me. Never told Jason. He wouldn't have spent so fucking long here, would he, if he had someone to go back to?' He stared at me, then sniffed and softened. 'That's why we're all here. You, me. We have no one else, Alex. No one to come looking for us and disturb the peace. We got too many connections, we're not allowed to stay, not since . . .' He shook his head.

'Not since Sully?'

'Kurt doesn't like outside influences.'

I remembered Domino saying something like that to me before, and it made me think about my own situation. No brothers, no sisters, no parents. No friends to speak of. No one to give a shit. No one to come looking for me if I didn't come back to England.

'The people here, Alex, *they* were Matt's family. Your family too, now. He had anyone else, he'd have gone to them a long time ago.'

'It still doesn't seem right,' I said. 'It feels like we should tell someone.'

'Who would you tell? We have our own way of dealing with these things.'

'This has happened before?'

Michael looked down at the ground, pursing his lips in deep thought before looking me in the eye. 'You know what would happen if they came up here, took a close look at the way we live?'

I didn't reply.

'You know what they do to people in this country when they catch them with drugs?'

I shrugged.

'They execute them, Alex. I heard about people getting put up against trees and shot without so much as a sniff of a judge. So what do you think's going to happen when they come up here with their guns and they find a bunch of crazy foreigners? Drugs, dead body. I wouldn't be surprised if some of them thought it might be fun to have some hunting practice out in the woods.'

'That wouldn't happen.'

'No? You think it wouldn't?'

I was about to reply, but Michael turned his back on me and continued moving towards the rear of the longhouse. 'They'll be waiting on us,' he said. 'We better get a move on. Show some respect for our friend.'

I followed him to the back of the longhouse where there was a small outhouse with a crooked wooden door covering its entrance.

Michael pulled back the door, the lower corner arcing in the groove worn in the hard dirt. He leaned into the gloom, half in and half out, taking something in his hand and passing it back to me.

'Take this,' he said, holding the *cangkul* out to me. A cross between a pickaxe and a shovel, I'd never seen anything like it at home. A smooth wooden shaft like a pickaxe handle, with a flattened blade fixed at a right angle at one end. I took hold of it and waited for him to pass out another.

With one in each hand, I stepped away from the outhouse, allowing Michael to come out, he too with a *cangkul* in each hand. He closed the door with his foot, pushing it into place.

'What about his neck?' I said. 'Did you see Matt's neck? The bruises on his face?'

'I didn't see nothing.'

'It looked like—'

'Enough talking,' Michael said. 'We got digging to do.'

I stayed where I was, undecided. We were going to bury a man without any contact with the authorities, and the notion of it was absurd to me. I came from a place where everything was steeped in law and formality, where our lives were governed and confined by every rule we had to obey. And yet here we were making our own laws, our own rules. It felt unnatural even if it was the most natural thing in the world.

'So we're gonna just bury him?' I asked. 'And that's it? No doctors, no police? As if nothing has happened?'

Michael came close to me, let me feel his size. 'You think of anything better?'

'What if he's not dead?' Even as I said it, the thought filled me with cold horror.

'He's dead,' Michael said. 'You saw him just like I did. There's no way Matt's alive. Anyway, Kurt's a doctor.'

'A kind of doctor,' I said. 'And no one seems to know what that means.'

'We already talked about that, Alex. You ask too many questions. Maybe you're not ready to be here with us.' He walked past me, making it clear he didn't want to talk any further, so I kept quiet and followed him out of the main clearing and along the path I'd taken last night.

The sun was creeping higher and its rays were penetrating the canopy above us. I looked up, seeing the sky among the firs, no clouds to dampen the sun. I wished that I was away from the forest, that I was sitting where I had been with Domino when I first laid eyes on Danau Toba. I wanted to see the sun glittering on the surface of the water and I wanted to taste the breeze that skimmed its surface. Instead I was compelled to follow Michael, deeper into the trees, closer to the place of execution where I'd been last night. Closer to the place of burial.

A couple of paces behind him, I watched as Michael trudged the path, both *cangkuls* in one hand, balanced over his shoulder. As always, he was without shirt. The muscles were tight in his back, bunched and sinewy, running the length of his torso and trailing into the top of his shorts. I wondered how long he'd been in this place, subject to the rules that I assumed to have been created by Kurt. He'd said the people here had no one to come looking for them, and it split my feelings between sadness and a sense of belonging. If what he said were true, then these people were just like me.

25

We came into the clearing where the execution stone lay cold, but Michael continued walking, back among the trees again, deeper into the forest. After a few minutes I saw people standing in a group, surrounding a patch of ground swept clean of leaves and pine needles. I could see where they had used their hands to tug foliage from the soil and throw it to one side to leave the ground exposed. They were standing around the bare patch in silence, apparently waiting for Michael and me to arrive.

A little further away, Matt was lying dead. Kurt and Jason sat beside him.

When we came closer, some of the people stepped aside to allow us through, and Kurt and Jason stood, coming over to meet us. They each took a *cangkul* from us and we moved apart far enough so as not to hamper the digging.

Jason struck the ground first, and the rest of us followed. The soil was dense and moist, shot through with a nervous system of roots, some like shoelaces and others as thick as my forearms. The digging was hard work, the *cangkuls* struggling to cut through the thickest roots, but everybody took their turn. The sweat was heavy on my brow when Alban tapped me on the shoulder and took the *cangkul* from me. I nodded as I handed it over and stepped away to let the digging continue.

I watched the hole become deeper and wider as each of us took a turn, and before long I found myself watching Domino hefting the tool over her shoulder and driving it into the soil. I saw the exertion on her face, the sweat forming in her hairline and the way her chest flushed with the effort. It reminded me of the day I had watched Helena cutting the tree.

When Chris took the *cangkul* from her, Domino came to stand beside me, breathing hard. Her hand reached for mine, encircled it and squeezed. I looked at her, seeing her eyes ringed red. She forced a tight smile and nodded.

By the time everybody had taken a turn at digging, the hole wasn't deep enough, so we began stepping in once again, taking over from those who were tired. I found myself digging with Helena, both of us standing waist deep in the hole that was now only big enough for two. I listened to her breath and I remembered what I had seen last night. I tried to understand why my mind had played such a trick on me. It must've been because of what happened in the lake. If it hadn't been for me, we might've already had one burial. Two bodies. I shuddered at the thought and found myself slowing in my digging, stealing glances at Helena until Alban stepped forward to relieve me of my duties.

Standing with the others again, none of us speaking, I watched Helena dig until she, too, was relieved, this time by Kurt, who resumed with great fervour, as if he, as leader, needed to assert his strength and resolve.

Helena climbed out of the hole and went to stand at the opposite side from me. For a moment our eyes met, and she held my gaze for a second longer than she needed to before she glanced at Domino and then looked away.

In all, the digging must've taken two hours, and it surprised me how quickly I became used to the idea that Matt was dead. This burial process was a catharsis for the group. By being physically involved in what was happening, we each bore a part of it, and I understood, right then, that what we were doing was not wrong. A benign acceptance came over me and I began to feel calm, almost glad to be here. This was his family, and a family is entitled to bury its kin.

My mind was only brought back into focus when I noticed a

shape, maybe twenty yards further in among the trees. It was difficult to make out what it was, but it wasn't natural. It wasn't a tree or a plant, the shape was too regular. It looked as if it had been made by man. No more than two feet tall, solid, square, out of place.

I leaned to one side, trying to see better, but whatever it was, it was partly obscured by the fronds of a fern. All I could see was hard-edged shapes in the forest. I could count at least three, but I had no idea what they were. A trick of the light, perhaps.

'Enough,' I heard Kurt say, bringing me out of my daydream, and I turned to watch him lay the *cangkul* aside and climb out of the hole. He dusted himself down, knocking the soil from his naked torso, then put out a hand and someone passed him his shirt. He pulled it over his back and buttoned it, looking around at us, saying, 'It's time.'

Jason climbed down into the grave and took hold of his friend as Michael and Kurt lowered him in. He held Matt under the shoulders and put him in the bottom of the hole, deep enough for him to be out of sight from those of us encircling his final resting place.

At my mother's funeral, the men had worn dark suits, dark ties. The women had worn dark dresses. Some had worn hats. Old women holding handkerchiefs to their faces. People even brought black umbrellas, but there was no rain that day.

When I looked around Matt's grave, the picture was very different. A truer representation of what Matt had meant to the people who were here to put his body into the ground. Sarongs, flip-flops, batik and bare chests. Fifteen of us like that. Fifteen faces turned towards Matt's grave. Fifteen people willing to participate in this ritual; the burial of someone they had lived with, slept with, eaten with. Fifteen people who considered themselves isolated enough to settle into this life without concern for that which they may have left behind them. Men and women who were barely even men and women.

I cast my eyes around the motley collection of people who believed themselves alone enough to adopt this lifestyle. A common bond dragging them together, forming a surrogate family that meant they were no longer alone. I wondered how many of them had found what they were looking for and how many of them had simply stayed because it was easy. Or because they had been persuaded by Kurt that this was what they wanted. And, for that reason, I was not like them. I was here only for Domino.

Jason climbed out from the grave and stood at the edge, looking down at his friend. He ran a hand across his short, untidy beard. The beard that tried to hide acne scars not more than a few years old. After a moment's silence he took a deep breath and spoke, his eyes still lowered.

'I . . . I don't really know what to say. You all knew Matt. He was a good guy. Never did anything to hurt no one. Never said a bad thing. Liked to have a good time. I suppose he could be a bit of a dick sometimes, you know, be a bit annoying, getting so bloody hyped up, running about like a lunatic, but . . . yeah, he was a good bloke. I'm gonna miss him . . .' He stopped speaking and swallowed hard, fighting back his emotions. He looked at Kurt, who nodded, urging him to go on.

'He was kind of like a brother to me,' he said. 'To us all, I know, but . . .' He looked down again and sniffed hard. 'He was like me. Brought me here. Found exactly the kind of place we were looking for. He told me he wanted to stay here for ever, chilling out, getting high, having a good time. He said . . .' Jason's voice became strained. He stopped speaking and we waited. I expected him to say something else, the way he'd finished, but he lapsed into a long silence, which was finally broken when Kurt stepped forward and handed a *cangkul* to Jason.

Jason took it and shovelled the first heap of dirt onto Matt's body. With nothing to protect him, the hard patter of soil fell on cloth and skin, like heavy rain on hardened ground. A prosaic and necessary end. It scattered across his stomach, fell into the spaces between his arms and his chest and, as with the digging, each of us took a turn at returning the soil to the hole we'd made. The ritual was coming to a close and we were hiding Matt beneath the trees. We were erasing him from the community, from this world, with only our memory of him to account for his existence. Once he was lying, dark and decomposing, becoming part of the forest, he would be gone, leaving nothing behind.

We each stepped forward when it was our time, and we kept our solemnity as we took the *cangkul* and threw the soil. I tried not to look at him when I cast it over him, tried not to imagine him sitting up and dusting it off or suffocating underground with the musty scent in his nostrils and a silent scream in his clotted throat. I tried not to imagine the grit beneath his eyelids.

The last part of him to be covered was his face, perhaps no one wanting to be the person to throw the dirt onto the one thing that identified Matt as our friend. But that honour fell to Jason, who stepped forward and said one last farewell to his friend. And then Matt was gone.

When the final heaps were placed on Matt's grave and the dirt that wouldn't fit back in the hole was smoothed out, Kurt stepped forward to the edge of the freshly turned soil and addressed us all. 'Matt loved this place so we give him to it. Everything comes from the earth and everything must go back to it. We won't mourn him, we'll celebrate him.' He looked around, making eye contact with each of us, finally staring at me. 'We all need to remember what's important; why we're here.'

Filtering back through the trees, I saw Kurt and Michael walking together in conspiracy. I hung back, catching just a snippet of their whispers, '. . . need to go see them . . .' and something about sending a message, then Domino took my hand and waited for them to overtake us. They stopped talking as they passed, Kurt nodding when he caught Domino's eye.

We stopped until they were out of sight, Domino telling me she wanted the others to move ahead before we continued. When we came to the area with the execution stone, she turned away from the path leading back to the main clearing and headed into the trees, moving deeper, towards the sound of rushing water. After walking for a few minutes, we broke out of the forest onto a hillside that was covered with rough scrub growing around black stones. We were above the place where the water fell from a crack in the rocks and splashed into the pool below.

'You remember when you jumped?' Domino said. 'You were pretty cool. What did you say? *You don't have somewhere higher?*'

'I don't really remember.' We stopped near the edge and I looked out at the water. 'Did *you* do it?' I said.

'Hm?' She looked round, jerking her head. 'Did I do what?'

'Jump.'

'Oh. Yeah. Everyone does.'

I sat down. 'You didn't get pushed?'

'Nope.' Domino remained standing, her hands on her hips. 'But it took me a while to build up the bottle.'

I looked up at her. 'Kurt brought you here, didn't he?'

'Uh-huh.' She watched my reaction, then cast her eyes back to the lake again.

'He was your boyfriend?'

Domino looked down at me again. 'Would that be a problem?'

I watched her for a moment without replying, then sighed and looked back at the lake. I didn't want to care that Domino and Kurt had once been together. I wanted to be care*free*, but I didn't want to imagine her with anyone else either, and I was angry with myself for feeling that way.

'Anyway, *he* brought me here,' she said, realising she wasn't going to get an answer. 'Introduced me to Freia, Michael and S— Well, there were only a few people here then.'

'You were going to say Sully.'

'Yeah.'

'It's a big deal he left, isn't it?'

'I don't want to talk about Sully.'

'OK.' I turned my face to the lake. 'So, anyway, you stayed. With Kurt.'

Domino sat down beside me. 'Yeah,' she said. 'With Kurt.'

'Did you ever bring anyone else here?' I turned to look at her.

'Only you. And I'm not with Kurt, if that's what you're going to ask next. He's—'

'I don't need to know. After what I've just seen, I don't think anything matters.'

'You think it was wrong to bury Matt?'

'Yes,' I said. 'And no.' For a moment, among the trees, I had seen it with clarity. I had understood it all. But now, away from everyone else, my acceptance was fading again. As if the distance weakened Kurt's spell.

'It's what he would've wanted,' she said.

'I suppose.'

'You hardly knew him.'

'True. But it didn't look like an overdose to me.'

'What?'

'Didn't you see the bruises on his face? I kind of forgot about them when we were . . . well, when we were in there digging. It was like we were somewhere else, all of us caught up in the moment, but now, out here, cold light of day and everything, I remember. He had some kind of mark across his throat, too. Like he'd been strangled or something.'

'Strangled? What the hell are you talking about, Alex? You some kind of expert?'

'No. I just . . . Oh, I don't know.' I paused, remembering something else. 'Has this happened before?'

'What?' She stared at me. 'No. Why would you ask that?'

I watched her, trying to read her hasty reaction.

'What made you say that?' she said, changing her expression, softening it.

'Everyone seemed to know what they were doing,' I said, still studying her. 'No discussion, nothing. It's like everyone just knew what to do.'

'Oh.' Her face softened further. 'We've talked about it before. You know, one of those discussions you have when everyone's stoned or drunk.'

'Yeah, that's common,' I said. 'Get high and talk about burying each other in the woods.'

'Come on, Alex, you know what it's like here. Surely you can understand? The people here, this is their family. It's where they want to be. Everyone's agreed it's what they want.'

'Even you?'

She turned away and looked at the lake.

'Look, I just think maybe we were in too much of a hurry to put him in the ground. Like maybe someone was trying to hide something.'

'Something like what?'

'I dunno, but don't tell me you didn't see those bruises.'

'So what would you have done, Alex?'

'Get someone to look at him, maybe.'

'Like who? Like an outsider? Shit, you have any idea what would happen if—'

'Save it. I already had that lecture from Michael.'

'Well, maybe you need to hear it again,' she said.

I was disappointed that I'd received the same reaction from Domino as I'd had from Michael and I understood that Kurt and this community were more important to Domino than I was. I'd hoped that I could tell her how I felt about what had happened, but I could see I was going to have to keep my thoughts to myself.

'So what do you do when you go back to Oz?' I changed the subject.

'Not much,' she said. 'Why?'

'No reason. Just getting to know you better, that's all.'

'You know me well enough.'

'Do I? I reckon I hardly know you at all.'

'Oh, I dunno, I think we know each other well enough.' She reached around and put her hand on my crotch.

I sighed and reached down to stop her. 'That's not what I mean, D.'

'Don't call me that. You never call me that.' She snatched her hand away.

'Kurt does.'

'You're not Kurt.'

'No, I guess I'm not.'

'And my life away from here doesn't matter. Only time I'm really me is when I'm here. *That's* the person you know. Can't that be enough for you?'

'It's only one part of you, though. I want to know more if I'm going to—'

'All right then: I see a few friends, get a job, earn some money, come back. Is that what you want to know?'

'So you *do* have friends, then? And you don't tell them about this place?'

'They wouldn't understand.'

'You mean you never told *any*one?'

'Some, but it doesn't matter. They'll never come. They'd never find it.'

'But if something happened to you, they'd have some idea where you were, right?'

'Nothing's gonna happen to me.'

'But if it did. It's not impossible. Look at everything that's happened to *me* since I got here.'

'They'd know I was in Sumatra. That I'd come to Lake Toba.'

'But not where?'

'Right. Not where.'

'So what about Matt?'

Domino shook her head. 'What about him?'

'Was he like you? Are there people who might know where he is? People who might come looking for him, like they came looking for Sully? People who might find out we just buried him in the woods?'

'If Kurt thought anyone would come, he wouldn't let him be buried there.'

'What, then? What would he have done?'

Domino shrugged. 'I don't know. Find somewhere to leave him, I guess. Somewhere he'd be found but not connected with us.'

'Find somewhere to leave him? That's fucking crazy, Domino. You can't just bury people without telling anyone and you can't just leave them lying around like a piece of meat. Like they're inconvenient.' Now that I was away from the group and the rest of the community, away from the forest and the burial, I could see the madness in it all again. It was as if my senses had returned to me. And even though I knew Domino was a part of it, I had to say it aloud, just to make sure I wasn't as mad as they were. 'You just can't do that. Not even Kurt.'

'Why'd you say it like that?'

'Like what?'

'Like that. *Kurt*. Like saying his name leaves a bad taste in your mouth.'

'Why do you care how I say his name?'

Domino and I stared at each other for a moment before I sighed and looked away. 'You have feelings for him, don't you?'

Domino stood up. 'I'm going back to the others.'

'Think I might stay here a while. Look at the lake for a bit.'

'Suit yourself.' She turned to leave.

'Stay with me,' I said. 'I don't want to argue.'

'It might be too late for that,' she replied without stopping.

I didn't watch her go, and it wasn't until the sound of her footsteps had faded into nothing that it occurred to me that she hadn't told me why she'd brought me out here.

26

Kurt had said something about celebrating Matt, not mourning him, but when I came back into the clearing, hoping to find Domino, I couldn't see any evidence of celebration. Helena was sitting on the steps of the rice granary with Alban, neither of them speaking, and I couldn't see anyone else around. The tables were empty. The place was quiet. It was hard to believe that just an hour ago, we'd all been in the forest, burying one of our friends.

I stood for a moment, surveying the area, wondering where everyone had gone, when something caught my eye and I turned to see Michael strutting from the back of the longhouse. He was carrying a tin of paint in one hand and a brush in the other. He nodded a kind of greeting before coming towards me.

'Where is everyone?' I asked.

'Gone.'

'Gone? Gone where?'

'Different places. Some just down to the *kampong*, get a few things. Others maybe over to Parapat – who knows?'

'And Domino? Has she gone, too?'

'Saw her and Kurt going down the track. She looked pissed off about something.'

I stared across the clearing, wondering if I could do the same. The prospect of escaping for a while was an enticing one. If I left, saw something other than trees for a while, breathed some different air, maybe I'd come back to Domino as a new person. Maybe things would make more sense.

'You should stay here,' said Michael from behind me.

'Hm?'

'I said you might as well stay here. They left twenty minutes ago. You probably wouldn't catch them till you get all the way down. And there's nothing you need to do down there.'

I looked at him, standing shirtless with a paint tin in one hand and a brush in the other.

'There isn't, is there?' He narrowed his eyes. 'Anything you need to do, I mean.'

'No, I just—'

'No one you need to talk to.' He put down the tin and brush, drew back his shoulders. 'Nothing you need to tell anyone.'

'No.' I shook my head. 'I wanted to see Domino, that's all.'

'She'll be back.'

'When?'

'Why not help me out? Do some painting. You'll be surprised how relaxing it is. Good thinking time, and I reckon you need a bit of that. When we're done, she'll be back. You can make up then.'

'Make up?'

'Something pissed her off, Alex, and I'm guessing it was you.'

I stayed where I was, looking at Michael then back to the path again.

'C'mon, Alex. What d'ya say?'

'I think I'll go after them,' I said, making a move.

'I don't think so.' Michael came forward and put his hand on my shoulder. His grip was tight. 'I think you should stay right here and help me. Give yourself some of that thinking time I told you about.'

I made myself relax, not wanting to cross him. Perhaps there would be a moment, later, when Michael turned his back. If I was going to get away, it would have to be then.

'Put things into perspective,' he said.

'OK,' I submitted. 'So, what are we doing, then?'

His scowl became a smile. 'We're making the place look pretty. Come on, we need a couple more things.' He sauntered back to the small hut behind the longhouse from which we'd taken the *cangkuls* that morning. I waited while he opened the door and leaned in. To my right, I saw a flash of colour and turned to watch a butterfly flitting among the trees. With movements that seemed almost haphazard, it blinked in and out of view until it came into the clearing and settled on the ground close to my feet. As if to display its beauty to me, it opened its wings to parade its vivid orange and white and black markings, almost like a tiger's. Seeing it right there, barely any movement, an image of Hidayat's butterflies flickered through my mind, but then Michael retreated from the hut with more paint and the spell was broken. The butterfly lifted without a sound and retreated the way it had come, disappearing into the forest.

Together we set up two trestles fashioned from rough pine trunks. The unplaned wood still had its bark, covered with rivulets and beads of resin, which had oozed like blood from its wounds and hardened. There were nail heads protruding in places, large and round, not completely hammered in. We stood them close to the longhouse that served as our home, laying a crooked plank across them and climbing up, taking the paint tins with us.

'You ever painted a longhouse before?' he asked.

'Sure,' I said. 'I do it all the time.'

'Then you'll know what you're doing.' He stared at me like he wanted to put his fingers round my throat and squeeze. Maybe he would, if it weren't for Domino.

'How hard can it be?'

'It ain't hard,' he said, popping the tops off the tins, revealing the paint inside. Red, black and white. The only colours that were on the main longhouse, the one that was already decorated.

'You paint the other one?' I asked.

'Mm-hm.'

'It looks good.'

'It does.' He arranged his tins and brushes so they were within reach.

'Did it take long?'

'Couple a months.' He handed me a brush.

'What's inside?' I ran my fingers over the tip.

'Nice try.'

'You don't like me,' I said. 'You don't trust me.'

'I thought you were one of us. But the way you were talking this morning, I think you still got a long way to go.'

'That's why you stopped me from leaving? That's why you didn't want me to go after Domino? Because you think if I leave I'm going to tell someone?'

'This place is important to us,' he said. 'To some more than others.'

'I can understand that.'

'So we have to protect it.' He looked at me. 'Domino likes you, you must be OK. Maybe I was a bit hard on you.'

I shrugged. 'Nah, not really. It's just weird, that's all. I mean, we buried someone this morning. Like it's normal.'

'It *is* normal.'

'Is it?'

'I'm trying hard to like you, Alex, but you're not giving me any reasons. Matt was our friend and we loved him. We did what he woulda wanted.'

'Sure. Of course. Sorry. So are we going to do some painting, then?'

There were designs all over the side of the building, some larger than others, and I watched Michael pick out a carved relief of a lizard and begin painting. I followed suit, choosing a large *singa*-mask design that had been carved into one of the thick wooden struts.

'How long you think these have been here?' I asked, changing the subject. I could see traces of paint etched into the veins of the dark wood and I used the barely discernible colour as my guide.

'Years. Maybe hundreds.'

'No idea who built them?'

'Nope. Nor who lived in them. All I know is we fixed them up, made them somewhere to live.'

'You put the roofs on as well? Most of the ones I've seen have corrugated iron.'

'Me and some others. Kurt, Freia. Took a long time collecting all that fibre. And it has to be higher at the front. Took us a while to get that right. It's supposed to mean the father of the house wants his children to reach higher in life than he has.'

'And we're all Kurt's children,' I mumbled to myself.

'Hm?'

'Nothing.' I reloaded my paintbrush.

'And did you know the father always sleeps at the front, with the children in the back?'

'Kurt told you that?'

'Yup.'

'So, me sleeping right at the back means something?' I said. 'Like I'm the least important.'

'You got that right. Only advantage to being *there* is that there's an emergency exit.'

'Emergency exit? I never noticed it.'

'Well, it's there,' he said. 'Right by your bed. Only alteration I made of my own. Back door. Always gotta have an exit strategy.'

'Is that so?' I squatted down to paint the lower section of the *singa*.

'Oh yeah.'

'So how long did it all take?' I asked, keeping him talking. 'Fixing it all up?'

'Still doing it.'

'But up to this point?'

'Few years.'

'A few years? How long have you been here?'

Michael didn't even turn to look at me as he spoke. 'Four, maybe five years. Sometimes it's hard to remember.'

'But you leave from time to time, right?'

'What's it to you?'

'Just making conversation.'

He paused, his brush coming to a stop on the wood. 'Yeah.' He looked down at me. 'I leave sometimes.'

'You go home?'

'*This* is my home.'

'So where do you go?'

'You ask a lot of questions.'

'Getting to know you. Give you a few reasons to like me.'

He smiled, a twitch, then it was gone. 'You know Kuta?'

'In Bali?'

'Yeah, in Bali.' Michael loaded his brush and continued painting, the muscles in his forearms bulging and relaxing with his movements.

'You go to Kuta? We're talking about the same place, right? Bars, clubs, partying. *That* Kuta?'

'That's the one.' Now Michael was smiling, too. A real smile. It was the expression I'd seen when I first came to the group. 'My guilty pleasure.'

'I bet Kurt loves that,' I said, wiping the tip of my brush, using a different colour for the *singa*'s black eyes.

'You'd be surprised.'

'But I thought he hates places like that. I mean, the way he talked to me about it—'

'Sometimes talk is just talk, Alex. Even people like Kurt got to party sometimes. And he's full of surprises. Just like Domino.'

'Oh yeah, she's full of surprises all right.'

'You like her.'

I used to think I was falling in love with her, but after our last conversation, I wasn't so sure. But I was still drawn to her. There was still something strong. 'Yeah, I like her.'

'Like me and Helena.'

'You're together?'

'Kind of.' He avoided a real answer, changing the subject. 'It bothers you Domino's gone off with Kurt. I can tell.'

I stopped painting, the brush still touching the wood, and I pictured Domino and Kurt walking down to the *kampong*. Perhaps he would put his arm around her, pull her close.

'It shouldn't,' he said.

I started painting again, rubbing the brush hard against the rough wood, pushing the black paint into the crevices.

'He's her brother,' he said. 'You know that, right?'

'Yeah, I know that. We're all brothers and sisters here, right?'

'No,' he smiled. 'I mean, like, they really are brother and sister. Kurt is Domino's brother. They're blood.'

Michael didn't let me out of his sight that day. Not once. He even followed me to the dunny, but I was too preoccupied with my own thoughts to care too much. What he had told me about Kurt and Domino made so much sense. It explained their closeness and, despite myself, I couldn't help feel as if a threat had lifted. I had tried not to care about their relationship, to be relaxed about it, be more like Domino was, but the stain of jealousy had always been running below the surface of those thoughts. No matter how hard I tried to be someone else, I hadn't been able to suppress myself, and there was a degree of relief now that I didn't have to bury that any longer.

We painted for the rest of the morning, but I had no idea how long we were at it. I still couldn't help looking at my wrist, even though my watch was long gone. I'd wanted to try to relinquish my control over everything, and this place was helping me to do that. Without the touchstone of time, there was no way for me to slot everything into its place.

We stopped for an hour or so at lunchtime and sat to eat fish and rice. Helena was there, but she was quiet and I thought maybe she was still thinking about the burial this morning. I would've liked to talk to her about it but when I tried to make conversation, Michael distracted her and she became quiet and withdrawn.

We painted some more after lunch, going right through until dusk, when we sat round the table again for something to eat. There were only six of us at the table for dinner: me, Michael, Helena and Alban, who had loitered near Helena all day and was drawing vicious looks from Michael. Jason stayed in camp, but had been quiet, moving in and out of the woods, saying nothing to anybody, joining us only when there was food on the table. Evie was there, too – a petite girl, maybe the same age as me. From behind she could be mistaken for a boy. She had elfin features and a good nature, always smiling. She generally stuck close to Alban, making me think they were together, but today he'd been showing a lot of interest in Helena.

After we'd eaten, Michael said he had a few things to do and disappeared into the longhouse that was kept locked. I watched him go in, then I went to the fire by the kitchen and sat down to drink a warm beer. My neck was aching from looking up at the longhouse all day, and my eyes were beginning to close because I'd hardly slept last night.

Helena came over and sat down beside me, offering me a joint. 'There's stronger if you want it.'

I accepted it, saying, 'No, this is enough for me. I didn't take anything at all before I came here.' I thought about Matt and wondered what he'd taken that was strong enough to put him in the ground. If that's what had really happened. I stared at the fire for a while without speaking, then handed the joint back to her. 'You come over here to avoid Alban or talk to me?'

She laughed. 'You noticed that? He's been hanging round me all day. I thought Michael was going to burn a hole right through him the way he was looking at him.'

'Yeah, I think he likes you. Michael, I mean. But I get the feeling it doesn't go both ways.'

'He isn't my type.'

'Have you told *him* that?'

'He doesn't listen. Won't hear it.'

'I can believe that. Kurt already told me he has a short temper, that I don't want to fall out with him.'

'Kurt said that?'

'Yeah. And someone else told me he once killed a man with his bare hands.' I held my fingers like claws in front of me. 'You think that's true?'

Helena smirked. 'I've seen him angry, but . . . Who told you that?'

'Jason, I think. Maybe Matt.' Saying his name made me think of his body lying there in the dirt, with those marks on his neck. I wondered if the marks had been made by a man's fingers. The kind of man who could kill another with his bare hands.

'Well, if it's true, then I guess you should keep away from him.'

I looked at her, seeing a serious expression before her mouth cracked a smile.

'I'm just kidding,' she said, but behind the smile, there was a glint of something else in her eyes. As if there was a little doubt.

'So, anyway, where did you guys meet?'

'Me and Michael? Sari Club in Kuta. You ever been?'

'No.'

'I thought he was pretty cool, but he's different here.'

'I know that feeling,' I said, and we fell into a comfortable silence before Helena spoke again.

'About what happened . . .' she started. 'I—'

'It's OK,' I said, not wanting her to thank me again for saving her. 'Anyone would have done the same thing.'

'What d'you mean?' She looked confused.

'I'm not brave,' I told her. 'I just swam faster than Michael so I got to you first. Not sure he was so pleased about that, though.' I was proud of what I had done that day in the lake, but I didn't want to make a big deal of it; partly because there was a risk of angering Michael, but also because I'd seen *her* face when Domino came to me in the forest. I was worried that what I had done for Helena was confusing my feelings for her. If she felt like she owed me something, she might be more inclined to attach herself to me.

'Oh,' she said. 'No, I meant—'

'I thought Alban was with Evie,' I deflected her.

'What?' She watched me for a moment, then shook her head and looked at the ground. 'Oh yeah. Kind of. I'm not sure really.'

'So why's he chasing *you*?'

'You think I'm not worth chasing?'

'I didn't mean that. Of course you're worth chasing. You're beautiful.' The words came out before I realised I was going to say them and I was surprised to feel my cheeks flush.

Helena noticed it, her eyes lifting to mine as soon as I said it. She smiled and I looked away.

'Sex and death,' she said, taking a drag. 'Maybe that's what got into Alban. Something makes them go together, isn't that what they say?'

'I haven't heard that.'

'Don't you feel it, though?' She glanced around before putting her hand on my knee. 'I don't mean like violent death. Not like that. I think it's about the grief. About wanting to be with someone. The *right* person.'

'I don't know. Maybe.' I stared into her blue eyes, then looked down at her hand on my knee. She had long fingers, not one of them adorned with a ring. Her wrists were also without jewellery of any kind. I tried to think about Domino, but couldn't picture her in my mind. Instead I saw Helena, as I'd imagined her when I was in the forest.

'Alex?'

'Hm?'

'I wanted to talk to you about before. Last night. This morning.'

'This morning?'

'Yes. In the forest. We—' But even as she felt for the right

236

words, Michael came out of the second longhouse, turned as he reached the bottom of the ladder, and stared over at us.

'Don't reckon he's too happy about us talking,' I said, raising a hand to him.

'No,' Helena answered.

Michael began to acknowledge the greeting, then he shook his head and stalked over to where we were sitting. 'I need some help,' he said, his face serious. His eyes were on me but I wasn't sure if he was talking to me.

'More painting?' I asked. 'In this light?'

'Not you.'

'Me?' said Helena.

'Mm-hm. There's stuff to deal with back here.'

'OK.' Helena held up her joint for him to see. 'Just let me finish this and I'll be there in a minute.'

Michael faltered between leaving and staying. He opened his mouth to speak, but closed it again before turning on his toes and returning to the longhouse. He looked back once, before climbing the ladder and disappearing from view.

'What's in there?' I said to Helena.

'You didn't ask Domino?'

'No. It didn't feel . . .' I let my words trail away. 'I think maybe I was afraid she wouldn't tell me. I don't want to be unimportant to her.' Just like I hadn't asked her about Kurt. Part of me didn't want to know the truth – didn't want to *face* the truth.

'Stay with her long enough, you'll probably get your own key.'

I looked at Helena, seeing a change in her demeanour. I wondered if I'd said something wrong.

'Only three people have one,' she said.

'Should you be telling me this?'

'You're one of us now, right?'

'I guess so.' I thought once more about what we had done this morning. I had been a part of the ritual, too. I had stood with the others and buried Matt. And it felt wrong. 'You said you wanted to talk to me, before. Was it about Matt?'

'No.'

'What, then?'

'It can wait. The moment's gone.'

I studied her expression, wondering what had changed her mood. She wouldn't look me in the eye. I waited for her, but she continued to stare at the longhouse where Michael was expecting her. 'So what *is* in there? You'll tell me, won't you? Now I'm one of us.'

'Our livelihood. It's where we keep what we sell.'

'Sell? You mean drugs? You sell drugs?'

'*We* sell drugs.' Helena nodded.

'I . . . Jesus.'

'Does it bother you?'

'I don't know,' I said. 'Yes. No. I mean, I know about drugs here, but . . . isn't it dangerous? Doesn't it bother *you*?'

'It's mostly just grass. Some wacky stuff. Hippy shit, not killer shit.' She said it like it was nothing.

'No, I mean dangerous like what if someone gets caught?'

'I never thought about it like that. Kurt has someone who looks after that.'

'You never thought about it? But they execute people in this country, right? That's what Michael said. He said they shoot people for drugs here. Surely it's gotta be worse if you're selling the stuff.'

'Wouldn't happen. Kurt has someone.'

'Kurt has someone.' I sighed and looked across at the longhouse, thinking the more I found out about this place, the less I wanted to stay here. I wanted to be with Domino, but didn't want to put my life up for it. Didn't want to be *executed* for it. 'And they keep them in there?' I said, wondering how much was inside, how many bullets it would buy for us all. Would they line us all up together, or would they shoot us one by one?

'It was a while before they let me in. I suppose they wanted to know they could trust me, that I was going to stay here. Won't be much longer before they ask you to earn your keep.'

'How d'you mean?'

'Sell,' she said.

'What?' I thought about what Domino had said, what Michael had told me. One of the reasons they didn't want to tell anybody about Matt's death was that they didn't want anyone to come here, to find what we had in the community. Now I understood that a little better. What we had here wasn't only for our own use. And to take it away from here, to sell it and risk detection – I knew right away that I wouldn't ever want to do *that*.

'You remember those guys who came up here the other night?'

'Of course.'

'I guess they have other people, but we sell for them on Samosir and around Parapat.'

'All of you?'

'Some more than others. *I* don't go out so much. Kurt still likes me to stay close. Says it's 'cause I'm a good cook, that I'm good at looking after everyone, but I think he's worried I still have doubts after . . .' She bit her lip and looked over at the longhouse.

'After what?'

'Nothing.' She forced a smile, still staring. 'Anyway, the tourists take to us better. Kurt says they like to see a white face, something familiar. Makes them trust us more. So we do the selling. Keep it in there, take it down and sell it. The money goes in there, too.'

'So this place is basically just a drug factory,' I said.

'Hardly. We don't sell enough for it to be that. This country isn't the backpacker haven it used to be. And you know this place is much more <u>than</u> that, Alex. This is just to make a bit of money.' It sounded almost like a line, a way of justifying it. Someone else's words, perhaps.

'I bet Kurt takes his cut, though.'

Helena shrugged. 'I don't know why he would. He never goes anywhere. And anyway, who cares? We have enough to eat and to drink.'

'And that's all you want? It doesn't matter you're risking your life?'

'Kurt says that won't happen, that he has a man—'

'In the police, yeah, yeah.' I shook my head. 'I don't know, Helena; drugs, burials, guns – this place is starting to scare me.'

'Enough to leave?'

'Not sure it's what I want any more. It's not turned out to be quite what I expected. It's not exactly paradise, and I don't fancy getting shot.' I thought about Domino, but watched Helena, our eyes meeting now, long enough for it to mean something. 'And you?' I asked, still holding her gaze. 'You ever thought about leaving?'

'Yes.' Her eyes shifting to the longhouse. 'I have.'

'And?'

'It's not that easy. I don't have anywhere to go.'

'Nowhere?'

'Nowhere. No *one*. Just like you, just like everyone else.'

'Except Domino and Kurt. Brother and sister.'

'Yeah.' Helena turned her body towards me, stealing a look at the longhouse before leaning closer and lowering her voice. 'Alex, can we talk later?'

'Of course. What's wrong?'

'Not here,' she said. 'Not now.'

'When?'

'Later. Somewhere quiet.' She moved away from me and stood up as we heard voices.

Others were coming into the clearing. Kurt and Domino were the first, their expressions serious. Then Freia and Morgan, carrying rucksacks on their back, heavy from the look of them.

I stood, intending to go straight to Domino, but she immediately looked away when she saw me approaching. She said something to Kurt, then broke off from the group and moved quickly towards the longhouse Michael and I had been painting earlier that day.

'Leave her for a moment,' Kurt said, coming to me. 'She needs some time alone.'

'Is she OK?' I could see the resemblance. Brother and sister. That's why they had always looked so well suited to each other.

The others moved around us, going about their business, lighting lamps, preparing food. Michael climbed down from the longhouse, locking the door behind him.

'She's had a rough day, what with Matt and . . .' Kurt shook his head and looked at the ground for a moment before putting his hand on my shoulder. He turned me towards the fire and encouraged me to walk with him. 'Come on,' he said. 'Let's get something to drink.'

I glanced back at the longhouse, seeing no sign of Domino, then resigned myself to spending a few moments with Kurt while he regaled me with more of his stories and philosophies. I'd go after Domino later, tell her I was sorry.

Kurt stopped beside Michael, asking, 'How have things been today?'

Michael looked at me and shrugged. 'OK,' he said. 'Pretty quiet.'

Kurt nodded, not saying anything for a couple of seconds before re-setting himself once again as if he'd forgotten the smile he'd shown me a few moments ago. 'Let's have a drink,' he said. 'We brought beer.'

Morgan and Freia set down the rucksacks they'd been carrying and opened them. They began taking out bottles of Bintang beer, placing them on the table in the kitchen area. I could see that the bottles were still cold, condensation sweating on the green glass, soaking the red and white label.

Michael let out a loud cheer and went over, the first to take a bottle. He put his mouth on the top, pulling off the cap with his back teeth and spitting the jagged metal out into his hand. He raised the bottle to us all, turning once on the spot, said,

'To Matt. Our friend and brother,' then tipped back his head and drank the entire bottle in one long chug.

When he had drained it, he slammed it down on the table and helped himself to another. He used his teeth to remove the cap once again and raised the bottle to his mouth before stopping to look around at us all staring at him. 'What?' he said. 'We gonna have a party or not?'

27

The beer was good. Not cold enough, but good. Someone brought out a CD player and a set of fresh batteries, put some music on and turned it up loud. There were joints and pipes and beer, people dancing, letting off steam, so I guessed it was the kind of party Matt would've wanted as his farewell. This must've been the reason why they'd all gone down the hill today: to bring back supplies for the party.

Some of the others hadn't yet returned, but it wasn't long before they began appearing from the forest carrying rucksacks filled with beer and food that wasn't fish and rice. There was *nasi bunkus*, fresh fruit, *rendang*, bags of roasted peanuts, containers of chicken curry.

Within half an hour or so, the place was overflowing with food and drink and Matt's wake was in full swing. Perhaps we weren't so different here after all.

I drank my beer and watched the others with interest, but my eye kept straying to the longhouse, wondering when Domino would make her appearance.

'She'll come out when she's ready,' Kurt spoke into my ear. 'It's been a tough day.'

I nodded, staring into the fire, cradling a beer in my hands. 'I guess she liked Matt a lot?' I asked, remembering her mood when I last spoke to her.

Kurt shrugged. 'It's always hard when something like this happens. Domino's very emotional.'

'Mm.' In the short time I'd known her, I'd seen enough to confirm it.

'And death does strange things to people,' he added.

My mother's death had cut me free from responsibility and filled me with guilt. Helena thought death made her want to be close to someone.

'Don't worry. She'll come out when she's ready, but look.' He pointed to the far side where the last people were emerging from the forest. 'Something we have to do. You're going to like this, Alex.' He slapped me on the back and stood, encouraging me to follow him to the place where Chris and Eco were coming into the clearing, sweating with the exertion of what they were carrying.

'You like pork?' Kurt asked me.

'Sure, I . . .'

The pig was about the size of a large dog, but considerably fatter. Its black body was tied to a wide stretcher made from pieces of bamboo as thick as my arm. It wasn't fully grown, but it looked heavy and I could see the fat wobble beneath its thick hide. Chris and Eco put the stretcher down in a way that looked practised – as if they'd done it a number of times on their climb up to the community. The strain was evident in their faces, and I didn't envy them their journey, but there was a sense of appreciation, because as soon as they were among us, everybody stopped what they were doing and gathered round to look down at the animal. I had assumed that it was dead, but coming closer, I saw it open its eyes and roll them in delirium. The animal twisted in its newly returned fear, but the ropes that criss-crossed its body were too tight and all it could do was open its mouth and squeal.

Michael stepped to the front of the crowd and squatted on his haunches, slapping his hand on the pig's belly. He looked up at Chris and Eco, nodding, saying, 'Good pig.' He turned to stare directly at me. 'Alex, give me a hand.' He went to the front of the stretcher. 'Take the other end. Helena, bring my things.'

There was something in Helena's look – pity, fear, I wasn't sure what. The light from the fire was deceptive; it hid our true expressions behind shadow and false movement. I watched her for a second, then did as I had been asked. I went to the other end of the stretcher and bent my knees, taking the handles. I put as much into the lift as I could muster, not wanting to be inferior to Michael's obvious physical strength. Then, led by Kurt, we carried the pig across the clearing, into the forest and along a path I had come to recognise. We were going to the execution stone.

We moved through the trees like the funeral procession Matt never had. Around us, the others lit the route with torches, both electric and flaming. The muscles in my arms burned with the strain of the pig's weight, and my fingers began to slip from the bamboo grips. I tried to focus, estimating the distance left to travel, mindful of the pitfalls of the path. But when I stumbled, it was Freia who came to help take the weight of the stretcher. She nodded to me and winked before looking straight ahead, walking alongside me. As we moved, others took the weight on either side – Jason, Alban, Morgan – and when we came into the clearing where the execution stone stood, there were at least six of us carrying the beast.

We laid the pig down and waited while Kurt lit the torches, and I watched as Michael took his machete and cut the ties that held the pig in place. The animal struggled to its feet, but its ankles were still bound with rope and its cloven hoofs slipped between the bamboo slats of the stretcher, stumbling and skittering, the two hard surfaces clicking together until it managed to push itself upright and stand. Any chance of escape impossible, it moved across the clearing in faltering hops, its eyes rolling, its head moving from side to side.

Helena came through the gathering and handed Michael the things he had asked her to collect for him. The first was a long, narrow knife, which he slid into his belt, and the second was a short-handled axe, which he hefted in one hand before turning to look at his audience.

I took a step back so that I was among the others but Michael spotted my movement. 'You want to do it, Alex?' He held out his hand, offering his axe.

I shook my head.

'You sure?' He let his arm loosen, the weight of the axe dropping it straight down so it swung parallel with his leg.

'I'm sure.'

'Oh yeah, I forgot. You don't like to kill things.' Then, with no warning, he took a step towards the pig, raising his arm, the axe swinging high above his head. He brought down the back of the tool, the blunt edge of the darkened steel blade, in one movement, a swift and merciless gesture. The cold metal made a flat and hard slap against the pig's skull and the animal's legs buckled beneath it.

It fell dead without a sound.

'You ever see a thing like that?' Alban said into my ear. 'Didn't even have time to squeal.'

Michael leaned the small axe against the execution stone, then he slipped the narrow bladed knife from his belt and crouched beside the beast. Again, with just one fluid movement, he jabbed the blade, puncturing the pig's throat, and withdrew it as if he'd done nothing more than slide it into warm butter. He stood and stepped back, admiring the gush of blood that drained from the animal, spilling in a great pool by his feet. A dark puddle of life that glistened in the glow of the flaming torches, reflecting their dancing light.

When the flow had stopped, one or two others went over to help him drag the body away from the blood, and he took a flaming torch, passing it over the lifeless body, burning away the hairs that covered its skin, the singed smell mingling with the stink of fresh blood. They worked quickly, turning the pig over to rub the torch over its other side.

With that done, Michael put his hands on his hips and looked at those of us who hadn't yet participated in the slaughter of the animal. 'You wanna eat, you gotta help,' he said, looking directly at me.

I had already helped. I had carried the animal to this place. And anyway, I wasn't sure I wanted to eat it. Not after witnessing that.

'What's the matter?' he asked, seeing my discomfort. 'Where do you think meat comes from? A plastic bag?'

'No, I—'

But Michael didn't give me time to reply. He came straight to me, putting the narrow-bladed knife in my hand, curling his bloody fingers around mine, pulling me towards the body lying on the ground. 'Come on,' he said. 'Let's get you bloodied.'

I could feel it on his hands, warm and sticky.

'Here.' He squatted beside the pig, bringing me down with him and tightening his grip around mine on the handle of the knife. 'Let's do it together,' he said. 'Like brothers.' And before I could resist, he touched the blade against the animal's belly and drew it lengthways from between its hind legs, right along to its throat.

The sharp blade sliced through skin and fat and flesh. There was little resistance. There was an almost poetic simplicity to it. It wasn't repulsive – as I had thought it would be – but, instead, there was a mesmeric quality to the way the steel carved through the animal, separating its layers. Only when the viscera bulged out and spilled at my knees did I close my eyes so as not to see it, but then all I could see were visions of the bus crash, the mess of broken bodies, dismembered limbs, the man who had split like a wet balloon, the blood and the despair.

'Well done, brother,' Michael said, turning to look at me, our faces close together so that I could smell his breath, and although he called me 'brother' there was something in his eyes and something in his voice that suggested he might have preferred to run his steel across *my* belly, spill *my* guts at the foot of that execution stone.

All that remained now was for Kurt to remove the pig's head, which he did with several strong blows from Michael's *parang*, and some show was made of leaving it, along with the glistening entrails, beside the stone.

'An offering,' Michael said to me.

'To who?' I asked.

'Christ knows,' he shrugged. 'The gods?'

Later, I sat by the fire, drank beer and watched them dancing. There was still no sign of Domino and, although I had tried to go to her, Kurt had stopped me. So I sat alone and thought about how Michael had slaughtered the pig with such expertise, and I remembered the stories Matt and Jason had told me. The pig was butchered now, the carcass left out in the woods, and the flesh was cooking over the fire, but my hunger was not stimulated by the smell of meat. I couldn't rid myself of the cloying taste of fresh blood. It didn't seem to bother the others, though; most of them were on their feet now, moving to the beat of the music, some of them with their faces raised to the sky. I studied them through the numbed haze of my own alcohol-induced intoxication, admiring how freely they moved, as if they were alone, each of them twisting in isolation. Even Kurt was among them.

From the main throng, Helena caught my eye, her narrow hips swaying, her bare feet scuffing in the dirt, her skirt lapping at her calves. She flicked her hair from her face and held her hands out to me, still moving, beckoning. I smiled, shaking my head. I was no dancer. Even with the dope smothering my thoughts I was still too inhibited. In fact, the drug swelled my inhibition, brought it to the fore and the mere thought of dancing with the others induced feelings of paranoia. No matter what I tried or believed, I was who I was. I was never going to be anyone else. Since coming to this country I had always been following other people, always been doing what they wanted me to do, always been trying to be someone else. I could see that with a clarity I hadn't had before, and knew that all I needed now was the courage to walk away. But if I did that, I would be without Domino, and I wasn't sure I was ready for that.

Helena persisted, moving towards me, her body twisting like a snake. She smiled, tossing her hair, reaching down to hold her skirt higher, flicking it around her knees in time with the music, lifting it to her thighs before laughing and dropping it again.

As before, I shook my head at her, but she had no intention of giving up on me, coming right over, taking my hands and pulling me to my feet. I had no choice but to join her and the others; she had made it impossible for me.

I followed her and began dancing. Self-conscious and awkward, I angled my head to the ground, but Helena put one hand under my chin and raised my face to look at her, and she danced like that, one hand on me.

When the song came to an end, I took the opportunity to leave, moving away from the area where the others were dancing, but Helena pulled me back as another song began. A slow beat, quiet but building up to something.

'You don't like to dance?' She came close and spoke in my ear.

'Not much of a dancer.'

'Me neither,' she said, her lips almost touching my skin. 'This helps, though.'

She leaned back and held out her hand. A tablet. Similar to the one Kurt had offered me.

I glanced over at the longhouse, wishing Domino would come out, wishing she'd take me away from this place. 'I'm fine,' I said. 'I just want to chill out.'

'Forget about her,' Helena whispered in my ear.

'What?'

'Take it,' she said. 'You'll feel better. Dance. Have a good time. It'll be just like it was before.'

The others were dancing around us now, Helena starting to move again, her hand extended, the tablet rolling from side to side on her palm as she swayed.

Around us, the others continued, their faces contorted with

the efforts of their movement. Each of them moving faster now as the music began to build.

I noticed Kurt among them, caught his eye. He held me like that for a second, then closed his eyes and turned away. Behind him, standing still among the other dancers, Michael did not avert his stare.

I looked back at Helena, shaking my head again. 'I'm fine,' I repeated. 'Really.'

Helena persisted, snatching her hand shut, coming close to me again. I began to turn, made a move to leave, but she put her arms around me, pressed her body against mine, her thigh squeezing between my own, her pelvis crushing against me. She reached up with her right hand and touched the tablet to my lips. 'Take it,' she said. 'Take it and dance with me. Hold me. Do what you did before.'

'Helena, no. Stop.' I pushed her hand away. 'I should go and find Domino.'

'Please,' she said, grabbing my arm, one last attempt to keep me there, but I snatched it from her grip, making her twist and stumble. She put out her arms to steady herself, but she'd lost her footing and wheeled backwards, trying to regain her balance with each step. Unable to keep herself upright, though, she finally fell back, knocking into the other dancers as she collapsed in the dirt. The people whom she'd bumped simply glanced down at her and continued, their minds elsewhere, no doubt encouraged by the chemicals racing through their blood.

Helena stared up at me, shaking her head, an aspect of confusion. But even as I watched her, wondering what to do next, her expression melted, faded, dropped from her face only to be replaced by one of sudden understanding followed by embarrassment and shame.

I immediately felt my heart become heavier and I felt sorry for her, so pitiful in the dirt. She hadn't meant for this. She was trying to reach out to me, to make a connection.

I went to her, extending a hand down for her, but before I could get close, Michael appeared at my side, his fist driving straight into the spot just below my breastbone, taking my breath and dropping me to my knees.

I lifted my face to him, wanting to ask what he was doing, but my lungs were empty and I only managed to produce a sucking noise. Michael showed no mercy for my condition, though, and hit me square on the nose, knocking me sideways onto the ground as blood erupted from my face. My instinct was to put my hands behind my head, protect my face with my elbows and roll into as small a ball as I could manage. I felt Michael punch me once more, this time in my unprotected kidneys, then I heard Helena's voice calling him off me. But Michael hadn't yet had his fill and he hit me two or three more times before Kurt ordered him away. This time, Michael did as instructed and stepped back with one final kick to my ribs.

I stayed where I was, curled into a ball, wishing I were somewhere else. Anywhere but here. And, with blood on my face and bruises forming on my body, I decided I would leave this place. As soon as it was light, I would leave here and never return.

'C'mon, up you get,' I heard Kurt's voice and felt someone pull my hands from my head. 'Come on. It's all over now.'

I snatched my hand away and took my arms from their protective position. I looked up at Kurt and the others, humiliated and full of hate.

'No harm done,' said Kurt.

In response, I touched my hand to my nose and brought it away, contemplating the blood on my fingers before looking at our great leader.

'You'll be fine,' said Kurt. 'Some cold water, a towel, you'll be fine.'

I stood, staring at Kurt, then at Michael, who was standing behind him. There was murder in his eyes, his fist clenching and unclenching. He hadn't finished with me. If Kurt hadn't stopped him, I think he might have carried on beating me until I was dead. Killed me with his bare hands.

'Now, why don't you two make up?' Kurt said. 'It's been a

hard day for everybody. We don't want to start fighting among ourselves.'

'You saw what he did to her,' said Michael, still staring at me. 'Kick the fucker out. Kick him out or kick him in. I can dig another hole out there in the forest just for you.' He pointed at me.

Kurt spun round and slapped Michael across the cheek. 'Sort yourself out,' he said. 'You want me to kick *you* out? I'll have no one talking like that.' He looked round at the others, silent, the music still playing in the background. 'That goes for everyone. We're brothers and sisters here, so we'll fucking act like it. We have a disagreement, we sort it out. We shake hands and we bury it.'

'I'll bury *him*,' Michael muttered, earning another slap. He turned and glared down at Kurt, the two of them sizing each other up, Michael's face a contorted picture of aggression, Kurt's a calm mask of forgiveness.

'Time to make up,' Kurt said.

Michael remained fixed, then the moment broke and he turned his head to one side. When he looked back, he was the Michael I'd first seen. His smile was back and he was nodding at Kurt, stepping towards me, his hand outstretched.

I was too taken aback to do anything other than return the gesture and shake his hand.

'No hard feelings,' he said, leaning in to speak more quietly. 'Just steer clear of Helena. I see you do anything other than treat her like a lady, I'll cut your throat and leave you in the forest to bleed like a pig.' And all the time he said it, he smiled.

'Good,' Kurt said when we'd shaken hands. 'Now go get yourself cleaned up.'

'Let me help him.' Helena spoke for the first time since Michael had hit me. She came forward and said the words in a quiet voice. Almost a whisper. 'It was my fault.'

'How was it your fault?' asked Kurt.

'I . . .'

'Let him clean himself up,' said Michael, taking her hand and leading her away.

Helena looked back at me, an unspoken apology on her face. She hadn't meant for any of it to happen. She had been looking for something quite different that night.

28

I washed my face in cold water and considered going to look for Domino, but my whole body throbbed a reminder of what Michael had done, and I wasn't sure I wanted to talk to anyone right now. So instead, I took a couple of bottles of beer from the kitchen and wandered over to the line of trees at the furthest part of the clearing, beside the longhouse.

I leaned against the trunk of a pine, settled in the comfort of the near darkness and watched the party continue. As the dancers moved back and forth I caught glimpses of Helena, sitting like I was, not participating, watching things happen around her. I thought our eyes even met once or twice, but I wasn't sure she could really see me sitting in the gloom.

Michael was attentive, bringing her drinks, trying to make conversation, but every time she just shook her head and looked away. I was pleased he wasn't getting what he wanted from her. I would never be a physical match for him, so I felt there was at least some justice when I saw Helena dismiss him. He was persistent, trying everything before eventually turning his back on her. They sat together, as if each of them were alone, for at least half an hour before he gave up and went to join the rest of the party. I watched him laugh and drink and dance and I hated him.

I was so lost in my thinking that I didn't notice Helena coming over.

She lowered her head in shame as she approached. The others paid little attention, but Kurt was watching.

When Helena reached me, she asked, 'Mind if I talk to you?'

'You still high?'

'Not so much. I was just . . . dealing with it, I guess. What happened. I'm OK now.'

I searched the crowd for Michael.

'I'm sorry,' she said.

'You want to sit down?' I looked up at her.

She was biting the inside of one cheek, her mouth pulled to one side, her thin lips tightened. Her brow was furrowed and she hesitated before crouching beside me and speaking quietly. 'Can we go somewhere else? Somewhere more private?'

Kurt was still watching us, this time with Michael standing beside him. I could see that Michael wanted to come over, but Kurt held him back.

'Let's just stay here. Better to keep in sight of the rest of the group. Don't want people to get the wrong impression. Especially Michael.' I put a hand to my face.

Helena sat beside me. 'I'm sorry about that,' she said again.

'You didn't do it.' I was still watching Michael. Kurt was speaking to him now, saying something in his ear. Michael nodded, came through the dancers, glaring down at me as he passed, and disappeared behind the longhouse.

'And I'm sorry about trying to make you take the tablet. I just thought that if you had something to loosen you up a bit, you might feel better. You might . . .'

'Like I said before, Helena, I'm not much of a dancer.'

She pulled her legs beneath her and crossed them, hiding them under the folds of her skirt. One shoulder of her vest top slipped down her tanned skin, showing the lacy edging of a well-worn bra. She made no effort to cover it. 'You looked like you needed to have some fun. It's been pretty strange for you since you got here. It's not always like this, you know.'

'If it was like *this* all the time, there'd be no one here.'

She smiled and tilted her head to one side, dark hair falling across her face. She used her fingers to tuck it behind her ear. I thought she was going to speak, but she remained silent, watching me.

'So . . .' I tried to think of something to say, something to stop her from staring. 'Do you ever get out of here?'

She moved her head so the hair fell away from behind her ear and covered half of her face again. This time she made no attempt to move it.

'You ever go back to Sweden?'

'Sweden?' She sighed and looked away as if the answer was floating somewhere in the darkness by the trees. 'No.'

'There's no one you miss back there?'

'No.'

'What about other things, then? Is there anything else you miss?'

'Tell you the truth, there's not much I want. Maybe someone to get close to.'

'You have Michael.'

She rolled her eyes.

'You came here with him, though. You said you met in Kuta.'

'Mm.' She traced one finger in the soil by her feet, moving it gently from side to side, wearing a tiny arcing trench. 'But it was his friend I liked. I came here for *him*, not Michael.'

'Michael was with someone else?'

'His name was Sully. He said he had this cool place to show me.'

'He's the guy who disappeared.'

'You know about Sully?'

'Domino told me.'

'Told you what?'

'That there was a guy who left. Disappeared. It was Michael who told me he was called Sully.'

'He doesn't like to talk about him.'

'But they were friends, right?' I recalled Michael's reaction the day we cut the trees. He hadn't said anything about being friends. It was Matt and Jason who had told me that.

256

'They were,' she said. 'But they fell out.'

I looked at her and thought about the way Michael liked to keep her close to him; the way he was always around; the way he watched her. 'Because Sully was your boyfriend?'

She shook her head, still moving her finger from side to side. 'Not really. Never quite happened that way.'

'But Michael didn't like it. I get it. So where is he now, then? You think he went off on his own travels for a while?'

'Something like that, I suppose,' she said without looking at me. 'Just went without saying anything. His parents, they came looking for him, but I didn't know what to tell them.'

'You spoke to them?'

'Kurt wanted me to. I guess I knew him better than anyone else.'

'Better than Michael?'

She shrugged. 'It's what Kurt wanted.'

'So what did you say to them?'

'Not much. That he must've had enough, so he left. I don't know where he went.'

'But you stayed.'

'Nowhere else to go.'

'And you miss him?'

She stopped moving her finger. She thought about what I'd asked, then she nodded and reached out to brush her knuckle across my cheek. 'Sully was quiet like you. Strong inside.'

'You hardly know me,' I said, and looked away to the long-house again, wondering if Domino was ever going to make an appearance tonight. If she took too much longer, I'd go inside and look for her.

'You like her.'

'Who?'

'Domino. You like her.'

'You're not the first person to say it like that. You guys all feel protective about her.'

Helena raised her eyebrows and looked over at the

longhouse. 'That's what you think? That I feel protective about her?'

'I just thought—'

'She's Kurt's sister.'

'I know.'

'That's why Kurt's always watching you. But if she doesn't want you . . .' Helena looked at me. Our eyes met for a moment, then she looked away as if too embarrassed to finish her sentence. She didn't need to.

'Helena. I . . . I'm flattered . . .'

She reached out and put her finger on my lips. 'Shh. Don't say anything.'

I stopped and she took her finger away.

'I mean, why wouldn't she want you? I just meant that if something happened to her . . .'

'Like what?'

'If she went away or something, then . . .'

'Helena. Is this because of what happened?' I asked her. 'The other night? In the water?'

'No. You think I like you because you helped me?'

'*Do* you?'

'No,' she said. 'I mean, of course that helps, but no, that's not the only reason. You're a good guy, Alex. Different from the others. I like you because I like you, that's all.'

I didn't know how to reply, so I didn't try. I admired the way she was so candid about how she felt. It reminded me of Domino.

'And then last night,' she said, 'when you went into the forest with Kurt. You took the tablet.'

I nodded. 'Yes, I did.'

'I saw the way you reacted.'

'You were watching me?'

'For a while. Before I came to you.'

'You came to me?'

'Of course. But you're here for Domino. That's why you stay,

258

I understand that. It was just for that moment, but if you wanted it to be—'

'Hang on, Helena, what do you mean, you came to me?'

'I saw you leave; saw Kurt follow you. I was worried when he came back without you, so I came looking for you . . .' She stopped and her face fell. 'You *do* remember, don't you?'

'I remember.' My mouth went dry and I took another sip of my beer to hide my reaction. I looked at Helena, her head still on one side, her hair still cascading across the side of her face, creating a curtain between us and the others. She was waiting for me to say something, her expression caught between a smile and expectancy.

I lowered my voice. 'Does . . . does anybody know? Did anybody *see*?'

She shook her head. 'I left when I heard Domino coming. No one knows. Just us.'

And it all came back to me in a mad rush of colours and sounds and sensations. The rock and the blood and the souls and the feeling of being one with everything around me. I remembered how I'd felt when Domino came to me and we lay together on the soft needles. I'd been confused about something, though. I'd seen Helena's face instead of Domino's, but there was a perfectly good reason why that was so. I thought it was because I'd saved her life, and that doing so had brought her to the front of my mind, but the reality was quite different. It was because Domino had not come to me in the woods that night. Helena had.

29

I continued to watch Helena, not sure what to say, disturbed to find that it didn't upset me more. I'd thought she was Domino and she'd misunderstood that, but I had a thrilling memory of that night, and this revelation didn't diminish it. If anything, it made it more exciting, more forbidden.

'We can be together,' she said. 'If you want. We can leave here.'

'I like you, Helena . . .'

'But?' Her face fell.

'But things are getting way too complicated for me. I need to take a step back. Think about what the hell's going on. You do, too. I mean, think about Michael, about what he just did. And think about Domino.' My eyes went to the longhouse. She'd been inside for so long now. 'Maybe we should just forget what happened.'

'Forget it?'

'Well, maybe not forget it,' I said, remembering how good it had been. I looked at Helena, then at the longhouse again. I shook my head and began pushing myself to my feet, but Helena put her hand on my arm.

'Alex.'

'I better go see her.' Last time I'd seen Domino we'd argued and I thought it must be clouding my judgement. If I saw her, I'd remember what it was to be with her and it would push Helena to the back of my mind.

'Kurt said to leave her, Alex. Let her be alone for a while.'

'I should see if she's OK.'

'To block me out?'

'Hm?'

'Be with her, forget about me?'

'I'm sorry, Helena.' I moved past her, heading round to the front of the longhouse, all of the others still wrapped up in the music. All of them but Kurt. Kurt who noticed everything.

I was just a few yards away from the longhouse when he stopped me. 'You sort things out with Helena?'

'Yeah.'

'She's a nice girl,' he said. 'But you know she's Michael's, right?'

'They're not together.'

'They are in *his* mind.'

I sighed. 'There's only one person I'm interested in here.' But I knew it was a lie as soon as the words came from my lips.

'Good.' Kurt put his arm around my shoulder. That brotherly gesture again. 'As long as it stays that way.'

'Yeah.' I made a move for the longhouse again.

'She needs time,' he said, tightening his hold. 'Wait until she comes out.'

'I just want to check on her. Make sure she's all right.'

'Why wouldn't she be all right? You're really that worried about her?'

I glanced back at Helena. 'Yes, I really am. I think I upset her.'

Kurt smiled. 'It's not you.'

'What?'

'It's nothing to do with you.'

'You sure? I mean, we sort of had an argument and—'

'There's nothing you could do that would upset Domino. This is about something else,' he said. 'Something much bigger than you.' His words dug into me and I watched his face for some display of intent. I wasn't sure if he had meant to insult me that way, or if he was just saying it as he saw it. Perhaps I really didn't mean anything to Domino at all.

Kurt released his hold on me. 'Tell you what,' he said. 'I'll check on her.' His body language made it clear that he wanted me to stay back, the way he stood facing me for a moment, drawing himself up, puffing himself out like a wild animal protecting its territory. He knew I cared for his sister, he was saying, but there was no way anyone could care about her as much as he did.

'Stay here.' He fixed me with his hard stare before turning round, but even as he was just a few paces away, the door opened and Domino stepped out into the night. She came down the ladder and went straight to Kurt. She stood in front of him, speaking quietly, and I watched for a moment before turning round to see Helena watching them, too. She looked at me, then returned to the dancers, taking something from a pocket in her skirt and putting it into her mouth.

'Kurt said you were worried about me.' Domino put her arms around my waist from behind and held me tight. She spoke into my ear as Kurt walked past us, going back to the others.

'I was,' I said. 'You OK?'

Her arms tightened even further and she pressed herself against me. 'Let's find somewhere quieter.' She released her grip, took my hand and together we headed for the trees.

Approaching the fire, the light it cast was bright in my eyes and it darkened the forest beyond, making it nothing more than a black wall of emptiness. But as we passed it and my eyes grew accustomed to the darkness, I could see a figure crouched at the line of the trees.

Coming closer, Michael looked up at us. Now that we were almost on top of him, I could see him quite clearly, the glow from the fire glistening on his skin. He was squatting with what looked like a tree stump, a solid piece of dark wood, between his knees. Despite the cool breeze, he looked as if he'd been exerting himself. His skin was shining with sweat and there was a dusting of soil across one shoulder.

'How you doing?' He directed his question to Domino.

'Better,' she said. 'You?'

Michael didn't reply, he just nodded and took a drink from the bottle of beer beside him.

'Looks like hard work,' Domino said.

He secured the bottle by screwing it into the soil and picked up a narrow-bladed knife that was lying at his feet. It was the one he had used to bleed the pig. 'Yeah.' He returned to carving the surface of the wood.

'It's a Batak house,' Domino said to me. 'He's making a Batak house.'

'As close as I can get,' Michael replied, slipping, nicking himself with the blade.

'You not partying?' Domino asked.

He lifted his finger to his lips to taste the blood. 'Don't much feel like it right now.' He looked at me, then at his fingertip. 'And I want to get it finished. Maybe paint it tomorrow. It's for Matt.'

Then I understood. Michael was carving a shrine for Matt. Something to mark his grave. Something more than just a heap of freshly turned soil to give proof of his life. Not a brass plaque on a wall, but a solid piece of the forest, ingrained with his own sweat and blood. A tribute to a friend.

'You going out there?' Michael asked, looking at Domino.

'Get some space,' she said. 'It's been a tough day.'

'Hasn't it just?' Michael looked at me once more, then spoke to Domino. 'Be careful,' he said.

We hardly spoke as we walked. It was a fresh night, not cold, but the air had a slight chill and I felt goose bumps pulling tight on my skin beneath the ill-fitting, borrowed shirt. Being like that, wearing another man's clothes, reinforced my feeling of transience here. I couldn't imagine myself staying for a long time. Not any more. And when we came out of the trees, onto the hilltop where we had argued that morning, I had a sensation of being freed from tight constraints. I didn't feel as liberated among the others as they did. I hadn't lost my inhibitions as they had, and I still clung to the pieces of my life elsewhere. I'd taken the drug and I'd done the jump, but this wasn't where I was going to find myself. I had no doubt that the place and the people would have a profound effect on me, but they were not going to be my great eye opener. Maybe nothing was.

I expected Domino to stop when we came out into the open, but she continued walking, taking us both right to the edge of the cliff. There was a good moon that night, not so much cloud in the sky, and the platinum light wavered across the surface of the water. There was little breeze up on the cliff, so the water below was still, just a slight wave on its surface to break the glow that the moon laid down upon it.

'Don't get too close,' I said to her.

Domino tipped her head back and released my hand, taking a step closer to the edge. Her eyes were closed, squeezed shut, shallow wrinkles spreading from the corners. She lifted her hands and held them way out to her sides as if she were dying on a cross.

'Domino?' I reached out to her but didn't touch her for fear that she would pull away and slip. Fall.

'You ever wondered what it would be like to fall a long way down?' she said.

'I jumped, remember?'

'No,' she said. 'Not here. You jumped from further along. We're higher.'

I edged closer, leaned forward to look over and saw that she was right. Below us, at least sixty feet down, a shelf of black rock jutted from the side of the cliff, hanging over the water that swelled twenty feet or so below that. 'Shit, you're right. You don't want to jump here.'

'Don't I?'

'No. You don't. You go over here, that's the end. There's no climbing back up from that.'

Domino stayed quiet, her arms outstretched, her head back.

'Have you taken something?' I asked.

'No,' she said. 'Not a thing. Not this time.'

I glanced over the edge again, but it made me queasy so I stepped back and looked at Domino, watching her sway. 'Come and sit down,' I said to her.

'You think it would hurt?'

'Stop talking like that.'

'I mean, would you feel it, or would you just—'

'Come away from there. For fuck's sake, Domino, you're starting to scare me.'

She lowered her arms and turned round to look at me. 'I'm not gonna jump. I was just wondering what it would be like.' But the expression in her eye, the way her smile didn't come like it normally did, it made me think that it hadn't just been for effect. There'd been a moment, a split second, when she'd considered going over, and it had scared her just as much as it scared me.

'Come on,' I said. 'Take my hands. Come and sit down.'

She looked at me, then seemed to blow away the thoughts that had been buzzing around her head and she smiled, this time a proper smile, and she reached out to take my hands.

I led her a good distance away from the edge and pulled her to the ground.

'I'm sorry,' I said after a while. 'I was an arse today.'

'About Matt? Don't worry about it.'

'About Kurt. Why didn't you tell me he's your brother?'

'Oh, that. Well, I was going to. The night we arrived. You looked jealous and I wanted to make you feel better, but you stopped me. You said you didn't care.'

'I didn't want to. I thought he was an old boyfriend and I didn't want to care. I thought it would . . . that you'd think less of me.'

'Sometimes you're so tight, Alex. Think less of you?' She nudged me and I winced, a hand going to my ribs.

'What's wrong? You hurt yourself?'

'It's nothing,' I said. She didn't need to know what Michael had done. She couldn't see the redness on my face in this light. By tomorrow there would be bruises; we'd talk about it then.

'You sure?'

'Yeah, I'm sure. Is that what's bothering you?' I asked. 'That we argued? Kurt said you were feeling . . . I don't know, low, I guess. He said you'd had a hard day and that you wanted to be on your own.'

'And you think that had something to do with *you*?'

'Well . . .' I immediately felt foolish and embarrassed. 'I mean, after what happened with Matt, then I was giving you a hard time about Kurt.'

Domino allowed a half-smile to creep onto her lips, the same half-smile I'd seen before, and I felt as if I were losing her, as if she were going back to her thoughts; the ones she'd been having a few moments ago when she was standing over the precipice.

She shifted, lying down in the sparse grass, resting her head on my crossed legs and looking up into my face. 'Neither of those things,' she said.

'What, then?'

She closed her eyes and sighed, her mouth opening a touch when she breathed out. 'Something else,' she said. 'Something else happened today, something bigger, but I want to forget about it.' She reached up and touched my face. 'I just want to be with you and forget about it.'

'Something happened? When you went away, you mean? Where did you go? Down to the *kampong*?'

She put her hand behind my head and pulled me towards her mouth. 'I don't want to talk about it,' she whispered as she touched our lips together. 'I just want to be with you for a while. Talk about other things.'

'Like what?' I let her kiss me. 'What you want to talk about?'

'We could talk about you . . .' she said.

'Wouldn't take long.'

'. . . and about whether or not there's something going on between you and Helena.'

'Me and Helena?' I hoped she couldn't detect the shock in my voice. 'What do you mean?' A flash of our moment in the forest. Helena and me together. How good it had felt. I tried to tell myself it was the drug that had skewed my judgement, but I knew that somewhere beneath the lie there was something else. It was Helena's face I had seen. Under it all, I had known.

'I'm not sure, really. It's like you have a connection or something. I can see that Michael doesn't like it. It bothers him.'

'And you?' I asked, feeling guilt for my lie, but a vague triumph that she even cared. 'Does it bother *you*? Is that what's the matter?'

'*Is* there something between you?'

'Just that I saved her life. I think maybe she feels like she owes me something, that's all.'

'Like I saved yours?'

'I suppose so.'

'And do you feel like you owe *me* something?'

'No. I don't think so.'

Domino kissed me again and smiled. 'Good. And no, it doesn't bother me. You're mine, Alex, I know that. But there's something on your mind, I can tell. You seem different somehow. Is it because we argued? Is it because of what we did this morning? Burying Matt. You still thinking about that?'

I pulled back and looked down at her.

'It's OK,' she said. 'It's normal.'

I sat up straight. 'For a while I understood it.' I was glad to have changed the subject away from Helena. 'When we were all in the forest together, it felt like the right thing to do, just for a moment, but then it was gone. I mean, you can't just bury a person. It's not right.'

'It's what we did, though. All of us. And it's the way Matt would've wanted it.'

'Is it? It's not what I'd want. I'd want . . . Well, I don't know what I'd want, but I wouldn't want that.'

'How is it different from what happens anywhere else? There was nothing anyone could do for him. He was dead, so his friends buried him.' She paused. 'Has this got something to do with what happened to your mother, Alex? Is there something you want to talk about?'

'No.'

'It's just that when we talked about it before, at the hospital, I got the feeling there was something else. Something deeper.'

'This hasn't got anything to do with my mother,' I said.

'Sounds to me like there's something you need to get off your chest.'

'Other than burying Matt, you mean? For Christ's sake, Domino, you can't just bury people.'

'Why not?'

'Well, how did he die, for a start? For all we know someone could have killed him.'

Domino lifted her head from my legs and half-turned, eyes wide. 'What?'

'I was thinking about his bruises.'

'He OD'd,' she said, her body tense. 'We know that.'

'*How* do we know that?'

'Kurt's a doctor.'

'So everyone keeps saying, although no one seems to know exactly what kind of doctor.'

'You don't believe it?'

'What about the mark I saw on his throat? Didn't anybody else see that?'

'You think too much, Alex. You ask too many questions. Why don't you just let things be?'

'Because it doesn't feel right. I don't think Matt—'

'It's been dealt with,' she snapped.

'What?' I looked down at her. 'What d'you mean by that?'

She shook her head as if she'd said something she hadn't meant to. 'Nothing. I dunno.'

'You said it's been dealt with.'

'Yeah. I meant we buried him, that's all. There's nothing else to it. He's gone.'

'Is there something else?' I pressed her. 'Something you want to tell me?'

Domino pulled her lower lip between her teeth and bit on it as if trying to stop herself from saying something. She held that expression for a while, her eyes searching my face, then she finally shook her head and took a deep breath. 'No.' She forced a smile. 'Nothing. Let's not talk any more. Things are so much better when we don't talk.'

We watched each other for a while, her with a kind of hopeful expression, then she put her head back on my lap, averting her eyes and staring up into the sky. I turned my attention to the lake and my mind went back to this morning when we'd buried Matt in the forest.

It seemed like a long time ago that we'd all stood round the grave, the heavy patter of soil on his skin. I remembered how long it had taken and how my attention had wandered and I'd surveyed the woods around us. I remembered the unusual, uniform shapes further away among the trees. Strange silhouettes out of place. Over the course of the day, with so much happening, I'd forgotten about them, but now I tried to see them again. And then it came to me. My mind skipped to what I had seen just a short while ago when Domino and I had come into the woods, and in that instant I knew what those regular shapes were.

The object Michael had been carving; it wasn't the first shrine he had made.

30

I tried hard not to think about those silent shrines, skulking among the trees, just out of view, but they kept swimming back into my thoughts, and I found myself trying to count them from the picture I had in my mind. Once or twice, as we sat holding each other, I was tempted to ask Domino about them, but something pricked at me, telling me to keep it to myself.

We didn't speak as we drifted apart on the bluff overlooking Toba, and it was only when I realised Domino was sleeping on my lap that I woke her with a gentle shake and told her we should get back to the longhouse.

We made our way back to the clearing where the party had calmed down and the music was gone. There were still a couple of people about. I noticed that Alban was asleep at the table, his head hidden in the crook of his crossed arms, leaning on the cold stone. Evie was beside him, one arm around his shoulders. Another person was curled up by the fire, which was dying from neglect, but I couldn't make out who it was, because his sarong was loosened and pulled high over his head to keep him warm. I guessed he was too drunk to make the short trip back to his bed.

Domino and I crept into the longhouse, careful not to disturb the others. We made our way to the back of the building, glad for the warmth it provided, and found our own space. We lay on the mattress, still fully clothed, our backs pressed together.

When Domino was sleeping, I rolled over and stared into the

darkness at the apex of the longhouse, listening to the sounds of the sleepers about me. I dozed for some time, but my mind kept going back to those silhouettes among the trees, and the more I thought about them, the more I wanted to know.

I lifted my head and waited to see if Domino moved. I edged away from her, and when she didn't react, I was confident I wouldn't disturb her, so I pushed myself up into a crouch. I remained in that position for some time, scanning the darkness. I didn't want to risk waking anyone; this was something I wanted to do alone.

I took one of the several torches kept near the back entrance and opened Michael's trapdoor, keeping my movements slow and quiet. I slipped out, closed the door behind me and waited a few seconds, listening for sounds of disturbance. Satisfied that I hadn't woken anyone, I dropped my flip-flops, stepped into them and set off into the woods.

I kept to the path leading through to the execution stone and, for the first few steps, there was enough light from the moon for me to continue without the torch. But as I progressed and the canopy closed in above me, I switched it on and shone it ahead of me, keeping the beam low.

The root-veined, potholed track seemed longer than when I'd been this way before, and I began to wonder if I had taken the wrong route. I stopped and shone the torch around me, pointing it behind, then either side, into the trees. I looked for a fork where I might've taken a wrong turn, but the path was a single cutting through the trees; there were no wrong turns to make. It led only in one direction, never deviating from that, so I pressed on.

It wasn't long before I came out into the small clearing with the execution stone, and when I did, I stopped, playing the light over its surface. When I'd come here with Kurt, and the torches had been burning, the stone had looked so different. It had almost been alive. But now, in the cold light of the washed-out, battery-powered beam, the rock looked nothing more than what it was: a large, cold, grey rock. An ordinary object that had been used for extraordinary things. The ground close to it was dark with the pig's blood, which had soaked into the soil, and I could hear the frenzied buzz of flies' wings. And when I ran the torchlight over the ground, the beast's eyes glistened in its severed head, the entrails still in a saggy heap close by.

I moved past the rock and the carnage and pointed the beam at the ground around the edge of the small clearing, searching for the path that I knew led away from it. It was narrower than the one leading into this place, but it wasn't difficult to find, so I was on it within a few seconds. It was when it came to an abrupt end, giving way to the forest, that my search was to become more difficult. Once I was off the track, I would be in a no man's land of shadow and spectral beauty. Out here, I could truly lose myself.

I hesitated and glanced down at my feet standing on the edge of the path, then I took a deep breath, swallowed hard and pressed on.

I did not believe in ghosts and spirits, monsters and ghouls, but out there, alone, the ridiculous was plausible. Every time the breeze brushed through the treetops, and every time a twig fell, my heart beat a little faster. I fought the urge to turn back to the security of the longhouse, the renewed appeal of Domino's warm embrace, and I continued deeper into the forest, co-cooned in my tiny circle of weak orange light. I extended the cone outwards, sweeping the beam around me, searching for the shapes I'd seen lurking among the trees.

I had no idea what time it was, and it was easy to lose track of the minutes, alone and in the dark. The moon was high, just a few days away from being full, but that didn't tell me much. As I searched, I began to doubt that I would ever find what I was looking for. Perhaps I'd imagined those regular shapes. Perhaps I'd jumped to the wrong conclusion about what I'd seen. And even as I thought about it, the whole day began to feel as if it had been a dream. I was tired, my mind was confused, and everything merged into one. Dreams and reality.

The notion of returning to my bed, of closing my eyes and holding Domino tight, brought with it a physical memory of how it would feel to be warm and asleep. For a split second I forgot about the cool breeze, about the tiny noises from the forest, and my mind was elsewhere, in a more comfortable place than this. I decided that I should go back. I'd had my adventure. I'd been out in the night, stolen away like a thief. I had tried. I'd made my best attempt to satisfy my curiosity but now other things were more important. So I turned round, looking for the route I'd taken through the trees. And that's when I realised I was lost.

I stopped in my tracks, my heart beating faster now, and spun round in a circle, darting the beam of the torch to and fro, searching for a sign, any sign, that would tell me where to go. There was none. Forcing myself to stay calm, telling the rational part of my brain that panic was the worst thing I could do, I brought my breathing under control and closed my eyes, counting my breaths.

When I re-opened them, I switched off the torch and looked around once again. I was hoping that something from the camp would be visible through the trees, but I had come a long way. I had taken two paths, passed the execution stone; there was no way that light, even if there was any, would pass this far.

All around me was darkness.

I flicked the torch back on again, wishing it was stronger, and played it about the trees, across the ground, searching for a clue, wondering if it might be best to stay where I was rather than wander further. Wait here until daylight, even. But then I saw the mound of loose dirt. No more than a few feet away from where I was standing, and I knew where I was. I had a point of reference. Matt's grave.

I went towards it, careful not to hurry as I wanted, and kept my eyes on it, afraid to lose it if I glanced away for even a second. Once there, I positioned myself as I remembered I'd been standing that morning, turned round and shone the torch ahead of me, knowing it would be the way out. I took one step in the direction of warmth and safety, then stopped. I wasn't lost any more. I had a marker. I'd come here for a purpose and now that I knew where I was, there was no reason not to carry on. I would find those shapes.

I hardened my resolve and went back.

It took me a couple of minutes to find them, but once I spotted them, they were unmistakeable. The regular, angular, shapes were clear among the soft shadows and the curves of the forest.

I kept the beam of the torch centred on the closest of them and began walking towards it, once again afraid to take my eyes from it.

It was exactly what I had thought. A shrine. My fear had been that the shrines might be recent, but this one was very old. There were signs to suggest that it had once been painted, flecks of faded colour on the carvings, but time had taken its toll. The wood was worn, sheltered by the trees but still affected by the elements. Even here, the rain would penetrate the canopy.

I crouched to look closer, holding the torch in my right hand and using my left to dust away the dirt that coated the carving. A spider, small-bodied and long-legged, disturbed by my unwanted attentions, scurried over my hand, causing a sudden feeling of revulsion, making me wave my hand in quick, sharp movements. I shone the torch closer, shifting it across the surface of the shrine, checking for more creatures before I continued, taking away enough grime to read a name. *Sondang Sirayit*. No dates, but I knew it couldn't belong to a member of this community. The shrine was probably older than all of us.

Close by, another, similar in age, and again with just a name. *Tetty Sinaga*. No dates. I studied them both, comparing the craftsmanship, seeing the immediate similarity in their shape and design. There were others, too, perhaps four in this group, each of them a dozen feet away from the other. And behind them, another two, although perhaps not quite as old. These ones still had some of the paint clinging to the dark wood. I crouched in front of the smallest one, wondering if this person had not been so important, or perhaps a smaller shrine was meant for a child.

I imagined that these were the graves of the people who had once lived in the longhouses we now inhabited. Perhaps they had even built them, and the hands that had put them together now lay beneath my feet, a collection of bones.

I was saddened to find the graves, to know that people had been buried here, but I wasn't uncomfortable with it, and I was relieved that the graves were old. I was glad that these people had not been put in the ground by Kurt and his community, and I passed among them, crouched low in the ferns and other plants so that I could read their names. I was oblivious to the night around me as I picked out the individual burial places, discovering this for myself, with no one at my side to judge me.

Much further back, though, hidden behind a ragged growth of shrubs, I held back the foliage to find another, more recent shrine. And when I read the inscription, this one pinched my skin, tightening it to a constellation of tiny bumps, freezing the blood beneath.

Taking shallow breaths, I ran the torch beam over the shrine. A small longhouse fashioned from one piece of wood. The carving here was no older than a year or two. The paint was still clear, bright, vivid. The markings were less practised, almost crude. The work was less authentic. And the words on the shrine were not local. I was not familiar with the natives of this place, nor was I familiar with their language, but the words carved on this hidden shrine were western – '*Our Friend and Brother*' – and I knew Matt had not been the first.

I touched a hand to my chest and wondered whose shirt I was wearing.

31

There is nothing present in darkness that isn't present in light. Darkness is not a thing. It is a nothing. But when I switched off the torch and the night wrapped itself around me, I sensed the ghosts of the people buried here. '*Our Friend and Brother*', the corpse at my feet, with only soil to keep us apart. I wondered who had called him 'friend', but hidden him here, away from the others, away even from the place where Matt had been laid.

I had rarely felt like a true part of the community, but it was only now that I began to fear it. Whatever bad things had happened here, and whatever bad things were going to happen, I didn't want to be a part of them.

I glanced around me, my eyes becoming accustomed to the dark. From where I was sitting I could make out the shrines I'd first spotted, and as I scanned the forest, other shapes came to me from the gloom. It surprised me that once my eyes were allowed to settle, I could see well enough with just the light of the moon. In fact, the torchlight had hampered my vision, giving an unrealistic hue to everything, casting shadow, making me see only within its orange eye.

There were two other shrines, not far from where I was sitting, and something else that I hadn't noticed in the light of the torch. A mound, like a pregnant swelling in the earth. I wondered what the swelling was – the rest of the forest floor was quite flat, covered only by the patches of ferns and other flora that grew there. But this was no plant. This was something else. Something more solid and impenetrable. A crouching person maybe. An animal. Or a beast.

I waited, watching, but the thing didn't move, so I stood, and without turning on the torch, crept over, moving my feet slowly so as not to disturb it. When I came to it, though, I realised it was not a living thing but a mound of dirt. Loose soil. With two *cangkuls* lying across the top. And on the other side of it was a shallow hole. What I was looking at, illuminated in silver moonlight, was an empty grave.

It was only then that I saw the light among the trees, bobbing backwards and forwards, flashing between the dark trunks, killing shadows, allowing them to flood back again.

Someone was coming.

My instinct was to remain hidden and, almost without thinking, I hunched low, becoming smaller so I wouldn't stand out if the beams came close to me. As the torch continued to glitter and sweep in the forest, I dropped forwards into a crouching position and moved away from the shrines, going deeper into the forest, taking shelter behind an overgrowth of ferns. I lay down among them, facing the direction of the light.

It was almost ethereal, watching the light bobbing towards me but hearing nothing. A forest spirit come to visit the remains of its dead ancestors. But no matter what fanciful images came to mind, there was no denying what this was. Someone was coming to the spot where the dead were buried.

I kept low as the torchlight came closer, and as the beam widened, catching my eyes in one instant, I buried my face in my arms, which were crossed in front of me. I pressed my nose to the dirt and waited for the light to pass away from me before I dared look up again, trying to raise nothing more than my eyes above the level of my arms. I shuffled further back among the plants, eager to see who it was, what they were going to do.

When the progression of the light through the trees finally stopped, I heard voices, whispering, carried on the breeze. I saw figures. Not one, but three. At first they were difficult to make out. The person holding the torch was obscured from view by the thick trunk of a tree. All that was visible was the beam of light, directed at the ground, and the slight protrusion around the edge of the tree trunk. The others moved further forward, carrying something between them, and bent over to place it on the ground. When they stood, they stretched their backs.

These two figures were clearer, illuminated in part by the orange light from the torch but also by the moon and my improved perspective now that I'd allowed my eyes to grow accustomed to the night. The tall stature and wide proportions of the first man were unmistakeable. Since coming to Indonesia I hadn't seen a man as tall or as muscular as Michael. The other person was harder to make out at first, but when the torch bearer swung the beam up, towards his face, his identity became clear. Kurt.

It was impossible to tell what they'd been carrying – the angle was all wrong – but I had a keen idea. I tried to persuade myself that it was the shrine that Michael had been carving earlier that evening. It made sense they'd want to come out to place it by Matt's grave, and I guessed that the torch bearer would be Jason. He too would want to be there when they placed it. Only thing was, though, I could think of no reason why they would do it *now*. In the dead hours of shadow and obscurity. And they were not standing at Matt's grave. They were further in, close to the hole I'd seen. A hole that could have only one purpose in such a place.

When the circle of light settled on the ground, it fell upon the object they had been carrying, and although it was bathed in shadow, it confirmed what I had feared. A body. They had come here to bury another body.

When Michael and Kurt had rested, they spoke again, this time a little louder. I still couldn't hear what they were saying, or who was speaking, but some of the words reached me.

'. . . get it done . . .'

They leaned down, put their hands on the body and pushed, rolling it into the hole, dropping it in with a dull thump.

With the body out of sight, Michael and Kurt began scraping the soil back into the hole, grunting with the effort, while the torch remained fixed on the spot.

When the soil was all in place, the two men battered it flat with the *cangkuls*, then collected pine needles from the surrounding area, scattering them on the disturbed soil. With that done, they stretched again, then stood, hands on hips, looking down at the spot where they'd put the body.

'. . . should do it . . .' I heard one of them say, but neither of them made a move.

'. . . not enough . . . something else . . .'

Then more words, and the torch was redirected, sweeping the area around them, flashing past my hiding spot among the ferns, then returning and stopping.

Michael and Kurt turned to face my direction, both of them coming towards me, their footsteps becoming louder, their voices more audible.

'We need to cover it more,' said Kurt. 'Put some plants over it or something.'

'Plants? How we gonna do that?' said Michael.

'Pull some up,' Kurt replied. 'Replant them. Few days, it'll look like they were always there. Doesn't need to be too much; no one's coming out here.'

'We didn't do it to . . . to the other one.' Michael's head turned in the direction of the shrine I'd been looking at.

'Still can't say his name?'

'I can say it.'

'Yeah,' said Kurt. 'Sure you can. Well, anyway, he was one of us. He was our friend and he deserved better. You want to make one of your carvings for this wanker as well?'

'No.'

'So let's just get on with it, then, shall we?'

Now the figure with the torch was coming closer too, their whole shape obscured by the diffused glow of the light. They were nothing more than a dark silhouette, sweeping gently from side to side, looking for a good place from which to take a few plants.

The most obvious spot was right here, the place where I was hiding.

'Over here,' Kurt said, and my heart hammered hard in my chest. I would surely be discovered if they came this way. 'There's loads here.'

The torch jerked in my direction now, falling a few feet short of my crossed arms and protruding head. I ducked down and shuffled back among the plants, keeping as slow and quiet as possible.

Michael and Kurt came closer, blocking the torchlight, casting shadows, and the torch bearer moved the light to accommodate them.

Then Kurt spoke again, saying, 'For fuck's sake, D, keep the light still, will you?'

Now my heart stopped hammering. I stopped creeping backwards and lifted my head above my crossed arms. I stared at the silhouetted figure with the torch, but still couldn't make out who it was. Perhaps I'd heard wrong. Perhaps Kurt had said something else, uttered another person's name.

But then she spoke and I knew it was her.

'Can we just get out of here?' she said. 'I don't like this.'

It was Domino. The girl who had saved me, who had inspired me. The girl I had followed to Lake Toba.

'We wouldn't be here if it wasn't for you,' Kurt snapped. 'Christ, D, you don't half cause some shit.'

'And you better get your boyfriend to stop asking so many questions,' said Michael. 'And keep him away from Helena, or we're gonna have to dig one of these for him.'

'He's not interested in *her*,' Domino replied. 'She's the one trying to latch on to *him*.'

'Stop it, you two, let's just get this done,' Kurt told them.

I was frozen to the spot, my mouth open, my eyes wide. I lay paralysed by fear and indecision and incomprehension. I could do nothing but watch as Kurt and Michael came closer still, reaching the undergrowth I was hiding in. Kurt felt for the base of one of the plants and tugged, fixing his feet securely on the ground and leaning away, using the strength in his legs to pull up the plant. When it came loose, popping from the soft soil, he fell into a sitting position and the fern landed in his lap.

'Couple more ought to do it,' he said, throwing the fern at Domino's feet and repositioning himself. He lifted his head to Michael. 'Come on, then. Gonna be much quicker if we both do it.'

I heard Michael sigh, then he, too, felt for a plant and began tugging.

As they struggled to pull the foliage from the soil, Domino moved the torch, alternating between the two of them so that each would get light. On the third or fourth pass, sweeping the light from Michael to Kurt, each of them with their head down, the light flicked across my face and became still, highlighting me like a rabbit caught in the glare of a hunter's lamp.

I ducked my head low, once again burying it in the crook of my crossed arms, but I knew it was no use. Domino had seen me. She couldn't have failed to see me. It was the only reason why she'd stopped sweeping the beam. Slowly, I raised my head and looked at her, no more than a few feet away. I couldn't see her face – the glare from the torch ensured that – but I knew that if the darkness were replaced with daylight, we would be staring at each other. Each of us as stunned and shocked as the other.

She would've known I was gone as soon as she had awoken. Perhaps she hadn't even been asleep, and had known that I'd left the longhouse. But she wouldn't have known where I had gone. This was probably the last place she would have expected me to come in the dead of night.

I wondered if she had told Kurt I was gone.

Time crawled while Domino kept the light on my face, and my heart beat in slow motion, like a deep, heavy drum. The air was sucked out of the world, and my entire body felt as if a great weight were bearing down on it, crushing it, forcing the air from my lungs, squeezing my chest, breaking my bones. My legs were numb, my eyes wide, my mouth gaping. Then, as if the air rushed back into our world, she redirected the light, moving it to one side, the beam jerking erratically across the forest floor.

'A little light here, Domino,' I heard Michael say, from somewhere a million miles away, his voice coming to me down a narrow tunnel.

Then the beam was on him and, like a wild animal released from the spell of the light, I began to move again. I wanted to bolt, but instead, inched further back into the flora, afraid that Michael would see me, terrified that he would have a reason to dig another hole out here in the wilderness.

32

When they were done, Kurt and Michael picked up their tools and made ready to leave. They cast one final look around the site, then Kurt took the torch from Domino and they set off in the direction from which they'd come.

I watched the light moving into the distance, a will o' the wisp, flitting among the trees until it was gone. I waited, still prostrate among the plants, scanning the trees for any sign of their return – perhaps Domino would change her mind, decide to tell them I was here – but there was no more movement in the forest.

My heart was still drumming when I finally sat up and looked around. I remained that way, watchful, then got to my feet, collected my torch and crept to the spot where they'd been. In the dark, with just the moonlight, there was little sign they'd been here at all.

I stared at the spot where they'd buried the body. Where *Domino* had helped bury the body. She'd had a hard day, Kurt told me. She didn't want to talk about it, she'd said when we'd been together by the cliff. And now I understood why. In my naivety, I'd thought it was something to do with me, but now I could see that more serious matters had been troubling her. And with that understanding came a lucid realisation. I would have to leave this place.

Right now. Without changing my mind. It was time for me to take control.

I would have to leave the community. Leave Kurt and his

people, leave my examined life, and most of all, I would have to leave Domino. But even knowing what she was involved in, I felt a sense of loss. A sadness that she was not what I thought she was. No longer was she just a wild and eccentric animal. Now she was something more.

Coming back through the forest, I wished I didn't have anything to collect – that there was no reason for me to go back. But all the belongings I had in the world were in the longhouse. My money-belt, locked in the cupboard, right next to the place where Domino and I slept. It was all I had, and I couldn't leave without it.

The only thing standing between where I was now and escape from Kurt's camp was that money-belt.

The sky was starting to lighten when I headed back to the camp, but the light was not good, the brightness of the moon having waned, only to be replaced by the greyness of the approaching dawn. Looking up, I could see the clouds through the trees, no sun burning through them yet, just a dim and difficult light that made it harder to see than before. Everything had a sombre hue, the shadows closing in on me as I picked my way through, until eventually they thinned out again and I saw the shape of the longhouses in the main clearing.

The place was deserted. The fire had long since died and lay cold, waiting to be revived. The table was empty, the kitchen was desolate, the longhouses remained still. No music, no laughing, no voices. No movement of any kind.

Knowing this was my best chance to retrieve my belongings, I emerged into the clearing and approached the longhouse. If I left it much later, people would be waking, but for now they would still be sleeping off the after-effects of last night's party. I hoped that the gravediggers were asleep too, tired from their exertions in the forest, and was glad I'd been relegated to the back of the longhouse. Being the runt of the group had some benefits after all: at least I wouldn't have to pass everybody in order to get to my belongings. Just Domino.

I slipped to the back of the longhouse, prepared myself for what I was going to find, and nudged up the trapdoor. Michael's 'exit strategy'. I spied through the crack, but it was too dark inside to see much. Pushing it further and climbing in, I knew straight away that Domino was not there. Our thin mat was unoccupied on the floor of the longhouse. I scanned the interior for any sign of her, but saw nothing. I couldn't even tell whether Kurt and Michael were back in their beds.

I took the key from round my neck and slid it into the lock on the old cupboard, turning it until there was a gentle click. I opened the door, wincing at the quiet creak, reached in and felt nothing.

Without thinking I put one hand to my mouth while the other moved across the dusty surface of the empty shelf. There was nothing on it at all. I felt further, touching every surface, but the cupboard was bare.

I stopped searching and closed my eyes, pressing my hand tight against my mouth. I wanted to smash my fist into the cupboard door. I wanted to stamp my feet and tear the place apart, searching for my belongings. I took a deep breath to calm myself, sucking the air through my nostrils, the noise of it loud in the quiet longhouse.

I composed myself as best as I could and considered my limited options. Domino must have returned to the longhouse and taken my money-belt, realising that I'd leave. Perhaps Kurt had it now. Maybe Domino had told him what I'd seen and they were cutting off my means of escape. They might even be waiting for me somewhere outside. I squinted and looked down the length of the building to see if Kurt and Michael were in their beds. There were bulky shapes down there in the fading darkness, but it was impossible to know for sure.

I stared at the far end of the longhouse and made my decision. I'd run anyway. Just as I was. With nothing. Perhaps I'd go to Hidayat, take up his offer of help. When he'd fixed my shoulder, he'd warned me about this place, told me to go to him if I needed to. And if I could make it back to Medan, there was always the consulate. It made life difficult, but there wasn't much else I *could* do. They may have taken my best means of survival, but they still didn't have me. I wouldn't be the first traveller to lose his money and his passport. And there was always the police. If I went to them, I might even be able to retrieve my belongings.

I took one last look around the longhouse and turned to leave when something caught my eye. Someone close by, a few beds away, had moved and was now propped up on one elbow. A shaft of grey light fell through a crack in the roof and sliced across her shapeless form.

'Alex?' It was Helena's voice whispering to me.

I pushed the cupboard door to, left the key in the lock and tiptoed over to where she lay. I crouched beside her, putting my face close to hers, touching a finger to my lips. She nodded, moving her face into the shaft of weak light and I saw the puzzlement in her eyes. I shook my head at her once, then did something that took me by surprise. I leaned forward and kissed her on the forehead. And before she could say anything else, I stood and crept away from her, letting myself back out through the trapdoor.

I was halfway across the clearing – halfway towards the safety of the trees – when I heard the sound behind me. A quiet click. Feet on the rungs of the ladder. Soft footfalls approaching. I stopped and turned, knowing that she had followed me.

'You're leaving,' she whispered.

'Yes.' I looked around, feeling exposed standing in the middle of the open space, where the last of the moonlight fell through the open canopy.

'Let me come with you.'

I wasn't sure what to say. Part of me wanted to say yes to her but I had a strong feeling that if I took any part of this community with me, the malignancy of this dark paradise would follow me.

'You should stay,' I told her.

'No.' She shook her head, urgency clear in her quiet voice.

'You don't mean that. We have something, don't we? There's something there. We're friends.'

There was a desperation in her voice that I didn't want to hear. I didn't want her dependence. I didn't want her to project something on to me because I was her only way out. I didn't want her to attach herself to me as I had done with Domino. 'Of course we're friends.'

'Then let me come with you.' She held up a hand and for the first time I noticed she was carrying a small bag, the kind of bag someone might use to carry passports or tickets. It was her lifeline.

I sighed and looked at the ground, finding no inspiration there. Helena was desperate. Like me, she had no one. Like me, she was alone. I couldn't leave her in this place any more than I could stay here myself. 'All right, I—'

'You two OK over there?'

We both stopped dead, staring at each other, then turning in unison to look into the near-darkness of the shadows at the far side of the clearing.

I squinted, stepping closer, seeing the small, red eye of a cigarette lift, glow, then drop. I heard the exhalation of smoke, then Kurt spoke again. 'Come closer. Both of you.'

Now I could make out his silhouette, sitting at the table, and I cast my eyes around, wondering where Michael was. Perhaps behind us, knife in hand, waiting. So I had been right. Domino had told them what I had seen. She had told them and they had taken my belongings and they had come to wait for me. I tried not to be afraid. I tried to be strong, but in my mind I saw the blade of Michael's machete, the same one we had used in the forest when we had cut down the trees; the one Kurt had used to remove the pig's head. I saw the execution stone, livid blood on its dry, expectant surface. And I saw a grave, a fresh hole containing a fresh body and I heard, once again, the ugly patter of soil thrown onto dead skin.

I felt Helena reach out and her fingertips brushed against my own. I pulled away.

'Come on,' Kurt said again. He didn't raise his voice; it was a serpentine whisper in the night. Firm but quiet. Demanding.

We went to him, seeing only his shape, the tiny eye of the cigarette as it glowed and darkened, glowed and darkened.

'I know what's happening,' Kurt said.

Neither of us answered.

'I don't like it.'

'You don't own us.' I spoke aloud, my voice wavering at first, then becoming more confident. 'We can do what we want.' I wanted to tell him to go to hell. I wanted to tell him we were leaving and turn and walk away, the two of us departing this place for ever. But I knew he wouldn't let that happen. Something told me that if I tried it, Michael would step out of the shadows and cut me down like a tree. I was trapped like one of Hidayat's butterflies. Netted and ready to be pinned.

'Not here, you can't. Not here.' He paused. 'Helena, go back inside.'

I sensed her hesitation.

'Don't look at him,' Kurt said. 'Go back inside before Michael comes out. We both know what will happen if he sees this.'

Beside me, Helena moved. Once again, she touched my fingers, then she turned and went away. As far as I knew, it was the last time I would ever see her.

I listened to the faint sounds of her feet on the hard dirt of the clearing, then she was gone and Kurt spoke again. 'Come and sit with me for a while.'

'Why don't we just come to the point?'

'Sit the fuck down, Alex. We need to talk.'

I took a deep breath, stepping over to the table and sliding onto the bench opposite Kurt.

'Smoke with me.' He slid a packet of cigarettes across the table in front of me.

I stayed as I was for a moment, then reached out and took the packet. I slipped out a cigarette, fumbled the lighter and flicked the wheel with my thumb.

'So, I came out for some air,' Kurt said. 'A smoke, chill for a bit, and what do I see? I see people sneaking around in the night.'

I said nothing.

'I know what's going on, Alex. I've been watching you and Helena.'

At first his words surprised me. I expected him to ask about what I had seen earlier that night among the trees.

'Do you think we're fucking idiots?' he said. 'How long do you think it'll be before Domino realises? Or Michael? In fact, Michael's already getting ideas – bad ideas – and I don't want that. Not in my place.'

I let the cigarette smoulder between my fingers. So many thoughts were racing through my head. Domino hadn't told him. This wasn't about what I had seen. This wasn't about leaving. This was something else.

'Sneaking out together in the night, Alex? My sister not fucking good enough for you?'

'I . . .' I opened my mouth to speak, but I didn't know what to say. He'd caught me off-guard.

'Don't make any excuses, Alex, just tell me the truth. Is this the first time?'

'The first—'

'Is this the first time you and Helena have come out here alone?' His voice grew louder, erring away from a whisper. 'Is this the first time you've come out here to *fuck* Helena?' There was such poison in his voice now. This was not the gentle hippy he liked to portray. This was something else. Something sinister.

'I didn't—'

'The truth, Alex. Just tell me the truth. Is – this – the – first – time?'

'No . . .' I said. 'I mean, yes, I—'

'Well, is it or isn't it?'

'Yes,' I said, making a decision. 'Yes it is.'

Kurt sighed a heavy sigh into the night. 'OK. Good. I believe you, Alex.'

And for a long time he was silent. Only the crackle of his cigarette as he dragged on it, blowing out the last lungful and dropping it to the ground where he crushed out its light.

'I can see you have a connection, you and Helena,' he said, his voice calm again. 'You saved her life.'

'Yes.'

'But I told you to keep away from her. I mean, Domino would be upset, but Michael? I think Michael would kill you. Shit, I think he would have killed you the other night if I hadn't stopped him.' He leaned forwards on the table. 'If you want to stay with us, Alex, you're going to have to sort yourself out. Asking questions, pissing Michael off, carrying on with Helena . . .'

I wondered if I should tell him I would leave, but I knew he wouldn't let me go. No one ever left. That's what everyone said. And none of us had anyone to come looking for us. We were alone. All of us.

'The night you saved her, I told you I owe you,' Kurt said. 'So this is it. This is me paying you back. I'm going to go back inside, now. I've had my smoke and now I'm tired. I'm going to go back inside and I'm going to pretend this never happened. I'm going to keep it to myself. Michael and Domino need never know. And you're going to sit here and think about it while you finish your smoke. And then you're going to go inside, lie beside Domino, and wake up in the morning with all this nothing more than a bad dream.'

It was the first thing he'd got right. This was all a bad dream.

Kurt stood up and came around the table, putting his arm on my shoulder. 'Think about it,' he said. 'Think about it hard. Because next time, Alex, I'll let Michael beat you to death. Hell, I might even tell him to do it.'

And when Kurt was gone, I stayed where I was, letting the cigarette burn down in my fingers. And I thought about what he had said. And when I had thought about it enough, I stood and turned to look at the longhouse one more time. I felt for Helena, lying there, wondering what was happening out here, but there was nothing more I could do.

I turned and melted into the trees.

33

Morning had come to the hillside and when I emerged from the trees into the new day, I quickened my pace, a weight lifted from my shoulders. Now that I was further away from the community, I no longer needed to be so careful. No one would be looking for me; I had slipped past them and now I could disappear from their lives.

Except that meant leaving my belongings. And Domino. So beneath the feeling of release, there was a sense of the loss of what could have been, and I stopped and looked back.

There was nothing of the community to see from here. Behind me, trees growing thicker and closer together until there was nothing but a dense forest. But Domino was in there. She had brought me here and now I was leaving her behind without giving her the chance to justify herself. Perhaps there was a rational explanation for what I had seen. I found myself considering different options, wondering if there was any way I could stay in touch with her, but I kept coming back to the same thing. Whatever I tried to imagine, I always saw myself lying in the moonlight, watching Domino standing over the grave, lighting the way for her brother and his accomplice. She was involved in something I did not wish to be a part of.

I sighed, shook my head and turned away. There was no looking back now, I told myself; it was time to look forward again. I would not be fooled by anyone else on my journey. I had learned my lesson.

But as I began the trek down the hillside I saw a figure, not more than a hundred feet away, sitting in the scrub. Around her, a profusion of *spectabilis*, as if blood was seeping from a thousand broken hearts. And as I approached, the figure rose and faced me.

'You're leaving,' she said as I came to the place where she was standing. 'I knew you would, but you don't have to.' She held out my money-belt.

'Yes I do.' I snatched the belt. I wanted to walk past her. I wanted enough strength to leave her behind. She'd let me down. Disappointed me more than I'd ever known.

'Your face,' she said, raising a hand to touch me. 'What happened?'

'Michael didn't say?' I leaned away from her fingers.

'*He* did this?'

'I'm guessing it's not the first time, he was well practised. Look, Domino, you want to talk about my nose, or you going to tell me what's going on?'

Domino sighed and took away her hand. 'You mean last night?'

'Of course I mean last night.'

'What you saw, Alex . . .' She searched for the right words. 'What you saw was . . .'

'I know what I *saw*.' I wondered if the dampness in her eyes was real, or just an act. 'I saw you and your brother putting a body in the ground.'

Domino looked about her with alarm, as if there might be someone to hear us. 'No,' she said. 'What you saw—'

'How many others are there? How many more like the one you buried last night? How many more without a name or even a marker to say they're under there?' I was angry with myself for still wanting her. Angry that I didn't have the strength to just walk away. Angry that she had let me down. 'All that crap about Matt wanting to be buried there – how do I know he wasn't killed? How do I know that Kurt or Michael or even *you* didn't kill him? Killing people and burying them in the woods. Is that what you people are doing here?'

Domino shook her head harder now. 'Of course not. You've lived with us, you know it's not like that.'

'So who was the guy you put in the ground last night?'

Domino reached out to touch me again. 'Alex—'

I moved away. 'There's other graves there, too,' I said.

Domino dropped her arm and stared at the ground.

'Who's under there? How many other people are buried out there?'

She looked up, the dampness in her eyes growing, intensifying the colour, swelling into watery beads, which hung on her lower eyelids, welling until they were too big to be contained there. They spilled over, running down her cheek.

'And who's *Our Friend and Brother*?' I asked. 'Who's in that grave?' And as I said it, I realised I knew exactly who it was. In the forest, it was just four words on a shrine, but saying it aloud, making the sounds, it seemed so obvious. I had even heard Michael say those exact words when he toasted at Matt's burial. I stared at Domino, realising the darkness ran much deeper. 'It's Sully, isn't it?'

'What?'

'Sully. That's why he disappeared. Because somebody buried him out there in the woods.'

'No. He left. Sully left.'

'I saw his grave, Domino.'

'No. Where?'

'Who was it? Who buried him? Was it you? Did *you* bury him?'

'He left, Alex, I told you.'

'What happened to him?' I remembered what Michael had done to me last night; what Kurt said he would tell Michael to do to me if I didn't stay away from Helena. 'Was it him?' I asked. 'Did Michael do something to him?'

'Please.' Domino reached for me once again, but reconsidered and took her hand away, crossing both arms across her chest and drawing them tight. She opened her mouth as if to speak, then closed it again and shook her head. 'I don't know.'

'You don't know? You don't *fucking know*?' I looked back at the trees, wondering if Helena had lied to me just as the others had lied. 'Does *she* know? Does Helena know that Sully is buried out there?' But I knew that she couldn't. Helena was not like Kurt and his sister. I stared at the forest and wondered if I should go back for her, but I was too afraid of what Michael would do. I was sure that if I went near her again, he would kill me and I would join the others under the soil. She would be safer without me. Michael would protect her.

'*I* didn't know.' Domino looked up and, despite everything, seeing the tears made me want to take her in my arms. For someone who'd always been so confident, she looked weak and small. But I had to be strong. I had seen what I had seen. 'I promise you, Alex, I didn't. You have to believe me.'

'I don't know what to believe,' I said. 'But one thing I *do* know is that I don't want anything to do with this. I don't want to be involved.' I began walking again, showing her my anger, but feeling torn inside.

This time she grabbed my arm, pulling me back. 'Don't go,' she said. 'Please, Alex. Don't.'

'I have to.' I didn't look at her. 'I can't stay here.'

'But I need you. Why d'you think I didn't tell Kurt you saw us? It's because I *need* you here. I never wanted to be with *anyone* like this. You're so good for me, Alex, I think I lo—'

'Don't.' I took her hand from me and continued to walk, my legs numb. 'I don't think you need anyone.'

'Stop,' she said, her voice loud. 'Stop, Alex. Don't just walk away from me. You can't just walk away. Not after every- thing—'

'What?' I spun round. 'What you going to say? Not after *what*? After everything you've done for me? After all the help you've given me? That what you're going to say?'

'No,' her voice becoming quiet now. 'After everything we've had together. After everything I've felt for you.'

It stopped me in my tracks. I knew how I'd felt about Domino, but we'd never talked about it. I didn't know how she felt about me, not really, and I had always suspected that her feelings were not as strong as mine. I took a few steps towards her, then made myself stop. I shook my head. 'I have to go,' I said, a tightness in my throat. 'I can't stay. Not now.'

'Please. Just a while longer. After that we'll leave together.'

'No.'

'Then wait for me. Give me a chance to explain what you saw.'

'Tell me now.'

Domino glanced behind her and looked back to me. 'No time.' She looked around again. 'Not here.'

'Goodbye, then.'

'Stay at Toba for a while,' she said. 'A few days. A week. Go to Pulau Samosir Cottages. I'll find you there. It's a small place. Just wait for me. A week, Alex. Give me a week.'

As I thought about it, Domino came close to me and I felt myself melt, the hardness seeping out of me. She took my face in her hands and kissed me.

'Please,' she said, breaking away. 'Wait a while. We'll be together again.'

I didn't answer.

'It *is* what you want, isn't it?'

I shrugged and turned away from her. 'I don't know, Domino. I really don't know what I want any more.'

I didn't look back as I continued down the hillside, but I thought hard about what she'd said, knowing that I'd do as she had asked. I'd wait for her and her explanation. A week. No longer. I'd stay on Samosir, see the things I'd come here to see, but I wouldn't see them with the same eyes I'd had when I arrived in this country. I wouldn't experience them with the same heart.

34

In the *kampong*, I went straight to the shore and headed to the jetty where I'd seen the boats moored. I walked close to the water's edge, along the bank that was lined with *deke ramba*, stone tanks built into the side of the lake. The loose built edges allowed fresh water to circulate, but kept the captive fish trapped inside. I stopped and watched the *ikan mas* and *mujahir* – flashes of gold and silver fish darting for deeper water they'd never reach – then I looked over at the jetty and saw what I had come for.

There was just one boat that day, a red speedboat with a white hull and a single Evinrude engine. There was a set of water skis in the back, a coil of rope that looked old and worn. A couple of orange life jackets, the tough material split in several places. Beside the boat, sitting on a short, rough wooden jetty, a man, his trousers rolled to his knees, his shirt unbuttoned, his feet dangling in the water. He heard my movement and turned to look at me.

I stopped and watched him stand, his body language aggressive and suspicious. He drew himself up to his full height, a good few inches taller than me, and lifted his chest. 'What do you want?'

'It's Richard, isn't it?' I was hoping to see Hidayat, but Richard was the one with the boat.

'What do you want?'

I looked out across the lake and then back at Richard. 'A lift?'

His big shoulders dropped a touch, then he drew them back up again. 'Your comrades not tell you I don't give lifts?'

'My comrades?'

He flicked his head in the direction of the hill. 'Up there. Your friends. They send you on a supplies run?'

I shook my head.

'Food? Booze? Drugs?' He turned away from me, going to his boat, busying himself with other things.

'They're not my friends,' I told him. 'And I'm not planning on coming back. Hidayat said I could come to you if I needed help.'

He looked round at me. 'They kick you out? Christ, that's a new one. What they do? Smack you about a bit first? You look like shit.'

'You should see the other guy.'

Richard smiled, in spite of himself. 'First your shoulder and now your face. Shitty luck, mate. Looks like they dragged you around the forest.'

'Are you going to give me a lift or not?'

He sat down on the edge of his boat, unrolled the legs of his trousers, leaned back and took out a pair of flip-flops, which he dropped onto the jetty. 'That depends.'

'On what?'

'On how much money you got.' He worked his wet feet into the rubber flip-flops.

'Enough.'

'Don't get smart.'

'How much do you want, then?'

'Where do you want to go?'

'Samosir.'

'That's it? No idea *where* on the island?'

'Pulau Samosir Cottages.'

He thought about it. 'I know the place. Hundred thousand roops.'

I nodded and put my hand in my pocket, taking out a wad of

notes. I unfolded them and counted them out, coming short by a thousand.

'Not enough,' Richard said.

'I've got more.'

'Yeah? Well, lucky you, but you're gonna have to show me otherwise you're not going anywhere on my boat.'

'I've got it on me,' I said, thinking I'd dip into my money-belt once we were on the water. 'I'll give it to you when we get there.'

Richard showed me a knowing smile and shook his head. 'Uh-uh. You need to put the money in my hand before you step foot in my boat.'

'Look,' I said, 'I have the money right here. Can we just go, please? I'll give it—'

'No money, no ride.' He was enjoying himself. 'Unless you want to take that.' He pointed at a canoe that was lying at the end of the jetty, a hole in its hull. 'But you might need one of these.' He reached into his boat again and took out a large Blue Riband margarine tin. He threw it at me but I was slow and didn't catch it. The tin fell onto the jetty with a rude clatter that disturbed the morning calm. It rolled in a curve and I watched it run out to the edge of the jetty and drop into the lake where it floated for a few seconds before tipping to one side and filling. As it sank, the gold interior glinted in the clear water.

I wanted to show him two fingers and walk away, but I couldn't. I didn't want to go back up the hill to Kurt, and last time I'd ventured onto the path up the cliff, I'd fallen and dislocated my shoulder. I couldn't see anybody else around, so if I was going to get out of here, it was going to be on Richard's boat. 'For Christ's sake,' I almost pleaded. 'Give me a break, will you?'

'Why? Why should I give you a break?'

I touched my hand to my waist.

'You worried someone's gonna see your money-belt, is that it? That me or someone else will try to take your money. You think we're thieves round here?'

'No.'

'Then show me the money. Put it in my hand and you'll get your ride.'

With no other option, I sighed and reached for my belt.

I climbed into the boat and sat on the back seat, close to the engine, as Richard loosened the rope securing us to the jetty. He threw the rope at my feet and jumped in, settling himself behind the wheel and switching on the engine. Close to my ears, the motor started, drowning any other sounds.

I looked back up the hill, towards the line of trees as the propeller churned the water and took us out of the small bay, into the main body of the lake. And then, for the first time, I was on Toba, with the wind in my hair, and my trousers soaking up the water from the hard plastic seat. I continued to stare at the hillside as we sped away from it, leaving that part of my life behind, then I blinked hard and turned my attention to the rest of the lake.

On one side, the island of Samosir slipped by, and far away on the other, I could see the high black cliffs rising to pine forests. There were one or two boats here; small fishing vessels, not much more than canoes, the single occupants casting nets or drawing in woven pots attached to small floating buoys. They pulled in the baskets, winding the orange plastic string into their boats, checking the night's catch.

Richard took the boat around the tip of Samosir island, turning, taking us back in the direction of Parapat. Dotted along the edge of the island I could see small settlements. Collections of traditional houses and cottages that looked to be in failing order.

On the mainland side, the shoreline had the look of a 1950s European resort. Low-rise villas on the water's edge, metal railings, light blue paint on stucco, dry and split like slashed paper. There were rows of pedalos, too, red and blue shapes bobbing on the waves, waiting for one of the few tourists to wake and take them out onto the water. I watched them, my head turning as we passed, thinking that I might have been one of those tourists. Just a short while ago, I had intended to spend my time in places like this, along with the other people who came here, but my experiences had been quite unlike anything I had expected. So much life and death in such a short time. Kurt had been right about one thing, though: everything was different in his community. And now I was glad to be free of it.

With those thoughts, I hardly noticed that Richard had slowed the engine, and it was only when he cut the motor altogether that I looked up to see what was going on.

For a moment he just sat there with his back to me, while the boat bobbed in the water. The lake lapped at the hull, a hollow, calming sound. The engine ticked beside me. Somewhere on the lake a boat sounded its horn.

'What's the matter? Why have we stopped?'

Richard turned round and stared at me, a thoughtful expression, before pushing himself out of his seat and coming to sit opposite me. The boat rocked in the water as he came over, leaning forward, his face close to mine. 'Not often I get one of you people on your own.' I could see the lines at the corners of his grey eyes, the tiny points on his square chin where fresh growth was pushing through.

I leaned away from him. If Richard was trying to intimidate me, it was working.

He reached into a top pocket and took out a packet of cigarettes. Not *kretek*, not the clove cigarettes of the locals. These were Benson and Hedges, the gold box and the particular British branding looking out of place in his tanned hands, here in the middle of Lake Toba.

He put a cigarette in his mouth and lit it with a plastic gas lighter and I couldn't help but glance at the engine beside me.

'You worried I'm gonna blow us up?' he asked.

'What do you mean by that? "One of you people"?'

'One of Kurt's people.'

I shook my head and looked at my feet. 'I already told you, I'm not one of his people. I'm leaving. Going somewhere else.'

'See the sights?'

'Something like that.'

'Or maybe get some supplies for your friends? Do a bit of selling? They got you doing that yet?'

'I already told you—'

'Yeah. They're not your friends, and you're leaving.'

'Right. Anyway, you know me. I've only been up there a few days.'

'You went up there with that girl. Domino.'

'Yeah.'

'It not work out for you?'

I looked out at another speedboat passing us, a hundred metres away, its engine droning.

'Probably better that way,' he said.

When I didn't answer, Richard took a long drag of his cigarette and ran his thumb across his lips, the cigarette end coming close to his face, making him squint against the smoke. 'You know, I used to take you people across the lake all the time. A regular fucking ferry service until your man Kurt tried to spin his way out of paying.'

I thought about how determined he'd been for me to pay him before he'd allowed me to set foot on the boat.

'He tried to weasel out of it, getting all smarmy, but I wasn't having any of it. So then he got ballsy, lost his hippy cool and started shouting, calling me all kinds of things. One thing led to another and he ended up with some bruising. Bit like yours now. Nothing too bad, but the way I saw it, he deserved it. Deserved more, probably. I'm trying to make a living, you know. Gas costs money.'

He took another drag and studied the end of the cigarette. 'Then his man found Hidayat out looking for butterflies. Up on the hill there.' Richard pointed.

'His man?' I stared at him. 'Who?'

'The big guy. American.'

'Michael.' I touched my nose, remembering last night.

'That's the guy. Thought it would be a good idea to have a

go at Hidayat. He do all that to you?' He pointed to the bruise on my face, the dirt on my clothes.

I took a deep breath and nodded without intending to.

'We got something in common, then. Except he beat Hidayat even worse. Close to death. Broke his jaw, three ribs, perforated an ear. Wouldn't go out after that, not even for the butterflies.'

'What did you do?'

'I didn't do anything.' He sniffed hard. 'I would've gone up there and shot the fucker between the eyes if Hidayat hadn't begged me not to. He's the forgiving kind, and he doesn't want to spend what he's got left fighting with idiots like your man Kurt.'

'What he's got left?'

Richard looked at me hard. 'He has MS.'

I didn't know much about it, but I remembered the way Hidayat had dragged his leg – as if walking had been a struggle. 'Is it bad?'

'Good days and bad days, but it's getting worse, so we keep away from that little cult you people got going up there.'

'It's not . . .' I was about to tell him that it wasn't what he thought. I felt the need to defend the place, probably because I'd been there myself, enjoyed it for a while, but then I stopped. I reminded myself of the reason I'd left. Maybe I hadn't stayed because I'd enjoyed the place, wanted to be with Domino, but because it had burrowed under my skin and into my mind. Like a bloated tick feeding on me, sucking away my sense of the real world. That's why my initial reaction was to defend it.

Richard nodded like he'd seen straight through me. 'Saw it for yourself, didn't you? *Felt* it.'

I looked Richard in the eye before glancing away. The way he stared into me made me uncomfortable. And what he was saying, I didn't want to hear it, but I knew there was truth in it. Kurt had an influence over those people, even if it hadn't worked on me in quite the same way.

'You want to tell me what happened?'

I shook my head and watched a boat in the distance, not much more than a dark smudge on the surface of the water.

Richard leaned further forwards and tapped the cigarette packet on my knee to get my attention. When I looked at him, he offered them to me. I reminded myself that I didn't smoke, not before going up there, and shook my head again.

'Was it something you did? Something you said?' His manner softened. 'Something you saw maybe?'

I sighed and shook my head again. 'Can we just get going?' I said, feeling suddenly younger than my years; feeling that the man sitting opposite me was stronger and more knowing than I'd ever be. I'd fooled myself into thinking I'd grown in some way from my experience, but I knew now that I was still the same person I'd been when I set foot on the plane and watched the doors close on the non-life I was leaving behind.

'Sure,' he said, but made no move. Instead, he took another drag on his cigarette and lifted his head skywards to blow smoke at the clouds. He leaned over the side of the boat and touched the cigarette tip into the water before dropping it into a Fanta can that was tucked into an elasticated net pocket by his seat. 'You really liked her? That girl?'

'Yeah,' I said. 'I did. Maybe I still do.' But it didn't matter. She was gone now. Left behind. I'd do what she asked. I'd go to the hotel, stay a while, but I had a feeling I'd never see Domino again.

'You know, I never did understand the thing with women,' Richard said. 'Too bloody complicated. That's why I prefer men.'

I looked up at him.

'Don't worry,' he said. 'You're not my type.'

'Eh? No, I—'

Now he smiled. 'Don't worry about it, kid. I'm pulling your leg. You seem all right. Hidayat's usually a pretty good judge of character – better than me anyway – and he liked you.'

'That's why you're helping me?'

'I'm not helping you. You're paying, remember?'

'And that's it?'

Richard shook his head. 'Hidayat told you to come to us if you needed help, and I'll do pretty much whatever he wants.'

'I lost his cloth,' I said. 'The one he used for a sling. I promised I'd bring it back.'

'The *ulos*? Don't worry about it. It was probably just his way of trying to make you come back. Anyway, I reckon you got other things on your mind. Come on, let's get you over the lake. The further away from those people, the better. Consider yourself lucky to have got away.' He climbed back into the front seat. 'You know, people leave them alone up there because they don't do any harm, or because they got someone protecting them, but there's something not right about them.'

'They seemed OK,' I said. 'At first, anyway. Just a few people living how they want to.' But even saying it, I knew they were someone else's words. Kurt's words. Perhaps his spell had gripped me tighter than I'd thought. Or perhaps I was still standing up for Domino, but whatever it was, I'd seen how they wanted to live. I'd seen the graves, I'd seen the markers, and I'd seen the secret burial. And I'd chosen not to be a part of it.

'You know they had the police up there one time? A year ago, maybe a little longer.'

'I heard.'

'And did you hear that some people came over from Australia looking for their son? Hadn't heard from him for weeks. Last place he'd contacted them from was Lake Toba, so they came here to poke about. Police weren't much help, so they started showing pictures around, coming down to the lake, asking if people had seen their kid. I recognised the picture and pointed them in the right direction. I'd seen him going up to that place they've got up there.'

I couldn't help looking back, but the hillside was obscured now; all I could see was Samosir.

'Police had to follow up on it. As far as I know they had a look round but didn't find anything. Got told the boy stayed a while and moved on. No one got busted, though, not for anything. No arrests at all, but there's drugs up there, I know it. What the hell else are they doing up there? And I know your people sell on Samosir.' He paused for a moment and watched me as if waiting for me to give something away. 'I've seen them.'

'I'm not selling anything,' I said.

'They must've paid someone off,' he carried on. 'Hell, you can buy just about anything here. Buy your way *out* of anything. *Korupsi*. It's like there's a price list. A hundred thousand for a dope bust, add a bit for LSD, more for heroin, couple of million for killing a man.' He stopped again, watching my reaction. 'You don't pay, you're in deep shit, especially with drugs. You know what they do with druggies in this country? They jail 'em and shoot 'em.'

He turned back to the wheel and started the boat with the turn of a key. The motor was loud in my ear and I had to shout when I next spoke.

'What was their name?'

He looked over his shoulder and furrowed his brow. 'Who?'

'The people you said. Who came looking for their son.'

Richard closed his eyes like he was thinking hard. 'Sullivan, I think.' He paused as if checking it again. 'Yeah. Kid called himself Sully.'

I turned my head and stared at the water, lifting my eyes to see the shore. I remembered how I had seen the lake for the first time, the excitement and the promise. That moment when the cloud had broken and the sun had shone through like it was blessing the water. Then I thought about drugs and pigs and Michael's fists, and how I had hidden in the night, lying close to where we had buried Matt.

There was no breeze and the air was warm, but I shivered for Sully's unspoken death. For his shallow grave. And for his nameless shrine.

35

When we reached the eastern side of Samosir, Richard took us into shore where there was a gathering of dilapidated buildings close to the water. I climbed over the side of his boat, stretching to make it onto the concrete steps without falling into the water. I thanked him and he waved a hand as if to tell me it was no problem, like he'd done it for free, then he revved his engines and headed back into the lake. He turned the boat not in the direction of his home, but towards Parapat on the other side.

I stood on the concrete jetty, holding on to a set of rusted metal, pool-style steps that dropped into the lake. Two women were washing clothes just along the shore, white islands of bubbles drifting out in the dark water, and they watched me as I headed up towards the guest house. Now, as for the rest of the boat trip, I was thinking about Sully, wondering exactly how he had died. And I thought about the people who'd come looking for their son. Kurt had sent them away with the belief that he was still alive out there somewhere, not buried beneath the forest floor. Sully, a member of the community populated by lonely, impressionable travellers. Losers and drop-outs who had no one to come looking for them. But Sully *hadn't* been alone. Someone *had* come looking for him.

The Pulau Samosir guest house was an innocuous place, just a small collection of four, maybe five waterfront cottages, arranged so that each had a window looking out onto the lake. There were a couple more set back. Like everything else, the cottages were shaped like traditional Batak homes, but they were smaller, only meant for one or two guests. They were old and in failing repair, but there were signs of renovation. Some of them had been repainted recently, making me think of the work I'd done with Michael.

I wandered past the cottages and approached the main office, a saddle-roofed building with a wide veranda at the front where several tables were laid out. Each of them covered with a white paper tablecloth held down with clips. Knives, forks, spoons, glasses and coffee cups laid out on each one. There was a group of Europeans sitting at one table: three young men and two women.

I walked through the open door into the main building. This front area was small. A counter that served as a reception desk. An old bell fashioned from polished brass, the kind you hit on top to make it ting. A rotating rack with colour leaflets and pamphlets standing in one corner. A wooden unit to one side with guidebooks and tourist maps. To my left a swing-door led to a kitchen. Even now, this early in the morning, the air was scented with spiced cooking.

By the counter, close to me, a small woman was sitting in a rattan chair. Her eyes were closed and her head was bowed as if she were sleeping. I cleared my throat to attract her attention and she immediately looked up and smiled, her old face cracking into a dry mud-bed of fissures. She had long hair, tied into a tight bun. She beckoned me in and moved behind the counter, lifting a section of it to let herself through. She was wearing a white tunic and a sarong. Her feet were bare.

'Do you speak English?' I asked, but she shook her head and continued to smile. Her teeth were stained betel-nut red.

'Room?' I ventured.

The woman nodded and took a sheaf of paper from a pile at one end of the counter. She turned it round and passed it to me. It was a faded, photocopied list of prices and I was relieved to see that each one had a translation next to it. No double or single rooms, nothing like that, just different rates for different lengths of stay.

I pointed to the weekly tariff and held up a finger. 'One week,' I said. 'One room.'

She nodded and took out the necessary paperwork, which I completed and returned to her before she held out her hand and showed me that she knew at least some English. 'Pay now,' she said with a smile.

I took some money from my pocket and counted it out for her. It amounted to no more than three pounds a night.

She took the bills, folded them and crushed them in her fist while taking a key from under the counter with her other hand. Then she barked something in Indonesian that sounded like 'Pa!' and a skinny man, similar in age, came through the swing-door, bringing a fresh waft of cooking smells with him. The woman handed over the key and the man beckoned me to follow him.

I trailed him back along the path and waited as he went to the door of the cottage nearest to the metal steps where I'd first stepped foot on Samosir. He turned the key and pushed open the door, showing me into the room. Once inside, he opened the shutters and showed me the bathroom with a smile before saying, '*Selamat datang*. Welcome,' and leaving the room.

Alone, I sat on the edge of the bed. It was a simple room, but comfortable. Clean. The sheets were fresh, and the floor was free of dirt. Swept and washed. There was a table beside the bed with a stack of four or five well-thumbed paperbacks, and a lamp that looked as if it might not work. I reached over and tried it, surprised that it came on with a single click. I smiled to myself and went to the bathroom, looking in at the clean facilities.

A proper toilet, not just a hole in the ground. In the corner, a concrete tub, waist high, filled with water. I dipped my fingers in to test the temperature and found it to be stone cold. Resting on the edge of the tub was a stainless-steel bucket with a fixed handle. I didn't suppose it would be much different from the cold waterfall I'd grown used to, but was pleased to see that there was also a shower in the room. I hadn't realised, until now, how much I had missed hot showers, and the sight of two taps on the wall, one marked red and one marked blue, stirred surprisingly strong feelings of comfort. I turned it on, testing the water, feeling it growing warm.

Unable to wait, I stripped off, threw my clothes onto the floor and put the shower on full blast. While the water warmed further, I inspected my bruises in the mirror. I looked tired and drawn, my eyes bloodshot, the right one ringed black, blue and yellow. There was a day's growth of stubble on my face, streaks of dirt from my night in the forest. There were bruises along my ribs, too, some on my back where Michael had kicked me.

I turned away from myself and stepped under the hot torrent. The water and the free soap didn't wash everything away, but it made me feel better. The cold shower of the waterfall was already just a memory.

After that I climbed between the fresh sheets and slept. I didn't wake until early the next afternoon.

36

Feeling like a different person, I lay naked on the bed and stared at the ceiling. The sun slid through the slatted shutters and fell across me in golden bars. I tried to put the past days behind me. Focus on what I was going to do. I hadn't decided how long I'd wait for Domino, or if I even wanted to wait for her at all now, but I was glad of the change of scenery and made up my mind to make the most of my time here. And the first thing I needed to do was find something to wear.

I counted out a few notes into my pocket, glanced around the room that contained nothing of my own, and closed the door behind me. With my fresh mindset, I couldn't help but feel a kind of freedom. I was going back to the world with new eyes. Things were different away from the trees and the clearings and the swept dirt. Here everything was open and colourful. It was warmer, too, as if the sun had finally agreed to burn through the cloud and shine on me. There was life and there was sound and there was openness by the lake – something that had been missing on the hillside.

I wandered back towards reception with a confidence that had eluded me. There was a bounce in my walk as I followed the stepping stones – no hidden paths and secrets here. I took in everything around me, soaked up everything I saw, watched people going about their business, saw the other tourists and travellers experiencing the island. I wondered why I'd ever considered staying cocooned on the hillside with Kurt and his people, and realised that this was exactly the reason Kurt didn't want people to leave the community too soon. Because, like me, they'd see that it was not the life they wanted. Up there, people were not themselves. Up there, people thought they were free, but they weren't. Instead, they were a primitive, shadowy version of themselves. That was no paradise. It was another world; something darker.

I took a seat at one of the tables and waited no longer than a few minutes before someone spotted me and came out to take my order. I'd missed more than one meal, and my stomach was complaining. I was going to eat something other than fish.

Using only my index finger and my smile, I ordered chicken curry, rice and a Bintang beer from the menu. And when the food came it was good, hot, tasty and free of grit. The beer was cold and the clean glass sweated in the warmth of the early afternoon. It was perfect.

When I'd finished eating, I leaned right back in my chair, put my hands across my stomach and closed my eyes. This was the best I'd felt in a long time. It was as if all my worries had melted away under the warm shower and now I had buried what was left of them beneath a good night's sleep, a meal and some warm sunshine. I even stopped thinking about what I'd left behind, and began thinking about what lay ahead.

I walked away from the lake, following the small map on the back of the price list the woman in the *losmen* had given me. A road, not much more than a track, led further inland, but I didn't have to walk far before I came across what I was looking for. A *warung*, a stall no larger than a bus shelter, with an array of goods hanging from it, covering almost every inch of its surface. T-shirts, shorts, caps, flip-flops, sandals, swimming trunks, sarongs, sweets, cigarettes, drink cans, everything. And beside it, tied through their front wheels with a length of chain, a row of bicycles and mopeds.

I bought some new clothes, basic toiletries, a small backpack, a cheap watch, and hired a moped for what was left of the day, setting off along the main road that snaked around the island.

'*Pigi mana?*' said the stall owner as he finished showing me how to use the moped. '*Pigi mana?* Where you go?'

I shrugged and swung my leg over. 'Don't know.'

'Don't know? *Tidak tau?*' He gave me a thumbs up. 'Good place to go.'

Keeping track of the time on my new watch was a revelation to me. By putting plastic and metal on my wrist, I was once again in control of my time. Time that had never changed. It hadn't quickened, slowed, stopped or disappeared, but I had lost track of it, and felt secure in my regained mastery of it. I was recapturing control of my own life. I was making my own decisions and doing the things I wanted to do. I wasn't following anybody.

It struck me that I had been swept along by so many emotions and intentions. I had been controlled by the community, sapped of my ability to be myself, and by not refusing to go along with its strange rules and rituals, I had been carried into extraordinary circumstances. Kurt had told me that the community was a place to be free, but he was wrong. Out *here* I was free. Out *here* I made my own choices. And, blessed with that feeling of great relief, as if a shroud had been lifted from my mind, I thought I had seen the last of Kurt and his people.

I rode through one or two small villages, stopping to look around in each one, and passed many shrines along the road. The first few reminded me of what I was leaving behind me, the night I'd spent hidden in the forest, but once I'd seen so many, I hardly noticed them any more.

At about four o clock I stopped by a village stall to buy a bag of rambutans, which I ate by the roadside, peeling the hairy red skins and savouring the sweet white flesh. Further down, on the other side of the road, there was a dilapidated longhouse with a rusted roof. In front of it, colourful fabrics were held up on poles, a makeshift sun shelter, and there was a group of people beneath it, the women with their hair tied back, all wearing *ulos*, traditional Batak cloth, woven with fresh and vibrant colour. Even the men, in shirts and trousers, were wearing *ulos* over their shoulders. I could see blackened pots over wood fires, a line of children watching from a stone wall beneath a small grove of trees. I could hear singing from inside the longhouse, the sound of instruments, drumming, the beat fast and alien to my ears. It was a colourful and joyous spectacle and only when I saw the coffin being carried from the longhouse did I understand that this was a funeral. I watched for a while longer as they carried it around the house, and my thoughts turned to the funerals in my recent past. I thought about what I had seen in the forest and I thought about Domino and I thought about Helena, feeling a tinge of guilt that I had left her behind. I watched the mourners circling the house with the coffin and I wondered what I could have done for her. What I could *still* do. But I told myself that Helena would be fine. That she was safe. Then I stood, turned the moped round and headed back the way I'd come, thinking that tomorrow I would venture further.

Back in my room, I stripped off, throwing my borrowed shorts and T-shirt into the dented brass bin in the far corner of the room. I showered again, shaved and dressed in my new clothes. The batik-print shirt still smelled of the ink that had been used to produce the vivid pattern, and the flip-flops smelled of rubber, and I liked it. Everything I wore smelled unused. Fresh. Mine. I was a new person and the next part of my trip had truly begun.

With the sun almost gone from the sky, I left my cottage and took the path to reception. There were a few electric lights on already, not much more than bare bulbs hanging from wires in the ceiling. The group of Europeans I'd seen when I arrived was there again, sitting at the same table, a collection of dishes laid out in front of them.

They glanced at me as I went to the table I'd used at lunchtime and I was about to sit down when I changed my mind. I wouldn't sit in the same place. I'd choose a different table. And I would do that each day and night I was here. There would be no pattern, no habits. This was a stop on a longer journey. I would be here and then I would be gone.

The old woman with the bun and the smile came to my table almost as soon as I was on the chair, her sarong whispering around her bare ankles. She placed a menu in front of me and managed a short English phrase. 'Good evening,' she said.

'*Selamat malam*,' I returned, and we smiled at each other, being able to do little more. I ordered a beer and looked over the menu, settling on something I'd never heard of.

At the back of the covered veranda, against the outside wall of reception, two dark-skinned men were sitting on a worn rattan bench, deep in conversation. Behind them, on the wall, two guitars. I'd only just started eating when one of them took down an instrument, strumming a few notes, twisting the tuners, then starting to play.

By now, there were people – Europeans or Americans, I guessed – at one or two of the other tables and most of them stopped talking, looking up at the guitarist. When he started to sing, the sound he produced was loud and smooth and deep. The second man, the older of the two, joined in from time to time, making movements with his hands as if telling a story, and occasionally he made loud clicking noises deep in his throat. Then he took the second guitar from the wall and turned it round, using the wooden back as a makeshift drum.

I watched and listened as I finished my meal, disappointed when they stopped. They accepted applause before settling themselves back on the bench as if nothing had happened.

I overheard the people on the table next to me discussing the singing and I turned to look at them, catching someone's eye. A small guy, in his twenties, short blond hair and ruddy cheeks.

'Hey, man, you on your own?' he said. They were the people I'd seen when I arrived.

I nodded, not sure I wanted to speak to anyone else. I'd been enjoying my own company all day, getting to know myself better than I'd been able to among the trees and the people.

'Travelling?' he asked.

I hesitated, remembering Kurt's disdain for travellers and tourists, then I smiled and nodded. 'Yeah. Travelling.'

'Brave man.'

'Brave?'

'Travelling on your own. Most people, they have someone with them.'

I had a vague recollection of Domino saying something similar. I'd never thought of myself as brave. 'Or maybe just stupid,' I said.

He laughed at that, looking round at his friends and nodding. Then he leaned over the table and held out his hand. 'I'm Bas,' he said. 'Sebastiaan. And this is Christina.' The girl at the table lifted a hand and smiled. She was petite with dark curly hair cut short and unflattering.

'Alex,' I told him.

'And these two crazy guys are Gaz and Paulie.'

Still shaking Bas's hand, as if he didn't intend to let me go, I raised my left hand and said, 'Hi.'

'You German?' I asked, narrowing my eyes at Bas. 'That a German accent?'

He laughed. 'German? No fuckin' way, man. Dutch. Not these two guys, though. These two are your countrymen.' He pointed at me and put his head to one side. 'English, right?'

I smiled and nodded.

Bas invited me to come over and sit with them, asked about my black eye. I told him I slipped getting off the ferry and they all nodded with sympathy. He said he and Christina met Gaz and Paulie a couple of days ago, showed them the best places to chill out on the island and told them where to get the things they wanted to smoke, shoot, sniff or pop. He said he'd do the same for me if I liked; he knew a girl – 'white, not some dodgy Indonesian' – who could get anything, but I shook my head, telling him I wasn't into that stuff. And I wondered if I knew his dealer. We might have even shared a longhouse.

'Not into it? You *are* English, right? I thought all you guys were into it. I mean, you gotta be into it here. It's the right place for it. *The* best place, man. You're not into it, you never tried it.'

I just showed him a brief smile, thinking about the tablet Kurt had given me. I imagined it was just the kind of thing that a guy like Bas was looking for. Maybe he'd even like it up there with Kurt and his gang.

'I can show you places,' he said to me. 'Places like you never seen.'

'You'd be surprised,' I said.

Bas gave me a curious look. 'Yeah? You know somewhere?'

I shook my head. 'Nah. Not really.'

I had a couple of drinks with Bas and his friends, saying goodnight at around half ten. By then we were all quite drunk and Christina was clinging to Bas like he was the best catch she was ever going to get. She had her arms wrapped around him and I envied him in a way. Earlier on, sober and in daylight, I'd thought I could forget about Domino, but now, in the cool darkness, wandering back to my guest house, alone and drunk, I didn't feel so clear about that any more.

I followed the path using the light that spilled from one or two of the other cottages, leaving the sounds of the dining area behind me. I let myself into my room and sat on the edge of the bed for some time, listening to the lake caressing the shore, feeling alone. In the corner of the room, where the white wall met the ceiling, a gecko was sitting, waiting for something tasty to come its way.

'Eat them up, little guy,' I said aloud. 'Keep the little buggers from biting me.'

It waited, motionless, before giving up and moving away, its body waggling from side to side as it searched for another corner, another spot to lie in wait.

I climbed into bed in just my shorts, and looked up at the gecko once more before switching off the light.

Somewhere around midnight, according to the luminous dial on my cheap watch, I was woken by a low rumbling. I sat up in the darkness and strained my ears. Again the sound came, this time louder, longer, and I climbed out of bed and threw on my shirt and put on my flip-flops. I left my room and went down to the lake.

The water was beginning to chop, a cool wind cutting over its surface and somewhere in the distance, further east from where I was standing, thunder rumbled once more. I sat down on the concrete jetty and watched lightning flash on the other side of the lake. Bright and daring, followed by the low growl of thunder, rolling and breaking in the electric atmosphere, with nothing to stop its progress. As the minutes passed the storm grew ever closer, a beast approaching, the lightning reflected on the surface of the lake and the thunder shaking through me, surprising me every time it bellowed. And when the rain came, hard and heavy, I stayed where I was, letting it soak right through me. The dense, cleansing downpour battering the lake, crashing down on me, the earthy sound of the drops bringing to mind the scatter of soil on dead skin. I closed my eyes and turned my face to the sky and I thought about the story Domino had told me. About how the lake was formed.

And I wondered if something had angered the gods.

37

When I woke, the morning air was sweet with the scent of wet grass and damp soil. There was a brightness which I hadn't seen since coming here. A freshness. The rain had washed everything clean. It had rinsed the cataracts from my eyes.

I'd slept well after the storm, settling in my comfortable bed as the beast had rolled on, moving overhead, searching for other places to wipe clean.

Showered and dressed, I ate alone – no sign of Bas and his friends – taking a plateful of the ripe, fresh fruit on display. Papaya, pineapple, rambutans, mangosteens and bananas. A colourful array of the sweetest things the country had to display. In the palms by the veranda, bright birds, bee-eaters, swooped to snatch insects from the air, their bodies a flash of green and blue and red.

Feeling as cleansed on the inside as I did on the outside, I set out on the road, making for the place where I'd hired the moped. Early as it was, the stall was open and the man was smiling just as he had been yesterday, happy to take my money. He unlocked the chain, wheeled the first of the mopeds over to me and exchanged it for a wad of cash, which he tucked into his pocket.

The moped was slow and noisy, but I was glad to be out and on the move. I passed paddy fields and small settlements of Batak houses, many with corrugated iron across the saddled roofs, much of it rusted and worn by the elements. Clothes were strung on wires between them, and great mats were laid out before them with rice spread out to dry in the sun.

I passed through Tuk Tuk without stopping and drove on to Ambarita. Kurt would've scoffed at me signing up for a guided tour with some of the other pale tourists, but I'd left that behind now, and gathering with the others made me feel as if I were raising my fingers at him. Rebelling. Hell, I might even go and find that hotel shaped like a fish.

Our guide was a serious-looking man, hardly a smile. A pink and white striped shirt, white trousers and sandals. He gathered us all together using English that was thick with accent but far better than my '*Bahasa Indonesia*'. I looked around at the other tourists, wondering if they even spoke English, and it struck me that whoever these people were, wherever they came from, the most assured way of being understood was to speak English.

There were a lot of children running around, pulling at our shirts, trying to sell chewing gum, sweets, T-shirts. I bought Chiclets from one of them, maybe ten years old with a worn, dirty T-shirt, shorts that were too big for him and nothing on his feet but dust and scabs. I wanted to do him a favour, but it just encouraged the others. They thought I was the only one going to buy anything so I was worth a shot, all of them crowding round me like I was a pop star. They were disturbing the guide's patter, so he chased them away with harsh words, taking off his sandal and slapping one of them hard as he ran away.

He must've seen the look on my face because he waved a hand and shook his head. 'My son,' he said.

A few people in the small group laughed, bringing a wry smile to his face that was gone within a couple of seconds. I turned away and watched two scruffy dogs, amber fur, sniffing and dismissing each other before parting ways, ignoring the chickens that scratched in the dirt.

I didn't listen much when he took us into the longhouse and told us how the Bataks used to live. This longhouse was empty, but I'd been into ones with life soaked into their walls. Coming out of the house, he took us down to the stone chairs. This was what Kurt and Michael had tried to recreate in their own community by dragging rocks from further up the hillside. These chairs were not just rocks, though, they were *carved* from rocks. The guide told us this was where the council would have been held, then became enthused when he recounted the gory bit. The part Kurt had so relished.

'This,' he said, leading us to the execution stone, 'was where they took people to be punished.'

We followed him like sacrificial sheep, listening as he talked over the sound of a cockerel that crowed not far away. We studied the stone, this one mottled and old, the surface almost white in places where the elements had pounded it. It was a different shape from Kurt's. This one flatter, more square, and there was another stone close by that was used as a block, a place to behead rather than disembowel. The guide told us about the cannibalism. Dragged his son over, blindfolded him, made him lie on the rock. He took a dark, patterned *ulos* cloth from beside the stone and put it over his son's face and explained how the ancients would have sliced him open. Then they moved to the block and the boy got to his knees and, as the guide spoke, he chopped the edge of his hand down across his son's neck and the boy gave a less than convincing death rattle and slipped sideways off the rock. The gathering of tourists laughed, the young boy stood and bowed, then his father described how the ancients ate the dead man's organs and drank his blood. A tale well practised, told time and again for entertainment and revulsion.

Seeing it like this was strange. Not at all like it had been to see Kurt's execution stone. This felt less real, as if I were watching it all on a screen. It was nothing compared to what I had seen among the trees. Up there it had been more sinister, more *possible*. Without the jokey re-enactment, without the laughing tourists. With just the wind and the trees and the dirt and the dark.

After the mock execution there was a photo opportunity for

the tourists, taking turns sitting in the bench seat, putting their arms around the stone figure. I'd had enough by then, I didn't need to visit the gift shop, so I slipped away, decided to go it alone, get back on my moped, head out to the water's edge and stare at the lake for a while.

On my way over to where I'd left the moped, though, something caught my attention. The sun was high and the shadows were short, but the spaces between some of the iron-roofed buildings were shaded from the sun. In one of those spaces, grey without direct sunlight, were three figures, not wanting to be seen.

I moved to one side of the track, slowed my pace and watched them conducting their deal. The two with their backs to me, blocking the third from view, looked like tourists. Young, no older than me, small packs on their backs, making some kind of exchange. I guessed drugs, and thought about the penalties if they were caught. Prison. Death. Up there it hadn't felt so dangerous. Nobody was there to see; everything was shielded by the trees and the sense of otherworldliness. But down here, it was different.

I carried on walking, pretending not to notice, surprised at how quickly it happened. Within a few seconds, the young tourists were coming out of the shadow, rejoining the track and walking towards me. They looked at me as they passed, one of them hiding a guilty look that stained him, his eyes averting as soon as they met mine, going to the ground, thinking of something to say to his travelling partner.

I glanced over my shoulder once they'd passed, shaking my head a little, and when I turned back to the road, I saw the dealer come out of the shadow and I recognised her immediately. Freia.

I'd planned on going to a few other places before heading back to my guest house, but after seeing Freia, I didn't much feel like it. It reminded me what I was escaping from, and I realised that I hadn't gone far enough. I'd languished, avoided making a decision. I'd hung around close to Domino, waiting for an explanation – as if anything might be good enough to justify what I'd seen. Coming down from the hillside was coming back to reality, but it was only now that my epiphany came. I could hardly believe I'd even considered waiting. I made myself imagine not seeing Domino again. I pictured myself leaving Samosir today, and I knew it was the best thing to do. Domino had been an image, not a reality. I didn't need her. I didn't want her. I didn't want any of it. The drugs and the graves were all I saw now.

So, returning to my *losmen* that afternoon, I decided I'd waited long enough – that what I was waiting for was not worth it. I was going to leave that place. I was going to put my toothbrush and my new T-shirts and my spare trousers into my backpack and take the ferry to Parapat. I'd buy a proper rucksack, some more clothes, a few necessities, then I'd do all the things I'd planned on doing with my mother's money. I'd take the bus to Brastagi and climb the volcano. I'd see the apes in Bukit Lawang, go to Aceh, then head out to Bali. I couldn't wait any more.

I returned the moped to the *warung* and headed for my room, spotting Bas and Christina coming in the opposite direction. Bas held up his hand, a half-wave, and they stopped in front of me. 'Alex,' he said. 'You been telling me lies? I thought you said you were travelling alone.'

'I am.'

'So who's the girl?' he asked, glancing at Christina, then punching me on the arm like he was my buddy. 'She's pretty, Alex. No wonder you kept her quiet.'

'She's sexy,' Christina said.

'Where?' I asked. 'Where is she?'

'Over by reception.' Bas pointed a thumb over his shoulder. 'I heard her asking about you.'

'Thanks,' I said, walking past.

'Hey,' called Christina. 'You want to get together, the four of us, we can . . .'

But I lost the end of her sentence as I made my way along the path, my stomach turning. I was not going to be persuaded. Whatever Domino had to say, I would tell her how I felt and what I was going to do. I was going to leave, no matter what.

I turned the corner, heading for reception, expecting to see Domino waiting for me, sitting at one of the tables, or standing with her back to me. But it wasn't Domino.

I stopped, shook my head as I approached. It wasn't the first time I'd expected Domino but got Helena instead.

'Alex,' she said, pushing out a chair so I could sit down. 'Drink?' She looked good. Her dark hair loose, her blue eyes smiling.

'How did you know I'd be here?' I was pleased to see her, glad to know she was safe.

'Domino told me.'

'She told you? Why?'

Helena waved her hand, attracting the woman's attention and raising her bottle. The woman nodded and went inside.

'She wanted me to come and see you. Kurt sent me and Freia down to make a few sales—'

'After what he said that night? He let you leave?'

'He thinks you're gone, Alex. He knows I have nowhere to go. And I guess he thinks it's time I start earning my keep. Make me one of them.'

'I saw Freia. In Ambarita.'

'You speak to her?'

'She didn't see me. Does she know you're here?'

'No one knows except Domino. Kurt's pretty pissed off about you leaving.'

'Good.'

'But he'd let you come back if it's what *she* wanted.'

'I'm not coming back.'

She drained her beer and put the bottle down on the metal table. 'What happened up there?' She flicked her head in the direction of the hillside, an almost imperceptible movement, as if she'd made it without thinking. 'To make you run away like that? Is it because of Michael? Your bruises . . . I'm sorry, Alex.'

The woman came to the table with two bottles on a tray, two glasses. I poured my beer into the glass and took a sip.

'She wants you to come back. That's what she asked me to tell you.'

It was ironic that Domino had asked Helena to bring the message. 'She doesn't know about us, does she?' I asked.

'No.' The smile she offered made her look a little sad.

I studied her face. 'Why didn't she come here herself?'

Helena shrugged. 'Maybe she thinks you've seen what you're missing. That you'll be bored and go back to her. She didn't need to come.'

'She said that?'

'No, but she'll be thinking it. She won't leave that place for you or anyone, Alex. It's part of her. And she'll never leave her brother, either. You said it yourself. It's what makes them different from the rest of us. They have someone.'

'That can't be true, though. The others, they must have people. What about Alban and Evie? They're together.'

'Not really.'

'You and Michael.'

'You're joking now.'

I reached out for my beer. I took a drink and held it in my hand, resting the bottom of the glass on my thigh. Condensation soaked through my trousers. 'I was about to leave the island. I was going back to my room to pack my stuff. I've had enough. Can't believe I even waited this long. I shouldn't have come here.'

'So why *did* you come?'

'She asked me to wait, but I guess you already know that.'

She shook her head. 'We almost made it the other night.'

'Yeah. But when Kurt was there and . . . I just had to leave.'

'I know. But then she persuaded you to wait for her.'

'Yes.'

'So what changed your mind? What made you want to leave now?'

'I saw Freia in Ambarita and it was like something just clicked. A wake-up call. I can't believe I've been such a bloody idiot. Maybe it's that place, maybe it got under my skin more than I thought. Her, too.'

'And you're not going back? Not even for Domino?'

'No.'

Helena twisted her glass with one hand, spreading the condensation mark across the tabletop. 'We didn't get a chance to talk about what happened. That night. I know you said to forget it, but I can't. I like you, Alex.'

'Because I pulled you out of the water.'

'No.' She shook her head. 'How about you? You like Domino just because she helped *you*?'

'Probably. Now I think about it, yeah, probably.'

I looked at her hand on the table and we were quiet for a while before Helena spoke again.

'Alex? Can I ask you something?'

'Mm-hm.'

'If things don't work out with you and Domino, I mean, if you really don't want to go back up there—'

'I already told you I'm not going back. I mean it.'

'Do you think we could go someplace together, then?'

I looked at her.

'As friends, I mean. We could travel together.'

I said nothing.

'I need to leave too, Alex, but I don't know if I can do it alone. I've been there so long.'

'How long?'

'A year? More? I don't know; that place gets in your head. You know that. You lose time.'

'Yeah.' I leaned back in my chair and stretched my feet under the table, thinking how everybody said that. Whenever I asked anyone how long they'd been there, none of them was able to give me a straight answer.

Early evening and the sun was bleeding in the sky. Everything carried a scarlet tint. As the colour faded, so the old woman put on the lights, bringing the bugs to the tables.

'I should go back,' Helena said at last. 'Freia doesn't know I'm here; she'll have to go back alone. They'll wonder where I am.'

'What will they do? Send a search party?'

'Not tonight. Maybe in the morning.'

'Really? They'd actually come looking for you?'

'I came to sell. There's more than just Kurt interested in what I bring back.'

'Alim?'

'And Danuri.'

'Yeah, well, I could make life difficult for Kurt,' I said, drawing a questioning look from Helena. 'Oh, never mind,' I told her, thinking about what I'd seen in the forest; what I'd seen Domino do with her brother and Michael. It hardly seemed real now. A bad dream. Drugs and death. I could tell someone, the police maybe, but I knew Kurt had protection – I'd heard it said more than once. Besides, I wasn't sure it was the kind of adventure I was looking for. You can't just drop information like that and run.

'Why don't you stay?' I asked her. 'Have something to eat, talk. You can sleep in my room. Screw their search party.'

Helena stopped with her glass at her mouth. She watched me over the rim before lowering it and wiping her lips. 'Really?'

'Why not? We're supposed to be travellers. Free spirits. We don't have to keep Kurt happy; we can do whatever we want.'

Again, an almost imperceptible glance in the direction of the hillside. Then a hesitant nod and a rebellious smile. 'Free spirits?'

'Free spirits,' I said.

We ordered food from the old woman and ate like we'd been on a desert island for a year. We talked like we hadn't talked to another soul for all that time, too.

'Last person I really talked to like this was Sully,' she said, taking my mind back to the marker I'd seen among the trees. 'Since then, Michael has always been there.'

'You didn't try talking to *him*?'

'Michael? God, no. He's not the understanding type.'

'And you never thought of leaving?'

'At first I didn't – not when Sully was there. And after that, it felt like I was part of the family, but it's not like that any more. I'm not like the others any more.'

'What changed?'

'I don't know. I think maybe it was you. Because I could see you weren't part of it. Because you questioned what we did.'

'So why didn't you just leave?'

'I have nowhere else to go.'

'Sweden?'

Helena shook her head. 'That would be too close to *him*,' she said. 'My father. That's why I came here. I suppose I was running away. He was a "hands-on" dad. Only the hands were always fists and fingers.'

'And you ran *here*?'

'Kuta,' she reminded me. 'Bali. It looked like a good place. When I needed to get out of the house, I used to sit in this café on the corner, browsing websites and wondering where I could go. It was the best way for me to lose myself and forget. I used to look at pictures of places and imagine myself going there – getting away. And one day I saw pictures of Kuta and it looked like so much fun. Bars, beaches, people having a good time. It seemed like it would be a good place to run away to, so that's what I did. Just like that and, God, I felt so brave. And then I met Sully and Michael and . . .' She shrugged.

'What about your mother? You couldn't have—'

'She died when I was six years old.'

'Shit, I'm sorry.'

She gave a humourless laugh. 'Seems like there's always someone leaving me behind.' Then she shook the thought away. 'So is it the same for you, Alex? Is there something you're running away from?'

I remembered a similar conversation with Domino, that night when we had sat on the hospital steps. 'He might not be there any more,' I said. 'Your dad, I mean.'

Helena sighed. 'I can only hope.'

'So you ended up coming here. With a guy called Sully you met in a bar in Kuta.'

'Sounds a little slutty, doesn't it?'

'Not really. Not much different from how I got here.' I watched her, remembering the last time I had seen her, outside the longhouse, confronted by Kurt. She was so much more simple than Domino. So much more like me. 'I was worried about you.'

'But you left me alone.'

'I thought it was safer that way. Better for all of us.'

I heard voices behind me and turned to see Bas and his crew coming in our direction.

'Time to go,' I said, pushing back my seat. 'Let's go for a walk.'

We went to the lakeside, sat on the stone bank and watched the lights on the water. Somewhere over the highlands thunder sounded, low and long.

And sitting there, with the cool breeze and the darkness, and Helena beside me, everything felt calm and right. 'Just now you asked me if I was running away from something,' I said.

I sensed her turn to look at me.

'Well, I suppose I am, in a way. I mean, I never really thought about it like that – *running away* – but . . .'

She said nothing while I collected my thoughts.

'My mother died. Just before I came out here. She was ill and I looked after her for a long time. Then all I ever saw was hospitals and medicines and . . . she wasn't in any pain, but she was . . . just lying there. She could hardly even speak in the end.'

'It must've been hard.'

'The thing is, I felt like my whole life stopped. And sometimes I hate myself for feeling like that; like she ruined my life. She didn't ask for it to happen.' I met Helena's gaze for a moment, then looked away. 'She asked me to help her.'

'Help her? You mean—'

'Yeah.'

'And that's what you're running away from? Because you helped her to die?'

I shook my head and stared out at the lake again. 'No. I *didn't* help her, Helena, that's the thing. I wonder if I should've done – sometimes can't get it out of my head – but part of me thinks she wanted it for my sake more than hers. Because she thought she was ruining my life. But I always hoped that she'd get better. I mean, the doctors told me she wouldn't, but I couldn't help hoping.'

'I can understand that.'

'Can you? Domino said she couldn't let that happen to someone she loved, that she'd have to do something.'

Helena made a dismissive sound. 'What does she know? Why wouldn't you hope for your mother to get better? My mother died when I was almost too young to remember her, but if I could have done something to keep her alive, I would've done it. I would've done the same thing as you did, Alex.'

I glanced down at her hand resting on the pale stone bank and I thought about reaching out to take it. Instead, I folded my fingers together and watched her as she looked out at the lights glistening on the surface of the water. Helena had made me feel better about my decision. She hadn't rid me of my guilt, but she had dulled it a little, and I wanted to do something for her. She thought that everybody abandoned her: her mother, her father. She even believed Sully had left her. 'Your friend Sully,' I said. 'You really don't know what happened to him, do you?'

She shifted to face me but her attention was caught by something flitting across the surface of the lake: a bat, flickering as it pursued an insect over the water. She shook her head. 'One day he was there, and the next he was gone. Just took his stuff and left. I guess I'll never know why he left.'

'You were close, though?'

'That's what I thought. I mean, we were never really together, not like that, but I thought maybe . . . Well, I guess I was wrong.' She looked at me. 'Am I wrong about you, too?'

If she had any idea Sully was buried out there in the forest, she hid it well. 'There's something I think you should know,' I said. 'I don't think Sully left you.'

'What do you mean?'

Helena was quiet when I told her about the shrine I'd seen. She stared out at the lights from Parapat on the other side of the lake and said nothing for a long time. Eventually I spoke her name, 'Helena,' and she put her head on my shoulder. She buried her face and I felt the dampness of her tears on my neck.

'Michael,' she said.

'Michael?' I stared at the lake, feeling the cool breeze coming across the water. It wasn't cold, but I shivered. If anybody was capable of such a thing, it was Michael. I'd heard what he had done to Hidayat.

'He was always so jealous.'

'You really think he could do something like that?' But I was sure he could. He had beaten *me*, leaving me only when Kurt had called him off like a dog. If Kurt hadn't been there, Michael might have crushed the life out of me with his bare hands. I'd heard stories of him doing such a thing and I hadn't believed them at the time, but perhaps it was true. Perhaps he had done it to Sully. The thought of it brought memories of Matt's injuries, of my night in the forest, of the secret burial. I wondered if I should tell Helena what I had seen, but she'd heard enough already today.

'Yes,' she said. 'I think he could. I saw what he did to you. What would he have done if the two of you had been alone?'

I struggled with the idea, didn't say anything for a while because my mind was numb. Then I lifted one hand to stroke her hair. 'I think Domino knows. I asked her about it before I left.'

Helena sniffed and raised her head to look at me. 'What did she say?'

'She said she didn't know, and I really wanted to believe her. Maybe that's why I came here, agreed to wait.'

'I'm glad you did.'

'But I don't think I *do* believe her. Not really. I'm not even sure Matt OD'd.'

'What, then?'

'I don't know, but you shouldn't go back. There's things going on up there you don't want to know about.'

'What things?'

'There are other shrines up there.' The first drops of rain broke the surface of the lake. Thunder sounded, this time much closer, followed by a brilliant flash that lit Danau Toba. 'I didn't look at all of them. D'you think . . . Did you ever hear of anyone else going missing? Just leaving?'

'Not since I've been there.' She lifted a hand and wiped a raindrop from her face. 'There was only Sully.'

'Christ, I thought it was supposed to be a peaceful place.'

'We should go in,' she said. 'Storm's coming.'

'Let's stay here a while.'

'We'll get soaked.'

'You'll be surprised how good it feels,' I told her as the rain reached us, gentle at first, then growing heavier.

We pulled closer together and waited for it to come.

'I think I always knew,' she said after a while. 'Inside. Somewhere deep. I think I knew what Michael had done.' The tone of both sorrow and relief. At last she knew. And she hadn't been abandoned.

We watched the storm advance across the lake until it was on us with all its cleansing violence. We let ourselves be drenched, Helena wincing at the force of the drops on her skin, turning her face to mine, her eyelashes and nose dripping, raising her voice over the sound of the storm. 'This is amazing,' she said. 'I've never felt this before.'

'We should remember it,' I shouted over the sound of the torment on the water. 'Whatever else has happened, we should always remember *this*.'

'Our Toba,' she said.

'Our Toba,' I replied.

Back at my room I showered and changed into clean shorts and a T-shirt, telling Helena she should do the same, asking, 'How long since you've had a hot shower?'

'A while,' she said, closing the bathroom door.

I lay on the bed and shut my eyes, waiting, listening to the last of the storm as it passed over. The sound of the rain merged with that of the shower, and I thought about Helena standing beneath it. I remembered what she had done that night when I had taken Kurt's pill, how she had looked, and how confused I had been to see her face, not Domino's. And I felt it now, with great clarity, that I had experienced no disappointment. Even when she told me what had happened, I felt no anger, no betrayal. Helena was not Domino and I was glad of it. She had some of Domino's strength, but she had more of her vulnerability. And those were the moments I had come to long for in Domino – the moments when I truly felt that she was mine. But I understood that it would never be so. She would always belong to Kurt, and she would always be that *other* person. Now, with my eyes open and nothing to blur my vision, I knew what I really wanted.

When Helena came out, she was dressed in a pair of my shorts and a T-shirt, her towel held close to her chest. Her hair was damp and hung in tails around her face.

'I'll take the floor,' she said. 'I'm used to it. I just need a sheet or something.'

'There's room here.' I moved along, pulling down the cover.

Helena held the towel tighter to her.

'Really,' I said. 'Come on.'

333

She put the towel on the floor by the bathroom door and came over, climbing onto the bed beside me and lying flat, facing the ceiling. I pulled the sheet over us and lay beside her so that just our shoulders were touching.

'You OK?' I asked, not looking at her.

'Yeah,' she said.

I reached over and switched off the light. 'Should we tell someone?'

'Who? Who would we tell?'

I turned my head on the pillow, looked at her silhouette. She sniffed once and I turned away again. 'We should go,' I said to her. 'Tomorrow. We should leave.'

'Together?'

'Yes.'

'Like we were going to before?'

'No. This is different.' This time I wanted her to be with me.

'Where shall we go?'

'Anywhere.' I could sense her relief and it gave me a good feeling. 'It doesn't matter. Somewhere quiet.'

'I need to go back,' she said.

'What?'

'I have a few things. Some money, my passport. If I'd known, I would have brought them with me.'

'Leave them,' I told her. 'I have money and we can go to your consulate, get another passport.'

'You think it'll be that easy? No, I need to go up there and get what's mine. It's all I have left.'

'I know what that's like.'

'Anyway, I want to say goodbye to Sully.'

I tried to imagine how she would be feeling. 'You're not going looking for Michael? Do something stupid, I mean.'

'Maybe if I was braver.'

I smiled in the darkness. 'It's not a good idea. We should just go.'

'I have to, Alex. Sully was my friend. Someone has to say goodbye to him. It's not right to leave without doing that.'

334

'I think I can understand that, but they'll want to know where you've been. How will you get away again?'

'They won't even know I'm there. I can go through the trees. I know my way around that place.'

'And if they see you?'

'They won't.'

'Then I'll come with you.'

'No. It's not safe for you. They'll make you stay.'

'I thought you said they won't see you.'

'Well, if they do, it won't matter so much – I'll make an excuse – but if they see *you*, they'll make you stay. Please, Alex, just wait for me to come back.'

'I've heard that before.'

'I know, but *I* mean it.'

I turned my head towards hers again and she did the same, our breath meeting.

'I'll go first thing in the morning,' she said. 'If I'm not back by twelve, you should leave without me.'

38

At first light we left the room together, walking further along the shore, where we found a boat to take her across the water. I gave her money, told her that Richard would bring her back if she told him about me, and stood on the bank as the boat moved out of sight beyond the headland, then I turned and made my way back to the *losmen*.

I waited until noon but Helena did not return.

I sat in my room, I paced the shore, I watched, but there was no sign of her. When the hands on my cheap watch reached one o'clock, the air felt colder despite the bright sun. An uneasy feeling crept into me. I shouldn't have let her go back up there. I shouldn't have let her persuade me. There was too much waiting for her in that clearing.

I went to the shore and squinted out at the lake, looking for any sign, even a glint on the surface of the lake that might be a distant boat. I strained my ears for the sound of an outboard, but every time I caught a hint of an engine, the boat was far off-shore and moving slowly in the water.

For all I knew, Helena might have been sitting safely among the others, eating, smoking, playing mah jong, but I began to imagine the worst. I worked hard to persuade myself that she was fine. The trip across the lake would have taken at least half an hour, with that much again to reach the community. One hour travelling, perhaps longer, and an hour or so once she was there. She was fine. She would arrive any moment. There was no need for me to go after her.

By two o'clock, with my stomach turning and my mind awash with thoughts I didn't want, I decided to settle my bill at the *losmen*, have everything ready so I could leave as soon as Helena returned. And if she wasn't here within the hour, I would go after her. I would look for her. I wouldn't leave her behind this time.

Stepping from my guest house, closing the door behind me, I heard Helena call my name. I stopped, one hand still on the key and watched her running up from the lake.

Before she reached me, I could tell that she was distraught: the tone of her voice when she called my name. The frantic manner in which she ran.

Behind her, Richard's boat was bobbing on the surface of the lake. Richard's face was turned towards us, but I barely registered that he was there, my concentration was so taken by Helena, who came to a halt by my side, her shoulders slumping as if bearing a heavy weight, her eyes closing, her head shaking.

'What?' I asked. 'What happened?'

Helena opened her mouth to speak but all she could do was shake her head.

I put my hands on her. 'What's the matter? Tell me what's happened.'

Helena looked at me, taking a deep breath, pursing her lips.

'*What happened?*'

'I was in the trees, coming back from the shrine . . . from Sully . . . and I saw . . .'

'What?' My hands gripping her slim shoulders, squeezing until I could feel the hardness of the bone beneath her skin. 'What did you see?' Flashes of being woken by Domino, seeing her in a similar state.

'Men,' she said again. 'With guns.'

'What men?'

'Danuri.'

'Danuri?' Even now I remembered the way he'd looked. Calm and intimidating. The man who had pointed his rifle into the trees the night Domino had stolen Alim's pistol.

'They beat Domino.'

'What?'

'I saw them hit her, drag her away.'

'Drag her where?'

'I don't know.'

I took my hands from her shoulders and pulled her close. 'Are *you* all right?'

'They were looking for Kurt,' she said against my chest. 'Shouting for him. Everyone ran, but they caught Freia and Jason. Domino, too.'

I looked down at her, putting my mouth on the top of her head.

'They started hitting them. Said they'd keep doing it till he showed himself.'

'And did he?'

She shook her head, said nothing, so I held her tighter, tried to be strong for her. I felt the same creep of fear that I had felt that morning in the forest, when Domino came to tell me about Matt, but muted. I experienced it as though by proxy, as if it flowed from someone else.

When she spoke again, her words came in a whisper. 'They cut Freia's throat.'

I stood back. 'What?'

'Jason, too.'

I felt cold.

She came closer, pressed herself against me again.

'Are you sure? I mean, maybe it just looked like it?' I reached for another explanation. It was too unreal. As if there was insufficient drama to accompany such news. 'Maybe they're still OK.' But she couldn't be mistaken. You can't be mistaken about a thing like that.

'No. There was blood. So much . . .'

'What about Domino?'

'They hit her.' Helena looked up at me.

'Did they . . . ?'

'No.'

Everything was a muddle in my head. It had all changed so much. What had once seemed good and calm had twisted beyond any recognition. As if some malevolent darkness grew out there, easing itself among the trees, corrupting everything it touched. But there was nothing mysterious about the polluting forces at work. The darkness that resided there was born in the hearts of people like Kurt and Michael, and they spread their poison with false promises of freedom.

'And he didn't come forward?' I asked. 'Kurt?'

'I didn't see him.'

'You mean he let them beat her? He hid in the forest and let them *kill* people?' There were many things wrong with the way they lived, but Freia and Jason didn't deserve that. All they had wanted was a different life – to belong – and I had a vague sense of that because there had been rare moments when I, too, had felt a part of that community. But something had always made me step back and now I understood that nothing had changed in that place. It had always been heading in this direction. Something like this was always going to happen.

There were tears in Helena's eyes and I knew that beneath the fear and the revulsion and the loss, there was guilt, too. Like Kurt, she had remained hidden. She had done nothing.

I touched my hand to her face, wiped away a tear with my thumb. 'It wasn't your fault,' I said, feeling stronger, calmer, focusing on Helena. 'You couldn't have done anything.'

'He said he'd kill Domino. If Kurt didn't give himself up, he'd cut her throat.' She reached up and put her hand on mine. 'Then they took her away.'

'Shit, so where *was* Kurt?'

Helena shook her head. 'I didn't see him.'

I imagined him scurrying into the forest like a frightened animal, trying to arrange his thoughts, see past the blood and the death and the fear. 'And Michael?'

Again, she shook her head.

'We have to do something,' I said.

'I just want to get away from here.' She pressed my hand against her face.

I nodded. 'Me too.' But we couldn't just walk away. If Kurt didn't help Domino, no one would. She would die. 'I should do something.'

Helena stepped back and looked at me.

'We can't just leave her,' I said. 'We can't leave thinking she's going to die.'

Helena continued to stare.

'She's got no one else to help her.'

'What about the others?' she asked. 'Michael? Kurt? She has them.'

'Does she? You said you didn't even see them.' I looked at the ground, walked away running both hands over my head, came back to her. 'She meant something to me, Helena.' I made fists, unable to relax. 'Last night you asked if I liked Domino because she helped me.'

'You said "maybe".'

'Right. And that's why I have to help her. She helped me when I needed it, and now she needs me. I *have* to do something. I can't just let her . . .' I could hardly believe I was saying it. It wasn't real. It wasn't happening to me.

'How would you ever know? We leave now, don't look back, you'd never know.'

'I don't want to not know. I don't want that. It's like you wanting to say goodbye to Sully. You want it behind you.'

'What can we do, though? We can't go back up there.'

'You don't have to do anything. You can wait here. I'll get Richard to take me to the police. Let them deal with it.'

She thought about it for a moment, shaking her head. 'Don't leave me on my own.' She took my hand. 'Let me come with you.'

It felt good to know she needed me. I didn't want to be alone, either. 'I'll understand if you want to stay here.'

'No.' She squeezed my hand, seemed to stand a little taller, her back straighter. She was strengthening herself. 'We'll do it together.'

I threw my backpack into my room, then took Helena's arm and, together, we went back along the path towards the water. We didn't speak as we walked.

When we came to the boat, Richard held out his thick arms. 'She didn't have enough, but said you'd be good for the money, and seeing as how I like you now and she looked so sad—'

'You know where to find the police?' I said.

'Police station?'

'Will you take us? Show us where?'

'What you want to go there for?'

'Something's happened,' I said.

'Up at Camp Weird? Someone get busted?'

'Someone got murdered.'

'Murdered?' He half laughed, searching my eyes for the hint of a joke, but saw none. The smile fell from his face. 'Seriously? Murdered? Who?'

'Some friends,' I said. 'Maybe more if we don't go now.'

'Jesus Christ.' He sat down and ran a hand over his head, looking at Helena. 'I thought you looked upset, but . . . I'm sorry. You want to tell me what happened?'

Helena looked at me for reassurance, so I nodded and told her to go ahead. I wanted to hear it again myself, now that she was calmer. So she spoke it aloud again, it still feeling unreal, and when she was finished, we lapsed into silence, even Richard finding it hard to take in.

He lit a cigarette and took a long drag. 'You sure you want to get into this?' He was serious now. 'You might be better off just walking away. Kind of luck *you* have, they'll think you did it.'

'We can't walk away,' I said.

He whistled through his teeth. 'Well, I'll probably regret it but I could do with some extra cash. And Hidayat'll be proud of me.' He looked at Helena. 'You clean?'

She nodded.

'Nothing on you at all? You don't want to go walking into a police station loaded with powders and pills. You know what they'd do to you, right?'

'I'm clean,' she said.

'OK, then. Climb aboard.'

39

Crossing the water, Helena and I sat facing each other, not speaking, only the sound of the engine until we neared the far shore. As Richard took us closer I looked out at the other boats here, idling in the water, some moored to the narrow, precarious jetties that reached out into the shallows of the lake, others discarding passengers or moving back out onto Toba. There was more noise here than I had heard in a while, a great and colourful agitation of life. Shouting and singing, people everywhere, loading and unloading, children running and laughing, jumping into the water. A truck stood in the shallow water, its tyres half submerged, as three boys carried baskets of live chickens from the flatbed and loaded them onto a waiting boat. From its exhaust, a blue-grey stream of fumes bruised the air, wafted across the surface of the water and faded into nothing. Richard took us a little further along the shore, away from the main throng, and brought his boat to a standstill by a section of concreted bank.

Richard moored the boat, then he led us across the busy road saying he'd take us right to the police station. On the other side of the street, a large open square surrounded on three sides by battered and neglected concrete buildings. Two-storey blocks with balconies and rusted tin roofs, the ground levels filled with ramshackle shops spilling out into stalls that filled much of the square. There were lean-tos less functional than the one we'd had in the forest clearing, some of them adorned with torn plastic sheets around the sides to protect the stall owner's stock.

A giant go-down had enormous sliding doors pulled wide to reveal a cornucopia of batik shirts, kris knives, Batak carvings, *ulos*, rolls of material and assorted touristy trinkets. There were mats laid out on the ground from which cross-legged women sold goods from colourful piles of exotic fruits and spices. Powders that were brown or black or grey – as red as blood or as yellow as the sun that burned above us. There were canvas ponds filled with live fish, baskets piled high with dried ones. There were chillies and bananas and rambutans and mangosteens and other fruits and vegetables I had never seen. There were stalls draped with colourful cloths, and there were even vendors who carried their entire stall with them, around their neck, trays laden with cigarettes and sweets and plastic toys. Two buses, end to end, their matching paint jobs of dark blue with yellow stripes and complex lettering. Both had bare-chested men on their roofs, stacking baskets higher than their heads. The bus closest to me had a detailed painting of Lake Toba on its rear. There were mopeds and bicycles and people passing to and fro among the stalls and the grime. The ground was loose with standing water and discarded produce, the air filled with the smell of petrol fumes and rotting fruit and open drains.

We passed it all by, making our way along the road, beside a building site where men were sitting on an unfinished roof, their legs dangling, drinking from tin cups as they followed us with curious eyes. Behind the new building, other concrete constructions, their white walls stained, rose up the hillside.

A good twenty minutes' walk from the commotion of the market, we came to the police station, a squat building of just one storey, bricked, plastered and painted white. Three or four other buildings stood around it, some of them stained around the roofs where the rain had leaked down the walls, marking the whitewash.

There was a high fence around the small compound, something like chicken wire crowned with barbs, and wide gates, which were now open. At the mouth of the enclosure, next to

344

the gate, a police officer was waiting for the opportunity to raise the red and white striped barrier that was on a counterweight across the main entrance.

Richard nodded to the man, spoke a greeting and passed to the side of the barrier. Helena and I followed him, grateful for his help.

The main road into the compound curved in a circle, and there was a sign with an arrow pointing the direction of traffic flow. Right now, though, the only vehicle in sight was a white van – a strange, squat contraption with a short flatbed and a bubble-shaped cab. Across the front, in black lettering, the word *Polisi*. We passed the van and approached the main building.

Richard was first up the steps, pushing his way through the green painted door, holding it open for us. We went inside and allowed the door to swing shut on its sprung hinge.

'You want me to do this?' Richard turned to me.

'It should be me.' I looked over at the policeman behind the desk, his posture deliberately intimidating. He was sitting straight up in his chair, staring directly at us, both hands on the table as if he were about to push himself out of his seat. In front of him were several piles of papers, a couple of pens and a nasty-looking baton.

'You speak Indonesian?'

'No,' I admitted, accepting that Richard knew the customs, the language, the culture far better than I. 'Thanks.'

He approached the desk as the man behind it began to speak. Conversation passed between them, but I understood none of it. To me it hardly even sounded like a language.

'You speak any at all?' I asked Helena, keeping my voice low.

'Not much.'

The man behind the desk rummaged in a drawer for papers, started taking notes. On occasion, Richard turned his head in our direction as if he were talking about us.

After a few minutes I put my hand on Richard's arm. 'What's he saying?' I asked.

'Just relax. I'm doing what I can.'

I stepped back, biting my lip. I was beginning to feel more anxious.

'It'll be fine,' Helena whispered, taking my hand. 'I'm sure it's going to be fine.'

'You understand *any* of what they're saying?'

'A little,' she said. 'From what I can make out, Richard's telling him what happened. Saying that Domino's been abducted.'

I took my hand from hers. 'They need to get up there and look for her. Why isn't he in a hurry?'

Helena shook her head. 'Everything works like that here. Everything is slow.'

'We can't afford to be slow,' I said, snapping my attention away from Helena when I heard a chair scraping on the concrete floor.

The policeman at the desk was standing now, still speaking, but holding his hand out to Richard in a gesture I recognised. He was telling Richard to stay put. Wait here. He looked around Richard at me, his eyes lingering on Helena for longer than they needed to, before he spoke a few more words and disappeared through a door to the side of his desk.

'He wants us to wait,' Richard said as soon as he was gone.

'I gathered that. What else did he say?'

'Said he needs to get his superior.'

'So are they actually going to do anything?'

Richard sighed. 'Sit down a minute. He's gone to—'

'Sit down? That's the last thing I want to do. I want to make sure they're going to *do* something. The longer this takes, the less chance she's got. Maybe *I* should talk to him.'

'Probably better not,' Richard said.

'Why?'

'You start making a fuss, Alex, and they'll kick you out of here so hard you won't know what day of the week it is. This isn't England. You give them any reason to, they'll either lock

346

you up or forget you ever came in here. You think they actually *want* to do anything? That guy, all he wants is an easy life.'

I closed my mouth and stared at him. Helena took my hand and pulled me towards the chairs, but I remained standing.

'Sit,' Richard said. 'Please.'

I sighed and sat down, putting my head in my hands, sensing Richard and Helena taking seats on either side of me.

'Things take time here,' Richard said. *'Jam karat.* Elastic time. Nothing ever happens *now.* It always happens later. In a moment. A few minutes, an hour, a day.'

'A day?'

'It won't take that long,' he reassured me. 'But if you want to find out what happened to your girlfriend—'

'She's not my girlfriend.'

'OK, whatever, but you're going to have to be patient and stay calm.'

I sat forward on my seat, as if in prayer. After a while, Richard leaned back and took a cigarette from his packet. He offered them to us but neither of us accepted.

He sat beside me without speaking, the smoke drifting into my eyes.

Richard was grinding the butt into the ashtray on the desk when the policeman returned, holding open the door for the man who followed him. A man I'd seen before. Danuri.

He stopped in the doorway, hat in hand, checking us each in turn, his dark eyes narrowing. He tightened his lips, the small wispy moustache moving as he did so, then he showed us a smile that wasn't a smile and came further into the room. We stood up as he moved behind the desk, placing his hat on the surface, then he sat down and waved the other policeman away.

He steepled his hands and pressed his thumbs against his mouth as if devising a great theory, but when he finally lowered his hands and spoke, he said, 'So you've come for your friend?'

I was surprised to hear him speak in English and it must've showed on my face.

'I went to school in Penang,' he said. 'English was compulsory.'

I took the opportunity to come forwards, forcing out my words, not wanting to betray my fear of him. 'Where is she? Here?'

'Perhaps.' He snorted hard and looked me up and down. 'Who are you? I don't remember seeing you.'

'A friend,' I said. 'I just want to know she's all right.'

He glanced at the door before leaning back in his chair. 'That depends.'

'On what?'

'On whether you can give me what I want.'

For a moment I didn't know what to say. 'But . . . ? I . . .'

'How much?' Richard asked.

The man shook his head, the smile dropping from his face. 'Not *how much*,' he said. 'Not this time. This time it's *who*.' He leaned forwards again, placing his hands on the table. 'This girl, she's in big trouble. *Big* trouble. I have *shabu-shabu*, *putaw*, all the makings of a drug factory.'

'Heroin and crystal?' Helena interrupted. ' There's none of that up there.'

'There could be. If I wanted there to be.'

'No way,' Helena said. 'You know where all that stuff comes from. You do anything, we could—'

'You'd like me to have you taken out of here?' Danuri raised his voice. 'Put in a cell with your friend?'

Helena took a step back.

'So she *is* here?' asked Richard.

'I think we can help each other. I have someone you want and you have someone I want.'

'Who?' I asked.

'Kurt.' He leaned back and rested his fingers on the handle of the pistol that he carried in a leather holster at his hip. 'And his friend. The American. You could save me the trouble of trying to find them. It would be in your friend's interest if I see them soon. I can wait a day, maybe two, but after that I will have to process your friend and . . . well, drugs . . .' He shook his head. 'The courts are hard. If she's lucky, she might be with us for a while. If not . . . You know how we execute our drug criminals here?'

I stayed quiet. There was nothing to say.

'Firing squad,' he said. 'A thing like that can be quick or it can be slow.'

'It would never happen,' Richard said. 'She's Australian, right?' He looked at me. 'It would never happen.'

Danuri sighed. 'We don't always wait for a trial, sometimes we just find a quiet place, but maybe you're right. Maybe it wouldn't happen like that. But our prisons are not so nice. There are worse things than being shot.'

I didn't even want to imagine what he was talking about.

'All those narcotics,' he said. 'It would be a long time before she ever got out. And when she did, you wouldn't recognise her any more. She might not even recognise you.' He laughed. 'She might not even recognise *herself*. It can be arranged.'

'She hasn't been processed?' Richard asked.

'Not yet.'

'If she hasn't been processed yet, she's invisible,' Richard told me. 'No record, nothing. No one knows she's here. If you can get her out now, do it. If you know where Kurt is, give him up.'

'So if Kurt comes here, you'll let her go. Just like that?' I said to Danuri.

He smiled. 'Just like that.'

'What if we can't find him? What if we don't know where he is?'

Danuri shrugged. 'Bad news for your friend, I think.'

'Why can't *you* find him?' I asked. 'You're the police. You've been up there. Find him yourself.'

Danuri stood up and put his hands on the desk, leaning all his weight. He studied the polished surface for a few moments before releasing his weight and standing upright. 'I don't have the manpower for that. This is not police business. This is *my* business.'

349

'Just what are we talking about here?' There was an edge to Richard's voice now. '*Your* business?'

'You don't need to know. All you need to do is find Kurt. Tell him if he comes to me, I will let his sister go. He knows where to find me.'

'We'll find him,' I said. 'I'll tell him. I'll *make* him come to you.'

Richard looked at me when I said it, the expression on his face saying that he didn't think I could do it. Even if I found him, I couldn't make him come. Not even for his sister. 'We want to see her,' Richard said, turning back to Danuri. 'Make sure she's OK.'

Danuri thought about it, eyes on Richard because he had become our spokesperson. 'No,' he said. 'Impossible.'

'Impossible? Why?'

He came round the desk and strode to the front door. A man in a military-style uniform, but there was no upright stance, no discipline in his motion. This was the lazy and untouchable arrogance I had detected in his gait the first time I had seen him, outside Alim's place, and then again in the clearing. He pushed through the door and held it open – not an act of courtesy, but a threatening pose. Not an invitation to leave, but a demand for it.

'Is she even here?' Richard asked.

Danuri remained silent.

'She's not, is she?'

Still nothing.

'I know the senior policeman in this area,' said Richard. 'I play cards with him once a month. A quiet word, a few dollars, and I'll have her out of here in a day. Maybe have your job, too.'

Danuri let the door swing shut and he came close to Richard, one hand on the butt of his holstered revolver. He stood toe to toe with Richard and looked up into his face. Like David and Goliath. 'I could have that girl raped, tortured and butchered in less than an hour. She'd disappear like she never existed.'

Richard held his stare.

'Just find Kurt and give him the message,' Danuri said. 'Leave the rest to me.'

'Let me see her and we'll do it,' I said. 'Let me see that she's OK.'

'Find Kurt and you can see her all you want.'

'I have to see her first,' I said, surprising myself. Perhaps *this* was who I was – the person who faces up to a man like Danuri.

He tightened his brow, clenched his jaw and looked away. There was sweat on his forehead, beads of it around his moustache, dark stains around the armpits of his uniform. 'One minute,' he said. 'Follow.'

I glanced at Richard as Danuri pushed the door wide and strutted from the room. We fell in line behind him, walking around the building towards a small, fenced area that was hidden behind it.

'So I guess this is Kurt's protection.' Richard kept his voice low so that Danuri wouldn't hear. 'The man keeping him out of trouble. I wonder what went wrong?'

In my mind I saw shallow graves in the ancient darkness. 'I don't know.'

'And did you know who this guy was?'

'No,' I said, looking at Helena. 'Did *you*? Did you know Danuri was a policeman?'

'No.' Helena shook her head as we came to a corral, maybe fifty feet by fifty feet, surrounded with heavy chain fence topped with razor wire. Within it, four men sitting on the grass, doing nothing but time. Like animals in a zoo. At the far end of the enclosure there was a small hut with no door, and nothing inside but shadow.

Danuri stopped ten feet from the fence and signalled to one of the guards, who unlocked the gate and went in, heading straight for the hut. He pointed his rifle at the shadows and within a few moments, Domino emerged into the sunlight.

I could see, even from here, that she was in a bad way. Her body was stooped and she adopted a protective posture as if she knew what to expect. Her clothes were dirty, torn in places, and her face was bruised and bloodied. She walked from the hut with a pronounced limp.

When she held up her hand to shade her eyes from the sun, she caught sight of us and I saw relief descend over her. She stood straighter and started towards us, but Danuri barked an order and the guard moved in front of her, raising his rifle.

'What have you done to her?' I felt anger and frustration boiling in me. Not fear.

Danuri waved a hand, and the guard pushed Domino back into the shadow of the hut. 'Now you have seen her.' He glanced at me as if I were something he'd found dead in the road. 'You want to get her out, you know what to do.'

'If you hurt her . . .' It was an empty threat. 'You can't do this.'

'Of course I can,' he smiled. 'I can do whatever I want.'

40

Leaving the compound, Richard spoke quietly. 'My advice is get her out. Let me talk to this man I know.'

'You heard what Danuri said. An hour. That's all it'll take him, probably less. I can't risk it. If he found out . . .'

'You got money?' Richard asked.

'Some.'

'You'd be surprised how quick money can swing a thing like this. Have you got dollars?'

I nodded.

'Even better. A hundred bucks'll get you off a drug charge, two hundred for murder. You just have to know the right people. It gets harder and more expensive once they're processed – which she isn't.'

'I don't want to risk it.'

'You have to. How you ever going to find Kurt? Where would you even look?'

'He'll be up there.'

'Maybe, but you saw what state she was in. You two go looking for Kurt, even if you find him, she might not be breathing when he comes down. *If* he comes down.'

'He's right,' Helena said. 'Think about it. And even if he did come down, do you really think Danuri's going to let her go? You think he'd keep his word?'

We were outside the compound now, standing beside the road.

'I could go right now,' said Richard. 'It's not that far from here. Do you have money with you?'

I looked at him. 'Why are you helping us?'

Richard stopped. 'I don't like Kurt. I don't like his little cult, or what they do, but that . . .' He motioned his head towards the place where we'd seen Domino. 'That's not right. She doesn't deserve that.'

'No,' I said. 'She doesn't.'

'So you want me to help you or not?'

I considered my options, but I had no choice. Richard and Helena were right; I could look for Kurt, but there was no guarantee I would find him. And although I thought he would give himself up for his sister, I couldn't be sure. But I had to do *something*. 'OK,' I said. 'Let's find your friend.'

'I'll have to go on my own,' he said. 'He's not going to want an audience for this.'

'So I have to trust you?'

'Yeah. If you want my help.'

We returned to the market place and I handed over six one-hundred-dollar bills. Unused, crisp and with the unmistakable smell of new money. And, with mixed emotions, I watched Richard board a bus, taking the only hard currency cash I had left. I didn't like to see it go, but I knew it wasn't much to pay for a life.

'You've done what you can,' said Helena as we watched him leave.

'You think we can trust him?'

She thought for a moment. 'We have to. What else can we do?'

When the bus was out of sight, Helena and I wandered through the market, but neither of us was much in the mood for sightseeing or shopping, so we headed back to the shore and climbed into the boat to wait.

We sat on opposite sides, facing each other, wanting to be closer but feeling it wasn't right. For now, my concern was for

Domino. Once she was free and safe there would be time to unravel everything else and put things back in the order they belonged.

After an hour, there was still no sign of Richard and we were both beginning to get hungry now that the excitement had waned and we'd had time to realise we hadn't eaten. We wandered over to the market, bought fruit, which we took back to the boat and ate in near silence.

It was about four o'clock when Richard returned. He was not alone when he climbed off the bus. Shuffling beside him, like a soldier retreating from the battlefield, Domino clung to his arm for support.

Helena and I went to them, taking her weight. I put her arm around my shoulder, while Helena did the same on the other side.

Domino managed a smile when she saw me, and she leaned her head on me as we walked. Her injuries looked worse close up. The bruises on her face were more livid, the dried blood around her nose was more noticeable. And when I looked in her green eyes, I couldn't help but feel the betrayal of my thoughts for Helena, even though hers conveyed almost no emotion at all.

'She hasn't spoken,' Richard told us. 'Wouldn't even look at me.'

'She needs help,' I said. 'We should get her to a hospital or something.'

'No hospital,' Domino said. 'Danuri.'

'She's got a point,' Richard shrugged. 'If Danuri's going to look for her, it would be a good place to start.'

Domino lifted her head from my shoulder as if it were too heavy for her. 'Where's Kurt?' Her speech was slurred. 'I need to see Kurt.'

'We need to get you sorted, then we'll go look for Kurt.'

'No.'

'Domino,' I pressed her. 'Let us help you.'

'I need to see my brother.' She was weak but she struggled

355

against me, taking her arm from around my shoulder, pushing herself away, stumbling and falling.

I put my hands on her, trying to help her up, but she pushed me off and looked up, saying, 'I need to see my brother, Alex. Please.'

'We don't know where he is.'

'He'll be waiting for me. Planning something. Maybe even to give himself up. He wouldn't leave me.'

'Where?' I said. 'Where will he be waiting?'

'At home.'

'Up there? You want to go back up there after everything that's happened?'

Domino nodded. 'I have to. I have to let him know I'm out. Please, Alex. Please help me warn Kurt.'

'You're never going to make it up there,' said Richard. 'You can't even stand up here where the ground's flat. Come on.' He reached down and took hold of her, hauling her to her feet.

'Let me go.' She tried to struggle against him, but Richard was strong, and once her energy was drained, he lifted her into his arms like she was a child and carried her back to the boat.

I went with them, seeing how compliant she was now as she lay across the damp seats, her eyes closed, exhaustion taking her. I stroked my hand across her head, moved the hair from her face and watched the rise and fall of her breathing. Just a few days ago she had meant everything to me. 'Maybe I should go look for him. I feel like I owe her.'

'No,' Helena said. 'You've done enough. You don't owe her anything.'

'And you know Danuri will look there, don't you?' said Richard. 'He might even be there now, or watching us, looking to see where we go. We should get on the water. Get out of here.'

'And then what?'

Richard shrugged. 'Listen to Helena. You don't owe them anything.'

'I know. I *know* you're right, but I have to help her. I have to do something.'

Richard clenched his teeth and shook his head at me, then told me to come with him, away from the boat. I glanced at Helena, then agreed, stepping down and walking ashore, out of earshot.

Standing close, Richard took a deep breath. 'Look,' he said. 'I don't want you talking about going back to that place. I'll take her to Hidayat. He'll clean her up and she can rest at our place. Then we'll decide what to do.'

I stared at him. 'Really? You'd do that?'

'Didn't I just say so?'

'Why, though? I mean, you hate—'

'I don't hate,' he said. 'I don't hate anything.'

'OK, but why are you helping us?'

'I'm not. I'm helping *you*.' He sighed and ran a hand through his hair. 'You and Helena. You're good kids, Alex, and you shouldn't be mixed up with those people. When I first saw you, I thought you were like them, but you're not. They didn't get into you. Didn't turn you. Hidayat was right.' He leaned closer, looking over at his boat before meeting my eye. 'And the way you looked at that girl Domino when you first came into my house, it was the same way I looked at Hidayat when I first met him. That's why I remember it. The only difference is I still look at him the same way. You, though?' He shook his head. 'You look at the other one like that now. Helena.'

'I . . .'

'Don't try to fool yourself. Don't try to change it or fight it. It's the right way to feel, Alex. She's better.'

'I still have to help Domino.'

'Sure you do,' he said. 'Because you want to do the right thing. That's who you are, not some fucking drop-out like the rest of those people up there. You don't want to turn tail and run away. And maybe you taught me something. Maybe that's why I'm helping you. 'Cause it's the right thing to do. Hidayat'll be proud of me.'

357

41

When we came ashore at the *kampong*, my ears were buzzing and my head felt numb from the thrumming of the outboard. The evening was closing in, the clouds darkening in the sky, the temperature cooling. An eerie light fell over the lake as we made our way to Richard's place. I was close to that other world now.

Domino refused to allow Richard to carry her from the boat, letting no one other than me support her while she struggled to his house. As soon as we were inside, she asked to be left alone to clean herself. Hidayat led her to the bathroom and when she emerged a while later, we took her into the only bedroom, where she collapsed onto the bed. We did what we could to make her comfortable before Hidayat ushered us out.

Helena and I sat stiff on the time-worn sofa and Richard sat across from us, unspeaking. When he rose and went into the kitchen, Helena took my hand, but when he returned with glasses of sweet, black tea, she let go, as if reluctant for Richard to see. There was no sound from the bedroom except for the occasional suggestion of movement, and our own silence was amplified in the small room. Outside, the lake maintained its continuous but gentle assault on the shore.

'You think he'll come here?' I asked after some time. 'Danuri?' I shivered, picturing Domino coming out of that darkened hut like a beaten animal, her face bruised and bloodied.

'He doesn't know who I am,' Richard said. 'Doesn't know where I live.'

'He couldn't have followed us?'

'I don't think so. Not on the lake.'

I had watched the water when we were coming here, and I had seen nothing keeping pace with us. Fishing boats and passenger boats, the odd water skier, but nothing more.

'Anyway,' said Richard, 'I have friends who outrank him.' But I didn't find his words reassuring. No one outranks violence. No one outranks the finger on the trigger. If Danuri knew where we were and he chose to act upon it, there would be no way to stop him. He had been there in the clearing that day when Alim had shot at Matt. I don't think he would have cared if the bullet had found its mark, crashed through Matt's skull and taken his life.

When Hidayat rejoined us, he moved with a jerk in his hip and I remembered what Richard had told me of his illness.

'There's very little I can do for her,' he said without looking at any of us. 'I've cleaned her cuts and bruises – they'll heal well enough – but I think there are other injuries that will run far deeper.'

'What kind of injuries?' Richard asked the question that was on all our minds.

Hidayat shook his head and looked at the floor. 'She wouldn't let me examine her fully. Given our history, I can understand that, but I think there's something she doesn't want to share. Something the men did to her.'

'You mean they . . . ?'

'Yes.' He looked at me. 'I'm afraid so.'

We fell into silence and I turned to stare at the closed bedroom door.

Later, sitting outside by the lake, beneath an avocado tree just beginning to flower, I looked across the water, wondering if any of the boats out there belonged to Danuri or his people. I still couldn't help thinking about what he had done to Domino, and I couldn't understand how someone could do such a thing to another human being. I didn't know if he had laid his own hands on her, but he had surely ordered others to. He had told them to rape her and beat her.

I spoke to Helena, saying, 'I can't imagine what she went through.'

'No.'

'I can understand why she wants her brother. He's all she has.'

'She has you.'

I smiled a smile that had no humour in it. 'No.'

'You sure? The way you helped her—'

'Because she helped *me*. And because, for a while, I thought maybe I was falling in love with her.' I felt embarrassed saying it, but it was good to say it aloud.

'And now?'

'And now I don't. I thought she was what I wanted to be. She was so free and I was so constrained. I thought she could teach me to be something else.'

'You don't need to be anything else.'

'You *can't* be something else. I can see that now. I didn't need Domino or Kurt to teach me that.' I paused. 'Or maybe I did.'

'You're a good person, Alex.' She touched my hand, traced a finger along the creases on my palm.

'Am I? I don't know. I'm an OK person. A bit stupid, I suppose. A bit weak, maybe.'

'You're a person who does the right thing. You just lost your way for a while. I did, too. It's what that place did to us.'

'Not that place.' I turned to look at Helena, then I glanced down at our hands, the fingers entwined. 'Those people.'

'We should leave,' she said. 'Now.'

'What?'

'Take our things and go. Right now. Just stand up and walk away. No more Kurt, no more Michael, no more Danuri.'

'What about Domino?'

'What about her? You've done all you can. Hidayat will look after her now.'

'I can't expect him to.'

'But he will. Ask him and he will.'

I sighed and turned back to the lake. The late afternoon sun tilted and banked on its surface, rippling with the movement of the water. Far away, the black cliffs rose to a sky that drifted with the slightest wisps of cloud. 'Part of me wants to do that. Just like you said. Get up and walk away.'

'Then let's do it.' She gripped my hand tighter. 'It's the only way we're ever going to leave this behind us.'

I imagined myself walking away and I knew it was what I really wanted. Something inside felt a duty towards Domino, but I told myself I had fulfilled that duty. I had repaid that debt. But it wasn't just about debt. Domino had meant something to me. 'I don't know.'

'What are you going to do? Keep hanging on to her? Let her control you for ever? Alex, you need to get away from her, get away from this whole place. We should leave just like we were going to. Don't think about it too much,' she said. 'Don't think so *bloody much*, just do it.'

'You sound like Domino when you say that.'

'I'm not her.'

'I'm glad.' I took my hand from hers and stood up. 'You're right. We should go. Domino will survive without us.'

'Really?'

'Yes. Really.'

As we walked back along the shore, it felt good to have reached a decision. Like the moment I had left the community, it felt right to be making progress again; to be making steps to leave. Only this time I wasn't alone, and I had a new purpose.

Richard and Hidayat were both asleep when we went into the house, Richard sitting up on the sofa, Hidayat resting with his head on his shoulder. The creak of the screen door woke them and Richard stood up, blinking away his tiredness. Hidayat remained seated.

I watched them both, wondering how I was going to thank

them for their help and explain to them that we were going to leave, but Richard just nodded at me. 'You're leaving,' he said.

'Yes.'

'It's the right thing to do.' He rubbed his eye. 'Hidayat and I were talking about it before.'

'Don't worry about her,' Hidayat added. 'We'll take care of her.'

'When she's well enough, I'm pretty sure she'll do whatever she wants,' I told them. 'She won't stick around.' But I couldn't help wondering what she *would* do, how she would get back in touch with her brother.

I turned to Helena. 'Let me say goodbye.'

'She's sleeping,' Hidayat said.

'I'll be quiet,' I told him, going over to the bedroom where Domino lay resting. 'I just want to see her.' I eased down the handle and opened the door just enough to look in. And I stopped. And stared. Then I turned to look at Richard.

'Where is she?' I asked. 'Where the hell *is* she?'

42

Domino was gone. She must have left while Richard and Hidayat were sleeping. Slipped away while Helena and I were sitting by the lake, making our plans to leave. And I knew where she would be headed. 'We have to go after her.'

Helena followed me outside and, together, we jogged along the shore until we were at the edge of the *kampong*, looking up at the hillside. We stopped and searched for any sign of Domino, but all I saw was the tips of the long grass leaning with the breeze, and the birds flitting in and out of the bushes, searching for the cicadas and crickets that creaked and hummed from somewhere within.

'She's gone,' Helena said.

Behind us Hidayat struggled, dragging his foot, holding on to Richard for support as they followed us out of the *kampong*.

'Let her go,' Richard called as they neared the spot where we were standing. 'It must be what she wants.'

'I agree,' Helena said. 'Let's just do what we were going to, Alex. If we don't go now, we'll never get away from here.'

If I had been able to see the truth in Helena's words, I would have listened; I would have taken her hand and left, but instead I shook my head. 'You saw what she was like. She could hardly walk.'

'I have to agree with Alex.' Hidayat spoke through laboured breathing. 'She wouldn't let me examine her properly. I don't know the full extent of her injuries, but she was very weak. She might have got a few hundred yards and collapsed.' The walk had been hard for him. He leaned against Richard, his body bent, the pain and effort clear in his face.

'She might be out there right now,' I said. 'Lying on the hillside.'

'So you want to save her again?' Richard asked.

'I have to.'

'Then let me come with you.'

'No,' I told him. 'Helena will come with me. We'll find her. Together we're strong enough to bring her back. You stay here with Hidayat. In case she comes back.'

He knew what I was saying. Hidayat needed Richard right now.

'*Will* you come with me?' I asked Helena. 'I can't leave her out there like that.'

Helena closed her eyes and turned away.

'Please.'

'And then we leave?' she sighed.

'And then we leave.'

Richard was reluctant to let us go alone, but there wasn't much he could do, so I shook his work-hardened hand and thanked Hidayat for all his help. I was surprised when Hidayat dismissed my offered hand, instead putting his arms around me and hugging me, but I returned the gesture with a deep feeling of friendship and gratitude.

'I came here to have a good time,' I said to Helena as we made our way up the hillside in the darkening afternoon. 'I did it to see something different, to *be* someone different.' We continued walking, the sound of our feet beneath us, the breeze in the grass ahead of us, the trees looming closer. 'I thought Domino . . .'

'You thought she was part of that,' Helena said.

'Yeah.'

'She is. *Was*. But that part's finished now.'

'Maybe.'

'Well, almost finished.' Her words came in heavy breaths,

the effort of hiking. 'You found the truth of this place quicker than anyone. It took me too long to realise it wasn't what I wanted, and it was you who made me realise it. I got stuck here. I didn't leave quick enough like you did.'

'And now I'm coming back again.'

'Yeah, but once we've found Domino, we can go wherever we want. Together.'

I looked at her, studying her face. She was tired, heavy bags under her eyes, a strain in her expression. Her hair was untidy, her clothes unwashed and dirty. 'Yeah,' I said. 'Together.'

She nodded. 'Come on. Let's pick up the pace, get this over with.' She quickened her steps, lengthened her stride, and I did the same to keep up. 'She can't have got *that* far.'

'What if we don't find her?' I said. 'What if she's out here somewhere and we can't find her?'

'We'll find her.'

'But what if we don't?'

'We'll have done what we can.'

We continued up the hillside without stopping, and by the time we were among the trees, the muscles in my legs were burning. It was hard to believe that Domino could have made it all the way up to the clearing. 'We can't have been away from the house for more than an hour,' I said. 'She might have half an hour on us, but no more.'

'She's obviously stronger than she looked.'

Coming into the clearing, though, everything was forgotten.

I was shocked to see such destruction. As if a force of nature had passed through, touching only the things that were not natural to this place. Where the kitchen had once stood, now there was just debris and deadwood. The uprights were torn down, pulled from the ground and thrown aside. The roofing was strewn across the far end of the clearing. A mess of palm fronds, wooden crosspieces and tarpaulin littered the once clear ground. Michael's building work had been solid, but not solid enough to withstand the corrupting strength of those who had determined to destroy this place.

Amidst the remains of the kitchen, there were the sundries of everyday life in the community. Aluminium plates and cups, spoons and forks, cooking implements, pans, tins and packets of food. Bottles of water smashed and split, rice scattered like confetti.

At the opposite end of the clearing, the longhouses had vomited their contents through their small trapdoors. Mats, thin mattresses, their possessions thrown out into the wilderness to pay for the deeds of the person who had founded this place. Kurt had given these people a new home, a new way of life, a separation that I had considered for myself, and he had ultimately led to its destruction, leaving them all with nothing.

Among the clothes and the personal effects, among the mattresses and the mats, among the trappings of a simple life, the most horrible thing. Half-buried beneath their own violated belongings lay the bodies of people I barely knew. And as I stared at the limbs that protruded from beneath the mattress closest to me, I remembered what Kurt had said. That these people had no one to come looking for them.

Except, perhaps some of them did. Perhaps, like Sully, someone *would* come looking for them, but would find only this.

Beside me, Helena was speechless. It was a moment for which there were no words. We stood, side by side, at the edge of the clearing and considered the devastation before us. This had been Helena's home for longer than it had been mine. I could only feel a fraction of what she felt.

I watched as she moved forwards into the clearing. She went without direction or purpose, her head turning this way and that, the movement slow and deliberate, her brain absorbing the information her eyes were feeding it as if trying to suck it through a dense sponge. Nothing getting through, just snatches.

She stopped in the centre of the clearing, beside the stone table, and she eased herself to the ground, sitting with her back hunched, pulling her knees to her chest and staring at the place where the bodies lay.

I went to her, squatting beside her and putting my arm around her. I looked to the spot she was watching and wondered how many were buried beneath. It would need a large hole, out there among the trees, to bury these children of Toba.

'Why did they do this?' Helena said. 'Why would someone do this?'

I opened my mouth, about to tell her what else I had seen when I found Sully's shrine – the shallow grave, a secret burial – but something stopped me. Helena didn't need to know. All this, right here, was enough. Instead I shook my head and kept quiet, wondering whose body was out there in the unmarked grave, whose death had led to this terrible retribution.

We sat like that for some time, the evening folding in to embrace us, the temperature dropping, and I kept my arms about her.

'We should get moving,' I said. 'We'll look inside, see if there's anyone there.'

So we headed over to the longhouse that had been our lodgings and, in the fading evening light, I could see a number of bodies, many of them almost completely hidden beneath the contents of the longhouse, just an arm or a leg visible, and I was reminded of the crash that had brought me here. But here, only his lower half covered by the odds and ends, was Jason. He was lying on his side, his head pulled back, his throat cut so that I could see the meat inside his neck. The blood was dry, and there were flies around the wound.

I stopped, my eyes on the injury, deadened by what I was seeing, as if it were unreal. Like a special effect, a movie wizard's dummy with fake blood and gristle. Jason wasn't Jason any more; he was just a carcass. It's all we are when life is gone: bones and blood and meat. No one is any different then. In the end, we are all the same.

'We have to know,' I said, more to myself than to Helena.

'We have to know.' And I began moving the debris, shifting it, dragging it, throwing it aside as I uncovered the remaining bodies. Helena was silent and immobile, watching my struggle before coming to my side.

Together we uncovered them and, even though we could see who they were, we rolled them over so their faces were toward the night.

'What about the others?' I said, when we had finished. 'Where are *they*?'

'Maybe they got away.'

'That's good,' I nodded. 'That's good.'

Alban's tufty blond hair was matted with soil and leaves, his shirt thick with the blood that had spilled from his throat. His dull grey eyes were wide and staring, his bloodied and beaten mouth open in a silent scream, his broken teeth twisted and shattered in dry gums. There was no sign of Evie, perhaps she had escaped or perhaps she was elsewhere, but Morgan and Chris were there, eyes rolled high, limbs twisted, bodies broken. The three metal rings had been torn from Morgan's lower lip, leaving a ragged tear that complimented the other marks on her face where rings and studs had been ripped away. Eco had received the same care and attention at the hands of his murderers. And Freia was there, too: Freia who had encouraged me to join the group when I had felt alone; Freia who had first come to help me carry the pig when I had stumbled; Freia who I had seen in Ambarita. Now she was dead. Her baggy T-shirt torn and bloody, her face so broken it was unrecognisable. Inhuman.

There was no serenity in their deaths. No dignity. No closing of eyes, no gentle sighing of escaping life. No paradise.

43

The longhouse was empty. Everything was cleared out. The men had been thorough in their destruction. Everything inside had been gutted and removed, but the building itself was left intact. Michael's work was not all in vain. Something had made the men stop short of demolishing the buildings. Whether it was because they were unable to destroy such craftsmanship or whether it was because they lacked the tools to do it, I couldn't guess. If it was the former, it would be worse – that they could bring themselves to disfigure and murder the people they had left outside along with the detritus, but not to disfigure wood and paint and nails.

Outside I had retrieved a torch from the debris, and now I switched it on, sweeping its light into every corner, but there was nothing to suggest that anyone was hiding here. 'Let's try the other one,' I said, waiting for Helena to descend the ladder first, switching off the torch as I followed her.

Helena was almost invisible now in the darkness. The shadows passed over her as if she were not there, smothering her and making her part of the night as we moved over to the second longhouse and went inside.

Training the light over the walls and across the floor of the building I had never been allowed to enter, it looked much the same as the other one, if perhaps a little better renovated. There were long tables, probably constructed by Michael, that may have once run the length of the house but now lay twisted and uneven, broken like the discarded bodies outside. There were overturned containers of food, boxes ripped open, bags split, sets of scales, small brass weights, but if there had been drugs stored here, they were gone now.

'No one here,' I said.

'We should go now. Maybe she left already. Found Kurt and left.'

'You're right.' I looked round at the torn sacks of rice, the sweet potatoes loose on the floor. 'Nothing we can do. Come on,' I said. 'Let's get the hell out of here.'

The torchlight and shadow were kind to her. They hid the dirt on her clothes, the mess of her hair, the exhaustion on her face. I looked at her, thinking it hard to believe that she had no one to come looking for her; that she was so alone in the world she had cast herself under the control of a man like Kurt. A man who, in fair times, was capable and eloquent, but in rougher times hid in the shadows and waited for the right moment to emerge.

I put my arms around her and pulled her to me, placing my hand on her head and pressing her into my shoulder. We stayed like that for a while, holding each other, interrupted only by the sound of the trapdoor creaking open.

The sharp noise in the otherwise silent space startled me and I released Helena, turned, raised the torch to point it at the entrance to the longhouse. I half expected to see Domino coming into the building but, instead, the nose of a rifle poked in, and a familiar face followed it.

'I'm surprised you came back here,' said Danuri, climbing in. 'If I were you, I'd be long gone.'

Behind him, another man, short and thin, wearing jeans and a light jacket, trainers on his feet.

I moved in front of Helena and looked at Danuri, the torch beam on his face, but not powerful enough to dazzle him.

'After all, you got your girl. Made sure she was released before I could do anything.'

I shook my head. I didn't know what to say. I didn't know how to feel, but something inside punched an icy fist right through me, gripping my guts and freezing them. Danuri might have been waiting for us, but I was more afraid that he had followed us here – afraid of what he might have done to Richard and Hidayat.

'You have influential friends. Or at least, your friend does. The one who helped you. I've seen him before,' he said, removing his left hand from the assault rifle, taking a soft cigarette packet from his top pocket. It was a calm motion, the act of a man who was in control. 'He runs a boat on the lake, right?'

I lowered the torch, gripping it in my fist, readying it for the first opportunity to swing it at him.

'Where does he live?' he asked. 'I thought I might pay him a visit sometime. Keep an eye on him.'

'I don't know.' I spoke around my fear.

'Hm. All in good time, then. But what about the other one? Where is *she*?' Danuri took a cigarette with his teeth, his right hand still on the grip of the rifle. 'The girl who was in my care. Domino. You not interested in her now that she's been used?'

Again the icy fist.

'I'm not sure she enjoyed it so much, but the men? I think they had some fun.' He popped a match with his fingernail and touched it to the cigarette. 'Perhaps *she'd* enjoy it more.' Danuri motioned the muzzle of the rifle at Helena. 'But I'd say she doesn't look as strong as the other one.' He blew clove-scented smoke above his head. 'Wouldn't last so long.'

'What do you want?' I managed.

'Kurt.' Danuri shouldered the rifle, took the cigarette from his mouth and blew on the lit end, making it crackle. 'I want Kurt. Where is he?' he said to the glowing tip. 'That's what you came back for, right?' He looked up at us. 'You found him?'

He spoke in Indonesian to the second man, who nodded, circling around us.

'I don't know where he is,' I said, watching the man move

out of view. 'We haven't seen him.' My attention torn between the two men.

'Maybe you can help with something else, then. Maybe you know what they did with my brother-in-law.'

'Who?'

'Alim,' he said. 'My business partner. My brother-in-law. One day he was there and the next . . .' He shook his head. 'And the next day he was gone. No sign. Nothing. Last thing anyone can tell me was that they saw him with the *orang putih*. The white man. And now my sister is very upset that her husband has gone.'

I shook my head, realisation dawning. 'I don't know, I . . .' I thought about lying on the forest floor that night, shrouded by the dark, concealed by the forest, watching Domino and the others putting a body in the ground, hearing the heavy patter of soil, and I knew. I knew who they had buried that night, and I wondered if I should reveal to Danuri the things I knew. I wondered if it would soften his demeanour towards me; if it would take the murderous look from his eye and the stone from his heart. But I was sure that if I told him what I thought, that his brother-in-law was buried out in the forest, Danuri wouldn't walk away and leave us. I had seen what he had done to Domino and the others.

'You know what I think happened?' Danuri asked, but I had nothing to say. I didn't know what to do. He came close to me, his face inches from mine, his breath stinking of stale *tuak*. The bloodshot vessels in his eyes were livid against the whites, vile tributaries of angry blood. 'You think your friend Kurt could kill a man?' he asked. 'You think he could do that?'

'I don't know.' I cast a glance at Helena, not knowing the answer to Danuri's question. I didn't know if Kurt could kill a man, if he had that kind of cruelty within him. But I knew of another who did. And I was certain that if Kurt had asked Michael to kill Alim, Michael would have done so.

Danuri's face relaxed and he leaned away from me, snorted and spat. 'So, you don't know where Kurt is, you don't know where Alim is. You don't know much, do you?' Danuri looked at me, his eyes not seeing me, as if he were staring into space, a moment of daydreaming before he refocused. 'OK,' he said, smiling. 'I suppose that's it, then. Thank you for your time.' He turned towards the way out, taking a few steps before stopping. He dropped his hands to his side and turned round again.

'Doesn't feel right. I feel . . . What's the word I'm looking for?' He waved his hands as if trying to conjure the word from nothing, the glowing tip of the cigarette writing a scribble of light in the air. 'Ah yes. I feel *unfulfilled*,' he said. 'I came here for something and I've left with nothing. I guess you'll just have to do.'

He said something in Indonesian and I felt hands grip me from behind, passing under my armpits and linking behind my head. The man was small and probably not as strong as me, but the movement was quick and sudden and it caught me off-guard, making me drop the torch.

As soon as the man behind me took hold, Danuri came forwards, holding the cigarette to my face. I twisted my head, an instinctive movement, but Danuri put one hand on me to keep me steady and pressed the glowing tip against my skin, once, twice, three times, close to my eye.

I let out an involuntary shout as the flesh burned and when Danuri withdrew, my body anaesthetised the wound, dulled the pain. The air around my nostrils was filled with the scent of cloves and burned skin and flesh. Something like spiced bacon.

The man behind me released his grip and pushed me away from him so that I stumbled. I put out my hands to break my fall, putting them against Danuri, who pushed me back. This time I fell to the floor, at Helena's feet.

'I would've kept my word, you know. If you'd done what I asked, I would've let her go.'

I looked up at him, my fingers going to the burns on my face.

'There was no need for any of this.'

'I don't know where Kurt is,' I said, wishing that I did. I wasn't made for this; I didn't want to be here; I didn't owe Kurt anything. If I'd known where he was, I'd have given him up in an instant.

Danuri blew on the tip of the cigarette again, twisting it while he watched me. 'I don't believe you.' He came closer, waving the cigarette in Helena's direction. 'And how about that girl? Domino. You went to a lot of trouble for her. A lot of expense. You must know where *she* is.'

The man behind us took hold of Helena this time, gripping her hard as Danuri put the cigarette close to her face. I could sense how hot the glowing end would feel next to her skin; I had the burns on my face to remind me.

'I don't know,' I said, wishing there was something I could tell him, something to make him stop. 'She left.'

'Well, that's unfortunate.' Danuri was in full swing now, enjoying himself. Helena let out a sharp cry of pain as he pressed the tip of the cigarette to the skin on her cheekbone. She snapped her head back and I immediately caught the scent of her burning.

Danuri let the glowing end hover over her left eye.

'Stop it,' I shouted. 'Stop it. I told you the fucking truth.'

Danuri sniffed hard. He snorted and spat to one side. 'Just one more thing, then,' he said. 'I need to know where the other man lives. The man who came to the police station with you.'

'In the *kampong*,' I told him. Feeling the shame of it straight away. I was glad to be telling him something. I needed to give him something that would stop him from hurting us, but I was betraying Richard and Hidayat. After all they had done for us. 'On the waterfront.'

'Good.' Danuri stepped back as the man holding Helena released her, and pushed her to the ground. Then he put the cigarette in his mouth and drew on it, grimacing at its taste. 'Just one more thing I want to do before I go.' He looked at Helena.

Beside me, Helena rearranged her dress, covering her skin. I was surprised she wasn't crying. She was stronger than she looked.

'Don't touch her,' I said.

'Why? What will you do?' Danuri asked. 'Will you try to stop me?'

I glanced at the rifle on his shoulder, the pistol holstered on his hip.

He dropped the cigarette, ground it with his foot and lowered his hand to the pistol. 'Think you could take it?'

I looked at his eyes.

'And what would you do if you could? You think you could use it? That you'd even know *how* to use it?'

I looked away from him, defeated. There was no point in showing defiance. There was nothing I could do.

'You know,' Danuri said after a few moments, 'I don't really need you any more.' I looked up to see that he was watching me. He slipped the rifle from his shoulder and tilted his head at Helena. 'You want to say goodbye to her before I do this?' He raised the weapon and pointed it at my face.

The next few moments passed in a haze. My initial response was to find a bargaining chip. A way out. I had to say something that would stop him from doing this; stop him from pulling the trigger. I opened my mouth but no words came out. My mouth worked in silence, my tongue dry, my head empty of coherent thought. I almost didn't even notice Danuri lower the weapon. I almost didn't hear him speak when he said that on second thoughts, the rifle was not a good idea. He didn't want to warn Kurt he was here. Kurt might be close by.

'No,' he said. 'It would be much better to cut your throat, let you bleed quietly.' But even as the man behind me took the knife out of his pocket, snapping the blade open, I heard a shout from outside, a voice calling, someone climbing the ladder. And then Kurt's face was at the trapdoor, a look not of surprise but of knowing, of *expectation*, when he saw what was happening inside the longhouse. In an instant he was gone, ducking back out of sight as Danuri reacted, turning, raising the rifle, firing a burst of shots that lit the room in a strobe of muzzle flash. Lead slammed into wood as the bullets tore into the floor around the trapdoor. The raw power of the weapon dazzled me. The sound terrified me. And the smell clung in my nostrils like fireworks on bonfire night.

Danuri edged towards the entrance, holding the weapon high, sighting along the barrel. 'Kurt?'

I listened for anything to suggest that Danuri had hit him, but there were no sounds from outside. Nothing.

'Come in,' Danuri shouted at the empty space that was the open trapdoor. 'Come in, Kurt – we need to talk. There are a few things we need to say to each other.'

'Come in there?' I heard Kurt reply. 'I don't think so.'

'You want me to shoot your friends?' Danuri motioned back to the second man, hissing something in Indonesian. The man grabbed Helena and brought her forwards, all three of them standing in front of me now, leaving me forgotten.

The man holding Helena pressed his knife to her throat.

'They're not my friends,' said Kurt. 'Fucking shoot them for all I care.'

'Then what did you come back here for?' Danuri replied. 'Why else did you come here?'

'Because I knew *you'd* come back here,' Kurt replied, and for a second I saw Danuri falter, as if confused. 'You tried to use my sister, but I called your bluff. You came back.'

Now it was Danuri's turn to be lost for words. But it was a moment that lasted no longer than a fraction of a second before movement filled the longhouse.

Michael materialised beside me as if from nowhere, passing me without making a sound. In one movement, he grasped the hand that was holding a knife to Helena's throat and he kicked out at Danuri. Danuri hadn't even had time to register that something was happening when Michael's foot caught him in the small of his back, thrusting him forwards so that he stumbled onto the space left by the open trapdoor.

Danuri missed his footing, stepped into the hole and fell through the opening, dropping the rifle, catching his chin on the frame as he went down. The sound of his teeth clashing together was quite clear, and then he disappeared into the darkness.

In front of me, Michael wrestled the other man away from Helena, pulling his knife arm straight back and hitting him hard on the side of his face. The noise of his fist on the smaller man's jaw was flat and dull, a heavy slapping sound. The man's knees buckled and he crumpled to the floor. He wasn't out cold, but his eyes were rolling in his head and he struggled to push himself up. Michael watched him, thinking about his next move, then kicked him hard in the head, immobilising him.

Michael went back to Helena. 'It's OK now,' he said, staring over her shoulder at me. 'I'm here.'

Throughout the brief but intense sequence of events, I had not moved. I was rooted to the spot, as if nailed to the floor, mesmerised by the speed and brutality of what I'd just witnessed. A simple, effective, vicious attack.

Michael released Helena, backed away from her, then turned to the trapdoor. 'You OK down there?' he called.

'Couldn't be better,' came the reply. 'How are things with you?'

Michael looked back at us, a reassuring smile for Helena and a scowl for me. 'Yeah,' he said. 'All under control.' He glanced down at the man on the floor, seeing that he was beginning to stir. 'Coming out now,' he called back to Kurt.

Michael picked up the pocket knife the man had been carrying. He threw it into the back of the longhouse, letting it clatter to the floor somewhere in the darkness. For the first time, I noticed that Michael had a weapon of his own – the *parang*, covered by a carved wooden sheath, attached to a piece of orange plastic string, which he had put across himself like a bandolier. The weapon hung loose at his side.

He went to Helena, asking again if she was OK, then ushered her towards the trapdoor, saying, 'You go first.'

'Lucky for you there's a back door,' he said, coming back to me.

'Yeah,' I said. 'Lucky.'

'You didn't think about doing something?' he asked.

'Like what?'

He shrugged. 'Anything.'

Maybe he didn't understand that up until the point when Kurt had showed his head above the door, I'd thought I was going to die. I thought that Danuri was going to take my life and leave me here, forgotten, with no one to come looking for me.

'Me, I couldn't just stand there and let it happen. I'd have to go out fighting.'

I stared at him.

'Shit, I'd have to do *something*,' he said.

'There wasn't any—'

'You were going to let him kill Helena.'

'No . . .' I stopped. He was right. I *was* going to let him kill Helena. Not because I wanted to. But because there was nothing I could do and because I was afraid. I had been afraid to die and all I could think of was begging for my life. Perhaps that was what I had come here to learn: that I was a coward.

'Come on,' said Michael. 'Time to go.'

'What about him?' I looked at the man lying on the floor. He was moving now. Slow, heavy movements as he tried to lift his head. There was blood coming from one of his ears, his mouth too.

'Don't worry about him,' Michael said. 'I'll deal with him.'

I went over to the trapdoor and began to descend the ladder, looking down, checking that no one was waiting for me with malicious intent. When my face was level with the floor, I stopped.

'You going to kill him?' I asked.

Michael looked down at me. 'Why? You wanna do it?' He

whipped the machete from its sheath and touched the edge of the blade to the man's neck.

I shook my head, paused for a moment longer, then took the final rungs and placed my feet on the soft ground.

44

The last light of the day finally receded from the trees, leaving the wrecked community smothered in a misty wash. The air was fresh and cool. By my feet lay the once-living inhabitants of the longhouse. The sound of flies was a constant and high-pitched hum in the darkening night. I didn't look down. Instead, I looked across at the figures bathed in the spectral light.

Kurt, the all-conquering lord of our community, was standing tall, Danuri's rifle in hand. Beside him was Domino, her posture more crooked, her shoulders slumped. Helena stood away from them, not far, but far enough to show that she was not with them – not *of* them. An unwilling part of the scene that was playing out before us. I admired her for it.

At Kurt's feet, Danuri. On his knees, his head bowed in defeat.

Domino came towards me now, expectant, but I knew that whatever had existed between us was gone. The living desire that pulled us together, the need we'd had for each other had now dissipated, become a part of the mist that surrounded us. And just as the sun would finally begin to shine tomorrow, to burn away the mist, so it would be for us. Whatever it was that had bound us together, it would fade to nothing, seared away by the events we had experienced here in these woods. But this was not over yet. Between now and then, there was more for me to witness – a spectator, not an actor. Maybe that's who I was. A tourist in other people's lives.

'What are you doing here?' I said to her. 'You're supposed to be—'

'This is where I belong.' Her eyes were wide, her pupils dilated by whatever drug she had taken. She put her hand out to touch me. She ran her fingertips across my face as if to reassure herself that I was there. She hesitated when she came to the painful places Danuri had seared with his cigarette, then she took my hand and pressed my palm against her own cheek and closed her eyes as if feeling the familiarity of a favourite soft toy. She spoke my name once before she moved my hand, took it away from her face and let it drop as she put her arms around me. 'I love you,' she said, but it wasn't true. Our circumstances had brought those words to her lips.

It wasn't long before Michael emerged from the longhouse, bringing the other man with him. The man who had restrained me now stumbled and flinched as Michael goaded and prodded him with the sheathed *parang*. His face was battered, his shirt stained with his own blood. He hunched and cowered as he moved, his manner displaying that he was resolved to total submission. I did not pity him. A base part of me would've liked to see the man killed for what he'd done to Helena and me – a part of me that I cursed for delighting in my suspicion that the man's ordeal was not over yet.

Michael stopped beside me and leaned in close. 'You thought I was going to kill him, right?' I could smell his stale breath, the strong odour of sweat. I could even feel the heat emanating from his skin. 'Not yet,' he said. 'We've got something special in mind.'

'You ready?' Kurt asked Michael as he came closer. He handed him the pistol that had been at Danuri's hip. Michael tucked it into the back of his waistband and slipped his arm through the string on the *parang*'s sheath so that it hung loose at his side.

'Come on,' Kurt said to the rest of us. 'We have things to take care of. Michael, you and Alex can bring Jason.'

Michael came back towards me, tapping me on the shoulder and beckoning me to follow.

He slipped his hands beneath the dead man's armpits and signalled for me to take the feet.

I shook my head.

'Just get over here and do it,' he said.

'No,' I told him. 'I don't want to be part of this. Let us go.'

'Us?'

'Me and Helena.'

Michael shook his head. 'You're already part of this,' he said. 'Now get the fuck over here and help me carry him.'

'I'm going to leave.' I turned and looked across at Helena. 'Any of you can come with me.'

'The fuck you are.' Michael dropped Jason's shoulders and came towards me, head lowered, his intentions clear. Michael and Kurt were my enemies now, just as Danuri was, and, not for the first time that night, I wondered if I was going to leave this place alive.

Cornered and afraid, I stepped back and raised my fists ready to defend myself. But Michael was too practised. His hands found their way through my feeble guard like snakes through long grass. He gripped one hand round my throat and slapped me hard across the face with the open palm of his other hand, catching the place where Danuri had burned me.

'I thought you were gonna be tougher than this, Alex,' he said. 'The way you jumped off the bluff with a witty quip. The way you swam straight out to help Helena.'

'I'd rather save lives than end them,' I said, my voice constrained by his fingers gripping my throat.

'Then maybe you want to think about saving your own and doing as you're fucking told.'

'Leave him, Michael,' I heard Domino say, and when I looked over, I saw that Helena had stepped forward, too. But there was indecision and fear in her face. She knew what Michael would do if she chose me over him. But Michael took no heed of either Helena's reaction or Domino's words. He was too caught up in the pleasure of the moment.

I tried to pull his hand away, but his grip was too strong, so I reached with both hands and grabbed the loose skin under his arms, six inches above his elbows. I took the tight folds between finger and thumb, twisting and pulling at the same time. Michael let out a cry of pain and jumped back as if I'd electrocuted him. He released his grip, but the victory was short-lived. He swung his right fist up under my chin, clattering my teeth together, forcing my head backwards so that I caught a brief glimpse of the canopy before he thrust his left elbow into the side of my neck, felling me with ease.

He hurried to stand over me just as Kurt called to him, but Michael glanced across and held up a hand before grabbing the scruff of my shirt with both hands and pulling me to my feet.

With blurred vision, I was able to see that the others were standing in more or less the same positions as before. Michael's attack had been fast. I could see the expression on Helena's face, even in my current state. She was begging me, without words, to do what Michael wanted. There would be another time, another opportunity to get away from here.

'OK.' I held up my hands. 'OK. Stop. I'll do it. I'll help.'

'I should fucking think so.' Michael released his grip and straightened my shirt for me. 'After everything we've done for you.'

I put a hand to my face and stared at him.

'After you, then, Alex. We haven't got all night.'

He waited for me to move over to where Jason lay; then he followed. I gripped Jason's cold, naked ankles and together we carried him back to the others.

'Ready now?' Kurt glanced back at us.

Michael nodded, 'Ready,' and we began walking.

45

We moved in silence, led by Kurt and his captives, weaving through the forest, walking to the stone, passing it and heading out to the place where we'd buried Matt. Night had settled and the feral darkness was lit only by shafts of electric torchlight piercing the trees, creating a mosaic of light and shadow on the ground. Here and there, the light moved among the trunks as if it were a solid entity, given shape by the lingering mist that rested a foot or so above the forest floor.

When we came to the spot where Matt was buried, Kurt told the two men in front of him to come to a halt. We put Jason down and moved to one side. I could see, just in front of us, a space where someone had been digging. A hole, squared at the edges, perhaps ten feet by six feet. It was no more than a foot deep.

I guessed that, when they'd been hiding in the forest, Kurt and Michael had already made a start on a single grave big enough for all our friends.

'This is where you buried Alim?' said Danuri. 'All the way out here?' He snorted and spat. 'Like a dog.'

'Not here,' Kurt said. 'This spot is for those who lived here. Your friend is buried over there. Like a dog. He doesn't deserve to lie in this spot.'

As Kurt spoke, Michael stepped around the hole in the ground, going to the far end. He picked up two *cangkuls* and threw them at Danuri's feet, where they landed with a clatter.

'What?' asked Danuri.

'Dig,' said Michael.

'We need to bury our friends.' Kurt nudged the muzzle of the rifle into Danuri's back.

Danuri took a deep breath and nodded his head, stepping down into the hole and telling the other man to do the same. They went to opposite ends of the hole and began digging, slinging the loose dirt to the side.

Michael glared at me and pulled Helena close to him before squatting at the far end of the grave, his eyes on the two diggers. Kurt remained where he was, rifle at the ready, a half-naked tribesman.

Taking the opportunity to be alone with Domino for a moment, I grabbed her sleeve and took her back, away from Kurt. 'What the hell's going on?' I asked her. 'Kurt can't do this.'

Domino looked at me in a daze, and I could see that her pupils were still dilated. 'For Christ's sake, Domino, do you even know what the fuck is going on here?'

'We're going to bury our friends.' Her words were slow.

'I can see that, but what about *them*? You do know he's going to kill them?'

Domino raised her eyebrows, blinking her eyes as if trying to focus. 'What?'

'We can't let Kurt kill them.'

'Why not?' she said. 'You saw what they did to our place. Our friends. Look what they did to *you*.' She raised a hand to my burns.

'What about Michael? Does *he* deserve to die for what he's just—'

'And look what they did to me.' She went on as if she hadn't heard me, turning her face to show me the bruising. 'And that's just what you can see. There's other marks I could show you, Alex. And some you'll never see. Men are pigs.'

I looked away and closed my eyes. It was unforgivable. What this man had done was unforgivable, but I still couldn't bring myself to accept that Kurt was going to kill him. 'It doesn't make it right.'

She pulled her lower lip between her teeth, then looked down and away. She shook her head. 'They killed Matt,' she said.

'I thought you said he OD'd.'

'That's what we told everyone. Kurt didn't want people to be scared, he wanted to protect us, but it doesn't matter any more. It's all gone now.' She sighed. 'You didn't believe it, though. You saw the bruises on him. You knew.'

I pressed the heel of my palms into my eyes and rubbed hard. I wanted it all to stop now.

'It was a warning from Alim and Danuri. "Do as you're told." Remember when they came up here?'

'A warning? Because you'd been sneaking around in their house?' I said, knowing this could have been avoided. It all led back to one thing. One person. Domino.

'Yeah, because of that. And because Kurt didn't like it that they wanted to cut our pay. And because Michael put his hands on him. They wanted to let us know who was in charge, Alex, so they taught us a lesson.'

'But why Matt? He wouldn't hurt anyone.'

'He was an easy target? He was the first person they saw? He did something to piss them off? Who knows, Alex? Ask Danuri.'

'So Kurt decided to return the favour? They kill Matt so Kurt . . . what? He sends Michael to kill Danuri's brother-in-law? Alim. The man I saw you burying.'

'No,' said Domino, kept going only by whatever drug she had taken. 'You have to believe it wasn't meant to be like that, Alex. We went down there to talk to him. Me and Kurt. After the funeral.'

'You and Kurt? Not Michael?' He seemed like the ideal person for that kind of work, but even as I said it, I remembered it couldn't have been him. Michael and I had worked on the longhouse that day.

'Just me and Kurt. That's all. We went down to straighten it out, make it all better, but things got out of hand. He started touching me like . . . like that time *you* were with me. You remember what he was like.'

'So *Kurt* killed him?'

Domino shook her head.

'Who, then?' But it could only have been one other.

'An accident.' A look of defiance coming over her face. A look I'd seen before. 'But I'm not sorry.'

I stared at her.

'I pushed him off me. Pushed him away and he fell. Didn't get up again.'

I shook my head in disbelief.

'Buffalo horns,' she said. 'Went right through his neck.'

I imagined Alim half lying, half sitting, skewered on the horns tied to the central column of the longhouse. Gurgling. Drowning in his own blood.

'And that bastard down there deserves the same.' She looked over at Danuri. 'For what *he* did to me. And to the others. To our home.'

This knowledge of Domino did not surprise me as much as I might've expected it to. I'd been through so much that was unexpected since meeting her, I was beginning to think nothing would surprise me any more. But I hated myself for being such a fool. I'd fallen for her, I'd followed her, and I had even helped her. My money had paid for her release from the very place she belonged. 'Look,' I said, 'I can understand why you feel that way, but—'

'No, you can't. You can't have any idea what they did to me down there. What they made me watch right here, in my own home.'

'Domino . . .'

'Don't ask me to stop,' she said. 'Just stay with me.'

'Stay with you? You want me to stay with you while you do this? And then what? And then Kurt turns on me? On Helena? Are you going to kill *us*, too?'

'No.' She put her hands on me. 'I won't let them touch you, Alex. You can't think that. And Michael would never hurt Helena.'

I shrugged her off and turned to face away from her, away from everything that was happening, putting it behind me, wishing that not seeing it would make it all go away.

'You got a problem back there?' I heard Kurt say.

I didn't hear any reply, but Kurt didn't speak again. I stayed where I was, staring ahead of me into the forest, thinking that I could run. Keep running and not look back. They probably wouldn't even bother chasing me because they had Danuri and his partner to deal with. I could make my way back down the hillside, get a ride in Richard's boat, go to Medan and catch a flight home. I still had my passport. I could get more cash, be away from this place within two days, sitting back in England, breathing the cold air, feeling the familiarity of my home. But if I ran now, Helena would be left alone with them, and I knew I wasn't going to desert her.

Instead, I did as I was told. I helped place Jason's body in the hole and then rested for a while before returning to the main clearing to retrieve the others. And each time we came back with more of our friends – Danuri and his man carrying, too – Kurt walked behind us, rifle firm in his grip.

When we returned to the grave for the last time, we laid the remaining bodies alongside the others and stood in silence while Danuri and the other man threw the soil over them. Jason, Alban, Freia, Chris, Morgan, Eco. These people would go unremembered except by those of us who had survived them, those standing around their grave right now, and those who had escaped the brutality of Danuri's visit, scattered to the wind as if they had never been here. Matt and Sully had their markers, but we would have to leave this place now – there would be no time to prepare a shrine for them, just as there had been no time to prepare individual resting places for them. A mass grave in a remote forest. Like the dirty secret of a despotic ruler.

I tried to distance myself from Domino, stay closer to Helena, knowing that if we had an opportunity to get away, we'd have to take it. But such an opportunity didn't present itself, and when the grave was filled, Domino came close, speaking into my ear.

'One last thing to do,' she said, looking over at Kurt's prisoners. 'And then we can leave.'

46

I knew. As soon as we came into the small clearing, exhausted from the carrying and the digging and the fear. As soon as Michael pushed the two men to stand either side of the rock and stepped back to join us. As soon as Kurt looked at each of us in turn before addressing the two men. I *knew* what he intended to do to them. And I was forced to consider my own position once more. The only things that stood between me and Michael's blade were Domino and Helena, and I had begun to wonder if even they would be any match for Michael's anger when it reached its darkest ferocity.

The air was clear and dawn was pushing in among us when we came to the place where it was going to end. The trees reached up around us, impervious to the acts that were being played out in this dark paradise. The rock in the centre of the clearing, however, seemed to live, and I saw it as I had seen it in my hallucinations, smiling, waiting for its thirst to be quenched. The pig's blood that still marked the ground here, the drying entrails, the vacant porcine head – these things were not enough. The rock wanted a different kind of sacrifice.

'You know what this rock is for?' Kurt said to Danuri.

'I'm not Batak. And neither are you.'

'No matter. When in Rome . . .'

'You should stop this now,' said Danuri. 'You won't get away with what you're doing. You will be caught.'

'Maybe,' said Domino. 'But you'll be dead.'

Kurt held up his hand to Domino. This was his time now.

'Let us go,' said Danuri. 'Walk away and don't come back. It's not too late. Not yet.'

'Of course it's too late. It was too late the moment you got rid of Hendrik. He was a good guy; I could deal with him. It didn't feel so . . . I don't know, it didn't feel so dirty. It felt like a way to survive, everybody getting along, no one wanting too much. But you? You make it unclean. You make it like it's a bad thing. You bring guns and attitude. You couldn't just let it flow. You got greedy and you pushed your partner out, probably cut him up and buried him deep, and now you're paying the price. It's fate. Karma. Whatever you want to fucking call it, it's unavoidable. You set it all in motion.'

'What are you talking about? Let us go,' he said again. 'We can put this behind us.'

'You're begging,' said Kurt. 'That's what you're doing, right?'

'No.'

Kurt went to the rock and put his hand on it. 'Begging for your life.'

The man beside Danuri said something in Indonesian, the pitch of his voice rising, panic in his eyes. Danuri ignored him, locked eyes with Kurt.

Kurt ran his hand over the surface of the rock, as I had once done, and I remembered the night he told me about it – how he and Michael had built the stone circle themselves. But this rock had always been here. This rock had seen life. And death.

Danuri shook his head. 'You don't have to do this.'

Kurt smiled at him.

'We're not going to die,' Danuri said. 'You're going to let us go.'

'*He* doesn't think so,' said Michael, pointing his unsheathed *parang* at Danuri's partner. The man was a sweating wreck now, his eyes flickering this way and that like a frightened animal looking for a way out. He had been digging and carrying all night but his body would be preparing itself, supercharging his muscles for flight. He was searching for a chance to escape

391

and it reminded me of how I felt. I, too, wanted to get away from here and although I didn't expect to die here, it wasn't beyond the realms of possibility. I had stepped into an insane world where almost anything could happen. It wouldn't take much for Kurt and Michael to turn on me.

'If you're trying to frighten me, it's not working,' said Danuri. 'Let me go, Kurt. We can make a deal.'

Kurt walked around the rock, staring at him, then coming away, stalking towards his prey.

'Let us go. Please.' Danuri finally accepted Kurt's commitment to this task. 'You don't have to do this.'

Kurt came closer to him, their bodies just inches apart. 'Of course I do,' he said.

'What about you?' Danuri looked at me. 'Are you going to let them do this? Do you think they're going to let you go after this? What makes you think you're so different from me? They'll kill you, too. They'll kill me and then they'll do the same thing to you. They can't let you tell anyone about this.'

If it hadn't been in their minds, it was now. Kurt and Michael both looked at me, but Domino spoke for me. 'He's one of us. Aren't you, Alex?'

'Yeah. Yes. I am.'

As I said the words, though, Danuri's partner let out a loud scream. The sound was alarming, shocking us all, giving the man a few seconds before anyone could react. He used those precious moments to take a few steps away from us, moving like a rabbit, bolting for the trees. If he made it in there, he stood a chance of outrunning Michael, losing himself, saving his life. If he was fast.

And he *was* fast. But not fast enough.

Michael squatted low as the man passed him, hefting his unsheathed machete, catching him in the hip and bringing him to the ground in an instant. The man yelped and curled himself into a ball, bringing his arms into his waist, one hand going to the spot where Michael had hit him. Almost immediately, blood began to darken his shirt.

As Kurt stepped back and swung the rifle up to point at Danuri, Michael took one of the other man's hands and hauled him to the rock, leaving a bloodstained scrape in the dirt. Michael leaned him against the rock, breathing hard, and turned to Kurt. 'This one first. And you'd better get on with it or he's gonna bleed out.'

Kurt nodded.

'I reckon you got a few minutes, then he's drained.' Urgency and excitement in his voice.

Kurt turned to look at Danuri. 'Criminals and volunteers,' he said. 'That's who lies over this rock. And you . . . what you did to our friends . . . to my sister.' Kurt shook his head. 'You know how this happens, right? You know what they used to do?'

I had the sense that Kurt was drawing this out, making Danuri wait longer for the inevitable. Kurt wanted to frighten him, make his last few minutes unbearable.

'If you think I'm gonna eat any part of him . . .' Michael said.

'Time to judge them.' Kurt turned to the rest of us. 'Domino?'

'Guilty,' she said.

'Michael?'

'Guilty.'

'Helena?'

Helena was silent. She opened her mouth but no words came out. Like me, she wanted no part of it. She didn't want to be here. She didn't want to see men die.

'I . . .' Helena looked at me, her eyes pleading, looking for the answer, looking for the way out.

'Don't look at *him*,' Michael shouted.

'I need an answer.' Kurt kept his eyes on Danuri. 'Now.'

'I can't,' she said.

'You can't? What do you mean you can't?'

'Just say "guilty",' Michael said. 'Let's get it done.'

'It's not right.'

393

'Not right? Were you here when they came to our home?' Kurt asked.

'Yes.'

'And did you see what they did?'

'Some of it.'

'And you saw them kill Freia? The others?'

'Yes.'

'And you saw them beat Domino. And you know what they did to her down there. You *saw*.'

'Yes.'

'So he's guilty.'

'Yes, but—'

'Good enough,' said Kurt.

Then he turned round and looked at me. 'Well?'

I stared at him. I looked across at Michael, the bloodied machete in his hand. I glanced at the others, Helena and Domino, both of them watching me, waiting for my answer.

'You said you're one of us. Prove it.'

I didn't know what I was going to say. This man was guilty. He had done the things they accused him of, but we were not judges. We were not gods. We were barely even men and women. It was not our position to punish him. 'This isn't right,' I said, feeling as Helena must've done. 'It isn't up to us.'

'Of course it's up to us,' said Kurt.

'We should take him to the police.'

'He *is* the police.'

'But—'

'He was going to kill *you*,' said Michael. 'He was going to cut your throat.'

So was Michael. He, too, had threatened to kill me, and I suspected he had already killed before. His friend Sully. The words were on my lips but I stopped them, knowing what consequences they would bring. I hoped Helena would have the sense to do the same.

'Screw him. Four out of five is enough,' said Michael.

'It's supposed to be unanimous,' said Kurt.

'And if he says no?' asked Michael. 'You telling me you're going to let them go? He's not one of us, Kurt. He doesn't belong here.'

Kurt considered for a moment. 'You're right. We're going to do this anyway.'

He nodded to Michael, who grabbed the wounded man by the scruff of his neck and dragged him to his feet. Limp as he was, the man was nothing more than dead weight and, although Michael was strong, he could not keep hold of him with just one hand. As soon as Michael turned him round and tried to force him, face forwards, over the rock, the man understood exactly what was about to happen. Despite being wounded and afraid, he was not ready to give up. He summoned his last reserves of strength and began to twist and writhe, forcing Michael to drop his *parang* and hold on to him with both hands. Michael managed to turn him round and push him down onto the rock, leaning across him and holding him as he jolted and bucked like a rodeo horse.

'Alex,' he shouted. 'Get over here.' His voice was uneven with the struggle.

I stayed where I was, rooted to the spot.

'*Now.* Hold him down.'

I couldn't comprehend what they wanted to do. After everything I had just said. Michael was asking me to hold down a man while he cut him open, hacked off his head with a machete. It was almost too much for me to process and I was unable to move. It was as if the message from my brain was interrupted somewhere on the path to my feet.

'Help him.' It was Kurt this time, a voice from somewhere outside the place I was now retreating into.

'Fucking get over here,' Michael said again as the man struggled beneath him, desperate to escape.

I tried to shake my head, to make some sense of how I was feeling, but the movement was nothing more than a slight turn to one side. I was underwater, drowning in air.

Michael was trying to hold the man with one hand. He had

one foot on the ground, the other one raised because he had his knee in the small of the man's back. His left hand was gripping the base of the man's skull, pushing his head forwards onto the rock. Blood was spilling from his wound, washing the grey rock, soaking into it, joining the blood of those who had been executed here before him.

With his right hand, Michael was stretching, searching blindly for the handle of the *parang*.

I watched, still rooted, as Domino stepped forward, reaching down, making contact with the dark blade, pulling the machete closer as Michael tried to secure his grip on their victim. Then Domino curled her fingers around the wooden handle. She began to lift the weapon, raising it high over the man's neck.

Domino had been everything I wanted to be. She was without constraint. She faced the world and the things it threw at her with her head high and her feet firm. She was freer than anyone I had ever met, but I realised, now, that it was not so admirable after all. Domino and her friends were *too* free. They were so untethered that they felt able to act in any way they wished. They were not confined by the same rules as I was, and they were prepared even to break their own. Their almost limitless freedom and their taste for experience had led them to this.

I managed to open my mouth, hearing myself speak one word, 'No,' then the man twisted to one side, a violent motion that unbalanced Michael, releasing the pressure of his knee. The man slipped from the rock and Michael's knee crashed down on it, giving no support, and he fell forwards, hitting his face, then slipping to one side, knocking into Domino.

Danuri took advantage of the distraction, making a break for the trees. Kurt raised the rifle and fired after him, a burst of shots, which crashed around the policeman. Danuri faltered, stumbled, clipped by one of Kurt's bullets, but he carried on running. Kurt held the rifle tight to his shoulder, aimed and fired again, a rattle of reports. Danuri jerked, twisted, fell and disappeared from view. As the echo of the shots dissipated,

Kurt ran to the edge of the forest, searching this way and that before he stopped and pointed the rifle towards the ground, where Danuri was lying. He paused for a moment, then fired another succession of shots.

Seeing his opportunity, the second man took off in the other direction. Despite the vicious wound in his hip, he had spotted his chance to save his life and he intended to take it. Michael scrambled to his feet and threw himself at the wounded man, but he was out of reach and within a few seconds, he was safely among the trees. Michael snatched his machete from Domino and chased after him.

Kurt left Danuri's body in the undergrowth, coming back to us, stamping his foot in frustration and pointing the rifle into the trees, but both Michael and the other man were now invisible, as if they had never been there.

47

'Why didn't you help him?' Kurt came to me, wanting someone to blame. 'Why didn't you fucking help him?' He waved the rifle in front of my face as if deciding whether or not to point it at me.

'Leave him alone,' said Helena. 'It wasn't his fault.'

'It wasn't anyone's fault.' I flinched away from the weapon.

'Yeah?' Kurt pointing the rifle at me now. 'You reckon? You could've helped, you know. This would all be over.'

'Killing Alex isn't going to make you feel better.' Domino still had feelings for me even though mine for her had evaporated. I was no longer infatuated. I was afraid of her. And I was afraid of her brother.

Kurt lowered the rifle and turned away from me. 'Why couldn't they just leave us alone?' Almost childlike in his anger. Someone had spoiled his game. Someone had ruined his kingdom. 'Why couldn't they just leave us in peace? This place was perfect. Fucking *perfect*. I just wanted it to be . . . Shit, we'll have to leave here now. If he gets away.'

'We have to leave anyway,' Domino said. 'It's finished.'

'We could've started again.'

'No,' said Domino. 'It was finished when—'

A single shot. A flat report from somewhere among the trees, making us all stop, listening to the silence that followed. Even the insects were muted by its intrusion. An empty space in our world that gaped for a while before it began to close as the insects resumed their chorus and time started once more. Then the distant sound of disturbance in the undergrowth.

Domino cocked her head. 'You hear that?'

We all listened to the approaching footsteps.

Kurt raised his rifle.

Heavy footfalls moving among the trees.

'Michael?' Kurt called. 'Is that you?' He tucked the rifle to his shoulder and waited. 'Michael?'

Then he appeared from the thick forest, grotesque and horrifying, like some untamed savage. He was out of breath and sweating, the moisture glistening on his skin. Michael still held the *parang* in his right hand. The blade was dark with blood, his naked torso splattered. In his left hand, the trophy, which he raised to show us, as Perseus might have raised Medusa's head. The hair was tangled in his bloodied fingers, matted and vile. The man's eyes were open as if to turn us to stone, and his mouth was contorted in a scream of fear and panic. Among the broken teeth there was a glint of gold.

'Got the little fucker,' he said to Kurt with a grin. 'Had to use the pistol to stop him running, but I got him.' Then he looked over at me, his body becoming tense. 'And as for you . . .'

Michael dropped his grim prize and strode towards me with great purpose as my mind reeled in horror. Without pausing, his right fist still clenching his weapon, he came at me and crashed the butt of the machete into the side of my head. For a moment everything was numb.

Then nothing.

It was the third and last time Michael hit me. I'd never been hit before I met him. Never been in a fight of any kind. I'd *seen* fights. Seen them on the streets at night, when the pavements were wet and the streetlights were reflected in shop windows. Ugly and blunt and unpleasant.

I hadn't even had time to register it was going to happen

when Michael hit me. And when I opened my eyes, I realised he must've knocked me out this time. The feeling in my head was much the same as it had been when I woke from the bus crash that had led me to this point. A pounding beneath my skull, the sensation that my brain was swelling like a sponge in water, ever expanding, pushing against its containment, determined to break free.

Everything was ending as it had begun.

I opened my eyes and looked up, the treetops swaying and spinning above my head.

'Get off him. Michael! Jesus Christ, you trying to kill him?' I think it was Domino who was shouting, but I couldn't be sure. Her voice was distorted, reverberating. I tried to turn my head to see if it was her, but my neck was stiff and painful and refused to do what I asked of it.

I blinked hard, opening my eyes in a stare, taking in too much light and immediately feeling a sharp pain behind them, forcing me to close them again.

'If that's what it takes,' said another voice. 'Yeah. Why not? Everything's gone to shit since he turned up.' A man speaking. Could have been Michael. Or maybe Kurt.

Then someone was beside me, putting their hands on my head. I opened my eyes, not much more than a slit, and looked at Helena. She showed me a reassuring smile, but Michael yanked her away before I could focus on her face. 'Get away from him.' His temper burning beyond control, his lust for blood heightened to a frenzy. Helena lost her balance as she spun round and fell at his feet. Her place at my side was filled by Domino.

I concentrated on fighting the dizziness that brought on the feeling of nausea. I swallowed hard, determined not to throw up.

'Help him up,' Domino said. 'Help him.'

'I'll fucking help him.' Strong hands were on me, rough and unkind. I was lifted into a sitting position and dragged backwards.

'Be careful.'

I was propped against something hard – the rock, I assumed – and hefted up, hands under my arms. When I was turned round, I knew what they were going to do. I had seen what Michael had done to Danuri's man and I knew he intended to do the same to me. I put my hands against the smooth surface of the execution stone and resisted, but I was weak. They pressed me against the rock, hard so it restricted my breathing, my cheek against the cold surface.

I knew that men had died here. I could smell the death.

'Please . . .' was all I managed before a hand was on my head, pushing my face harder to the rock. I felt my teeth against the inside of my cheek, and then something touched the back of my neck. Something sharp.

'Stop it,' someone shouted behind me, and I was jostled as the hands left me and I heard the sound of a scuffle. Free to move, I twisted myself round, tried to stand, but the pounding in my skull beat harder. So hard, so hard. My legs buckled beneath me and I slid to a sitting position, leaning back against the stone as I had done that night with Kurt.

I closed my eyes again and waited for the drunken feeling to pass while I listened to the garbled voices talking, arguing, just out of my range of understanding.

When I had the strength to move again, I raised my hands to my face and rubbed some life into it. I looked up at the others – three of them staring down at me, Domino beside me, asking if I was all right.

'What does it matter?' said Michael, his words clear to me now. 'He's not one of us. He never was. Right from the start I didn't trust him. Let's just kill him and go.' One bloodied hand held the *parang* loose by his side; the other seemed to be controlling Helena, who had recovered from her fall.

'Leave him alone,' Helena said, looking in my direction. She wore a frantic expression as she pulled against Michael's grip.

Or perhaps she was holding *him* back, stopping him from coming to me.

'He's seen too much,' said Michael.

'He can't stay with us,' Kurt added.

Domino put her hand on my head, touching it to the spot where Michael had hit me. It felt wet and when she took her fingers away, they were tipped with blood. 'He's bleeding.'

'I can make him bleed some more.' Michael pushed Helena out of his way and stepped forwards. Kurt took her arm, held her tight.

'No.' She struggled. 'No.'

'No one's going to touch him.' Domino stood and faced Kurt. 'He came for me. Got me out of that place down there, which was more than you managed.'

'I was working on it.'

'And I like him.'

'Well, you can't keep him, D.'

'He's not a dog,' said Helena.

'He might as well be,' Michael told her.

Then they fell silent, each of them watching me, and I tried again to get to my feet. By wedging my back against the rock and using my legs to push backwards, I was able to shuffle into a crouching position. From there, it was much easier for me to achieve my goal. I turned, put both hands on the rock and pulled myself to a stand. I took a deep breath and faced them all.

'Just leave me.' The world swam around me. 'Leave me here. You go. I'll be fine. I won't tell . . . I don't even know where you're going. What can I do? Please. Leave me here.' I was struggling to think, could hardly speak, my breath coming in halting rasps. If they left me here, I might die alone – but rather that than Michael use his blade.

I looked over at Kurt, seeing double, trying to focus on both of him. Domino standing close to him, Helena wrestling his grip.

'Domino, Helena, you don't have to watch this.' He nodded

at Michael, who pushed me back against the rock and raised his machete. Inhuman with his naked torso and his bloodied skin.

'You can't do this,' said Helena, breaking away from Kurt. She rushed to stand between Michael and me. 'Leave him alone.'

'Helena.' Michael dropped the blade a touch. '*Move*.'

'Help him,' Helena said to Michael, putting her hand on him. 'Please.'

He looked down at her hand, the first real sign of affection I'd ever seen her show him. It seemed to calm his madness, bring sanity to his expression. He relaxed under her touch, looked into her eyes.

'Please,' she said again, putting her other hand on his face. 'I'll do whatever you want. I promise.'

He watched her, lowering the *parang*.

'Anything,' she said.

'You'll come with me?' His words considered. Deliberate. Slow.

'Yes.'

'Wherever I go?'

'Yes.'

Michael glanced across at his leader, who was standing with his sister.

'Please,' Domino said to her brother. 'I owe him this much.'

Kurt stared past her, his eyes on me, clenching his teeth, the muscles working in his jaw. 'All right. All right, we'll leave him.'

'We should take him somewhere.' Helena still held Michael's gaze, keeping him calm. 'He might die out here.'

'Then he'll have to take his chances,' said Kurt. 'Don't push your luck.'

Domino came to me and squatted at my side. She looked at me with sadness and leaned forward to kiss my head. 'It's the best I can do.' Then she stood and went to be with her brother.

'Forget about him,' Kurt told his sister. 'He's not one of us.'

Michael took one last look at me, shook his head as if I were a sick animal in need of mercy killing. Then he turned his back and walked away, pulling Helena with him.

Drained of energy and life, I watched them leave, the four of them. The last of them. They crossed the clearing where so much had happened, left the stone that had seen blood, and met the mouth of the path at the edge of the clearing. Kurt was the first to disappear from view, then Domino, Helena and Michael.

'Wait.' Helena's voice, then she was re-emerging from the trees. She ran across the clearing and crouched beside me, taking my hand. 'I'm sorry,' she whispered, speaking in a hurry. 'We should've gone. After that night on Samosir, I shouldn't have come back. We should've left.'

Behind us, Michael called for her. His fury was rising.

'As soon as I see a chance, I'll leave him.' A tear fell from her right eye. It trailed the length of her nose like a heavy raindrop and settled on her upper lip.

Michael was out of the trees and coming across the clearing. Walking fast, swinging the *parang* in his right hand.

'Kurt's wrong,' I said.

'About what?'

Closer now. Michael's face set hard and grim, his fingers tight around the wooden handle.

'Saying we don't have anyone to come looking for us. You have me. I'll find you.'

Helena bit her lip, her eyes glistening. 'How?'

Michael's heavy footsteps pounding the soil. Close.

'Just remember *Our Toba*,' I said. 'You can remember that.'

'*Our Toba?* Like that night? I don't understand—'

'Just search for it. *Our Toba*.'

Now Michael was behind her, the tall savage in his dark paradise. 'We have to go. *Now*.' He leaned down and grabbed her arm, pointing his *parang* at my throat, daring me to stop him.

Helena reached out and touched the fingers of my right hand. '*Our Toba*,' she whispered as Michael pulled her up. '*Our Toba*.'

And then our connection was broken. And Michael was dragging her away, taking her out of my life.

48

I don't know how long I stayed there, delirious by that rock, thoughts swimming like wraiths in my broken mind. Terror spinning and wheeling. The fear of dying in that lonely place. Images of death ploughed through my thoughts like the bus that had brought me to these dark horizons. I saw Domino, a vision of deceitful beauty with her golden hair and easy nature and malign intent. In my confused and demented dreams she stood over the body of the man she had killed, side by side with Michael, upright and lithe, his heavy-bladed machete in hand, blood decorating his skin, shining in the light of fire. But now they were not in the forest, they were under the glow of the hospital lights and they were surrounded by the dead and the dying, the awful moans and the stink of fresh blood. And then I saw the woman's eyes. The old woman who had spilled her life onto the road in front of me. The woman who had *so* needed that final human touch.

I was not going to die. Not here. I would not die in this place. Somehow I forced all thought but that from my mind. I willed my eyes open and I refused to succumb to the enticement of sleep. And with the evanescence of those horrors, I focused on reality. I concentrated, and I summoned the strength to move.

Using the rock that was to have been my execution block, I stumbled to my feet and tested my strength. I put one foot before the other and I took the path back to the main clearing, seeing nothing around me, thinking only of making my body work for me, forcing it to take me where I needed to go. One step at a time. And there was only one place I *could* go; only one person to whom I could turn for help. Richard.

I remember little of my long and laboured journey down the hillside and out of the forest. It was the last time I would be among those trees, see that view of the lake, but I don't remember it. Perhaps it was better that way.

I found strength I didn't realise I had, and I made my way to Richard's place where Hidayat treated me well, kept me hidden long enough for me to recover from my injuries. I told them both what had happened, and at night I sometimes heard them talking to one another, their tone one of concern. But Danuri's disappearance from the world and the horrors of the community didn't touch us again. The only thing that connected any of us to that place and what had happened up there was Richard's friend – the one who had organised Domino's release – and I suspected that was why nothing came of it. *Korupsi* had worked in our favour.

I don't know if anybody found Danuri's body or the graves in the forest. No one came looking for him. He was no different from any of the others who had died there.

49

I stayed with Richard and Hidayat for just over two weeks, and as soon as I was well enough, I left Lake Toba. I had come away looking for something that I hadn't found. And now I saw the terrible irony of that place in the trees. It was only when I was away from it, as I had been on Samosir, and for those few moments I spent alone with Helena, that I was ever really myself. *That* was what Domino and her community had taught me. It had shown me not who I was, but who I was *not*.

When my bruises were faded and the burns close to my eye had hardened, Richard took me across the lake one last time. 'You'll have some good scars,' he said as I stepped off his boat. 'A few stories to tell.' Around us the world lived. The noise of children in the water, of boats and trucks. The sounds and the smells of the market were just as they had been before.

'Who'd ever believe it?' I asked. 'And who would I tell?'

'Are you sure you don't want to stay longer? Last chance.'

I shook my head.

'And you're not ready to go home?'

'There's nothing for me to go back to.' We had discussed it already, Richard and Hidayat sitting together, me feeling embarrassed and grateful for their concern. 'Anyway, I still want to see the things I came for. And I need to see if I can find Helena.'

'You really think you'll be able to?'

'There might be a way.' I was clinging to the faint hope that

Helena was still here somewhere, that I would somehow be able to contact her.

'Well, I hope it works.'

'Yeah.' I stared over at the market and I remembered the many stalls. 'Wait here,' I said. 'A couple of minutes.'

'OK.'

I jumped onto the jetty and jogged along it, dodging the children who were using it as a diving board. I went across the road to the market and found the stall I was looking for.

When I came back, Richard was sitting in his boat, smoking a cigarette. A man was trying to sell him an ornamental knife with a brass handle but Richard waved him away.

He stood and I gave him a package wrapped in brown paper. 'For Hidayat. It's not much but . . .' I shrugged.

Richard felt the weight of the package. 'What is it? You didn't need to buy anything.'

'It's the least I could do. And tell him I'm sorry about his *ulos*. Kurt put it on the fire.'

Richard looked at the package. 'That's what this is? A replacement?'

'Not so much a replacement,' I said. 'I know they mean something. Symbolic.'

Richard smiled. 'This one will, too.'

From Parapat I took a bus to Brastagi, where I found an internet café and created the means for me to reach out to Helena. My actions were born from hope rather than expectation, but I'd thought about it while I was recovering, wondering how I could find her, repeating the words *Our Toba* over and over in my mind. I heard them now not as I had said them the night of the storm, but as I had heard them from my own mouth that day by the execution stone. As if they were spoken by someone else, slow and laboured, a fragment of an idea behind them, and there was only one way I could think of using those words to find Helena.

I remembered Helena said that when she needed to lose

herself she had gone to a café on the corner, looked through websites, and I thought she might do that again. So I signed up for a free site and started putting something together. Something basic with a few photographs of Toba I stole from other sites to decorate my own. Seeing them reminded me I had no record of my time there. Nothing at all to show for my experience. When I arrived, everything was taken from me, and when I left, I had nothing. 'You're never free to do what you want until you've lost everything you got,' I had said to Domino, but what I really wanted now was to be myself. And to find Helena.

While I waited for her contact, I saw the sights, met other travellers like me, climbed the volcano Sibayak and saw the crater. I went to Bukit Lawang, saw the orang-utans, the feeding stations. I stayed in a jungle hut for several days, experiencing the rainforest, soaking it into my pores, but everything felt empty. I wouldn't be comfortable until I knew what had happened to Helena, and out there I was too far away from civilisation. If she tried to contact me, I wouldn't know.

So I went to Medan, dirty and crowded though it was, and I checked my site at the earliest opportunity.

Among the photos on the screen there were short notes I'd written, hoping that Helena would see them. Details of my travels around Sumatra and where I would go once I moved on to Bali.

I scrolled down and saw the message.

'We should have gone that night, Alex. After the storm. We should have left it all behind.'

Three sentences. Seventeen words that meant nothing to anyone but me. There were other messages above and below it, some even referring to 'Alex' and 'that night'; messages from travellers who'd stumbled across the website without knowing what it was or what it meant. Travellers, backpackers, hippies, wistful tourists. People whom Kurt would despise. People who'd been there, said it was part of them, too. I'd made it easy for anyone to leave a message, so I'd attracted those who felt the need to leave their mark. Individuals looking for a sense of belonging, wanting to share *their* Toba. Something larger had grown from the tiny seed I planted there in the ether, but those seventeen words were the only ones that meant anything, and I knew they were from her. No one else could have written them.

'We should have gone that night, Alex. After the storm. We should have left them all behind.'

I stared at the words and wondered why Helena hadn't told me where she was or given me any way to find her. Perhaps the message was incomplete. Perhaps something, or someone, had stopped her. I replied and for a day or two I waited for another message, but none came and I imagined Michael looking over her shoulder, watching everything she did. Controlling.

Helena might have typed the words from across the world, but there was a chance she might still be in Indonesia, so I decided to stay close, for a while longer at least, and continue as I'd originally planned. I took a plane to Bali, spent a few days in Kuta, the place where Michael and Sully had first met Helena. It was a world away from the quiet isolation of the community in Toba. It was noisy and crowded, an assault on the senses. I only stayed as long as I did because I knew it was a place that Michael favoured and I half hoped that he might go back, that I might see Helena there. But I found no sign of her.

Moving on, I made Ubud my base, among the rice paddies of Bali's central foothills. I visited Kintamani volcano and Pura Besakih – places both beautiful and worthy, but unable to fill the void inside me. I began to think I would never find what I was looking for, that what I wanted was lost on the slopes of Danau Toba.

And then I saw her again.

50

Sitting in a *losmen* in Ubud, I turned away from the computer screen while waiting for it to start up and I stared through the dirty window. Outside, people passed on the road. There were more than usual and I watched them for a while, the different faces passing, young people meeting and talking. I didn't notice the lack of smiles, the uneasy tension in their body language. I was watching them, but I wasn't seeing them.

Inside, amid the smell of a thousand travellers who had passed through this place, sat on this chair, put their fingers on this keyboard, I ignored the babble, tuned out the conversations of others. I drew inwards, shutting out the noise, and turned back to the monitor as I browsed to my site expecting to see only what I saw every time I looked at it. It had been weeks, eleven at least, since Helena and I had parted but still there was nothing from her since that first message.

As I expected, the site was barren of anything useful. I sighed at the screen and clenched my teeth, hoping she was all right, that she hadn't given them any reason to hurt her. I counted those seventeen words, read them and reread them, wishing there was something more I could do, knowing I'd look at them again that day.

'. . . bomb . . .' I heard the word from behind me and I glanced up, beginning to wonder at the unusual activity. There were five other computers and people were grouped around them, pointing at the screens, putting hands to mouths, shaking their heads. At the table beside me, a couple were staring at their monitor, the girl with tears in her eyes. I watched her for a moment, then turned to scan the room, seeing others in a similar state. Shock. Despair. And I kept hearing that word.

Bomb.

I went back to my own screen, closed the page so that my website dissolved and was replaced with the homepage. And in the centre of the screen, beside a small photograph, was the headline for a news item. 'Bali Terror Attack.'

I clicked the link and there, staring out from my computer was an image that stole my breath.

It was her. Unmistakeable. Helena was looking out at me from my computer screen.

With a trembling hand, I clicked the article and filled the screen with her image.

She was standing between two people I didn't recognise. To her left, a woman, and to her right, a man. The man, his pale trousers streaked with dirt and his shirt ripped open to his waist, appeared to be supporting most of her weight. He had one arm around her shoulder, the other across her waist as she struggled to stay on her feet. The woman, dark hair cut short, white shirt smeared red, was also helping to keep her upright. She was holding her hands, their fingers intertwined, searching for comfort. Needing human contact.

Helena was wearing a black vest, the same one she'd worn that day in the forest when she'd cut the tree and shown how strong she was. A vest that had once been soaked with sweat but was now soaked with something so different.

Her dark hair was matted with blood, pushed away from her face, which was bleeding from one side. It was difficult to tell exactly where she was hurt, there was so much blood. Her eyes were unfocused and her face was half-turned away from the camera, but there was no doubt it was Helena.

Seeing her like that stopped my heart and filled me with an overwhelming clutter of relief, fear, longing, anger. She was alive, or at least she was when the photograph was taken.

I looked for a date, seeing that it was posted in the early hours of the morning.

There were other pictures – of fire in the dark, of twisted motorcycles, of two young men carrying a girl between them, her head lolling back, her hair hanging heavy with concrete dust. I tore myself away from the images, trying to read the copy, trying to find a sense of the scale of what had happened. My eyes scanned the words, but I had difficulty filtering their meaning through my emotion. Something about a bomb in a nightclub in Kuta, possibly two. The details were vague. Speculation. Confusion. Most of the reporting centred around the destruction. Many were killed. A senseless tragedy. Eyewitness accounts, but nothing about *her*. Nothing about Helena other than her face staring out from the screen.

But I knew where she was. I had seen her. She was close.

I pinched my eyes for a moment and concentrated. It took me less than a minute to decide what I was going to do. Perhaps I already knew. Perhaps I knew what I had to do the moment I saw the photo.

I printed the picture, logged out of the computer, paid the tariff. Now I had a purpose again. A destination.

As I returned to my room to collect what I needed before I made the trip back to Kuta, I looked at the picture in my hand. The expression on her face, the blood, the wreckage behind her. It reminded me what I'd been through. It reminded me why I needed to go to her. I had made a promise to Helena, and I wasn't going to let her down.

In the reception area of my *losmen*, the television was on, continuous footage displayed on the screen, the incomprehensible voices reporting over the top. Images of fire, of destruction. Police vehicles and ambulances, blasted buildings, smouldering fires, faces twisted in agony. And so much blood.

There was a throng of young people here, westerners and locals, crowding inside, looking in at the open windows, all standing silent and watching the violence. There were tears and open mouths and eyes wide with disbelief. This was supposed to be paradise.

For a moment I looked around at these people and I thought about our own paradise in the trees, and how easily *that* had been shattered. I thought about Helena, lurching from one nightmare to another, and I remembered the others. Poor dead Freia. Matt, Jason, Alban, all of them lying buried beneath the soil. And when I thought about Kurt and Michael and Domino, I realised it was the first time I had considered they might have been caught up in it. And I knew that I didn't care what happened to them. They didn't matter any more. All that mattered was Helena.

I turned away and headed out.

The bus to Kuta was busy and tension was heavy in the air. For once, there was no music blaring, and the other passengers were sombre. Many of them westerners, making a pilgrimage to their former place of worship or, like me, looking for someone who was lost.

Beside me, squeezed into the small bench seat, a girl, younger than me, her face a mask of worry, her eyes staring ahead, her hands clasped together.

I folded the printed picture of Helena and put it into my pocket. 'Looking for someone?' I asked her. It felt wrong, speaking aloud like that, but there was no way of escaping the truth. Not talking about it wouldn't make it go away.

At first she didn't reply, as if she thought I was talking to someone else. When she did speak, it was to her hands. 'Yeah,' she said.

'Me too.'

She kept her head down. 'You think you'll find them?' Her voice was filled with worry.

'I have to think that,' I said. 'Yes. I'll find her.'

Now she looked at me. Her pale skin, her wide eyes. 'They didn't want to see Kintamani. Said they wanted to stay by the beach for a bit longer.' She turned and looked at the girl sitting behind us. 'So we went on our own.'

The girl behind leaned forward and put her hand on her shoulder. 'Don't worry,' she said. 'They'll be fine.'

'We should swap seats,' I said, feeling intrusive. 'You sit here.' I moved into the aisle, squeezing through the standing passengers.

Both girls thanked me with a forced smile, but neither of them spoke again. For the remainder of the journey, they sat close together, their arms linked.

The bus came to a standstill on the outskirts of Kuta, trapped among the other vehicles flooding to the area. For a while we all stayed where we were, rooted to our seats, then a murmur began at the front of the vehicle, working its way back to me, people beginning to speak, beginning to move. Following the crowd, I left my seat and shuffled off the bus.

Coming out into the day, I could see that the bus wasn't going anywhere. The streets were gridlocked, yet quiet. There wasn't the usual shouting and honking of horns that went hand in hand with an Asian traffic jam. The mood here was different from what I had seen before.

Further ahead, men in police uniforms, rifles over their shoulders, signalling to vehicles to stop. The roads were sealed off, and I guessed that we must be close to the site of the bomb. I moved to one side of the road and took the photograph of Helena from my pocket. It was creased where I had folded it, a cross on the page, intersecting the face of the woman who was helping to keep Helena on her feet. I stared at the picture, then looked up at the scene before me. She was out there somewhere. She was out there and I would find her.

51

Moving past the stationary vehicles and through to the roads that the police had sealed off from traffic, everything seemed normal. Quiet, but normal. There were fewer people on the streets, but there was nothing to suggest anything of magnitude had taken place. I even saw westerners in swimming trunks and costumes going about their business as if nothing had happened. Life goes on. Some things touch only the lives of others. Some are spared.

I looked at each of them in turn, searching for any sign of Helena.

I moved down the street leading to the nightclub, thinking that the best way to find Helena was to go to the hospitals, but something was drawing me onwards. Something wanted me to see what had happened. I could've gone round, avoided the horror of what lay somewhere ahead, but I wanted to pass through it, to see it, to satisfy myself that Helena was not there, among the walking wounded. Or lying dead on a street with only a thin white sheet to protect her dignity.

Pressing on, subdued, normality was crushed by dreadful intrusion. I passed two police cordons, slipping through crowds of onlookers that had gathered. Here the damage was more obvious: shop fronts blown out, debris across the road. Shattered glass was strewn about the street, crunching underfoot, and when I finally came to it, the scale of the devastation crushed me. The Sari nightclub, which I'd seen when I was last here, was now just a skeleton of steel and concrete. Ragged rebars of metal were exposed in the broken columns that had once held a roof. A dark hole had opened up nearby, leaving nothing but twisted fingers of metal, charred wood and seared concrete. The neighbouring buildings were gutted from the force of the blast and the ensuing fires. The smell of burning was thick in the air, challenged only by the smell of death. I stopped, awestruck by the scene before me: wisps of smoke rising from the piles. Men sifting, searching. Bystanders staring. Cars overturned, scorched, tyres melted. One vehicle with its doors blown open, its roof bulged and burst. Hell on earth. This was a long way from the beauty of Toba.

Teams of policemen combed the debris, searching for survivors and evidence. A group of men, each of them wearing blue tracksuit trousers and blue shirts, carried a stretcher high on their shoulders. The occupant of the stretcher lay limp, one arm dangling. Police, like soldiers in their military uniforms and their shouldered rifles, tried to keep people away, while remaining tactful, understanding the grief of people unable to tear themselves from this place.

I approached a woman who was standing alone, watching the policemen. I took the photograph from my pocket and held it up to her, asking if she had seen Helena. She stared through the paper as if it wasn't there. She had nothing for me; she was holding a photograph of her own. I moved on, passing an impromptu Hindu ceremony in the rubble, attended by people whose faces were blank with disbelief. Candles were lit and prayers recited. I sensed that the world had moved on. It had changed, mutated by fire and smoke and hate.

Coming away from the site, heading towards the beach, I saw many people, wandering, dazed like zombies, grief contorting their faces as they searched for their loved ones and tried to come to terms with what they had experienced. In the road ahead of me, a small group was talking to an older couple, shaking their heads, tightening their mouths. The older couple thanked them and headed towards me. Something inside me wanted them to carry on, pass me by, but they slowed their pace, looked at me with hopeful eyes.

'We're searching for our daughter,' the man said. 'Simone. She's about this high.' He raised his hand to shoulder level. 'Dark hair. Pretty.' His eyes were ringed red. 'Sixteen. Just sixteen years old. She was with her friend.'

His wife remained quiet, her eyes begging me to know where her daughter was.

I shook my head. 'I'm sorry,' I said. 'I . . . I haven't seen anyone.'

The man looked down at the photograph in my hand. 'Are you looking for someone, too?'

I nodded and lifted the picture. He studied it for a moment before looking back at me.

'Have you tried the hotels?' he asked. 'Some people have been taken there. The ones with burns . . .' He took a deep breath. 'They've been putting them in the swimming pools to ease the burns.'

'Thank you,' I said.

He forced a smile and moved on, heading towards the place I'd just come from. I turned and watched them go, hand in hand, searching for their daughter. When they rounded the corner, I continued to stare for a while before shaking myself and making my way to the beach. The man's advice had been kind, but I had seen the photograph of Helena and I knew that she was not burned. She was here somewhere and she was alive.

On the beach more candles, more grievers sitting vigil for the dead. The eerie quiet, the breaking of the waves on the shore. There were many westerners and locals together, bringing flowers to this spot. I watched a Balinese child, three or four years old, smiling, running to the surf, casting flowers into the waves.

I trudged the sand, searching for Helena, asking at every opportunity, but I was just one of many looking for the lost – people exchanging photos, names, stories, sharing a common bond. I showed my picture to a group of Australians, three big men, who shook their heads, 'Sorry mate,' and showed me a picture in return.

'No.'

'You tried Sanglah?'

'Hm?'

'Sanglah,' he said again. 'The hospital. Someone said that's where they took everyone. Well, most of them. We're going there now; you wanna tag along?'

'Sure.'

We walked to a spot on Jalan Raya Kuta where a number of dark-blue Bemos had collected to ferry passengers to Denpasar. Fixing a price with the driver was usually a matter of good- or sometimes bad-natured haggling, but this time the pricing was a muted affair as one of the four men I had joined nodded to the driver and we all climbed in.

There were one or two others inside already, facing each other on the bench seats that ran lengthways inside the vehicle. On a normal day, the walkway between us would be a death trap of luggage, household belongings and animals, but today was not a normal day. Today was the end of the world.

After a few minutes, the minibus started and we pulled away, leaving Kuta and heading towards Sanglah hospital.

As the vehicle swayed and rocked, I looked down at my hands and realised that I still had the photograph of Helena clutched in my fingers. I studied it once more, then refolded it and slipped it into my pocket.

'Girlfriend?' asked one of the Australians.

'Not really,' I said. 'Well, maybe. Yeah. I suppose she is in a way.'

Under other circumstances he might have considered my answer strange, but he just smiled a tight-lipped smile and nodded his head. He looked out of the window behind me, then he glanced at me again and extended a hand. 'John,' he said.

'Alex.' I took his hand and returned the shake.

'And these guys here are Danny and Angus.'

I leaned forwards to look along the line at the man sitting two people down from me.

'It's the red hair and the freckles that got him the name,' John said. The touch of levity that had skimmed his voice disappeared when he spoke again. 'We're looking for his brother. Jamie.'

'What happened?'

John shrugged and shook his head. 'We were in the club, drinking too much beer, having a good time. I guess we were lucky being right at the back. The ones near the front . . .' John stopped and gazed across at his friends. 'Shit, we only got here yesterday. Went straight to SCs.'

'Sari Club?' I asked. 'You were in the Sari Club?'

'Yeah,' he said. 'There was a bang. An explosion, I guess, then, about ten seconds later another one. The second one, though, that's what knocked me off my feet. All that smoke, the heat, we tried to stick together but I dunno what happened to Jamie.' He let his eyes fall on Angus, who was hanging his head, wringing his hands.

'Shit, I saw things . . . when we got out of there. The whole place was like something out of a movie. A war movie. People trying to help. I tried to help, too, but . . .'

I glanced over at Angus, doubting that he wanted to hear what John was saying, but at the same time I understood that John needed to purge himself. You keep things like that inside you, they eat you alive.

John lowered his voice. 'This guy. Crawling along the street. I went to help him, pull him up, get him standing, but when I got to him.' He stopped speaking, swallowed. 'He had no feet, man. No feet. And there was half a woman, just lying there. A kid, younger than me with his eyes burned right out of his head, screaming.' John's own eyes glazed over as he spoke and a dampness welled around the lower lids. He squeezed his eyes and the tears formed, bulging and running down his cheeks. He put his hands to his face to cover himself. It was probably the first time he'd stopped to think about what he'd seen.

52

Arriving at Sanglah hospital was as close to a living nightmare as I ever wanted to come.

I hadn't witnessed the horrors of the previous night, but what lay in wait for me here was bad enough. There were people everywhere outside the main building. Locals looking for loved ones or just come to see what was happening. Soldiers trying to organise the crowds, nurses in long white dresses with petite hats perched on their heads. Men in jeans and shirts with masks covering their faces, bystanders pulling their shirts over their mouths and noses to cover the smell of death. Onlookers peering over the opaque plastic that was wrapped from pillar to pillar around one veranda area that now housed rows of bodies shrouded in white sheets. No more room in the morgue. Bags of ice strewn among them in a vain effort to keep them from the cruel heat of the sun.

I stayed close to John and his friends, and we followed the makeshift signs that led us to a crisis centre on the second floor where we were met by westerners in the attire of holidaymakers. They looked tired, drained, and I guessed they were volunteers. People who had stopped to help. I admired their calm understanding in the face of so much pain and desperation.

A young man took us past the crowded noticeboards overflowing with pictures and names and numbers, people thronging round, fighting to leave their messages. We came to a reception desk on a worn, red-tiled terrace where we offered the names of the people we were searching for.

'Jamie Biggs,' John told the woman behind the desk, and as John and his friends looked through the list with the woman, another volunteer spoke to me.

'Who are you looking for?' he asked.

'Helena.' It was only then I realised I didn't know her last name.

The man looked at me. Anywhere else, on any other day he might have told me I was wasting his time. But this wasn't anywhere else. It wasn't just any day. 'Helen?'

'Helena.'

He showed me a sympathetic smile. 'This might take a while,' he said, running a finger down his list. 'Helena?'

I nodded and studied the upside-down list, chasing his finger. I became oblivious to everything around me. I didn't hear the weeping, the shouting, the frustration. I didn't take any notice of the volunteers distributing cups of tea and cheeseburgers. It was only when someone tapped my arm that I resurfaced and the sounds came rushing back.

I turned to see John, smiling beside me. 'They've got him,' he said. 'Jamie. He's downstairs somewhere. They're taking us now.'

'Oh. That's great,' I said. 'Brilliant.'

'You?'

'Nothing yet.'

'Well, good luck, mate.'

'Yeah. Thanks.'

John paused, a moment of understanding passing between us, something shared, then he turned and followed his friends into the crowd.

'I'm afraid we don't have anyone called Helen,' the man said from behind the desk.

'Helena.'

'Sorry. Yes. Helena. No one at all. These are just the known patients, though. There's something else we can try.'

I followed him to another room, air-conditioned, where he passed me into someone else's care and, under the harsh fluorescent lights, we trawled through a list of missing people, then a list of those who were known to be dead.

'She's not dead,' I told the woman.

Another sympathetic smile.

'No, really,' I said, taking the picture from my pocket. 'Look.'

I unfolded the paper and held it out to her. She took it from me and studied it for a while as if she were trying to decide whether or not she'd seen her before. Then she shook her head and handed it back. 'I'm sorry.'

I sighed. 'So what now?'

'You could leave your picture on the board. Leave a contact number on it. An address. She might see it. Someone might know her.'

'It's my only picture.'

'You could leave her name. A message.'

I'd seen the boards, the people crowded round them, reading each name so closely that their noses were almost touching the walls. One name. Helena. It would get lost among all those other names. 'Is there anything else I can do?'

'Ask around?' she offered. 'You might get lucky. Or . . .' She hesitated.

'Or what? There's something else?'

'We have photos. It's difficult. Not easy at all.'

'Photos? What kind of . . . ? Oh. Oh, I see.' Photos of the dead. Unidentified husbands and wives. Boyfriends and girl-friends. Sons and daughters. I'd heard a voice in the crowd, one of many, speaking about dental records and I knew that even a picture might not be enough to identify some of the victims. I wondered who or what could have been so intent on destroying life.

'We can give you a numbered ticket. Someone will call you.' She looked over at a closed door that opened as I followed her gaze. The couple I'd seen at the bomb site, the parents looking for their teenage daughter, were coming out, holding each other, their faces crumpled, their world collapsed in on itself.

425

'No,' I said, holding out the picture for her to see. 'Look. She's not dead. Helena's not dead.'

'I'm sure, sir, but we have to try everything.' She led me to yet another desk. 'Marla will help you,' she said. 'Good luck.'

When she was gone, I leaned forwards, putting my hands on the desk. I stayed like that for maybe a minute before looking up at Marla. But Marla wasn't looking at me. She was looking at the picture that was still in my hands, flattened against the top of the desk.

Marla was pointing. 'I've seen her. I've seen that girl.'

At first I hardly knew what she'd said. My ears accepted the sound of her voice, the formation of the words, but my brain took longer to register them, to understand them. I was preparing myself for the possibility that I might never find Helena, not here, but now Marla was offering me hope.

'Downstairs, I think.' She vexed her brow, looked up to one side, remembering what she'd seen, trying to draw one image from countless others.

'You've seen her?'

'Mm.' Still accessing the memories.

'She's all right?'

'Yes,' she said, her words hesitant, not wanting to give me too much hope before the memory came back to her in its entirety. 'I think . . .' Then her face changed. A sudden dawning. Her eyes came back to look at me, her eyebrows lifted, traces of a smile touched the corners of her mouth and I knew – before she even told me – I *knew* that Helena was all right.

'She was downstairs,' she said. 'A few cuts and bruises but she was OK. She helped me with a lady who . . . yeah. She was nice. Hold on.'

She turned away from me, touching another volunteer's shoulder, asking him to man the desk for a few minutes, she had something she needed to do. I could see such relief in her features. I had given her something uplifting to do. She wanted to take me to where she'd seen Helena, share in one of the happy stories of the day. She'd seen so much death and heartache that even the faintest glimmer of hope might be enough to carry her through the rest of this ordeal.

'She was here earlier on,' Marla was saying as we descended the stairs, heading against the constant flow of people. 'I've only been on the desk,' she looked at her watch, 'a couple of hours, and before that I was helping down here. This girl, the girl in your picture—'

'Helena.'

'Helena, yes, she came in with some cuts and bruises, a bit shaken up, but not too bad. I helped the nurses clean her up. She could've gone, but she said she wanted to stay. Help out, you know. She might still be there.'

Marla led me to a ward that might've been a field hospital. Men in jeans and shirts, identifiable as doctors only by the stethoscopes round their necks, nurses in white dresses that were stained fresh red and stale brown. All the beds were full, trolleys pushed into the free spaces, multiple casualties sitting on the floor waiting to be treated. I felt a sense of everything turning full circle. I had seen all this before, on a smaller scale, and I wondered if I were doomed to forever visit hospitals, to always see patients crowded into corridors, to always be surrounded by the sick and the dying.

As we entered, to one side of the open doorway was a gurney, the mattress indented where a patient had once lain, blood pooled in the spot where their buttocks might have been. The thick red liquid, soaked into the thin mattress, dripping onto the floor beneath it like an over-watered plant pot.

A man lay in the first bed, turned on his side, the skin of his thighs and lower back completely seared, nurses leaning over him. Another patient, her head fully bandaged, another with bandages in place of an arm. Marla seemed not to notice the carnage around her, pulling at my sleeve, directing my sight, saying, 'There. There she is.'

'Where?' I moved my head to see among the people moving about, looking at Marla, trying to see where she was pointing.

'Right there.' She urged me further into the ward. 'By the far bed.'

I stopped and put a hand to my mouth. I could see where she was pointing. A young woman was standing by a bed, holding an intravenous drip, leaning over to speak to a man sitting up in the bed. She was still wearing the same clothes as she had been wearing last night when the photograph was taken. And it dawned on me that Marla and I had misunderstood each other.

I lifted the photograph and looked at it again. The woman in the picture, the one supporting Helena – the woman with her arm around Helena's shoulders – *that* was who was standing at the far end of the ward.

Marla was mortified. She had given me so much hope. She said nothing. She didn't need to. The pain was clear in her eyes.

'It's OK,' I told her. 'It's fine. I'll find her. Thanks anyway.'

Marla looked at me, a mix of sadness and weariness.

'It's my fault,' I found myself consoling her. 'My mistake. I should've been clearer.' The girl she had brought me to see *was* in the picture I had shown her. 'It's OK. Really.' I felt awkward, watching her face fall. Her need to help me had been so great and now she was crushed. I did something that didn't come naturally to me. I put my arms around her and held her for a moment, telling her again it was all right. She had tried. She had done everything she could.

'Anyway,' I said, stepping back, 'she might be able to help me. She might know where Helena is.'

Marla nodded.

'Come on.' It was a calculated risk. If the woman from the picture had helped Helena, there was a good chance she knew where she was. I was certain that Helena was alive – I had seen her, I had a picture, she *had* to be all right – and if Marla could hear the news too, perhaps it would change how she felt.

We picked our way through the ward, almost unnoticed. Like worker ants with a job to carry out at all costs, the staff and volunteers moved around us as if we weren't there. If the woman noticed us approach, she didn't register it, and even when I was standing right behind her, she gave no indication that she knew I was there.

'Excuse me.'

She turned her head, a slow movement, and followed it with her shoulders and the top part of her body. She looked at me just long enough to acknowledge that I was there, then she turned her head again, her eyes going to the window.

Outside, I could see the pandemonium being played out at the front of the hospital. Ambulances, cars, motorbikes, people everywhere. There were even people at the roadside, holding out boxes, asking for money to buy supplies, cash to fund the rescue. Occasionally, as a car or motorbike passed, weaving through the traffic, passengers would throw money from the windows.

'Is this you?' I said, holding out my picture, showing it to the back of her head. The picture carried signs of having been repeatedly creased and pushed in and out of my pocket. It was crumpled, softer than before, and the folded cross that had run through it was no longer clean and crisp.

The woman continued to stare.

'Please. This *is* you. I'm looking for the girl you helped. The one in this photo. From last night.' I moved around her, standing in front of her, holding the picture up to her face so she couldn't ignore it.

'Please,' I said. 'Help me.'

She seemed to shake herself, and as she did so, she shook tears to her eyes. Tears of grief, exhaustion, frustration, I had no idea.

'I'm sorry,' I said. 'I need to know.'

She swallowed hard, nodded. Cleared her throat and pulled herself together. She looked at the photograph. 'I remember her,' she said, then turned to look at the bag of fluid she was holding. It was more or less full. If she stood there, holding it like that until it was empty, her arm would be numb, drained of blood. Marla realised this before I had, though, and already she was dragging an unused stand towards us.

'She must've been in the club, too,' said the woman. 'At the back, where we were. I couldn't see much. All the fire and smoke. Dust. Managed to get out, though, across a courtyard or something. There were a few of us, the fire chasing us. She was there. That girl. She was hurt. Her face.' The woman touched the side of her own face as she studied the photo. 'We helped each other over the wall.'

Marla took the bag from the woman and hooked it up to the stand.

'D'you know where she is now?'

The woman continued to stare at the picture, shaking her head. I was waiting to see what the head movement meant. Part of me wanted to grab her, to get the information from her so that I could find Helena and get away from this hell. I wanted to shout at her, to tell her to pull herself together.

Marla took the woman's hand, encouraged her to sit on the corner of the bed.

'What's your name?' she asked.

'Steph.'

'Well, why don't you come outside for a moment, Steph? Have a cup of tea, a bit of a rest. This is hard for us all. There are other volunteers. Someone else can do this for a while.'

'I'm not a volunteer,' Steph said, turning to look at the man in the bed. Until now, I hadn't taken much notice of him, I'd been so concerned with my own problems. One side of his face was red, raw where it had been burned, seeping fluids. His eyes were closed and he looked dead but for the weak rise and fall of his chest. Seeing him, I couldn't believe no one was doing anything more for him. 'He's my husband,' she said. 'They told me he's going to die.'

We fell silent, our world pushing outwards, dismissing everything around us. I could hear no sound, see nothing other than what was immediately before me. I thought about what Steph was doing, and I knew it was what I had done for my mother. I had kept hoping and I had made her live. Whether it was a selfish desire to keep her with me or an unwillingness to quicken her death, it didn't matter. I would always carry the guilt of it, and I couldn't run away from it, but I was more able to accept it now, and I knew I would have felt worse if I had taken the other road, if I had done as Domino had said *she* would do, that night when we sat on the hospital steps. Perhaps I should have seen then that it was something that separated us. Domino was willing to participate in the death of another, but I was not.

I looked up at Steph. 'I'm sorry,' I said. 'I didn't . . . know.'

'Are you Alex?' she asked, taking me by surprise.

'Yes.'

'She was saying your name.'

'Do you know what happened to her?'

'I'm sorry.'

'She's—'

'Yes. She's OK. They brought us in the same ambulance.'

'Do you know where they went?'

But Steph was turning back in on herself again, and I sensed that she had nothing left to say. I thanked her and stood up, moving away from the bed.

'Is she going to be all right?' I asked Marla.

'I'll stay with her,' she said. 'For a while, anyway. Why don't you try the other ward. Your friend might be there.' She gave me brief directions.

'Thanks,' I said. 'Thanks very much.'

She smiled. 'Good luck, Alex.'

She had even remembered my name.

53

I followed Marla's directions in a daze of growing relief and excitement. Helena was all right. She was here somewhere and she was all right. I'd had the picture to reassure me all this time, but I now had Steph's testimony, and I knew that I was close to finding Helena. Soon, we would be together again.

I hurried along the corridor, twisting and moving to avoid collision, slowing only when I came to the other ward, taking a deep breath and steeling myself before I entered.

But I could not have prepared myself for what I would see.

I was looking for Helena, but it was Michael I found. I recognised him straight away, propped up in the bed, his naked torso spotted with blood, as it had been last time I saw him. He looked bad. Much of his left leg was bandaged and there was a large dressing on the side of his neck.

I stopped and stared. This was the man who had intended to kill me. My last memories of him were of his brutal savagery and his lust for murder, and I felt fear rise in me when I saw him there. But, although I was afraid of him, I told myself he was not a monster. Seeing him like this, I knew he was weak. He couldn't harm me. I also knew he was my best link to Helena, so I repressed my fear, pushed it deep, and approached him.

'Michael,' I said, looking down at him.

'Who's that?' He opened his eyes, but he didn't look at me.

'It's me. Alex.'

'Alex? Shit. What the fuck are you doing here?' The tone

fairly neutral. Tired, not angry. Perhaps his condition had subdued him, or maybe they'd given him drugs.

'I'm looking for Helena.' I was surprised I felt no pleasure at his discomfort. Without my fear, I felt nothing for him at all. I was drained. I had nothing left.

'I don't feel so good.' His eyes moved as he spoke to me, as if they were searching for my face.

'Have you seen Helena?' I asked.

He rolled his eyes high enough for me to see almost nothing but bloodshot whites. 'I haven't seen jack shit since . . . well, since whatever the fuck happened. Last thing I saw was a flash of light, fucking noise and then nothing. When I opened my eyes, everything was gone. And I mean *gone*. Doctor said it should come back, though. Said a few people've had it. Please, God, I hope it comes back. I'm sorry about—'

'You can't see?'

'Not a thing. Please, Alex, you—'

'Where's Helena?' He looked scared, but I wasn't interested. I had no time for him. 'Where is she?'

'I don't know. I thought maybe she was here before. Thought I heard her voice, but . . . you think she's all right? Shit, you gotta help me find her, Alex.'

I looked around, realising now why she wasn't here. 'She's left you. Probably long gone. Saw this as her chance to get away from you.' Maybe she would contact me through my site now she was free. She would write to me and we would find each other again.

'What you talking about? Why would she want to leave me? Why wouldn't she come find me? If she's OK, why isn't she here?'

'Because she's afraid of you, Michael; you don't need me to tell you that.'

'What? No. It was you. You changed her. You were always trying to take her away from me.' He closed his eyes and shook his head.

I looked down at him, this man whom I had hated. 'I always

wanted to ask you. *Our Friend and Brother*. On the shrine. That was Sully, right?'

'What?' There were tears running down his cheeks, but these tears were only for himself.

'I guess Domino didn't tell you I found it. The same night you went to bury Alim.'

'How did you—'

'He was your friend, but I saw where you put him. That *is* him, isn't it? And it *was* you who put him there.'

'Sully left.'

'You killed him, Michael.'

'No . . . It wasn't like that. I didn't mean to . . .' He swallowed his own words.

'I told Helena what I found. That shrine hidden in the forest. First thing she said was that it was you. She knows you. She knows what you are.'

'He wasn't good enough for her.'

'But you are?'

'Damn straight I am.' His voice cracking, even through such defiant words.

'So you got rid of him. And you would've done the same to me if Domino and Helena hadn't stopped you.' I stepped back and stared, remembering how I had last seen him, dragging Helena away from me.

'No, Alex, I wouldn't have done that. We're brothers, right? Brothers. You and me, Alex, we have to stick together now. It's just you and me.'

'What about Domino and Kurt?'

'I don't know where they are, what happened to them.'

'So you lost them, too.'

'Maybe they . . .' He wiped the back of his hand across his nose. 'Shit, man, this is all so fucked up.'

I watched him, finding no pity. 'You never thanked me.'

'For what?'

'You never thanked me for pulling Helena out of the water that day.'

'It should have been me.'

I didn't reply, I just watched him for a moment longer, then walked away.

Behind me, I heard him saying my name. 'Alex? Alex? You still there? Don't leave me, man. We're brothers, right? Don't leave me. Alex. We gotta stick together. I got no one else, Alex.'

I ignored him and went to the nurse at the bed nearest the door. I asked if she spoke English.

'A little.'

'I'm looking for a girl,' I said, taking the picture out once again and pointing to Helena.

The nurse nodded. 'I seen her. Nice girl.'

'You have?'

'A few minutes gone.'

'Here?'

'Right there. Looking at that man you talk to. I thought maybe she know him, but she say no.'

'Where is she?'

'Gone. She leave.'

'Where?'

She pointed and I thanked her, my hopes lifting further amid all this chaos, but before I could leave, she put a hand on my arm and stopped me. 'You know that man?' She looked over at Michael. 'He need help. He need a friend. Someone. If you're friend—'

'No,' I said. 'I don't know him. I've never seen him before.'

She released my arm and continued to watch me as I hurried from the ward.

With a new sense of urgency, I rushed down the stairs that had brought me into this terrible place. I took them two at a time, my flip-flops slapping the stone steps. I dodged among the doctors and nurses at the bottom and jogged through the hospital entrance into the warm air, skirting round the back of an ambulance that was parked at an angle, abandoned in a hurry. There were still many people outside Sanglah, a greater collection of locals now, probably come to see what was going on. Many of them were lined along the plastic-wrapped veranda. They were peering over the top, holding their shirts to their noses, looking at the lines of covered bodies. I looked down as I passed, and something caught my eye, making me stop. I stared down at the corpses, covered only with thin white sheets. The unmistakeable shapes beneath. Some with limbs protruding. But one in particular had made me stop.

An uncovered leg. White. An unmistakeable mark on the ankle. A single domino. Double six. And I remembered everything that had come before this moment. I remembered when she had first shown me that tattoo, lifting her foot onto the bed, and how I had thought she was so perfect. And, despite everything she had revealed herself to be, I remembered what I had first thought she was. And it was with a sad heart that I turned away from her. I had other places to go now. Domino was gone.

54

I moved through the crowd, searching for Helena, spotting the white faces, focusing on them each for a moment, hoping that one of them would be her.

There. Walking away. Not looking back. Showing no interest in what was going on. Blue jeans and a black shirt, her hair tied back.

'Helena,' I shouted her name, but there was little chance of her hearing me. I shouted again, calling as I passed among the people. 'Wait.'

I was forced to stop as a group of people carried an injured man into the hospital. I shifted from side to side, wanting them to hurry, to move aside. Helena was getting away, moving out of sight now. I craned my neck to see her.

As soon as the men had passed, I pushed on, picking up my pace, moving as quickly as I could, calling her name over and over. 'Helena. Helena.'

Now a group of young men blocked my path, westerners, built like rugby players. I edged among them without looking at their faces, intent on keeping my eyes on Helena, not wanting to lose her now.

'Alex,' said a voice, stopping me. 'We found him,' he said. 'We found Jamie. Look.' It was John and his friends, the ones who had shared the bemo with me. 'How 'bout you? Any luck?'

I pushed on, calling Helena's name.

'Guess not,' said John, moving to one side to let me through. Angus and his brother moved, too, opening up the way ahead, and as they parted, I saw her again. Helena. Right there in front of me.

She'd heard me calling. She was in the process of looking over her shoulder and, as she did so, she caught sight of me. I stopped a couple of feet away from her. I had found her. At last I had found Helena, and now I didn't know what to do. There was no slow-motion approach, no smiles, no rousing music. But I could feel the tension drain from her and the relief rush in to replace it. Her shoulders dropped and her whole face changed. She took a step towards me and closed her eyes. She couldn't even manage a smile.

'It's OK,' I told her. 'It's OK.'

'How did you know where I was?'

I pulled the picture from my pocket and showed her. She took it from me.

'I was on the news?' she said, looking at the photo.

I nodded.

Helena crumpled the picture into a ball and dropped it. She put one hand to my face. 'What now?' she asked.

'We'll go somewhere,' I said.

'Where?'

'I don't know. Anywhere. Somewhere quiet.'

'A good place to go,' she said, and we began walking, merging with everyone else, nothing special or different. Just two more people in the crowd.